A Little Sunshine,
A Little Shade

A Little Sunshine,
A Little Shade

Partly written at this beautiful hotel! I hope it now has a happy home

E.A. North 12.3-20.

– Elizabeth Anne North –

© Elizabeth Anne North, 2015

Published by Lagon Bleu Books

A CIP catalogue record for this book is available from the British Library.

ISBN 978-0-9930062-1-0

Book layout and cover design by Clare Brayshaw

Prepared and printed by:

York Publishing Services Ltd
64 Hallfield Road
Layerthorpe
York YO31 7ZQ

Tel: 01904 431213

Website: www.yps-publishing.co.uk

For John. Once again my love and thanks
for your patience and endurance!

For David, Claire, Emily and George with my love.

And in loving memory of my two favourite Liverpudlians

My Dad Michael
&
Brenda H. a very special friend

She settled in her chair, reached for the box at her side. The wintry alpine scene decorating it was beautiful. Snow covered chalets, bright red geraniums spilling out from window boxes. The red satin ribbon was now a little worse for wear. She lifted from the box the delicate white matinee coat she was in the process of knitting. It was intricate but would be so very, very pretty – perfect for Emily Elizabeth.

CHAPTER ONE

Quite a crowd was gathered on Oakfield Station the morning Jonas Hardcastle, owner of the local cycle factory, and his wife Maisie left for their supposed 'Grand Tour'. Their daughter Luci, ignorant of the true purpose of their trip, was there to see them off.

That true purpose, known only to Jonas, Maisie and Jonas' sister Philly, was to enable Maisie to visit the clinic of world renowned eye specialist Professor Franz Zeigler. After so cruelly losing her sight many years ago and failing to find a cure, Maisie's hopes had been raised when Philly had returned from her own trip abroad with exciting news. Whilst visiting Switzerland Philly and her husband Conrad had chanced to meet Eustace Franklin and his son Isaac, who were staying in the same hotel. Father and son were there so as to be close to Mrs. Franklin, a patient in Professor Zeigler's nearby clinic, where she had recently undergone pioneering surgery aimed at restoring her sight. The initial post-operative signs were hopeful they had told Philly delightedly. After enquiring about her progress and conversing at length with Mr. Franklin Philly had concluded that his wife's history and condition was very similar to Maisie's.

Philly had been so heartened by all the Franklins had told her that she couldn't wait to get home and persuade her sister-in-law to investigate the possibilities of similar treatment for herself. After much encouragement Maisie and subsequently Jonas had secretly arranged an appointment with the Professor. Having endured many years of disappointment Maisie had been anxious not to raise the hopes of those close to her, and so she and Philly had decided to use the excuse of taking Luci on the "The Grand Tour" as the reason for their trip abroad, pretending even to her that it was simply a holiday. Her beloved Jonas must know nothing of her renewed hope, she knew how desperately he would want it to succeed and his heartbreak if it didn't. Luci's romantic pursuit of Philip Richards the young, very handsome, very eligible new bank manager however had put an end to their plans. At the last minute Luci had changed her mind about the trip, decided she needed to "be around" if she was to keep the attention of the young banker and so finally Jonas had had to be let in on the secret.

Jim Sanderson, the Hardcastles' chauffeur, was currently employed tending to the many items of luggage which needed accommodating in the guard's van whilst Bernie, his wife and the Hardcastles' housekeeper, fussed over Maisie's hand luggage. Stanley Briggs, Hardcastles' factory manager, had temporarily left his deputy Dannah Delaney in charge and pedalled along to wish them 'Bon Voyage'.

Kathy Watson-Smythe was also there to say goodbye along with her teenage son Harry and her sister Miriam Foster, Miriam on crutches now and doing so much better after her stroke.

Philip Richards was expected to desert his post at the bank and dash across to say his farewells, but up to press – and much to Luci's displeasure – he hadn't yet arrived. Adding to Luci's annoyance was her Aunt Philly who for some reason was surely over-reacting, blubbing all over the place and clinging to Uncle Conrad as if she never expected to see her brother and sister-in-law again. Luci felt everyone should be happy for them. They were going on a wonderful holiday for goodness sake!

Philip arrived just as the train was about to pull out of the station, managing to reach the carriage door just in time to say his good-byes and give them his firm assurance that he would look after Luci.

The travelling proved to be much more arduous than Maisie had anticipated and she was glad of Jonas' strong arms and reassuring presence, quickly realizing how very difficult it would've been if she, Luci and Philly had been alone as planned. The pair diligently sent postcards home, usually identical ones for Luci and Philly. They wrote glorying in the sunshine, the air, the relaxation and the wonderful hospitality they experienced at each location. Eventually they reached their ultimate destination, Switzerland, and the clinic of Professor Zeigler. The first two weeks they spent together in an hotel close to the clinic, Maisie attending the clinic most days for assessments and tests. Towards the end of the third week Maisie was admitted to the hospital in readiness for her operation, one which it was hoped would restore her sight heartbreakingly lost many years ago. Professor Zeigler had spoken to them often and was optimistic. Each case was he said unique but he had been able to help in cases just such as this and he had high hopes of doing the same for "Meesez 'Ardcastle".

Jonas visited his wife early on the morning of her operation, stayed with her until she was asleep and watched tearfully as she was wheeled away. He had been advised to return to his hotel. There would be no news for several hours, the procedure being long and complicated, but he couldn't, he had to stay close. And so Jonas had found himself a seat, had sat outside staring at the beautiful snow-capped mountains, the beautiful alpine scene spread before him and saw none of it.

A bubbly young nurse who had been looking after Maisie eventually popped her head out of the door, saw Jonas and without a word sat quietly down beside him. Obviously off duty she remained by his side until sounds from inside told them that Maisie must be returning to her room. The young nurse got up, went inside. Minutes later she was holding the door open for Jonas beckoning him inside.

'Mees 'Ardcastle she est back in 'er room now but fas' asleep' she said. Jonas went to Maisie's side, looked down at her precious face swathed in bandages. 'She be asleep perhaps for many hours' said the nurse again. 'Maybe you go and get some sleep yourself yes?'

'No, no' replied Jonas. 'I'm going nowhere, I'm staying right here.' The room was in darkness except for one light turned away from Maisie. The hours passed slowly by and then suddenly he felt her hand reaching out from under the coverlet, she must be aware he was there. He took her tiny hand in his. 'All over my love' he whispered, 'All over.'

Eventually Professor Zeigler arrived, his young entourage following closely behind. He was dressed in his usual flamboyant fashion, rather alarmingly coloured spotted bow tie and multi-coloured checked jacket albeit covered with his startlingly white medical coat. He thrust his hands deep into his pockets and struck a pose at the bottom of Maisie's bed. He looked very serious.

'Mister and Meesez 'Ardcastle' he announced 'I am ver pleezed to be able to tell you that the operation 'as gone ver well.' Once having delivered that little speech he spread his coat tails and plonked himself down on the bed, took both Maisie's hands in his. 'I 'ave 'igh 'opes my dear Meesez 'Ardcastle,'igh 'opes indeed. Tomorrow we will remove one layer of bandages, the next day another and so on until – voila!' – he clapped his hands – 'there est no bandages!' Maisie turned her face to him, smiled her gentle smile.

'Thank you Professor Zeigler' she said. 'Thank you with all my heart.'

'No thanks whatever are needed Meesez 'Ardcastle. I am completely at your service.' And with that he rose to his feet, clicked his heels together and did a little bow. He ushered his entourage out ahead of him and made to leave. Jonas was quickly round the bed to him, held out his hand intending to say so much but was able to say nothing. There was no need. The Professor, seeing the tears glinting in his eyes, merely nodded his head.

On the morning of the seventh day following Maisie's operation when the last bandages were to be removed, Jonas arrived even earlier than usual at the clinic. He was anxious but had been buoyed up by Professor Zeigler's optimism, they both had.

The Professor was so confident of success that he had suggested perhaps Maisie might like to be outside on the balcony for her first view of the world. In spite of his profession which dictated he be realistic and logical the Professor was a true romantic, a dreamer, and this was his vision of how it should be, the sunshine on a beautiful snow-capped mountain. But Maisie Hardcastle too was a dreamer, and the first thing she wanted to see was the face of her beloved Jonas, she wouldn't countenance being moved outside on to the balcony.

At precisely two o'clock Professor Zeigler began to personally remove the remaining bandages from poor Maisie's ravaged face. His entourage of young students stood in awe. The atmosphere in the room was tense as Maisie very slowly struggled to raise her poor swollen eyelids. Her eyes were sticky and it took several attempts before her eyelashes were parted and her lids fully open.

'Oh Jonas!' she cried, 'Oh Jonas!' But they were cries not of joy, but cries of utter despair. Professor Zeigler, alarmed, quietly indicated to his students that they should leave. As the last one left he closed the door firmly behind them. To say he was surprised, disappointed, was an understatement. He had anticipated that at the very least Maisie would be able to determine light from shade. Clearly there was absolutely nothing. Whilst his brilliant mind flailed about wildly, outwardly he remained calm and in control. He explained that with so much bruising from the procedure it would perhaps take longer than he had anticipated for there to be an improvement. They must be patient he said. Jonas was devastated but knew he had to hang on for Maisie's sake. Maisie, equally devastated, knew she had to hang on for Jonas. They both assured the Professor very politely that of course they understood, and yes it was early days.

Jonas could hardly bear to leave his beloved Maisie that night and when he finally did he walked all the way back to his hotel in an unseasonal snow storm. He'd hoped he would feel better the next day, once he'd begun to come to terms with the disappointment. After all it had been a long shot hadn't it and they hadn't lost anything, they were in exactly the same position as before. The thing was he didn't feel better because they had lost something, their dream, the dream they'd been clinging to for many months now. Maisie did her best to remain optimistic, stay cheerful at least, and they spent the day gathering strength from each other. They spent many days doing exactly the same as there was no change in her condition.

Maisie was due to be discharged on the Saturday of the second weekend following her operation and Jonas arrived even earlier than usual that morning clutching Maisie's overnight bag. He was so early in fact that when he entered her room Maisie was still sleeping peacefully. He decided not to wake her, sat down beside the bed and very gently took her hand. He looked around the room. Everything was so white, he'd never noticed before just how white. He turned towards the full length windows leading on to the balcony, saw the snowy peaks of the mountains, too early yet for them to be lit by the sun. He felt Maisie stir, looked down at her as she tried to open her eyes, a little sticky even now.

'Jonas? Jonas?' she said. Of course it was Jonas, she could feel his big slightly hairy hand holding hers. 'Jonas my love, your eyebrows need a trim.'

'Aye well when we........' began Jonas and then he leapt to his feet, screamed out his joy, took her in his arms virtually lifting her from the bed. A nurse rushed in, alerted and concerned by Jonas' shouts. He turned, recognizing her as the little nurse who had sat with him, metaphorically holding his hand the afternoon of Maisie's operation. Realizing immediately what had taken place the nurse quite unprofessionally let out a scream of her own and before long the room was crowded. Word was hurriedly sent to Professor Zeigler. There was no shortage of volunteers ready to race to the Zeigler's bungalow and give the Professor what he had been so desperate for – good news of "Meesez 'Ardcastle".

In his very pristine, very modern bungalow in the grounds of the clinic where he lived with his wife Simone, Professor Zeigler toyed with his breakfast croissant. Simone had never seen him so distracted, he'd been like a bear with a sore head for the last week, not sleeping, being touchy and off hand, she was pleased that she was leaving today for a short visit to her parents. Simone was first to the door. The Professor, overhearing the conversation which was taking place on his doorstep, gave a whoop of joy and without a word raced past his wife, coat tails flying as he ran and ran towards Maisie Hardcastle's room. The room up to that point noisy with celebration fell silent as he entered. He went to her, took both her hands in his own, looked into the eyes which he knew could now see him.

'Meesez 'Ardcastle, what is it that I can say?'

'Professor Zeigler' whispered Maisie, 'How can I ever thank you?' Jonas had disappeared, was in a heap on the floor and crying like a baby, 'his' nurse on her knees beside him.

'There, there Meester 'Ardcastle.'

Maisie smiled down at her husband inconsolable in the corner, reached out her hand.

'Come here my love, wheel me outside to look at that beautiful mountain.' A wheelchair was hastily produced and Maisie was carefully helped into it. The room was empty when Jonas finally pushed Maisie on to the balcony outside to see the sun now gleaming on the snow topped mountains.

CHAPTER TWO

The postcards had come regularly to Luci and Philly saying how much Jonas and Maisie were enjoying their trip. Finally came one from Switzerland, to Luci completely innocent but to Philly momentous. Philly spent the next days in turmoil, agitated, short tempered, nothing anyone could do would appease her. When over breakfast one morning Fanny the maid handed her an envelope post-marked Switzerland her heart flipped over, her face blanched. Conrad looking up from his newspaper pretended not to notice when she surreptitiously slipped it unopened into the pocket of her gown. When she excused herself from the table some minutes later saying she felt the need of some air, she'd take a turn around the garden, he merely nodded and continued his pretended avid perusal of "The Times".

He gave her a while before going over to the French windows which opened on to the garden, followed her progress until she settled on her favourite seat under the old willow. He watched as she retrieved the letter from her pocket, slit open the envelope, saw her body literally collapse and her hand go to her eyes. He wanted to go to her, comfort her over whatever was causing her such distress, but somehow knew he mustn't. Conrad returned to his place at the table and waited until she appeared once more framed in the doorway, the sunlit garden beautiful behind her. In the end he had to ask.

'Your letter my love, was it important?'

'No, no.' She waved it in the air. 'Just Jonas.'

'Jonas writing a letter on holiday? I thought we only received postcards' he laughed.

'Oh, it's only the factory, nothing of any great importance but you know Jonas, can't leave work behind. Anyway if you'll excuse me' she rushed on 'there are things I must do.' She dropped a light kiss on his forehead as she made her exit.

Philly spent the rest of the day going over and over Jonas' letter. It told her nothing really, nothing that she didn't already know. He gave details of their journey to Switzerland and other little titbits of information and finished maddeningly with the single phrase 'all systems go.' She supposed this was good news, surely it must be, so why did she feel so anxious, so afraid? When Conrad returned from business later than usual that day he found his wife sitting at her dressing table staring vacantly into the triple mirrors. From whichever angle she knew she looked dreadful.

'Alright dear?' he asked casually, sitting himself down on the bed behind her. She stared back at him in the mirrors. He was shaken when without a word her head flopped forward on to the dressing table and heart rending sobs began to shake her whole body. Conrad was beside her in seconds, his arms around her, holding her close. 'Hey, hey there my love, whatever is wrong? Are you ill?'

'No, no' she struggled to speak at last, 'it's Maisie.'

'Maisie is ill?' he asked anxiously 'But what's wrong?' Philly pulled away from his shoulder, dabbed at her eyes with his proffered handkerchief.

'Well not ill no but..'

'Just calm yourself darling and then tell me everything. In your own time, I'm going nowhere.'

Philly went on to explain the true purpose of Maisie and Jonas' trip, that the 'Grand Tour' was just an excuse. How she had been instrumental in initiating it and how she now feared it was going to turn out to be absolutely the worst thing she'd ever done, falsely raising their hopes. Conrad could immediately see that there was no real logic in her concerns but equally recognized this as the stress and anxiety of such a huge secret finally taking its toll. After a while, once she was calmer...

'But love you have no reason surely from what you have told me to suppose that Maisie's mission has failed. Jonas didn't say that did he?'

'No, no' she said impatiently. 'I've told you what he said.'

'Then why my love? Why have you assumed the worst, you have no reason to do so.'

Philly, twisting the sodden handkerchief round and round her fingers, looked up at him.

'I just know Conrad, I just know, I feel it right here' and she pressed her hand to her heart.

Conrad Templeton was a devout Catholic, had hoped in the early days of their relationship that Philly would convert to his faith. To her credit she had tried. Before their marriage she had taken instruction, had actually been admitted into the Catholic Church. But it hadn't worked, not really, Philly even to her own distress had no belief. Conrad however had enough for both of them and quite uncharacteristically, for he had never forced his beliefs on her, he suggested they might pray.

'What? But I can't' wailed Philly, taken aback by his suggestion. 'It would be wrong of me, you know I have no faith.'

'If it would help you at all my dear, I'm sure God will be only too pleased' he smiled. Philly thought about it.

'But I couldn't, not here in my bedroom!' she cried.

'Then we'll go to the church. If that will make you feel more comfortable then that is what we shall do.'

In any other circumstances Philly would never have agreed but she was in total despair and as he pulled her to her feet he smiled so lovingly at her she no longer had the heart to argue. The house was in darkness now, Fanny and Collins long ago in their beds. They crept silently along the carpeted landing, down the stairs like trespassers in their own home. Conrad carefully pulled back the bolts on the heavy door and led the way on to the porch and into the darkness. Having parked his car as usual at the back of the house he was able to start the engine without fear of waking anyone.

The car purred to a halt outside the Church of The Virgin Mary. The building ordinary, built with rust coloured brick, was not inspiring from the outside, its most imposing feature the huge black and gold ornamental gates which were denied their true purpose being permanently anchored back to the wall. Hand in hand Conrad and Philly climbed the few steep steps and pushed open the solid oak door. The church was never locked, open at all times for anyone who needed its sanctuary, its peace. Conrad stood to one side as Philly dipped her finger in the bowl of holy water and signed herself with the sign of the cross. She watched as Conrad did the same but with a reverence she had been unable to muster. She knew she'd been wrong to come, you didn't just pick up God when it suited you. The church was chilly and dark lit only by candles on the altar and on the window sills, candles that would flicker and burn throughout the night casting shadows close around them. The draught from the door as they had entered had sent the flames into a mad flurry, shadows dancing where previously there had been only darkness. Conrad pulled out two tapestry hassocks in the front pew and together they knelt in silent prayer, Philly knowing full well that Conrad's would carry more weight than hers.

Father Daye in his vestry heard the creaking of the door being opened and footsteps on the stone floor as he tidied away after his last Office of the day. He peered through the gap in the door not wanting to disturb whoever it was. He saw it was Conrad Templeton and his wife, could sense they were in need of solitude and so he sat himself in his comfy old armchair prepared to wait. In the end he knew he must make himself known. Fiona McKinley his fearsome housekeeper would be in the presbytery next door waiting to serve his supper. With his outdoor cloak pulled around his shoulders he gently eased open the vestry door.

'Father.' Conrad was instantly on his feet. 'I'm so sorry, I had no idea you were here. If I'd known........'

'There is no need of apology my son' said the priest gripping Conrad's shoulder. 'This is the house of God, not mine, and here to use as and when it will bring you comfort.'

'That is kind of you Father but..' Father Daye held up his hand to silence him.

'Unless you need me I will leave you and be on my way.' Suddenly Philly put her hand out to him.

'But we do need you' she whispered. The priest sat with them.

'Then tell me your troubles my children' he said simply. No doubt his supper would be ruined and Fiona would be cross, probably for days, but he was needed here. And so Father Daye listened to the story of Maisie Hardcastle, Philly's hopes for her. Once he had heard everything the three prayed together not only for Maisie but for Philly too in her anxieties. Father Daye finally rose from his arthritic knees and made to leave. They followed him out and back to their car. As Conrad closed the car door behind Philly he was sure he heard 'Let me in for the love of God woman!' as the priest banged hard on the locked presbytery door.

The house was as they had left it in total darkness when Philly and Conrad abandoned the car at the back of the house and scurried round to the front and up the porch steps. Conrad reached into his pocket for his keys, flapped wildly around his body feeling in all his pockets.

'Oh God Philly I don't have my keys, I must've left them in the church, do you have yours?' In answer Philly held her arms wide. For once she didn't have her compulsory handbag hanging from her arm.

'Why no' she said 'I didn't think I'd need them.'

'Now what?' whispered Conrad. Suddenly Philly found the whole thing hysterical and began to laugh. Her giggles affected Conrad and suddenly they were both laughing like children.

'We'll just have to wake Collins' said Conrad and he began knocking on the door, at first timidly and then more forcefully having drawn no response until they at last saw a light making its way across the hall.

'Who is it?' demanded a man's voice, 'who's knocking at this time o' night?'

'It's me' said Conrad pressing his mouth close to the door.

'An' who's me?' persisted the man.

'It's me Collins, Mr. Templeton.'

'An"ow does I know yuz who ya sez ya are?'

Philly decided it was time for her to intervene. She bent down, pushed open the letter box.

'It's me Collins' she whispered through the gap.

'Ah right ya are then Ma'am', and without more ado the door was hastily unlocked.

The next morning Philly awoke feeling much brighter, almost serene. Conrad, delivering her breakfast on a tray before leaving for a two day business trip, was relieved to find her that way.

'Here you are my love' he said, placing the tray carefully across her knees. 'No need to ask if you're feeling more yourself, I can see you are.'

Philly's serenity was short-lived. Finding herself at a loose end that evening, Conrad being away, she decided to pay Luci a visit, check that she was alright. She arrived to find Luci agog and excited. Her parents had sent news that they were returning early from their trip, three weeks early to be exact. Philly was immediately indignant. Why had she not been told? Why had Luci not informed her!

'But Aunt Philly' Luci cried, 'I assumed you would've heard from them too, they've always written to us both at the same time haven't they?' She reached for the postcard behind the clock, handed it to her.

"Bored with the sunshine, bored with doing nowt, and missing you. Mummy and Daddy xx arriving early 25th". Philly was taken aback, of course Luci was right, up until now they had always received seemingly identical missives. It could only mean one thing, they were angry with her. And in any case why would they be returning early?

When Conrad arrived home to find once again Philly inconsolable he had no idea what to do. She wouldn't listen, simply wouldn't be persuaded that she was jumping to conclusions. In the end he gave up.

Luci had realized that she had only five days now before her parents actually arrived. She immediately flew into a frenzy of preparation. The factory had to be running smoothly. Thanks to Uncle Stan and Dannah Delaney it was. The house had to be running smoothly. Thanks to Jim's wife Bernie, the housekeeper, it was. Only one thing was left, Lennie, Maisie's much loved Labrador. Luci decreed he must have a bath and have his nails clipped, the two things he loathed in equal measure. Lennie had been disconsolate having no clue as to why his mistress was no longer there, why his days were so empty, so useless now. Certainly Jim and Bernie, and on the odd occasion Luci, took him for walks but it wasn't the same as being busy all day as he was used to being when his mistress was around. He succumbed to the dreaded bath and the nail clipping like a doomed dog. Immediately after, in retaliation he escaped Luci's all seeing eye and made for the garden, rolling over and over in the muddy vegetable patch which had recently been relieved of its crop of potatoes. Luci discussed favourite menus with Bernie, Maisie's favourite flowers were picked and arranged around the house.

Bernie and Jim, having been asked by Jonas to move into the main house with Luci whilst he and Maisie were away, now began moving their bits and pieces back to their little flat above the stable block.

Everything was ready, everyone in high excitement – except Philly. Her melancholia had deepened, she had wanted nothing to do with plans for their return home. She was convinced she wouldn't be welcome. By the time the day finally arrived she was adamant she wouldn't be at the station to meet them. Conrad had lost patience in the end, got annoyed with her, told her how bad it would look. He was having no nonsense he said she was going and that was it, even if he had to drag her there.

CHAPTER THREE

At three o'clock on a scorching hot afternoon the train carrying Jonas and Maisie Hardcastle pulled into Oakfield Station. Luci was there, Jim by her side, Philip expected any minute. Philly was there, albeit reluctantly, alongside Conrad who had a firm grip on her arm making sure she couldn't turn tail and run at the last minute. Kathy and Harry had seen them off and were there for their return. Stanley Briggs was there, anxious to assure his boss that all was well. And it was, he and Dannah Delaney had managed very well. If he was being honest Stanley had had misgivings over Dannah knowing that the man was equally as qualified and experienced in management as he was. Stan had feared he might be usurped. But he need not have worried. Dannah was only interested in doing the job he was asked to do and no more, he had happily taken instructions from Stan and had given him no grounds for concern. Only Bernie Sanderson was absent insisting she needed to be at home 'getting things ready' with Lennie.

Jonas as he was used to doing waited for the train to be empty of its passengers before stepping down to help his wife. Instead of rather clumsily manhandling her down as was normally the case, today he merely turned and offered her his hand. Maisie appeared in the carriage doorway and then carefully but nonetheless confidently placed one foot on to the narrow step and the other on to the platform.

Luci gasped, could barely believe what she was seeing as her mother then proceeded to walk straight to her, her arms outstretched. Maisie crying took her daughter into her arms, looked into her eyes.

'My beautiful Luci' she whispered. 'Just as I knew you would be.' Philip, hurrying up the slope to the platform having finally managed to satisfy a particularly tiresome client, stopped dead in his tracks. Luci, her eyes filled with tears, clung to her mother not knowing yet what had happened but so, so very glad that something had. All the tears, fears and frustrations of her mother's sightlessness hidden for so many years finally pouring out.

'Oh Mummy' she cried into Maisie's shoulder, 'You can see again can't you!'

'Yes my precious darling I can see again' she said simply. Not wishing to relinquish her child for a single moment she took her hand, led her to Philly, surely unmistakably dear, dear Philly, older of course, greyer as was she but still as pretty as she'd always been. Philly on the point of collapse stumbled, weeping, towards Maisie and the three women hugged and kissed each other, laughing and crying for sheer joy. Oakfield Station had never before witnessed a scene such as this. The rest of the onlookers went one by one to Jonas, left to one side for a change. They shook his hand, slapped his back, said how delighted they were. Stan even went so far as to hug him. Jonas, ordinarily mortified by such displays of emotion, took it all gladly.

After much crying and laughing and 'come and see me soons' Maisie Hardcastle finally headed for home climbing into the car, Luci at her side, Jonas in the front with Jim, Philly and Conrad following behind. Maisie looked with wonder at all the things she'd thought she'd pictured so well but quite clearly hadn't. Everything was so much bigger than she remembered. The streets so wide, buildings so tall. She held her breath as Jim slowed the car to pull through the gates and up the driveway. She remembered her house as being splendid, but it wasn't splendid at all, it was magnificent. The trees and shrubs planted along the driveway such a long time ago as mere saplings were tall, sturdy, and today bursting with leaves and blossom. As the car pulled up to the house, its mullioned windows glistening in the afternoon sun, Maisie said that if no one minded she'd like to go into the house alone. As Maisie picked her way carefully up the steps Jonas leapt out of his seat, held up his hand to his sister who was already scrambling out of the car behind.

'Nay lass' he called, 'Just give her a minute' and he gestured towards Maisie. Maisie put her finger on the brass doorbell, stood there as if nothing more than a visitor. Bernie opened the door wide in greeting, didn't immediately take in the fact that Maisie stood there completely alone.

'Oh my love how good to see you' she cried, 'have you had a good jour..?' She got no further. She could tell!

'Oh Bernie my love, my dear, dear Bernie' said Maisie, wrapping her arms around her old friend. 'And still as pretty as a picture! Why are all my family and friends so beautiful? I can see I'm going to have to buck my ideas up' she laughed. Lennie, snoozing on the rug in front of the empty fireplace, pricked up his ears. It couldn't be? It must be a doggy dream but there it was again. He leapt to his feet, raced towards her skidding on the parquet floor thanks to his newly clipped paws. He landed at her feet an undignified heap and looked lovingly up at her, she'd come back at last. Still holding

Bernie's hand Maisie bent down to the animal, kissed his cold black nose, tickled him behind his ears.

'Hello my love' she said gently, lovingly, 'and how are you?'

Arriving late at the station Philip had been bemused by what seemed to have taken place. Luci had been understandably fully occupied but clearly also a little annoyed with him over his late arrival.

'I'll see YOU later' she said to him through pursed lips as the family made their way to the cars. Conrad, catching the rather harsh aside, had gone to him, clamped his arm around his shoulder, explained what had taken place.

'Take no notice lad' he grinned, 'it'll be the shock nothing more, don't take it to heart.'

Philip knew he must get himself to the Hardcastles' as soon as possible. It seemed an eternity until the end of business that day. He faced a dilemma when a member of his staff recognizing he was in a hurry offered the use of a bicycle so that he might get there more quickly. His dilemma was not that the bicycle in question belonged to Miss Trowsdale and was therefore a lady's "sit up and beg" cycle complete with basket on the front. No, it was that the bicycle was a 'Carlson Celandine' manufactured by Hardcastles' fiercest rivals. The Hardcastles notoriously kind and fair minded did however have an achilles heel. Their bias towards their own machines was legendary and cycles of any other manufacture were treated with the greatest disregard and their riders with equal disdain. For this reason Philip, although perceiving himself to be in Luci's bad books for turning up late at the station, was reluctant to present himself at the Hardcastles' on such a machine fearing it could only add to his problems.

However needs must, on balance he felt it to be his best option, and so finally and with as much good grace as he could muster he accepted the offer promising to return the offending article the next day. In the absence of cycle clips – clearly Miss Trowsdale had no use of them – he gathered his fashionably wide trouser legs into two extremely strong rubber bands and set off taking as many back roads as possible not thinking it wise for too many of his clients to be witness to such a sight. He feared it might damage his credibility as the bank's manager somewhat.

Arriving at the Hardcastles' he carefully propped Miss Trowsdale's cycle along the side of the house, hiding as much of it as he could amongst the heavy blooms of a Rhododendron bush.

It was Luci who answered Philip's ring on the doorbell.

'Where have you been?' she hissed, 'Daddy's been waiting for you and Uncle Stan.' She looked past Philip. 'Is he coming? Have you seen him?' Her face worryingly still full of disdain changed to contempt when her eyes raking over him saw his trouser legs still trapped in the two rubber bands. Recently Philip had noticed a distinct change in Luci's attitude towards him, the doe-eyed adoration of their early relationship had subtly but surely changed, Luci had become at times quite feisty. Philip stood on one leg, hand resting on the door frame as he tried with great difficulty to extricate himself from the rubber bands. Luci was determined not to help him, watched him struggle until eventually one gave up the ghost and snapped, she found herself quite disappointed. Once free of the rubber bands and again respectable Philip was ushered into the house.

To say that everyone was happy would have been an understatement. As the true long term repercussions of Maisie's cure sank in everyone was ecstatic. Philip went to Maisie seated in the middle of the sofa, Bernie at one side of her Jim at the other. These two were very special to her, had quietly and unobtrusively helped her through many troubling times and now they were to enjoy with her everything that was to come, she loved them both dearly and wanted them to know it. She had insisted they sit with her, they were not waiting on anyone, she wanted them alongside her as dearly loved friends. Lennie didn't sit at her feet, he sat opposite her on the rug just wanting to look at her, make sure she wasn't going anywhere, for something had definitely changed.

Maisie rose to her feet as Philip – who else could it possibly be? – approached. He held out his hand but she held out her arms. He found himself wrapped in a loving hug. Eventually she pulled away from him, explored his face, his beautiful long-lashed deep brown eyes, his pronounced cheek bones and chiselled jaw, wide, open smile, all as Luci had so often described. Philip told her what wonderful news it was, how he could barely take it in. Maisie no longer had anything original to say in reply. 'Thank you my dear, that is very kind' was the best she could do.

Stanley Briggs arriving some while later went to lean his Hardcastle Super Deluxe against the house, noting with contempt the machine already there – a Carlson Celandine! He propped his own cycle at the opposite end of the wall as if being in close proximity to such an abomination might in some way contaminate his own fine machine. Having to pass the offending article to reach the door his eyes were drawn as if by magnet to the inferior style, the poor paintwork, the chrome! Stan let out a huge tut and averted his eyes.

Once Stan had arrived and been gathered into the fold the party of invited guests was complete and Jonas announced that there must be Champagne!! Bernie made to get up, go and deal with it, but Maisie held her back.

'No love' she insisted. Luci followed her father to the kitchen saying she would organize the glasses.

'Aye that's a good idea lass, that'll be a big 'elp, you do that.' Philip, still trying without much success to ingratiate himself with Luci, went to assist.

Luci had earlier taken her father to task. Asked how all this had happened and more importantly why hadn't she been told? Jonas had put his arms round her, nuzzled his face into her hair.

'Ah love, we didn't have 'igh 'opes you know, not of the operation being a success, and we didn't want you being disappointed. More than anything though your mother wouldn't have you worried. We decided it would be best to just pretend we were having a holiday. And we did too, we had a damned good holiday. Don't be upset love, just enjoy it, we kept it from you out of love, nothing else.'

'But how long have you known about it? I just don't understand, how did it all happen?'

'It's been planned for a while now, since your Aunt Philly came back from her trip. She'd met some people in a similar situation to your mother's and they'd had great success at this clinic and so they recommended it. At first your mother and Philly weren't even going to let ME in on the secret. They were going to use taking you on the 'Grand Tour' as cover for your mother's visit to the clinic. That was why it caused such consternation when you kept changing your mind, you little minx!' he grinned ruffling her hair. Luci was aghast.

'But I spoiled everything then didn't I? I feel terrible, I was being so selfish.'

'Ah you weren't to know where ya love? And it's all turned out bloody marvellous! So no more fretting, let's all just enjoy it eh!' Luci began to cry and her father was content to hold her for a while, soothe her.

As Jonas eventually headed off champagne in hand, Philip gently pulled Luci to one side.

'I don't think we'd better do it tonight do you?' he whispered.

'Course not, don't be so ridiculous!' replied Luci quite sharply.

In spite of their changing relationship Philip and Luci still knew they wanted to spend the rest of their lives together, in many ways their relationship was healthier now, more evenly balanced.

Luci had thought that at the end of their long exciting trip her parents might well feel a little down and so she had decided that she and Philip would announce their engagement the very evening of their return, she'd felt it would cheer them up. They planned that Philip would first of all speak with Jonas, ask for Luci's hand in marriage, and then announce it to everyone. As it had turned out any announcement from them would surely have diminished the euphoria over Maisie and neither of them wanted that. Their news could wait.

Once everyone's glasses were full Jonas raised his own, held it towards Maisie.

'To Maisie' he said.

'To Maisie' rippled around the room. And then Jonas held up his hand once more for silence.

'I've another toast to make' he said, 'a very important one. To my sister Philly, God bless her, without her none of this would've happened. To Philly.' This toast too was enthusiastically endorsed. Philly, settled in Maisie's chair, Conrad on the arm, tucked her head into his chest completely overcome.

Maisie took a moment to look around her musing on the pictures she'd carried in her head of these people – her nearest and dearest. Having known most of them before she'd lost her sight she'd had something to work with, imagined how the years would've changed them. How strange it was she reflected that in such a short time those pictures so long carried had almost disappeared, been discarded. In most cases her imaginings hadn't been too wide of the mark. Jonas was chunkier – she really must do something about that – obviously greyer, and somehow shorter. Philly was thinner, far too thin for a woman of her age and height. Maisie remembered Philly as being majestic. Conrad had changed little in stature but was now almost totally bald and what little hair he did have was snow white. When seeing herself for the first time Maisie had been thoroughly shocked, had looked critically at the wrinkles around the eyes, the crepe like skin, the sagging neck, the frown lines across her forehead, the greying curls framing her face. She determined to apply a bit of hard work. Some rouge perhaps, a touch of lipstick? She was surprised neither Luci nor Philly had never suggested it.

Maisie was exhilarated but becoming tired and everyone sensed that the time had come for the party to break up. As the guests began to leave Maisie went to Philly, tucked her arm through hers and asked if she would accompany her up to her room. In the quietness of the bedroom she took Philly's hands in hers fully intending a little speech. But it wouldn't come, the lump lodged in her throat wouldn't let it. The two women, friends for so long, each looked into eyes glistening with tears then hugged each other and sobbed uncontrollably. There was no need for words.

CHAPTER FOUR

Stanley Briggs closed his gate behind him, pushed his bike up the path round to the shed at the back of his house pondering on the Hardcastles' good news. It was good news for him too in a way because he'd been dreading what he had to tell Jonas. Stan's home, for a man of his standing, was not insubstantial. A three bedroomed semi-detached Victorian style villa wrapped round by gardens on three sides, it had long been his family home. He had been born there, lived there with his mother and father and his older sister Harriet until each one of them had been picked off by death leaving Stan to rattle around in it on his own. Hardcastles Cycles was his life, joining them as soon as he left school and not being one for hobbies other than fishing and a bit of gardening. The gardens being laid to lawn required nothing more than a bit of weeding and a trundle up and down now and then with the lawn mower.

What Stan had always enjoyed though were his holidays. Taken in his younger years with his parents and sister, he now went alone to Clenton-on-Sea, staying at the Sea Cliff boarding house, landlady widow Mrs. Mollie Shakespeare. When Harriet had sadly passed away Stan probably out of sheer loneliness began to increase his visits to Clenton-on-Sea taking advantage of every charabanc trip out of Oakfield heading in that direction. Over the years he had become friendly with Mollie Shakespeare, actually found himself becoming increasingly fond of her. Having considered himself a confirmed bachelor Stan had been taken by surprise by his feelings for her. When she confessed that the feelings were mutual he had been quite stunned but agreeably so, he'd thought any romantic entanglements had long passed him by. Lately Stan had been moved to take stock of his life. Mollie as she grew older was finding the demands of running a guest house on her own more and more difficult to cope with and yet she loved the life of a seaside landlady. The two had talked and eventually decided that by the beginning of next year's summer season they would be man and wife and running the Sea Cliff boarding house together.

And so although happy that he was making the right decision Stan was dreading breaking the news to Jonas that he would be leaving Hardcastles Cycles. He was a modest man but was aware he was Jonas' right hand man, knew how much he would be missed. But at least Jonas now had Dannah Delaney who had already proved his worth. With Jonas in such a happy state of mind was it unfair to burst his bubble of happiness right now? After all there was no rush. Or was this the best time to tell him?

CHAPTER FIVE

Philip Richards had his own share of worries. Since having decided to learn to drive Luci had become more confident, suddenly had opinions of her own which she wasn't afraid to express, and alarmingly not many seemed to coincide with his own. He was proud of her of course he was, she'd taken the initiative and been determined to carry it through. Alongside this new found confidence however went a certain harshness, particularly towards himself, which hadn't previously been there. Also it worried him that since aborting their plan to announce their engagement on the evening of her parents' return Luci had been unable or unwilling to suggest another time when it might be deemed appropriate.

Philip was worried too about his sister Julia. Having failed her final exams which would have qualified her to become a teacher she had been offered the opportunity to re-sit but he had deep misgivings about the outcome having seen little evidence of any revision taking place. If he were being totally honest he found himself disappointed in her, she seemed to have little in the way of ambition these days, being perfectly content going off to a temporary stop-gap factory job each morning to paint bicycles. Unknown to Philip something had happened to Julia over the summer to totally distract her. Something Philip, thanks to Luci, had absolutely no idea about. The two girls roughly the same age and of similar temperament had forged a close friendship, often sharing lunch on the days Luci condescended to go to the factory. Over sandwiches one day Julia had innocently asked why it was that Hardcastles did so little in the way of advertising. Luci quite unconsciously adopting the family line of supreme superiority where cycle manufacture was concerned assured Julia that Hardcastles had no need of such a thing, the Hardcastle name spoke for itself. Julia, fond of her as she was, couldn't help but laugh at Luci's pompous pronouncement and when Luci glanced over at her she too burst into fits of giggles.

'Well' she scoffed 'who could make an old bike look interesting anyway!'

That evening back at her brother's cottage and finding herself alone Julia went to her room, reached into the back of her cupboard and pulled out her long discarded painting materials. Julia was considered to be an extremely talented artist and if it had not been essential that she had a steady income she might have pursued it as a career. She spent the next few nights working into the small hours. At the end of that week during the lunch break she went in search of Luci. As expected she found her in Jonas' office, Luci having taken it over during her father's absence. Julia tapped on the door, didn't wait for a response.

'Got a minute?' she asked, her blonde head bobbing round the door.

'Course' grinned Luci. 'Come in do, I'm so devastatingly bored.' Julia plonked herself down at the other side of the desk, an oversized leather satchel by her side. 'What on earth have you got there?' laughed Luci, 'You're not leaving us are you? Or is it just an enormous packed lunch!' Julia bent down, pulled from the satchel a canvas, possibly twenty inches square. On the canvas was a painting of what was clearly a French gentleman complete with beret and obligatory string of onions around his neck, cycling past the Eiffel Tower on a Hardcastle Supreme no less. She pulled a second canvas from the bag, this one depicting a Hardcastle Super deluxe leaning against a rock on a beautiful golden beach, the turquoise blue sea glistening in the background. Another canvas depicted a Hardcastle Premier being pedalled past Big Ben. In all Julia produced five canvasses all in vibrant colour and exquisitely painted.

Luci clapped her hands together, rose from her chair to take a closer look.

'But Julia' she cried 'they're just beautiful, you've done them haven't you? I hadn't realized you were so good' she exclaimed.

In spite of herself, for Julia had always been quietly confident in her own abilities, she blushed.

'So what do you think then?' she asked. 'As advertisements I mean.' Luci was thoughtful.

'Well they'd definitely be wonderful for that, they're so colourful, so eye catching, but as I said before do we need to advertise? We never have before, and in spite of being a little backwater, we do already export abroad you know.'

'Exactly! But oh Luci where's your ambition? With advertising you could sell around the world! Sell millions of bikes! Everyone needs advertising these days Luci, even Hardcastles' she sighed wearily.

Luci picked up the canvasses, one by one propped them on top of the filing cabinets which lined the room.

The hooter went signalling the lunch break was over and Julia quickly got to her feet.

'Well I'll leave it with you' she grinned and went back to work.

Luci was on her own until the middle of the afternoon when Stan put his head around her door.

'Don't know if you'll be interested love but I've just had a call from 'Peltier', you know our paint suppliers in France, they're sending a new rep. tomorrow. A Monsieur Dubois' he said, reading from his notepad. 'Claude Dubois, sounds a bit posh don't he? Don't know they've ever sent us an actual Frenchman before!' he smirked, 'Would you like to meet him?'

'Oh you know I think I'd enjoy that Uncle Stan, just as long as you're not relying on me for any translating because all I can remember from my French classes is how to say hello and goodbye' she laughed.

'Nay I'm sure we'll not need that' he smiled, 'you know how clever these French buggers are!'

Whilst explaining the purpose of his visit Stan's attention had been caught by the canvasses spread around the room. He began examining each one closely.

'Well I'll be blowed' he said eventually. 'Where 'ave these come from?' Luci stood beside him.

'Julia did them, you know Julia Richards, Philip's sister. She thinks we're lagging behind our competitors not advertising. She thinks these would make good advertisements.' Stan slowly stroked his chin.

'An' she could be right at that' he said, 'certainly everyone else seems to be doing it. But these are really good, good in their own right I mean not just as adverts.'

'Oh yes' agreed Luci airily. 'Julia is a huge talent, somewhat wasted I fear. Anyway of course we can't do anything without Daddy's approval so I'll just leave them where they are and we can ponder on it you and I whilst we wait for Daddy to return, they certainly brighten up the office anyway.'

'Aye good idea lass, good idea, we've got enough on our plates any road at the moment 'aven't we! P'raps we should have the meeting with the French chap in here tomorrer do ya think? Reps always bring plenty of samples with 'em and there's more room in 'ere.'

'Yes, yes, good thinking' agreed Luci. 'I'll give it a bit of a tidy up first though!'

Monsieur Claude Dubois was immediately taken with the very English beauty of Miss Luci Hardcastle. He was also very taken with the colourful prints she had so very artfully arranged during the course of her tidy up.

'I zink theeze are ver good' he said, closely examining one. 'Oo ist ze artist?'

'Oh one of our workers' said Luci. 'She paints in her spare time.'

'But then she iz wasted' he declared rather flamboyantly. 'She should not be painting only in 'er spare time! May I perhaps meet wiz this lady?'

'Why yes of course,' replied Luci quickly, eager to please. 'I'll go and find her this very minute.' She found Julia busy at work in the paint shop. Paint splashed dungarees tucked into wellington boots, hair piled on top of her head just any old how, she was hardly in a fit state to meet anyone thought Luci, but needs must. She tapped on the window of the paint room trying to attract her attention. Julia could hear nothing above the hubbub of the room and anyway was deeply engrossed in her work. Luci went to the door, yanked it open.

'Julia, Julia!' she shouted. 'I want you, you're needed' and she beckoned to her. Julia reluctantly put down the spray she was working with, if she wasn't careful the paint would harden inside the tube and then she'd have an awful job getting it going again.

'What is it?' she hissed impatiently. 'I'm in the middle of something.'

'I know, I know' said Luci quickly, 'but honestly you really must come, this is important.'

When Luci ushered Julia into the presence of the very dashing Claude Dubois she knew instantly that something very special had taken place, they all did. Claude Dubois found Julia in her scruffy state completely captivating, her pale green eyes, her blonde corn coloured hair splattered with paint. He took her hand.

'I understand theeze are your paintings' he said spreading his arms wide. 'Forgive me but you are truly wasted in a cycle factory!'

'Oh well I'm not sure about that' blushed Julia 'But thank you anyway.' Claude Dubois was peering closely at each canvas.

'But your technique, it is superb' he gushed. 'So delicate and yet at ze same time so strong!'

Luci and Stan witnessed this exchange between the two with mounting fascination. When not ten minutes later Julia had agreed to dine that very evening with Monsieur Dubois their surprise knew no bounds. Julia returned to her post floating on air, not even a blocked paint tube could upset her. When the hooter sounded for the end of the day's work, Julia retraced her steps to Jonas' office where she found Luci.

'Not a word to Philip' she hissed at Luci. 'You're not to breathe a word do you hear?'

'Well only on condition that you promise a minute by minute report!' grinned Luci.

'Done' replied Julia as she pulled the door closed behind her.

CHAPTER SIX

Six months, or perhaps more significantly six months back in her own home, had seen a huge improvement in the condition of Miriam Foster, Katherine's sister, after her stroke. Surrounded by her loved ones she worked tirelessly with retired nurse Muriel Parker to regain strength in her legs and right arm, practising walking with sticks and going up and down the stairs until the carpet was beginning to wear thin. Her speech although not good was at least now intelligible especially to those who knew her and spent time with her. However in the opinion of Doctor Kirk, the local GP and close family friend, Miriam was unlikely to improve much more, a view which out of kindness he kept to himself.

When Miriam Foster had finally been able to return to her home after many months of rehabilitation following her stroke she had found her household much changed. On the fateful day of her stroke she had had no knowledge of her younger sister Katherine's imminent return from India. When almost fifteen years previously their father Frederick Broughton having found Katherine out in a deceit, had so cruelly banished her to one of his businesses abroad, he had also insisted that her name never again be mentioned, 'She was no longer his child'. Miriam and her mother had hoped, expected that he would eventually relent, that it was intended as a short sharp shock to bring Katherine back into line. They were never to discover if that had actually been his true intention as on the voyage to India Katherine, headstrong as ever, had met, and hastily married, Henry Watson-Smythe, a young diplomat en route to India to take up a prestigious new posting for the Foreign Office.

Henry had been jilted at the altar on the eve of his wedding. His bride-to-be Petronella Wyatt had decided that she couldn't after all leave her family and build a new life with Henry in Bombay. Devastated he had nonetheless continued with his plans but was not looking forward to arriving in India without his new bride on his arm. He had been more than happy to pursue Katherine and she had had her own reasons for encouraging him. They had been married on board ship and arrived in India as man and wife.

Katherine had written with her news informing her father that she would not be joining his business in Bombay, that instead she had found herself a husband. Frederick Broughton, incensed once more at the actions of his youngest daughter, instantly and permanently erased her from the family. No mention of her had ever been permitted and so when the family had moved from their home in Bardswick to Oakfield it had been assumed that the Broughton family was made up of Frederick, his wife Ava, daughter Miriam and her husband William Foster. Miriam had fallen in love with William Foster when he arrived at International Cotton Exporters to take on the role of chief accountant and they had married within months. To Miriam's great sadness theirs had been a childless marriage but relatively happy until Miriam much to her horror had found out the truth about William. William Foster was a homosexual but his secret had been kept from Miriam until after his tragic death in an accident in one of the Broughton's factories. It had later transpired that William was being blackmailed, had had no choice other than to give in to the blackmailer's financial demands or face prison. It was only after his death when the blackmailer turned his attention to his widow that Miriam's worst fears had finally been confirmed. Miriam had long harboured suspicions over his sexuality but had refused to acknowledge that someone she cared for so deeply could so cruelly deceive her. Prior to his death William had already paid out considerable sums to keep himself out of prison and before too long Miriam had found herself in considerable financial difficulties having to keep up the regular payments due to her insistence that her husband's reputation should not be tarnished. The secret she had kept to herself until an old friend of William's, Dannah Delaney, had unexpectedly arrived on the scene.

Dannah Delaney had been a colleague and friend of William's whilst working alongside him at the Broughton factory in Bardswick. Theirs had been a good relationship until slowly but surely Dannah had begun to suspect William's secret. When one day William had made overtures to Dannah he had been horrified not only for himself but for the risks he knew William was taking. Rebuffed in no uncertain terms, William had remained good friends with Dannah but undeterred turned his attention to another young employee. Dannah, unable to countenance what was happening, found it impossible to continue working closely with William and left Broughtons to return home to Ireland. Away from the country Dannah had been ignorant of William's tragic death until his return to England several months later. Although not knowing William's wife well, on hearing the news he had felt obliged to seek her out to pass on his condolences. The two had instantly felt a connection. Dannah, although a quiet man, had been able to make Miriam laugh, not an easy task, but more importantly make her feel like a woman again after being so cruelly betrayed by William. Miriam invited Dannah, temporarily jobless and homeless, to stay with her until such time as he got another position and moved on. But that had never happened. Miriam began to rely more and more on Dannah Delaney. Following William's death the business once so profitable had suddenly for her become unmanageable, people she had trusted let her down and eventually she had no alternative other than to sell. By the time Dannah had arrived her financial position was not good and in the end fearing she was about to have to sell her home, her one asset, she found herself confessing the truth to Dannah. He was shattered to hear of the blackmail and she equally to hear that he had known all along about William. The sadness and horror of the whole situation served to bring them closer together, both falling in love, each one with the other but ignorant of the other one's feelings, believing them not to be reciprocated. Dannah had wanted to go to the police insisting that the blackmailer must be stopped but Miriam would have none of it. William had been her husband and his reputation in death must be protected at all costs.

Much against his will but in an effort to help and protect this woman he had so come to love, Dannah had had no choice other than to assist Miriam, organizing payments and moving money from one account to another. Dannah soon came to realize that Miriam's finances were in freefall due to the blackmailer's unreasonable demands. He had warned her and so had her bank. She had ignored both. It was possible that the stress of the blackmail and her resulting financial difficulties had precipitated Miriam's stroke. Dannah, called back to Ireland due to the illness and subsequent death of his younger brother Fin, had determined that on his return to England he would allow no more arguments, the whole situation simply must be addressed.

When finally able to return Dannah had found Miriam in hospital, barely able to communicate and bedridden having suffered a stroke, her financial problems remaining unresolved.

The tragedy of Miriam's plight had forced their feelings for one another to the surface and they both had been able to finally acknowledge their love for one another, eventually making plans to marry once her condition improved. As well as being faced with Miriam's illness on his return home Dannah had also been met with the revelation that Miriam had a younger sister, one returned to England supposedly on a visit, and one who clearly didn't care much for him or his position in her sister's life. He had initially found her haughty and unpleasant as had the rest of Miriam's household, most particularly Peggy Barley the housekeeper cum cook. Peggy was initially highly suspicious of Katherine's claims having worked for the Broughtons for over a decade and never once having heard of another sister.

It had been Jeremy Kirk, Miriam's GP, who had been able to confirm everything Katherine had said. Indeed Jeremy Kirk had been party to the events which had led to Katherine's exile. Jeremy being many years older than Katherine and a senior doctor had barely acknowledged her existence when she began work as a receptionist at the same hospital. Eventually Katherine had decided she wanted to be more than a receptionist. Perhaps a nurse? Or even a doctor? She began to seek help from anyone who may be able to assist her in achieving her dream. Jeremy, totally unaware that Katherine's father was opposed to her choice of career, had happily encouraged her and given her every assistance he could. At the age of eighteen Katherine had ill-advisedly gone against the wishes of her father, shunning the family business in the hope of entering the medical profession. Jeremy had been concerned to say the least when, after her secret had been discovered, she had been dragged kicking and screaming back to the family business, but he had convinced himself that her father must simply be testing her resolve, her determination. He knew medicine, particularly for a woman, was a huge commitment. Katherine having begun to have feelings for Jeremy had been desperate that they continue what had now become an affair, insisting that her father would eventually come round. Jeremy, although alarmed that they must meet in secret, unwisely allowed himself to be persuaded and the relationship had continued to flourish. Until one day she had simply vanished, disappeared from his life. Hearing nothing from her and unable to contact her for fear of antagonizing her father he had concluded that she'd had enough of him, moved on to someone more her own age, more attractive. Jeremy had got on with his life.

And so when many years later on the evening following Miriam's stroke Katherine had promptly fainted at the sight of Jeremy Kirk as he called to acquaint Peggy Barley of her employer's condition, he was as surprised as she was, having never had the slightest notion that Miriam Foster had a sister, and certainly not one he had previously known as Katherine Broughton.

Once Jeremy Kirk had confirmed that Katherine – Kathy as he had known her – must indeed be Miriam's sister, she still found herself having to work extremely hard to ingratiate herself into Miriam's household. Incredibly however her past relationship with Jeremy was instantly rekindled, in spite of their many years apart.

Dannah Delaney's actual role in her sister's household was a mystery. He was also absent, apparently in Ireland. On his return the pair had initially disliked and mistrusted each other, only finally being drawn together in their efforts to support Miriam and resolve some of her problems. After sharing the proceeds from the sale of the family farm in Ireland with his brother Fin's young widow Sarah, Dannah had been left with a healthy bequest which he had no hesitation in using to solve some of his bride-to-be's financial problems.

Katherine's marriage to Henry had finally ended in an acrimonious split after fifteen years, leaving her to bring up her son Harry on her own, Henry insisting she return to England and that the boy must follow. Surprisingly Henry had settled a more than generous allowance on Katherine and so she too was able to assist in Miriam's rescue. By the time of the planned wedding Katherine, having learnt the truth about William, was just delighted that her sister had finally found someone to truly love her.

The nineteenth of June had been chosen by Miriam for this her second wedding day, she wanted blossom on the trees. A dressmaker was called in and Kathy helped her choose a length of rose coloured shot silk which was to be made into a slim fitting dress with bolero style jacket, her hat a tiny veiled pill box in the same colour. The day thankfully dawned 'bright and beautiful' mimicking the hymn especially chosen by Miriam for the choir to sing during the service. After helping her sister to dress Kathy had gone down into the kitchen to help Peggy Barley the housekeeper and her friend Nancy, the cook from the Henderson household next door, with the final preparations for the small wedding breakfast, promising to return to help with the finishing touches, her hair and hat.

Dannah had decamped to Jeremy Kirk's for the night, tradition and superstition dictating that he should not have sight of his bride until they met in the church. Not one for superstition however despite his Irish ancestry, he'd decided that he just had to see her. He called at the house already in his finery, popped his head round the scullery door. Kathy looked up in surprise, wasn't at all sure when he said he needed to see Miriam.

'Oh I don't......' she began, but he was gone, Peggy and Nancy tutting their disapproval.

Dannah ran up the stairs to Miriam's room anxious to say goodbye before he headed off to the church with his nephew Patrick who was standing as his best man. He tapped gently on the door, pressed his face against it.

'Don't worry darlin'' he said 'I'm not coming in, I know I'm not allowed to see you. I just want to tell you I love you.'

He expected to hear her laughing admonishment. When there was no response he cautiously peered round the door. And there she was in a heap on the floor, pill box hat ludicrously over one eye, very obviously dead. Dannah knew instantly, his poor body incapable even of making a noise. He knelt beside her, took her into his arms and cradled her, righting the ridiculous hat.

That was how Jeremy Kirk and Patrick found him when they came looking, anxious to get him to the church on time. Jeremy taking in the scene put his hands on Patrick's shoulders, steered him round back to the door.

'But what........? began Patrick frightened.

'It's alright, I'll see to this Patrick, you go back downstairs' said Jeremy. He was on his knees next to Dannah when he heard the animal cry from Kathy, heard her running up the stairs. The door was flung open.

'Oh no, Miri, Oh no!' she cried, unconsciously reverting to her childhood name for her sister. Jeremy got to his feet, went to her, took her in his arms wanting to shield her from the sight of her sister. Peggy and Nancy arriving breathlessly on the scene merely turned and quietly walked away knowing there was nothing to be done.

Eventually Jeremy persuaded Kathy to go back downstairs.

'Things need to be done, people need to know' he said. He took her himself afraid she may faint. Once having settled Kathy as best he could, leaving her to the ministrations of Peggy and Nancy, he returned to the bedroom, found Dannah still cradling Miriam's lifeless body, stroking back her hair, kissing her forehead.

'Come on old man' he said gently. 'Let's make her more comfortable.' Dannah looked at him.

'What?' Jeremy looked towards the bed.

'She'll be better on the bed' and he went to pull back the covers. The two carefully, lovingly, lifted poor Miriam from the floor laying her gently on the bed, her head resting on the pillows. Jeremy pulled the covers over her beautiful rose coloured outfit, only the sweetheart neckline still on view. Around her neck the wedding day present locket from Dannah glinted in the sunshine now cruelly streaming into the room. Jeremy went to the window, pulled the drapes across and then quietly went from the room leaving the two of them alone. Dannah laid down beside her, looked at her sweet, sweet face. Jeremy had closed her eyes but he was sure there was a tear resting amongst her lashes. He needed to wipe it away, as he had so often done during the frustrations of her illness. He tenderly brushed the tear away with his thumb, rubbed it along his lips and then sobbed as if his heart was breaking.

It was some time before Dannah was able to leave Miriam, let go of her hand. Finally he did, he stood away from the bed, bent down to kiss her, his tears falling into her hair.

'Sleep well my darlin' he whispered.

Kathy was beside herself with grief, couldn't believe that after waiting so long to be re-united with her sister she had so suddenly, so cruelly, been taken away. Arriving back in England to find her sister desperately ill after a stroke had been bad enough, it being months before they had been able to resume any sort of normal relationship. Still so many things had been left unsaid, unexplained, and now they never would be. The only blessing was that Miriam had finally found happiness with Dannah. Jeremy had insisted that Miriam would've known nothing, would've suffered no pain, merely faded away and so surely her very last thoughts must at least have been happy ones.

The days following Miriam's death were dark, the nights heavy with dreams, dreams which Kathy would awake from, happy momentarily, before remembering all that had taken place.

On the eve of Miriam's funeral Kathy and Dannah went to the funeral parlour to say their last goodbyes. Miriam was dressed in her wedding outfit just as she had been when she died, her hat not on her head but laid neatly at her side. Kathy gently kissed her cold, cold cheek, pushed back the dark curls from her forehead.

'Good night my love, sleep tight' she said and then stood to one side, watched weeping as Dannah reaching into his pocket took from the satin lined box the gold band he should have put on Miriam's finger on their wedding day. He lifted her left hand tenderly, slipped the ring on to her fourth finger. She hadn't lived long enough to take his name, her headstone would bear the name Miriam Foster, but in his heart at least she was his wife.

As the funeral cortege arrived at the church the blossom hung from the trees in the churchyard just as Miriam had wanted for her wedding day. The choir began to sing 'All things bright and beautiful' as Miriam was carried into the church. Kathy following behind knew that nothing would ever be bright and beautiful again.

Dannah sat alongside Kathy and Harry in the front pew, Patrick and Jeremy either side of them. The church was packed, Miriam had been well respected by everyone who knew her, much loved by those who knew her well. There had been no wake, neither Kathy nor Dannah could even contemplate it, just the simple church service followed by the burial. Petals from the trees fell like confetti on to Miriam's casket as it was slowly lowered into the ground.

CHAPTER SEVEN

With Miriam no longer there the house at Number Two Ladan Road had no focus. Even though she had been away from home for almost a year in hospital and then the convalescent home everything had been arranged around Miriam's needs, all thoughts had been for her and how to help her recovery. Now there was just a huge empty space. Much to Kathy's surprise, and also it had to be said her relief, Miriam's solicitor had arrived to carry out Miriam's last wishes as set out in her Will. The Will written several years ago after William's death stated quite categorically that her younger sister Katherine Watson-Smythe was her sole heir and therefore entitled to everything in her estate at the time of her death. Kathy was only too aware that Miriam had little money to leave, having been the victim for years of a heartless blackmailer, but was overjoyed to learn that the house at least would be hers free of any financial burdens.

Dannah couldn't stay, he'd known immediately that he wouldn't be able to. Just days after Miriam's death and even before the funeral he had arranged to speak with his boss Jonas Hardcastle. Jonas was dreading the knock on his door. When it came he called a hasty 'Come in' and was round his desk to Dannah before the door had even properly opened.

'Dannah son, how are you?' he asked gripping the other man's shoulder. 'Sit down, sit down.' Jonas rested his ample backside on the corner of his desk, waited patiently for the other man to speak.

'I'm going to have to leave Mr. Hardcastle.' Dannah ran his fingers round his collar as if it was suddenly too tight. 'I don't feel I can stay in Oakfield.'

'I can understand that lad' Jonas agreed sadly. 'You tek as long as you need. What is it you're intending to do, have you decided?'

'I'm feeling the need to go back to me home, to Ireland' said Dannah bleakly. 'I feel the need of some open spaces, a place to breathe. The chap who took my brother's farm has branched out, opened a few holiday cottages and I'm thinking that's where I'll go, spend a bit of time with me brother.' Jonas had been about to say how that would be a good idea, to catch up with his brother, and then something stirred in the back of his mind, hadn't he heard that his brother had died?

'Aye well you must do what you think's best lad, as I said tek as long as you need, come back when you're good and ready.'

Dannah felt uncomfortable, Jonas had been so good to him but he had to say it.

'The thing is Mr.Hardcastle I've come to hand in my notice. I don't think I will be coming back – ever. I'm sorry to be letting you down, you've been so good to me...' Jonas leapt in.

'Oh nay lad. It's not offen I give advice but this time I'm 'oping you'll tek it. It's not good to make big decisions at times like these. And there's no need for you to, we'll manage until you decide definitely one way or t'other. We won't be making any hasty decisions about replacing you and it'll be better if you don't neither.' Dannah really couldn't be spoken to kindly at the moment. He quickly rose to his feet, took Jonas's hand, gripped it firmly.

'Thank you sir, you don't know how much that means to me, I'll be sure an' get back to you the moment I'm clear in my own mind.' With that he let go of Jonas' hand and was through the door. Jonas, desperately sad, leaned his back against the door and sighed. A little sunshine, a little shade. Was one person's joy always followed by someone else's sorrow?

Kathy and Dannah were not drawn closer in their grief, each believing privately that their loss was the greatest, their loss the deepest. Kathy not having seen her sister for so many years had then had such a short time with her and Miri not at her best. Dannah had spent so many years protecting and secretly loving this woman and just when all their dreams seemed about to come true they had been so cruelly snatched away. There was no God as far as he was concerned.

When Dannah announced immediately after the funeral that he would be leaving Oakfield no one was in the least surprised. Certainly not Patrick who had already gathered together most of his belongings and stuffed them into his rucksack tucked out of sight under his bed. He was ready. He was going with his uncle and no matter what Dannah said he was adamant. Only Kathy, Jeremy and Harry were at the station to see them off. It was an early morning train and so the platform was crowded. Even station porter Joe Parker couldn't raise a cheery greeting, could only manage a small salute.

Dannah had decided he would probably stay a week or two at what was now Liam Barclay's place and then travel to Dublin to catch up with his brother Fin's widow Sarah and his nephew Patrick's younger brother and sister. After staying briefly with her parents following the sad and sudden death of Fin, Sarah and the children no longer lived with them. Having been a seamstress in her younger days before she met and married Fin Delaney, Sarah had used her half of the proceeds from the sale of the farm to buy a little shop and set it up as a dressmakers. Double bay windowed with two bedrooms above and a cosy kitchen and outside toilet to the rear it was all Sarah and her little family needed. She had chosen wisely, the shop was in the middle of a busy thoroughfare in a bustling little town not far from the city.

Sarah had replied to Dannah's letter telling her of Miriam's death saying how she knew only too well how his heart must be broken, the sadness he must be enduring and how she longed to see him. When she received news that he was coming to see her she was delighted, even more so when she heard that Patrick would be coming too. It was becoming clear that England would soon be at war and she wanted no part of that for her son. If she could persuade him to stay in southern Ireland she may be able to keep him safe.

CHAPTER EIGHT

Stanley Briggs had been one of the first to learn of Miriam's death. The happy couple had intended to spend their honeymoon enjoying the delights of Clenton-on-Sea staying at the Sea Cliff guest house with Mollie Shakespeare, as recommended by Stan. Miriam still experienced certain difficulties and so it had seemed sensible to go where her problems might be more readily understood and catered for. It had fallen to Stan to call Mollie and tell her the news, tell her they wouldn't be going. He had been quite taken aback, she'd been rather abrupt, seemed put out rather than saddened as he had expected. But then she was in the middle of dealing with a bedroom ceiling about to fall in due to an over-zealous bather in the room above. When he then had to tell her he was postponing the date when he would be leaving Hardcastles due to Dannah's still uncertain plans, she was sharp at first and then increasingly angry, blaming him for the fact that she would now have to employ someone to do all the jobs which would need doing in readiness for the following season. Stan chewed his lip anxiously as he listened to her hitherto uncharacteristic rantings. For the first time he began to have doubts over whether he was doing the right thing giving up his job, marrying Mollie. He mulled it over, spending many sleepless nights and then decided that at least Jonas should know that he wasn't quite as sure about leaving Hardcastles as he'd previously thought he was. Jonas had been stunned, shocked to the core when he'd first heard what Stan had been planning to do but had nonetheless assured him that he understood, and that Stan must do whatever he thought best, you only had one life.

Stan chose an afternoon when things were slightly less hectic than usual and tapped on Jonas' door.

'Got a minute?' he asked.

'Aye course lad, come in and tek the weight off' answered Jonas, pleased of the excuse to put some particularly irksome figures to one side. He leaned back in his chair, folded his arms across his chest. Stan sat down opposite Jonas, suddenly was hesitant, not quite knowing how to put it. It all seemed a bit daft really. Was he being daft? Jonas waited.

'Thing is' said Stan at last, 'I don't know if I'm having second thoughts. You know about leaving.' Jonas was surprised, in two minds how to play this, it wouldn't be fair to influence him either way. Course he would be pleased as punch if Stan stayed, it had been a huge blow when he had announced his plans, but just because it wouldn't be good for him or Hardcastles didn't mean Stan shouldn't do it. Jonas was an avid supporter of marriage and didn't want his friend to forego the pleasure which could be derived from it unless he was absolutely sure. After all Stan was no spring chick and it was unlikely another opportunity would come along. Stan was struggling to explain the reasons behind his sudden doubts.

'Tell you what' said Jonas suddenly sitting forward, resting his elbows on the desk. 'How about you and me talk about this over a pint in 'The Feathers'. Even better let's do it tomorrow straight after work and then you come up and have a bite of supper with me and Maisie, she was saying only the other day how she'd love to see you.' It was agreed that was what they would do.

The following evening the sight of Jonas running to keep up with Stan as he rode his Hardcastle deluxe en route to 'The Feathers' public house caused many a chuckle. Stan locked his cycle to a drainpipe as beside him Jonas struggled to get his breath back.

'Couple o' pints over 'ere Ted if you'd be so kind' shouted Jonas as he pushed open the door into the snug. The two men settled themselves at a table overlooking the street. Although the public bar was quite full – workers calling in for a pint on their way home – the snug was relatively quiet, at least they could hear themselves speak! As Jonas had expected Stan found it far easier to explain his misgivings over Mollie with a pint of best "Madsons" in his hand.

Jonas was once again only able to advise caution, after all it was a big decision and not one to be made in a hurry. It had been arranged that as Stan was to eat with them that evening Jim would collect the two men from the pub at seven o'clock and drive them up to the Hardcastles' house. The landlord had assured Stan that his bike would be quite safe chained up to his very substantial drainpipe until he could collect it either later that night or in the morning. Jonas keeping an eye on the road outside as they talked spotted the car as it pulled up and urged Stan to down what was left of his pint. Jonas bundled Stan into the back of the car and then got in beside Jim. Only it wasn't Jim behind the wheel, it was Luci!

'What the 'ell' cried Jonas in alarm.

'Calm down Father' she smiled. 'I'm more than capable, Jim has been giving me lessons.'

'Like 'ell 'e 'as!' exploded Jonas. Luci slowly let out the clutch and the car moved smoothly forward. Jonas clasped the door handle with one hand and the edge of his seat with the other, clinging on for dear life. He turned to Stan in the back.

'Ya can get out if you like lad' he shouted above the noise of the engine. Stan, Luci was pleased to see through the rear view mirror, merely grinned, unconcerned. Jonas although not a driver had to admit, but only to himself, that she wasn't actually too bad at it. Nonetheless when she manoeuvred it between the pillars either side of the driveway leading up to the house he shut his eyes and kept them shut until he felt the pull of the handbrake and the car come to a halt.

He opened his eyes to see Jim standing in the porch nonchalantly puffing on his pipe. Jonas got out of the car, stood on the running board and shouted to Jim.

'Why you're an old bugger aren't ya' he said pointing down inside the car towards Luci. Jim remained where he was, still smoking his pipe, smiling as Jonas passing him said out of the corner of his mouth 'Ya deserve a bloody medal son!'

Maisie, as was her custom these days, stood at the door arms outstretched to welcome Stan.

'Stan love how good to see you.' A simple greeting but one which these days carried so much significance. Stan grinned, a wide smile stretching from ear to ear.

'Why Maisie love you've always bin a right bonny lass, but 'ere, I don't know, you're even bonnier!'

'Aye and you always were a flatterer Stanley Briggs' she laughed 'But come in, come and sit down.' Jonas coming into the room pretending to be angry and followed by Jim, wanted to know if Maisie had been in on Luci's 'surprise'.

'I only found out this afternoon, but I'm so proud of her, hasn't she done well?'

'Aye well that's as maybe but I reckon she scared poor Stan 'ere half to death didn't she lad?' Luci had already sidled up to Stan, slid her arm through his.

'Uncle Stan thinks I did really well don't you Uncle Stan?' Stan looked from father to daughter, grinned.

'I think you did fine Luci love, just fine.' Jonas headed for the drinks trolley, poured himself a large whisky, the implication being that he needed one!

The banging of the gong stopped any further discussion on the matter.

'Dinner is served Sir,' Bernie announced with her customary ironic deference once the gong had ceased reverberating.

'Right that's it!' bawled Jonas, 'that's the pair o' ya sacked! You Jim for encouraging Luci in her hair brained scheme, and you Bernie.... well you know what for!' he blustered. Everyone apart from Jonas laughed heartily, ignoring him and making their way into the dining room.

When Jonas saw the table was set for four he was adamant that Bernie and Jim should join them.

'But I thought we were.........' Bernie began.

'Aye well the pair o' ya can bloody well go tomorrer' he said in mock frustration, causing everyone to roar with laughter once more. With Jonas at one end of the table, Maisie at the other, Luci and Bernie opposite Jim and Stan, the meal was a happy occasion with lots of friendly banter and much laughter.

When half way through the meal Maisie slipped away to help Bernie bring in the desserts, Luci quickly took a card from her skirt pocket passing it across the table to Stan.

'We're having a surprise party for Mummy Uncle Stan, it's her birthday in a few weeks and we thought it would be nice to do something really special after everything that's happened. We're having it down at the village hall so that we can have a little band and some dancing. We'd love you to come but it's a secret, she doesn't know' and she put a finger to her lips to emphasize the point. As Stan hastily put the invitation into his inside pocket he couldn't help noticing the date, the very weekend he was supposed to be visiting Mollie again. Stan telephoned Mollie the next day, anticipating she wouldn't be pleased and wanting to get it over. Mollie was furious and Stan's determination to begin a new life suffered a further blow.

CHAPTER NINE

Kathy was completely lost, had no idea what to do now that Miri was gone. For a while she even considered returning to India taking Harry back with her, after all she had many friends there, up to a point she'd enjoyed her life there. But of course without all the privileges which had come because she was Henry's wife, she knew a life there now would be a completely different story. She felt a desperate need to get away from Oakfield just as Dannah had, but unlike him she had nowhere to go.

Oakfield suddenly seemed to have nothing to offer her. She'd come back to England to be reunited with her sister and now there was just a huge empty space. The time she'd been in England had been spent supporting her sister, urging her on to a full recovery and now that reason to be here had gone. Somehow the affection between her and Jeremy Kirk, so quickly and amazingly rekindled from so many years ago, no longer seemed enough. Of course she had her son Harry, but for how much longer? He was growing up quickly, would in all probability soon be gone. His desire to become a vet would obviously mean many years of study, none of which could be undertaken in sleepy little Oakfield or anywhere close by for that matter.

Henry had finally made it clear he wanted a divorce, indeed insisted upon it. Within months now the divorce would become absolute, she would be free to re-marry and it had somehow become taken for granted that that was what would happen – that she would marry Jeremy. Jeremy thought he understood how Kathy was feeling, assumed that her gentle withdrawal from him now was simply a natural part of her mourning her sister. Kathy wasn't so sure. There remained the vexing problem of the house, although hers, with staff and maintenance it was still a considerable financial burden. It was a large house and in all honesty they no longer needed a large house. Peggy having served the family so well for so long was a critical part of any changes, having had no other home for the best part of twenty years. Lizzie Carson the maid, so much younger, was not such a problem, she would easily find another post or possibly before long marry.

Whilst Miri had been alive it had all seemed so simple. It had been assumed that once married Jeremy and Kathy along with Harry would live in the two floors above the surgery which Jeremy currently occupied, his widowed sister-in-law Jeannie remaining in her rooms on the ground floor. Miri and Dannah as Mr. and Mrs. Delaney would remain in the house in Ladan Road with Patrick and Peggy. But now everything had changed and huge questions hung over all their plans. Would Dannah return? Would Patrick return? Certainly he had been adamant that he would, had told Farmer Dearing he would be back, had begged him to keep his job at Landridge Farm open. Kathy knew she needed to move on but was unable to do so whilst everything hung in the balance, was so uncertain. She had expected to be relinquishing any financial responsibility for the house once Miri and Dannah had married but now with Miri gone and Dannah having left it could hardly be expected that he would be contributing financially. Henry's allowance had been more than generous but she knew it would not cover all their expenses particularly if Harry was to pursue his choice of career and she was determined he would, it was the very least she could do for him. Jeremy shocked, shamed, but delighted when Kathy had revealed to him that Harry was in fact his son – conceived unbeknown to her before she was exiled to India – had assured her that naturally he would help in any way he could particularly in relation to Harry. It was his duty he said and Kathy didn't argue. Harry's true parentage remained a secret between them, both realizing that even now any such revelation would seriously damage Jeremy's career. Even Harry remained ignorant, still believing that Henry was his real father, Kathy and Jeremy both fearful of his reaction should he learn the truth.

Kathy was left with no alternative other than to consider getting a job, although quite what she had qualifications for was anyone's guess and there were still very few openings for women, especially women of her age. It was Peggy who surprisingly came up with a possible solution. The house was big she said, why not make use of it? Why not turn Number Two Ladan Road into a small hotel or guest house? Close to the station it would be the first place that travellers would come across.

At first Kathy was none too keen, didn't feel happy about throwing her family home open to strangers but she quickly began to realize she didn't have a lot of choice, if she didn't do something she wouldn't have a family home anyway. Jeremy was aghast at the idea, not at all happy with the idea of his future wife being nothing more than a landlady, it didn't fit in with his image. Strangely Jeremy's opposition just served to make Kathy more determined to go ahead. It was decided though that initially only three rooms would be made available to guests.

It was a very sad day when Kathy had to empty her sister's room, clear it of anything which had been personal to her. Naturally she had to do the same with her room, only the best rooms in the house could be made available if this venture was to solve their financial worries. The infamous desk was once more man-handled out of the small dining room at the front of the house and into the hall, its presence indicating that the hall had now become the reception area. As the project progressed Kathy found herself becoming quite excited, taking pleasure in moving furniture around so as to provide their prospective guests with the very best accommodation. Lizzie, now highly responsible and capable, was given the title of head chambermaid, in charge of none other than her own mother Ruby.

After weeks of preparation and on the verge of finally opening Kathy was surprised when returning from her daily walk one afternoon she saw a rucksack leaning next to the desk in the hall. She made for the kitchen. Surely Peggy hadn't taken in a guest already, they'd agreed on next week at the very earliest?

Seated around the large kitchen table were Peggy, Lizzie, Ruby, Harry and next to him Patrick. They were all laughing, clearly happy to be together again. Patrick looked up, scraped back his chair and without embarrassment went to Kathy and hugged her. She felt the tears coming to her eyes, the first tears she'd allowed herself for some while now. After a moment she pulled away, held him at a distance.

'Patrick my dear how wonderful to see you, and you look well.'

'Aye I am' he grinned 'but pleased to be back.'

'And Dannah' she dared to ask. 'How is he?' Patrick shook his head as if that was a question he was unable to answer.

'Ah ya know, he's coping. He's keeping busy helping me Mammie. She's lots of jobs lined up for him, hardly stops to eat, but then p'raps that's for the best right now' he sighed. Patrick went on to tell them all that he and his uncle had been up to since they left Oakfield. He told them how the trip back home to their old farm had been a mistake, how one day he'd gone looking for Dannah, had eventually found him sitting cross-legged next to Fin's grave in the pouring rain seeming not to even know where he was. Patrick had decided to take control, had told his uncle they were leaving immediately, heading for Dublin and the family. His mother's business venture he said was going well and Dannah had become interested in improving not only the living accommodation but also the business premises. It was now quite a swanky shop, he grinned proudly.

Kathy was reluctant to ask if Dannah would be returning to Oakfield, for some reason it mattered too much. She decided to leave it, hope someone else posed the question. Patrick returned to his job at the farm accompanied by Harry who had actually spent most of his own summer holidays there.

The Ladan Road Guest House opened two weeks later to a fanfare of trumpets but not much else, certainly there were no guests. Kathy was beginning to despair when on a wet and blustery day almost a month after the official opening the door bell rang and they had their first paying guest, none other than a Monsieur Claude Dubois who was seeking accommodation whilst he visited his clients in the area, one such being Hardcastle cycles. Apparently Luci Hardcastle had thought on her feet when he had asked if there was anywhere locally that he might stay. Claude's stay was a resounding success not only for Kathy and her staff but for Claude himself who had found it a very agreeable and convenient way to spend time with Julia Richards.

Julia Richards was still proving a mystery to her brother. Philip had had severe misgivings over the outcome of Julia's examination re-sits. He was a bag of nerves waiting for the results. Julia on the other hand was completely unconcerned, and on the morning that the postman finally popped the dreaded envelope through the letter box it was Philip whose stomach turned over. Julia nonchalantly opened the envelope, unfolded the single sheet of paper, scanned the contents before waving the paper under Philip's nose.

'See' she cried 'Ye of little faith!' and with that she rose from the table and went upstairs to get ready for her stint at the cycle factory. Philip read, and re-read, the contents of the letter. She had done brilliantly passing all the exams with flying colours. So why did she seem so totally disinterested? When later that evening he said as much to Luci she agreed that 'yes it was certainly rather strange.' She turned away not wanting him to see the little smile which she knew would be there.

CHAPTER TEN

Stanley Briggs arrived at the village hall to find Maisie's party in full swing. Although official invitations had been issued the world and his wife were there as Jonas and Luci had also extended many casual invitations, wanting everyone to share in their joy at Maisie's recovery. Looking around for a chair on which to perch himself, for he had no intention of dancing, he saw that they were all occupied either by someone's bottom or a handbag.

'There's a spare chair here Mr. Briggs' called a voice from behind him. Stan turned and saw stationed behind the refreshment table none other than Jeannie Kirk.

'Why hello there Mrs. Kirk' he grinned. 'Didn't see ya hiding behind there. Are ya not dancing?'

'Well not at the moment, it's my back you know, but the doctors always tell me it's good exercise for me and I should do it more often. I do come down to the dance class they hold here sometimes though, trying to be good!' she laughed. Stan edged his way around the table, set the spare chair squarely down beside her and settled his not insubstantial frame.

'Aye, an' ya know what? Someone recommended it to me to try and get a bit of weight off.' He patted his stomach. 'Although I have lost a bit of late with all me walking.'

'Well I'm sure there's no need' said Jeannie. 'We don't all want to be skin and bone do we?'

'That's right kind of ya love' he grinned, tapping her hand, 'But I think you're being a bit economical with the truth there! Any road what are these classes like? Are they a bit formal? Is everyone else really good? 'Cos I ain't too keen on looking a Charlie.' Jeannie laughed.

'No, no not at all, and you'd be made very welcome, there's always a surfeit of ladies. I'm sure you'd find yourself very popular.'

The music suddenly stopped and the dancers began to vacate the dance floor and make their way either back to their seats or to the refreshment table. Jeannie was soon overwhelmed and so Stan, unasked, set-to to help her. Jonas passing by gave them both a cheery thumbs-up.

The tea interval over everyone eagerly took to the dance floor once more.

'How's about we give it a go love?' Stan invited Jeannie, 'I'll give it a try if you will, we can mek idiots of ourselves together.' About to decline, something suddenly stopped her.

'Yes, yes why not! Who cares what we look like any way.'

Stan carefully helped Jeannie to her feet and led her to the edge of the floor where he said 'they could cause least trouble!' It was a slow waltz and one which Jeannie and in spite of his protestations Stanley Briggs were more than capable of executing. Finding themselves enjoying the experience they stayed for the next dance and the next. In the end Jeannie had to accept defeat, said her back was starting to ache a little, and Stan solicitously guided her back to their chairs and then went off in search of an alcoholic drink for them both.

Towards the end of the evening Jonas mounted the tiny stage alongside the band whereupon he made a short but heartfelt speech. He told everyone how blessed he and Maisie felt at her recovery and how equally blessed they were to have so many wonderful friends to share it with. Friends who he said had helped to make some very difficult times bearable. There were many moist eyes that evening.

The band was still going strong when Jeannie told Stan that she really must be going.

'Then I'll walk ya home love' said Stan, 'I've just about worn meself out an' all.'

'No really I wouldn't hear of it' insisted Jeannie. 'I can see you've still got plenty of energy left and I'm fine making my own way home.'

'You'll do nowt o' sort, and that's an end o' it' insisted Stan, making it quite clear he would brook no argument. After finding their coats the pair went in search of Maisie and Jonas to say their "thank yous" and "goodbyes". Maisie thanked them for coming, said how lovely it had been to see them. There she went again, would she ever say that phrase without a lump coming to her throat? Jonas put his arm around Stan's shoulder.

'Grand to see ya enjoying yourself lad, and am I mistaken or are ya losing a bit of weight?' he laughed, playfully patting the other man's middle.

'Aye well I'm trying but I think it's all me walking.'

'All yer walking?' queried Jonas. 'And when did ya ever walk anywhere, yer backside's fairly stuck to yon saddle.'

'Not now it ain't, not since I 'ad me bike pinched.'

'Yer bike pinched?' asked Jonas, incredulous.

'That night we 'ad that pint at 'The Feathers', do ya remember? I went back forrit next day and somebody'd tekken bottom half o' drainpipe wi' me bike still attached!'

'No!' Jonas was scandalized. 'What's the bloody world coming to eh? Next time you'd best get a Carlson, no one'd want to pinch one of those buggers!' he laughed and the rest of them joined in.

When he arrived at the factory the Monday following Maisie's party, having diverted past the village hall to check dates and times of the dance classes, Stan opened his office door to find a spanking new Hardcastle Hopper propped against his desk, a rusting piece of drainpipe tied to its frame. He went next door, flung open the door without knocking. Jonas put down his pen, he'd hardly been able to contain his mirth as he'd heard Stan arriving.

'Ya daft so and so!' exploded Stan, 'you really are a stupid sod'!

'Aye well I allus knew you liked me' guffawed Jonas, thoroughly enjoying the situation.

'Yeah, well jury's out on that one!' responded Stan, 'but I'm not 'aving it so ya can just tek it back. I ain't 'avin no charity.'

'I tell ya what then, treat it as a retirement present if ya really are leaving' said Jonas, and once more took up his pen pretending to be thoroughly absorbed in what he was doing. In fact he was surreptitiously observing Stan's reaction to mention once more of retirement.

Stan's heart had literally sunk like a stone when the 'r' word was mentioned, more doubts about his decision seemed to creep in each day. He could see he was going to get no further arguing with Jonas over the bike, so muttering crossly to himself he closed Jonas' door with rather more force than necessary and returned to his own office resolving to return the cycle to the stores later in the day. Jonas was still laughing quietly to himself when Luci appeared.

'Whatever's got into you?' she asked hanging her jacket behind the door. Jonas couldn't resist, had to relate his joke to Luci – it needed an audience! In fact apart from being highly amusing Stan's reaction had been very revealing thought Jonas, clearly everything still wasn't cut and dried regarding his intention to retire. Selfishly Jonas couldn't help being delighted, but equally was determined to exert no influence.

Each morning for the next week Stan opened his office door to find the spanking new Hardcastle Hopper (drainpipe still attached) leaning against his desk and each morning he returned it to the stores. Into the second week Stan gave in, wheeled the cycle outside and wrote a thank you note to his boss saying he would accept the bike as an early retirement present (if he left) instead of a gold watch! Jonas finding the note on his desk tied to the piece of drainpipe, read it, roared with laughter, screwed it into a ball and fired it at the waste paper basket in the corner.

CHAPTER ELEVEN

Business was not booming at the Guest House. In the three months they had been properly open for business only once had they boasted more than one guest. When Oakfield hosted the annual Regional Brass Band Competition Miriam's old room was occupied by Somerville's Euphonium and one of the smaller rooms at the back by the French Horn.

Kathy was privately concerned about the lack of enthusiasm with which their venture had been greeted but had to constantly reassure Peggy that it wasn't her fault and that it had been a good idea to at least try it. Along with the worry over its apparent failure she was still unhappy over Jeremy's attitude. She had expected him to at least be supportive but he had been nothing of the sort, making it clear he felt it was a bad idea. As it turned out it seemed he probably had been right, it was certainly looking that way, but he surely needn't be so self-righteous about it.

It seemed too as if there was to be no 'Happy ever after' as far as Jeremy and Harry were concerned. Accepting that his mother and father were to divorce he seemed to have no problem with a friendship between his mother and the doctor, but the revelation that Jeremy was indeed his father, which at one time had appeared infinitely possible, seemed a very long way off now. Although polite at all times and superficially friendly there was no natural bond developing between the two. Jeremy was his mother's friend and as far as Harry was concerned that was all there was to it. Harry at the moment trusted his mother. Should he learn the truth she knew he would see her in a completely different light and it would surely change their relationship forever. She wasn't prepared to risk that and no amount of persuasion from Jeremy could change her mind. Harry indeed seemed to have inherited nothing from his real father. In looks he was like his mother and likewise intellectually. He was no high-brow, had no interest in music, history, the classics as Jeremy had. Harry was academic only in so much as it was necessary for his chosen career.

Kathy was acutely aware that as well as funding the household she would very soon be required to finance Harry's veterinary studies. Jeremy had offered to help and she had decided to accept, really she had no choice and in any case why shouldn't he? The house itself was safe, no money was owing on that at least, but it was still an expensive place to run. With three wages to pay, Ruby now also on the payroll, it seemed ridiculous that she would need to find employment herself simply in order to pay them. Of course she could've managed the house on her own but getting rid of Peggy and Lizzie simply wasn't an option, she had to find another way. Dannah had continued paying into the household in his absence but with it being several months now since he'd left, and it looking increasingly unlikely that he would ever return, Kathy knew that very soon she would have to relieve him of any financial obligation and take control herself. Somehow!

During Jonas' extended absence from the factory, ostensibly doing 'The Grand Tour' with her mother, Luci Hardcastle had felt it her duty to show a little more interest in the business just as her father had always hoped. With almost daily involvement it had at last slowly turned into a genuine interest. Her friendship with Philip's sister Julia had also helped to fuel the fire. Julia's insistence that Hardcastles should join other major companies and engage in some large scale advertising, along with her ideas as depicted on the canvasses, had begun to make Luci see the business in an entirely different light. Perhaps it didn't have to be the same old humdrum day in and day out she'd always perceived it to be. Having discussed with Stan the possible benefits of advertising, and weighing it up against the costs that would be incurred, they had agreed that it was certainly worth looking into but something which would naturally have to wait for the return of Jonas.

As Luci made her way to the village hall one Sunday afternoon to rehearse the chorus for the drama group's latest production, her eye was caught by a notice in the window of 'Sharps Ironmongers'. The shop would be closing she read due to retirement and a closing down sale would commence in two weeks time. Above the shop hung a large sign proclaiming the premises to be 'To Let'. The chorus were a complete nightmare that afternoon coming in when they shouldn't and being decidedly off key and Luci was impatient, distracted, for from goodness knows where an idea had come to her which had absolutely nothing to do with Jerome Kern or Oscar Hammerstein. As the rehearsals finally, mercifully, came to an end she went across the hall to Philip who had been busy in another corner coaching the principals, hooked her arm through his and told him there was something she wanted to show him.

Heading for home Luci pulled Philip to one side as they drew level with Sharps' shop.

'Look, come here and look' urged Luci, pressing her face against the window, cupping her hands round her eyes to keep out the light and give her a better view of the inside. Philip although having no idea at all why he was required to do this nonetheless obliged. Inside they could see the shop was crammed full, things hanging from every available space and stacked from floor to ceiling, dingy and old fashioned but to Luci it already held huge possibilities. 'Well?' she said turning excitedly to Philip. Philip was nonplussed.

'Well what?' he asked, puzzled.

'For a shop for us, silly!' she cried.

'A shop for you? You mean a shop for Hardcastles?'

'Yes, exactly' she said. 'Since Julia and I had that chat about advertising things have been buzzing in my head about what else we could do and as soon as I saw this shop I knew. At the moment we only sell our bikes locally straight from the factory, they're not displayed or anything so people aren't really able to compare, consider which model might be the best for them. If we were to have them on display in a shop it would be so much nicer and I'm sure we'd sell more.'

Philip certainly didn't want to dampen her enthusiasm. Whilst wanting to agree so as not to burst her bubble he still knew that he must advise some degree of caution.

'Well you might be right, but don't forget the overheads which would go alongside. The rent for a start, and then there would be heating and lighting costs and of course the cost for staff.'

Luci stamped her foot, turned from the window and without another word made off in the direction of home.

'Oh you!' she called over her shoulder, exasperated. 'Always the banker! Always the wet blanket! Have you no imagination, no creativity?' Philip hurried after her.

'Hey, hey wait a minute.' He grabbed her arm to stop her. 'I'm just pointing out some pitfalls that's all, that's my job, that's what I do.'

'And don't I know it!' shouted Luci fiercely, pulling her arm away, 'and what's more you needn't bother walking me home, I'll manage quite well on my own. And besides' she added sarcastically, 'you might even find a problem with that!' Philip knew when he was beaten, let her walk away.

That night as she got ready for bed Luci was still pondering on what he'd said. He could be right, she acknowledged that, but surely if you never tried anything! Over the last months Luci had come to have a little more respect for herself, a little more self-belief. She had been encouraged – and not just by Philip – to join the drama group and was now their chorus rehearsal pianist and much valued. Her budding interest in the business had been a revelation to her and she knew would delight her parents. Her romance with Philip had blossomed in spite of the odd inevitable spat such as this afternoon's. No, Luci's life had done an about turn and this latest idea of hers was going to come to fruition no matter what. She was determined.

The next time she saw Philip, she had calmed down and he was determined to try and be more supportive. He agreed that the shop could be a really good idea, but that there were many things to take into consideration and in his defence he said that was all he'd been trying to do when she'd flown off the handle.

Luci decided on this occasion to let his rebuke pass because she needed his help, needed help with the figures. Philip had to tactfully refuse saying he wouldn't want to give her father the impression that he was getting involved with the family business unless asked officially. Luci was disappointed but asked could he just help by getting details of the lease etc. He was quite happy he said to obtain details such as these which would be matters of general interest anyway.

A few days later Luci paid a visit to the ironmongery store supposedly desperately needing to purchase a new set of saucepans. She browsed for a while noting the layout and size of the premises, any changes which might need to be made. The shop was double fronted, a bay at one side and a large flat window at the other. In the middle were double doors with a small canopy above. What Luci saw impressed her and convinced her even more that what she was considering would work. Certainly the inside needed cleaning up, painting and re-organizing but that was easily dealt with. Just as she had been busy surveying her prospective premises Philip had been equally busy gathering together information regarding the lease and any other relevant details. All he would not get involved with were details pertinent to the business – profitability etc., that had to be entirely at the family's discretion he insisted.

By the time her parents had returned from their trip Luci had 'in her head' bought the shop, opened it and was doing a roaring trade. The news that her parents had brought with them turned everything on its head – nothing else seemed to matter – how could it? Maisie's recovery changed their world and for some while the family just basked in the joy of it all.

Philip and Luci's engagement announcement had been forgotten for the time being. Luci's new found interest in the business had also been laid to one side as she shared in her mother's new life. But inevitably things began to settle down, things once more began to be taken for granted.

Jonas was back at the factory and after a while much to his amazement Luci joined him. Her father had been interested and delighted to learn of his daughter's involvement whilst he'd been away and wasted no time in telling her so. Eventually Luci decided the time was right to put forward her idea of the shop. Mercifully the shop had up until now not been re-let, Luci had spent a nail biting time waiting for just that to happen. Although not 'Let' the shop was now empty, the closing down sale completed and Mr. and Mrs. Sharp had moved off to their retirement bungalow in a neighbouring village.

'Daddy' she began 'I've been wondering if it might be a good idea to have a shop?'

'A shop? What for lass? What would we be doing with a shop?' Luci went on to explain her reasoning, saying how they were bound to sell more cycles from an actual shop, people would prefer it to coming to the factory.

'And' she said triumphantly, surprising even herself, yet another idea appearing in her head, 'we could do repairs! I'm sure people are so busy these days they really don't have the time or inclination to be messing around mending punctures and things.' Jonas was wary of dismissing the suggestion out of hand, saying he would give it a bit of thought, talk it over with Stan. Luci was quite excited, normally he would politely ignore her suggestions.

Jonas did exactly as he'd said he would do, discussed it with Stan. They both knew that short of a miracle war was looming and if that were to happen there would be no need of shops to sell their cycles, fuel would be rationed and transport would become more difficult, pedal power would really come into its own, it would have to. His conversation over the shop with Stan was practical, when he discussed it with Maisie more emotional and personal, for with Luci finally showing an interest in the business they had no wish to dissuade her, they agreed to look into it further. Jonas called Luci into his office one afternoon, Stan sitting by his side, and told her that they'd decided to find out more, find out about the lease, in fact she could find out about the lease. Thanks to Philip Luci already had the details of the lease, thanks to Philip was fully up to scratch on all the finer details. She decided to give it a few days before divulging all she actually already knew. After thinking it over carefully and anxious to sustain Luci's belated interest in the business Jonas decided to go ahead with her proposal.

Julia still working in the paint shop prior to taking up a teaching appointment in the new term was thrilled for Luci and pleased that her influence had had a good effect on her. She knew her brother would have found life with a 'lady of leisure' tedious eventually and she really liked Luci, looked forward to having her as a sister-in-law. Philip although sad to lose Julia was thrilled that at last his sister would be taking up her new post, something which she had worked hard for, also pleased that she would at last be financially independent. He felt now was the time to push forward his own plans, most particularly his engagement to Luci. Unfortunately however the young lady in question was not of the same mind being completely absorbed with the shop which had rapidly become her "raison d'etre". He was happy for her, of course he was, happy to see her blossoming, just worried that not so very long ago it would've been he who would have been the cause. Luci had really been bitten by the business bug and there was no stopping her, he realized he would have to bide his time.

The contracts for the lease on the shop were duly exchanged and work began on both the interior and exterior of the premises. Luci knew just how she wanted it to be and she had her way, aided and abetted by Julia. On the day a delivery of Hardcastle cycles arrived Luci was delirious. The one thing that hadn't been entirely obvious was quite who would serve in the shop. At first it was thought a couple of the girls currently working in the factory would be the answer. But it wasn't for two reasons. The factory girls enjoyed the gossip and camaraderie of their contemporaries too much to be hidden away in a little shop pretty much on their own. Also the girls were all of an age where marriage and therefore retirement from the workforce was always on the cards eliminating any continuity.

Maisie alone knew that Katherine Watson-Smythe was looking for work, had become party to many of Kathy's woes and worries over recent months as she had unloaded her grief over her sister. Maisie was in two minds whether to suggest Kathy for the job. Might she be insulted? After all it was hardly some high powered post. It was quite a dilemma and one which caused her several sleepless nights.

In the end after first speaking to Jonas she put her qualms to one side, suggested to Kathy that it might be an option. Kathy was thrilled, although the salary wouldn't be huge it would be a help, and who knows she laughed, with commission she might soon make a fortune. Jeremy once again wasn't happy, made it quite plain that he considered she would be lowering herself. Brushing aside his reservations she accepted the offer, looking forward in any case to being out of the house, having something to do. The Guest House business had in fact picked up a little recently, was making a small contribution to expenses, but it was nothing that Peggy, Lizzie and Ruby couldn't handle on their own. No, she was best out of the way.

From the very first day Kathy loved her new job, revelling in keeping the shop tidy and eye-catching, making sure the books were up to date. Most of all though she loved the company, the walk to work each morning, the camaraderie with the other shopkeepers. To top it all trade was brisk and Kathy was kept busy which was just what she needed. For the first time in a long time she was tired at the end of the day, engrossed in things other than her own problems.

After locking up and taking a leisurely stroll home one afternoon Kathy entering the house saw a pile of luggage stacked against the desk. Things were certainly looking up she thought, all these cases couldn't possibly belong to one person, either that or whoever it was intended a long stay. She made her way down the hall to the kitchen and there they were chatting and laughing, Peggy, Lizzie, Harry, Patrick and Dannah. Either side of Dannah was a pretty little girl and a handsome dark haired boy. Next to Patrick was a stunning red head, hair falling softly around her shoulders. Dannah turned and saw her, pushed back his chair, stood up smiling his slow smile.

'Katherine.'

'Oh Dannah' Kathy said, tears sparkling in her eyes, 'How good to see you' and she realized in that instant how much she meant it, how much she had missed him. Peggy rose from her seat, in fact everyone seemed to as Dannah went to her and held her quite unselfconsciously in his arms. At length she pulled away, embarrassed and flustered, looking enquiringly at the strangers whilst knowing without a shadow of a doubt who they must be. Dannah went around the table to the young woman.

'Allow me to introduce my lovely sister-in-law Sarah' he smiled, putting his arm around her shoulders and pulling her close. 'And this here is my little darlin' of a niece Christie' he said as he bent down and lifted the little girl into his arms. Next he went to the boy. 'And this' he said proudly 'is our very own Nial, the good looking one of the family!' he joked.

'Aw, Uncle Dannah' said the boy, blushing to his roots, embarrassed.

CHAPTER TWELVE

Dannah hadn't been at all sure about returning to Oakfield. He'd expected his decision would come naturally but it hadn't. And so when over the breakfast table one morning, completely out of the blue, Sarah had made her announcement he had been wary.

'I'm thinking I'd like to be visiting me son Dannah' she said. 'It's bin a while now since he went back and with business being a bit slack over the summer I'm of a mind to take advantage of the little 'uns' school holidays and go over to England. What do you think? P'raps you'd like to come too?' Sarah knew only too well that her brother-in-law was struggling to decide what to do with his future, knew that something needed to be done to force him into action for it had been some time now since Miriam had died. They both knew that staying with her, being nothing more than a general dogsbody, couldn't go on forever. Sarah did indeed want to see her son, desperate to persuade him home to Ireland and away from the perils of impending war. Dannah privately thought she had little chance of succeeding. Patrick was a determined, stubborn young man but he knew equally she wouldn't rest until she had at least tried. In the end Dannah agreed to go with them to England recognizing, even if she didn't, that the journey would be difficult for a woman on her own with two young children.

Having not kept up a very good line of correspondence with the household and Patrick's news being rare and limited to his own activities Dannah had no idea of the changes which had taken place in his absence, Kathy getting a job and the house being turned into a Guest House. He had been more than a little taken aback when he'd seen the "Rooms to Let" sign in the dining room window, perhaps there wouldn't be room for them to stay? With business as it was however they were all able to be accommodated, especially when Nial was insistent on having a camp bed in the two older boys' room. When Peggy had explained Katherine was at work Dannah had assumed it must be some administrative post she had taken. When told she was working in a shop he was more than a little surprised recalling his first meeting with her when he'd considered her very 'upper class' and 'hoity toity'! Dannah's sudden re-appearance had caused a wealth of new emotions for Kathy. Her initial dislike of the man had been replaced she realized with feelings of comfort and reassurance, she was happier with him around.

As Kathy made ready to leave for work the morning after the family's arrival she found herself way-laid by Dannah.

'Christie and I were wondering if you'd like a bit o'company on your walk to work?' he asked.

'Why yes I'd enjoy that' she answered, 'Give us chance to catch up.'

Christie walked between them holding each of their hands and insistently calling for 'a swing' which they did laughingly, lifting her from her feet and swinging her forward every few yards. This was the sight that greeted Jeremy as he drove away from the surgery and along the High Street ready to commence his morning rounds. Pulling into the kerb alongside Dannah he went around the bonnet of the car to him, shook his hand warmly.

'Good to see you back old man' he grinned, 'you back for good?'

'Aw, of that I'm not too sure at the moment. P'raps just a wee holiday. I'm here with my sister-in-law and my nephew and niece here' he said, smiling fondly down at Christie. 'We've come to visit Patrick, try and persuade him home.'

'Oh. Well for whatever reason it's good to see you, very good indeed. But for the moment you'll have to excuse me, I really must crack on with my visits.' Jeremy smiled down at Christie patting her on the head.

'Lovely to meet you young lady.' He turned to Kathy, there was no greeting just a curt nod of the head.

'Of course, don't let us hold you up' grinned Dannah, stepping away from the car and pretending he hadn't noticed the frostiness between them. 'We'll maybe see you later? Bye for now.' The doctor got into the car, gave a small wave and slid the car into gear and away. Christie having kept tight hold of Kathy's hand during the exchange was anxious to continue their game. The trio arrived at the shop to see Joshua Chippings disappearing with his bike down the narrow passage which ran alongside. Kathy turning from unlocking the door met Dannah's quizzical gaze.

'Oh that's Josh, he does all our repairs, he works in a little shed out the back.' The bell tinkled above their heads as she led the way inside flicking on the lights as she went, the shop completely and thoughtfully refitted had all the latest amenities. Dannah was impressed with what he saw, rack upon rack of Hardcastle cycles of every shape, size and colour, some were even suspended from the ceiling. 'I'll just pop my head out, check Josh is alright' Kathy called from the back of the shop.

Joshua Chippings was more than alright, 'happy as laddie' in his new role. Recently retired as a foreman from Hardcastles he hadn't expected to work again, had anticipated spending his days doing a bit of fishing or yarning with his pals in the bar of 'The Feathers'. When he'd heard plans for a repair shop he'd been the first on Kathy's doorstep to apply for a job. How could she turn him down? Josh had built the machines – he would certainly know how to repair them!

Just as Josh loved his new job so Tommy Fletcher loved Josh. Now living just a stone's throw away with Mavis and John Tremmings and his big sister Joannie, Tommy loved and knew all there was to know about what went on in the High Street. When calling into the cycle shop one afternoon with his Auntie Mavis, taking a newly baked piece of Parkin for Miss Kathy to have with her afternoon tea, he'd been asked to take a slice to Joshua who was working in his shed out the back. Tommy loved the shed, the smell of it, the oily smell from all the bits and pieces which were necessary for Josh to do his repairs. That first afternoon Josh had produced a special little stool for Tommy to sit on, out of harm's way but close enough to see what was going on. They had become firm friends and from that day Tommy became a regular visitor to the shed, would sit for hours on the tiny stool, or on a fine day on the step of the shed singing away whilst Josh carried out his repairs. Today being a school holiday Tommy turned up earlier than usual, this time clutching a piece of Auntie Mavis' shortbread for them both to share at Josh's 'elevenses'. Dannah and Christie were still inside inspecting the shop. Christie was enchanted by a bright pink little girl's bike with a white basket on the front rather inaptly named a 'Pink Witch'.

'Please Uncle Dannah, pleese, pleese can I have it?' she begged. Dannah laughed.

'And how would we be getting it all the way home to Dublin may I ask? And in any case madam I didn't know you could even ride one.' Christie stuck out her chest and her bottom lip.

'I can learns, it would na take me long and then I could ride it all the way back to Dublin' she cried excitedly, clapping her hands.

'You're probably right at that' agreed Dannah solemnly, 'But who am I to take the risk of you tiring out your poor little legs?'

'Tis not fair!' pouted Christie, staring hard at her uncle. Kathy seeing only too clearly that the conversation couldn't possibly have a happy outcome decided to intervene. She knelt down to the now teary little girl.

'I'm sorry to say darling that I have to agree with your Uncle Dannah, you could hardly ride or carry a bicycle all the way back to Ireland. But I tell you what, if I'm not mistaken Joshua has a little tricycle about your size that he's busy repairing in his shed, how about you and I go and ask if you might borrow it for a while – see how you get on?' The child quickly rubbed the tears from her eyes.

'Really?' Christie's eyes shone. 'That would be real nice and I'm sure I'll learns quicker 'an any!'

'Well come on then' smiled Kathy reaching for her hand. 'We'll go right now if Uncle Dannah won't mind looking after the shop?' Dannah was smiling broadly.

'Aye go on away with ya you pair o' minx, leave a man to do all the hard work, why don't ya.'

Tommy was unhappy with an interloper in the shed and a girl at that, all she seemed to do was squeal. She squealed as Josh sat her on the silver three-wheeler and made out it was real difficult to push and pedal at the same time, she squealed as she and the bike were wheeled out into the yard. Miss Kathy was laughing and even Josh his friend was acting as though he found it funny. Girls! They really were useless! Irritatingly this Christie quickly got the hang of the pedalling and pushing and was soon being pushed proudly round the side of the shop and into the High Street by a smiling Josh and Miss Kathy. Tommy couldn't bear to watch, had had more than enough of the stupid girl and went to sit patiently on his stool to wait for Josh and normality to return. Christie was allowed to take the tricycle home with her to use for the rest of her holiday and when he saw she was finally going home he did reluctantly join in waving her off! 'Good riddance!' he muttered under his breath.

The next morning Tommy even earlier than usual raced round to the shed at the back of the shop but stopped dead in his tracks when he saw the silver tricycle already parked outside. He pushed his hands deep into the pockets of his shorts and turned on his heel to walk away. As he did so he heard another voice, a boy's voice this time, the squealing and giggling had stopped. He put his head round the door. The pesky girl stood demurely in front of Josh, chin on chest looking down at the floor.

'I'm real good at it now Mr. Josh, 'onest I am' she was saying. 'I rided all the way 'ere on me own!' The boy standing behind her, clearly older, scoffed loudly.

'You what! I had to push you up the hill because it was 'too hard' he mimicked in a girly voice. 'And then at the other side I had to chase after you 'cos you couldn't put the brake on, you're useless' he ended. Christie began to cry, heartbreaking sobs.

'Now, now' said Josh not used to childish wrangling. 'I'm sure there's nowt to fall art abhat, and look' he said relieved. 'Here's our Tommy! Hello there Tom and 'ow's you?'

'Oh I'm fine thanks Mr. Josh' he grinned, pleased to be able to help his old friend, he'd spotted his discomfort immediately.

'Tommy Fletcher' he said, holding out his hand to the boy over the girl's head.

'Nial Delaney' grinned the other boy. 'Pleased to meet ya, and this 'ere' – he pointed to the girl dismissively – 'this 'ere's me sister Christie' and he pulled a face.

'Aye I know who she is right enough' replied Tommy equally dismissively.

By lunch time all the dramas were over, Josh back on his own, Christie having returned home with her uncle and the two boys gone for a kick about on the Ovo, a piece of land where the old soap factory of the same name had once stood. Peace was restored and Joshua was grateful to be able to get on with his repairs. He hadn't honestly expected to be so busy, in his day people fixed their own bikes. Fixed their own everything! But not these days, no, people didn't seem to have the time no more. Mind you it was good for business, good for him, kept him from becoming an 'old woman' sitting at home.

Although thwarted so far in her attempts to persuade Patrick back home Sarah was at least enjoying her holiday, both children seeming to be fully occupied, Nial with his new friend Tommy and Christie with Dannah and the tricycle. Sarah was left to her own devices, taking long walks around the village, casting a professional eye over the many retail establishments. She also spent time with Peggy. Both experienced seamstresses and interested in needle craft of all kinds they found they had much in common.

Jeremy Kirk put in an appearance at the house in Ladan Road most days, but even to Dannah's untrained eye there didn't seem to be the same connection between him and Kathy. On the surface they were polite and seemingly enjoying each other's company but the spark that had been between them before was no longer there. But why was that surprising he mused, so much had happened to Kathy since she'd returned to England and not much of it good, how could she not have changed? The only thing was that as far as he was concerned she'd changed for the better. At first she'd seemed stiff, self-obsessed, verging on the pompous and intrinsically cold. Now after all that had befallen her she was much kinder, more thoughtful, caring, able to laugh at herself, small wonder then if she no longer fitted quite so well with Jeremy.

Dannah, as much as he liked and respected Jeremy, knew that he was very aware of his own importance, his position in the community. He was a very intelligent man and charming with it, but maybe that was no longer enough for Kathy? He chided himself however that it was Kathy's business, nothing to do with him, they'd sort it out for themselves. The only thing he had to worry him was his own decision, whether or not to remain in Oakfield. Dannah wasn't the only one to whom his decision mattered. When he heard of his return Jonas Hardcastle was anxious about what Dannah might finally decide, knowing he needed to take some time off from the factory, spend some precious time with Maisie.

Professor Zeigler whilst expressing delight at what he had achieved nonetheless had felt duty bound to point out that the long term prognosis for Maisie was uncertain. Whilst the procedure could last forever, equally it might not, there was simply no way of knowing. Jonas wanted to be with Maisie to share in her new found happiness, her new life especially if God forbid it should only prove temporary. They had to make the most of every minute. And then of course there was that ever present nagging doubt over war. If indeed war did come Jonas knew it would have serious consequences for everyone. He would lose a large proportion of his workforce, single unmarried men would be the first to be sent to fight and then possibly to be... Well it just didn't bear thinking about. There was the distinct possibility that his factory would be commandeered for the war effort, and he imagined in any case that the steel they used would be required for things far more important than bicycles. So everything hung in the balance leaving Jonas anxious to take time away from the business before events overcame them. Dannah Delaney was crucial to his plans, for if he stayed in Oakfield and returned to his job at the factory Jonas would more easily be able to step down for a while at least. Mercifully Dannah had no knowledge of all this for if he had his decision would not have been his own.

Philip Richards was also troubled by the news he read each day in the paper, in his opinion war was inevitable, just a matter of when, not if. Knowing that he would be involved made him even more convinced he wanted to be married to Luci and sooner rather than later, realized he wanted it more than anything in the world.

Luci now over the initial euphoria of her mother's cure, her success with the shop and Hardcastles' new advertising campaigns, would he felt be more susceptible to the idea of marriage. He decided to pose the question to her again.

He chose an evening having an intimate meal at his cottage to ask Luci if she was now ready for marriage. As he came through from the kitchen carrying a tray with the coffee he saw she'd moved away from the candle-lit table which he had so carefully arranged and was now settled on his small sofa, legs tucked underneath her. He placed the tray on the low table in front of the fire, sat down beside her turning to her to begin his prepared speech. Before he could say anything…

'Philip.' She seemed nervous. 'I was wondering... What do you think? Do you think now would be a good time to announce our engagement?' Philip burst out laughing. 'What? what?' she cried, 'Don't you want to anymore?' He took her face in his hands smiling his lovely smile.

'More than anything darling, more than anything' he whispered.

'Oh Philip I thought for one horrible minute you'd changed your mind.' For answer he gently kissed her on the lips. It soon became clear however that although their intentions had been the same, the reasoning behind them had been entirely different.

Luci had decided that if Philip was married and war was to come then he wouldn't be one of the first to be called up, one of the first to be sent to fight. It was assumed that it would be young single men who would be called upon first to serve their country and if Philip already in his late twenties was married he would be neither. Philip though knew that if war did come he would be one of the first to enlist, his pride wouldn't allow him to do any other and if he was to go away to war he wanted to enjoy being married to Luci if only for a short while. Philip knew he must be honest with her, leave her in no doubt as to his intentions. Luci was shocked when she heard his plans, so different from her own, felt she needed time to think it through, she certainly didn't want to end up a young widow. Philip was aware she needed time to get things straight in her own mind and agreed, albeit reluctantly, to give her as much time as she needed, she had to be sure he said.

Luci took her time, mulled it over, telling herself in the end that if he was brave enough to go and fight for his country then she must be brave enough to support him, she wouldn't want to marry a coward after all. In the end she told him how proud she was of him and that they must 'get on with it', organize their wedding.

The evening Philip asked Jonas for his daughter's hand in marriage was bitter sweet. Maisie and Jonas were happy for Luci, happy with her choice but deep down they secretly questioned the timing. Jonas was sad, terrified of what it might entail for his beloved daughter, but nonetheless proud of his future son-in-law, knowing full well that in his position he would've done exactly the same. At least thought Jonas he'd been honest with Luci and she bless her had been brave enough to accept it.

Jonas knew about war. When the last war had broken out, had immediately enlisted alongside Stanley Briggs and John Tremmings. He had stood in trenches up to his waist in water, rats sliding down the muddy walls and drowning beside him, floating next to his body. A big man, Jonas had returned home a shadow of his former self, but at least he came home, all three of them had. They had been lucky surviving bullets, bombs and fevers, left feeling guilty that the only effects for them had been arthritic joints. No, Jonas Hardcastle knew about war all right, equally knew that Philip was only too aware of the perils it would bring but nonetheless was prepared to go immediately and without question to fight for the freedom of his country. Although anxious for his beloved daughter he was proud of him.

Everyone was aware that this would be a very different war, not just fought in distant lands, in muddy trenches, but in the air and at sea, a war where people would be attacked in their own homes. When Jonas had come home all he'd said he needed was to see 'the sun and the breeze and the birds in the trees', that had been his mantra and was to this day. As long as he could do all of those he considered he should be content.

CHAPTER THIRTEEN

Tommy Fletcher had always disliked girls, could see no purpose for them, all they did was giggle or wail and he couldn't abide either. He especially disliked Christie Delaney. After a particularly irksome morning when she'd stamped her foot and insisted on joining him and Nial for their usual kick about he'd had enough. If Tommy knew anything he knew about bikes having spent so much time with his idol Josh. Irritated beyond belief with Christie he felt she needed teaching a lesson and decided to tamper with the brakes on her borrowed tricycle. Unnoticed he placed a thin wooden wedge in the mechanism to prevent it closing around the wheel 'That'll scare her' he thought, pleased with himself.

It was the next morning as he returned from his early paper round that he was forced to actually witness what he had done. Heading for the alley at the side of Tremmings Grocers which he now called home he happened to glance up the hill which was the High Street. Sure enough on the brow of the hill was the silver three wheeler with Christie astride. Following behind but at a distance was her Uncle Dannah. Tommy watched open mouthed as a cat shot out of a nearby passage and straight into Christie's path. Screaming with shock Christie was pulling hard on the brake but finding no resistance was careering down the slope at full speed, totally out of control, heading towards the edge of the kerb and the road beyond. Tommy could see a calamity of epic proportions about to ensue. Flinging his paper sack down he hurled himself at the bike as it whizzed past, frantically reaching out to grab the handlebars and pulling with all his might to bring the bike to a halt. Hanging on for grim death he managed to finally haul it towards him. The bike coming to a sudden stop jolted Christie from the saddle and she was dumped unceremoniously on to the pavement. Christie's screams brought Mavis Tremmings scurrying from the yard at the back of the shop where she'd been hanging out some washing, and Kathy from the shop at the end of the terrace.

With Christie finally quietened and taken to the back room of Tremmings' emporium to have her cuts and grazes attended to Dannah went to Tommy to thank him. In fact quite a crowd had gathered wanting to add their congratulations.

So grateful were Christie's family that Tommy was invited to a special tea at Number Two Ladan Road where every single mouthful was a torture. Tommy had been fortunate in so much as the wedge he had so carefully hidden had obviously come loose as the bike had eventually turned on its side and hit the ground, and so to all intents and purposes even to a trained eye the cycle appeared in tact and perfectly safe. Mavis Tremmings often said that you didn't need to go to church or spend all your time on your knees to be a Christian, in fact after the death of her beloved son Sammy she'd been unable to do either. Mavis maintained that God was your conscience, your conscience was God speaking to you. Until now Tommy hadn't known what she'd meant, but he did now. For although no one else knew what he'd done, he knew and always would, through his conscience this God was telling him he'd done something wrong, something very wrong.

For the rest of the holiday Tommy was nice to Christie. Everyone assuming he felt sorry for her nodded their heads in approval, which only served to make Tommy feel even worse.

It hadn't in fact taken Dannah long to reach his decision. Actually being in Oakfield had focused his mind and it had come quite naturally. He left telling Sarah until just a week before the family were due to return to Ireland. Taking one of their regular strolls and ending up as usual at the Haven he'd gazed out over the mud and stones, the murky brown water.

'I've decided to stay darlin'' he said not turning to look at her. Sarah likewise kept her gaze on the water.

'Well I can't say I'm surprised' she answered. 'It's certainly not beautiful old Ireland, but the people are great an' obviously think the world of you. So no, I'm not surprised and I'm pleased for you I really am. In any case should you ever have a change of heart you know we'll be there for you.' At last Dannah turned to her.

'You know I love you Sarah Delaney' he grinned. 'My brother was the luckiest man in the world to have had you, even if for such a short time.' He pulled her roughly to him.

'Ah get away with you' laughed Sarah still not able to face him. 'Twas me who was the lucky one to have him and his beautiful children.' Secretly Sarah was sad to hear his news. She had enjoyed having him with her in Dublin, had hoped he would be returning with them for good. Her idea to bring him back to Oakfield to finally push him into making a decision had been a risk she'd known but now they had their answer and they could all move on. Dannah belonged here now amongst people he loved and who had come to love him.

Patrick had not been persuaded to return with them, saying vaguely only 'one day maybe'. Sarah had had to be content with that. Tommy Fletcher was more than happy to wave Christie off when the family finally left to return to Ireland for she had become very clingy since his guilt had made him be nice to her.

Dannah's first port of call after waving goodbye to the family was the cycle factory hoping to see Jonas Hardcastle. There was no time like the present he'd said to Kathy. Jonas had been delighted to hear that Dannah wanted to return and was relieved that he wanted to do so immediately.

'There's nothing like work to tek your mind off things' he'd said. He felt confident now that he could spend the time he needed with Maisie, leaving the business in the capable hands of Stan, who had finally reneged on his arrangement with Mollie Shakespeare and decided he was not yet ready for retirement, and now Dannah. Yes he thought, the two of them would do very well. Luci appeared to have got over her 'business bug' for the time being and was happily planning her wedding with her mother.

Kathy was delighted when Dannah reported back on his interview with Jonas that evening over dinner. In fact everyone was relieved, considering Dannah a safe, supportive presence and feeling that was what would be needed to guide them through the possible storms to come. By mutual agreement Kathy and Dannah had decided that however awkward and unpleasant, finances needed to be discussed. They talked it over having coffee one evening in the drawing room. First on the agenda was the Guest House business and its viability. Although bookings had increased slightly it was only just making a profit and neither of them could see any reason why there should be any marked improvement. Was it really worth the disruption it caused? On balance they felt not but always there was Peggy to consider, it having been her suggestion. Who would tell her if they deemed it to be a failure? Once again – and rather cowardly they had to admit because neither of them wanted to upset Peggy – they decided to give it a little while longer. In any case who knew what the future held for the country?

With Dannah already contributing – indeed he'd continued to do so whilst he was away in Ireland – Kathy felt it was unfair when he offered to put more into the pot once he resumed work at the factory.

'Oh no' she cried 'definitely not, it's not even your house and you already pay more than your fair share for you and Patrick.'

'Whatever, we owe it to Miriam to make it work. You as her sister and me... well me because I loved her.' The sadness suddenly overwhelmed them both and yet again their financial troubles were put in abeyance.

CHAPTER FOURTEEN

The car slowly drew level with the church gate. Jim darted round the back of the car ready to open the door for the blushing bride. Lined up on the crumbling churchyard wall were many of the village children. In keeping with long tradition once the bride had passed through the gate a rope would be slung across the entrance and only once several bright new coins had been thrown to the assembled children would the bride and groom be allowed out to commence their new life together.

Her Matron of Honour stood waiting in the porch, beside her the page boy, his face wreathed in smiles. She felt the dampness seeping from the walls, the cold of the ancient flag stones beneath her delicate slippers. The organ began to play. The small procession made its way slowly down the aisle. Faces turned to smile, to wish her well. She hadn't expected there to be so many people. As she arrived at the altar the music reached a crescendo then faded away. She turned, passed her small posy over the head of her page boy into the waiting hands of her Matron of Honour. Joannie Fletcher pushed back her veil and looked into the adoring eyes of Jack Thorn.

Having declared himself to be the one 'giving her away' John Tremmings stepped back, took his place in the front pew beside Mavis, the pair having become surrogate parents to the orphaned Joannie and her younger brother Tommy. Tommy in his page boy finery squeezed in between them.

On the opposite side of the aisle Gladys Thorn stood proud but alone, a widow now, her beloved Bert being taken from her six months earlier. Taken before he was able to witness this happy day for his only child.

The ceremony over the happy couple returned down the aisle, smilingly acknowledging the good wishes of friends and neighbours. Joannie's best friend Cissie walked behind the happy couple. Tommy couldn't help a giggle when her husband Constable Downs gave her a huge wink.

Luci stood reflecting on her own wedding day almost a year ago now, Philip's arm protectively around her, her own arm resting comfortingly on her bump, beside her Maisie, Jonas and Bernie.

The guests made their way down to the Swan Hotel in Ladan Road, the small back room having been hired so that cake and wine could be enjoyed before the bride and groom headed off for their honeymoon. Jonas Hardcastle, lifelong friend of John Tremmings and employer of Jack Thorn, had generously insisted on loaning his car to transport the bride to the church and following the service the bride and groom to their reception. The rest of the wedding party walked with the exception of Tommy who insisted on travelling with his 'Joannie'.

The day following the wedding was equally momentous but distressingly sombre. The morning of Sunday the Third of September 1939 found the entire country gathered around their radios. Waiting. The inhabitants of sleepy Oakfield were no exception hoping for good news that wasn't to come.

The residents of Number Two Ladan Road hovered around the kitchen waiting for 11 o'clock when the Prime Minister Neville Chamberlain was to broadcast to the nation. In their hearts they knew what he would say, had been preparing for it for most of the year. In April when the Military Training Act had been passed requiring all able-bodied men between the ages of twenty and twenty one to undertake six months military training they knew the writing was on the wall. Winston Churchill's insistence in a magazine article that he believed Germany was keen to make war before the end of the year, coupled with the fact that that very same day 200,000 men were called up to fight in the 'event of war', merely added weight to their concerns. The 'trial run' for the blackout which had taken place in August had shaken those still in denial. When on September 1st German troops had invaded Poland, the evacuation of 3,000,000 women and children had begun and the Royal Air Force was officially mobilized, even the most optimistic had had to accept the inevitable. But there was always hope.

At 10.45 they took their places around the kitchen table. Dannah sat at the head, either side of him Kathy and Peggy, next to them Harry and Patrick. Dannah turned the knob on the bakerlite radio. It spluttered into life, crackled and then died. He whacked it on the top with the flat of his hand, classical music came – and went. Patrick leapt to his feet, himself gave the radio a smack, once again it crackled into life and died. They looked at each other aghast. Peggy Barley took control.

'Right that's it then' she said. 'We ain't gonna get much out o' that thing, best go next door, their's will be sure to be working, Edgar Desmond will've med certain o' that!' As one they hurried out of the door and down the scullery steps. Nancy appeared at the neighbours' door and Peggy explained what had happened.

'Course love, come in an' welcome, might as well 'ear the news together 'adn't we?'

And so it was that the Henderson and Ladan Road households heard the fate of their country together.

'I am speaking to you from the Cabinet Room at 10 Downing Street....'

Jonas, Maisie, Jim and Bernie sat together anxiously, sunshine streaming through the drawing room windows, listening intently to their radio.

'This morning the British Ambassador in Berlin handed the German Government a final note stating that.......'

Above the Tremmings' shop, John, Mavis, Gladys Thorn and Tommy Fletcher gathered around the radio on the sideboard next to the fireplace.

'unless we heard from them by 11 o'clock that they were prepared at once to withdraw their troops from Poland.....'

Luci and Philip Richards sat in their tiny living room holding hands, Luci's free hand resting protectively on her now restless bump.

'a state of war would exist between us........'

Jeannie Kirk was busy in the kitchen preparing Sunday lunch but still within earshot of the radio. Jeremy and Stanley Briggs sat as close as they could not wanting to miss a single word.

'I have to tell you that no such undertaking has been received and.......'

The newly wed Mr. and Mrs. Thorn cuddled together on the sofa enjoying their first day of married life alone, Gladys having moved in with the Tremmings for a week to allow them their 'honeymoon'.

'that consequently this country is at war with Germany.....'

Joannie pulled away from Jack, put her hands to her face.

'Oh Jack' she cried. 'Oh Jack you'll have to go.' Jack reached for her, pulled her back into his arms.

'I know love and I'll be glad to' he said more bravely than he actually felt. 'If it means helping to keep my loved ones safe then I'll be glad to.'

'I know' she said, 'I know, but Oh Jack' and her crying began in earnest.

Jeannie heard the low moans from the two men as she basted the roasting beef. She put the tin back into the oven and slammed the door, wiping her hands down her apron, went through to join them.

'So, it's official then' she said. Stan turned to look up at her shaking his head sadly.

'Aye, but nowt we weren't expecting.' Jeremy got to his feet, went to her, put his arm comfortingly across her shoulders.

'I'm afraid it certainly sounds like it my love. Come and sit down, gather yourself, even though we were expecting it when said out loud it sounds so brutal, so terrible. How has it come to this, weren't any lessons learned last time?' Stanley Briggs got to his feet.

'Tell ya what love, I'll be off, I'll not stay for me dinner, ya don't want visitors at a time like this.'

'No, no absolutely not!' Jeannie cried. 'We want you to stay, don't we Jeremy. Jeremy tell him.'

'Indeed we do' agreed Jeremy. 'It's at times like this you need your friends around you, need to be together. You must stay as we'd intended' he said, 'life goes on.'

Stan's regular presence on Sunday lunchtimes had rather crept up on Jeremy Kirk without him realizing it or knowing why. It had begun when Jeannie had started to go more regularly to the dance classes in the village hall. Apparently Stanley Briggs had decided to attend in order to lose some weight and had been an immediate hit with the ladies there, gentleman partners as always being in short supply. Stan had got into the habit of walking Jeannie home. What had started as a one off invitation had rather quickly developed into a regular event and he now spent most Sundays in their company. Not that Jeremy had any objection, he was happy for Jeannie and it eased his guilt when he spent time with Kathy although that seemed to be becoming less and less of late. Stan was persuaded to stay for lunch but they agreed that there was to be no mention of Mr. Chamberlain's message difficult though they knew that would be.

Luci buried her face in her hands and wept.

'Oh Philip no!' she cried. 'No, no I can't bear it. You'll go now won't you and I need you so much.'

'Of course I won't go yet you goose, how could you even think that? I won't get called up first at my age and I'll want to see you and the baby safe before I go. But I will go, I told you I would and you said you understood, you promised me you would.'

Gladys Thorn leapt to her feet.

'Oh my God no! That'll mean our Jack an' 'im only jus' wed!' Mavis was on her feet to the distraught woman, now her best friend, holding her tight. But what could she say?

'Oh love' was all she managed as Gladys burst into tears. Tommy Fletcher was bemused, looked across at his Uncle John.

'Ne'er mind lad, ne'er mind we'll sort it, I promise. Now look it's a nice warm day outside yonder, why don't ya tek yoursen off t'Ovo for a kick around? Do ya good an' I'm sure there'll be some o' yer pals there.' Tommy didn't need telling twice.

'Ya sure?' he asked.

'Aye I'm sure son, off ya go an' enjoy yoursen there's nowt ya can do 'ere, this is grown up stuff, we'll sort it.'

Jonas got up from his chair.

'Fancy a smoke lad?' he asked Jim. 'A turn round the garden?' Without answering Jim stood up reaching for his pipe from his pocket as he did so. Silently Bernie reached for Maisie's hand.

'My poor little Luci' whispered Maisie. 'My poor Luci and her little one.'

'Aye I know darlin' but she'll be alright you'll see' said Bernie simply. She knew nothing she could say would stop Maisie worrying – stop any of them worrying.

'Well leastways now we know!' said Peggy, putting her hands on the table to help her to her feet and scraping back her chair. She ran her hands down her pinny, looked around the table. Some too old to fight, to go to war. Some too young and yet too ready.

Peggy led the march home. There was no friendly banter as they took their leave of the Hendersons' kitchen.

'Best get our 'eads together over those war-time recipes love' she called over her shoulder to Nancy.

Patrick found the football, suggested he and Harry went for a kick around. Dannah headed off for a solitary stroll, there was no need of a coat it was a beautiful day. How could this be happening on a beautiful day such as this? Had the world gone completely mad?

Just Peggy and Kathy were left. Together they took two chairs from the scullery out into the sunshine of the backyard. Peggy looked up into the empty, brilliant blue sky wondering how long it would stay that way? How long before the skies became a hunting ground?

CHAPTER FIFTEEN

Impending war seemed to bring with it a rash of hasty marriages, people anxious to anchor themselves to home and family. Something to give them purpose and stability in an uncertain world.

Oakfield was no exception. When Peggy Barley was unexpectedly invited next door to take tea with her friend Nancy she had no clue as to what was to come. The invitation was unusual in so much as the Henderson household was a much more formal establishment than Miriam Foster's had been. The servants although treated well and fairly were never encouraged to entertain their own friends in the house and so for this reason it was an unusual and unexpected occurrence. Peggy had decided that in all probability it would be so that Nancy could show off with some fancy war-time cake she'd managed to make out o' nowt. She was to be greatly surprised.

Peggy had tidied herself for her afternoon out, taken one of her best 'day' dresses from her wardrobe. On arriving next door she found her friend had done the same. Nancy too was 'done up'.

'My Nance you look a rare sight you really do' she said admiringly as she entered through the back way. 'Yer not expecting King an' Queen are ya? Cos if ya are I'd best nip back next door for me tiara!'

'Nay, nay' laughed Nancy, 'chance'd be a fine thing! Sit yoursen down love.'

The tea was drunk and the delicate finger sandwiches eaten before Nancy settled back in her chair.

'Thing is love' began Nancy, obviously uncomfortable with what she had to say. 'There's something I need to tell ya.' The seriousness of her tone suddenly worried Peggy. This sure as anything weren't abaht any cake. Unable to guess at what it could be troubling her friend she sat back clasping her hands together. Finally Nancy took a deep breath.

'It's me and Mr.Desmond. Me and Edgar' she gulped, 'We're getting married.'

'Ya what!' Peggy couldn't help herself. Nancy looked across at her, clearly embarrassed.

'Well I know you'll be surprised love, I was, ya know when 'e asked me, but when 'e explained and I thought abaht it, well I think it'd be a good idea, be quite nice like. As ya know I've never bin married, not like you love and I know you've 'ad a lot to bear losing your Arthur the way ya did in the last war, and so young at that.'

Peggy didn't interrupt, didn't enlighten her, had never enlightened anyone about her marriage. How as soon as he'd got a ring on her finger the gentle soul that had seemingly been Arthur Barley had turned into a vicious cruel brute who abused her mentally and physically. She'd told no one of her sheer relief when the news had arrived that her husband had been killed in action. Certainly she'd played the role of the grieving young widow, mercifully childless, but inside much to her eternal shame her heart had been dancing. Over the years Peggy had had offers of marriage but had never once been tempted, turned them all down. She'd been fooled once, she wasn't prepared to take the risk of that happening again.

Although extremely surprised Peggy knew she mustn't spoil things for her friend. Who knew in any case? It might work out, she fervently hoped it would.

'Why Nance love, that's a surprise and no mistake but I'm real pleased for ya. Pleased for ya both, that's great news. Just 'ope he realizes what a lucky chap 'e is.'

'Well 'o knows how it'll work out? But we've decided we'd like to give it a go.'

'An' why not? But it'll mean big changes round 'ere. What do the Master and Missus 'ave to say about it?' asked Peggy.

'Oh they were right surprised too' laughed Nancy. 'But in the end they said they were pleased and we could stay on.'

'Well course and why not?' interrupted Peggy indignantly. She'd always felt that employers had far too much say in the personal lives of their staff, as long as they were doing their job that should be all that mattered.

'Aye but the thing is we're not wanting to. We're both getting on a bit and Edgar bless 'im sez it's time I took things a bit easier and 'e wants to an' all. He's got a bit set aside and I've got a little bit, only a little bit mind, and so he's wanting us to buy a little place. Down near the Haven mebbe, somewhere with a bit o' garden. Ya know 'ow Edgar does love 'is garden.'

Peggy was upset as well as being surprised now, knowing she would be losing her best friend, one she'd shared so much with over the years. No, this was a big shock and no mistake! However she knew she had to keep up the pretence of happiness. She clasped her hands together as if excited.

'But love that's just grand and no more than you deserve. An' when's all this gonna 'appen may I ask?'

'Oh well, soon as possible. Course we've got to find a place first but Edgar reckons now war's bin declared folk'll be selling up, get some money out of their properties while they can. Ya know in case they should get bombed an' 'em be left wi' nowt.'

Peggy arrived home some time later her own personal bombshell already having been dropped. Of course she was surprised, she'd had no idea there was anything between them. When she'd intimated as much Nancy had been quick in reply.

'Oh nay love, there's nowt like that. No, 'spect we'll just be like good friends really but living together instead of separate like. No, no love' she laughed 'there's nowt like that!' Peggy hadn't known whether to be pleased or sorry to hear that for in spite of her own experiences she felt that 'love' needed to be in the mix somewhere. However she'd had no wish to disillusion Nancy who clearly was excited at the prospect, and why not? She'd not had much to excite her up to press.

Nancy's plans forced Peggy to review her own situation. Things would definitely change apace for everyone with the war. Nothing could be even reasonably certain anymore. Certainly Dannah was past an age for any fighting so the guess would be he would be staying. Likewise Miss Kathy, but the two boys Harry and Patrick? Well even if not old enough to be called up she guessed they would try to go, want (foolishly in her mind) to go off and fight for their country having no idea of the horrors they would face. Would all the changes make Miss Kathy and the doctor hurry their plans?

Miss Kathy had confided in her about their previous relationship and how it had been rekindled when they had been so unexpectedly reunited, their intention to marry once her divorce was finalized. But that had been months ago. And was there still the same spark between them? She wasn't sure.

Sworn to secrecy until Nancy and Edgar were ready to announce their plans to the world Peggy found herself constantly mulling over her own future. Over the years it had become a sort of understanding that when she and Nancy were to hang up their aprons they would retire together and rent a little place. In spite of all Nancy's protestations to the contrary, her assurances that they would still be the best of friends, still spend lots of time together, Peggy knew that not having Nancy next door would change everything. Kind, ever polite chap that he was Peggy knew Edgar wouldn't want her around all the time. No she needed to instigate some changes of her own before they were made for her. Kathy and Dannah, even unaware of Nancy's plans, knew that Peggy could, but shouldn't be, left vulnerable by all the changes likely to affect not only the household, but the country.

Dannah and Peggy were not alone in their misgivings over the relationship between Kathy and Jeremy. So busily engaged with the shop Kathy was enjoying a life she had really never known before, at long last she was in charge of it, at the behest of no man. The relationship she had hoped for between Harry and his real father had so far not materialized, was no more than a polite respect on Harry's side. However Jeremy now seemed to be of the view that were Harry to know the truth he might feel differently towards him. Kathy was much less sure. As far as she could tell Harry was just relieved not to have a father in his life. Over the months the story of his difficult relationship with Henry had gradually unfolded and Kathy had been left with the guilt of not being able to tell him exactly why Henry, the man he believed to be his father, had eventually seemed to so dislike him. One day soon she knew she must find the courage to tell him but she knew he would blame her, would hate what she'd done, and she knew he would have every right to do so. She should never have pretended that he was Henry's son in the first place and here she was still pretending, to save herself, allowing him to imagine he was loathed by his own father. Kathy excused herself on the grounds that she'd had absolutely no idea of the cruelty being meted out. If she'd suspected anything other than that they'd enjoyed a normal father – son relationship then yes definitely she would've told him. Now it all seemed rather too late. She was convinced that once Harry really knew the truth he would despise her for being so callous and calculating, making him suffer for her mistakes. No, unlike Jeremy, at the moment she had no wish to enlighten Harry.

Quite naturally the difference of opinion caused friction between Kathy and Jeremy. She had begun to find fault with him, his pomposity, his stubbornness. She was under no illusions that he found her job – the fact that she worked at all – demeaning. She knew that once they were married there would be no question of the doctor's wife working. She was conscious that their relationship was now extremely fragile.

Jeremy too was concerned. At first he'd simply been happy to meet Kathy again, find his affection for her had not faltered, having always considered her to be the love of his life. And then when she had revealed the truth about Harry he had been overwhelmed to discover he had what he'd always wanted, a child of his own. Increasingly he felt Kathy distancing herself from him. He suspected it was because of her reluctance to do what she knew he so much wanted now, to explain everything to Harry. Oh he wasn't stupid or naïve, how could it possibly look to Harry? So young, so inexperienced, perhaps he would never forgive either of them but Jeremy desperately rather selfishly wanted him to know.

Jeannie, ever vigilant as far as Jeremy was concerned, viewed with alarm what seemed to be happening. He'd been so very happy, for a while seemed content, confiding in Jeannie over Harry, knowing she was the only person he could trust. But now he was like a bear with a sore head. When she'd pressed him he'd been quite brusque in his reply denying there was anything wrong and making it plain there should be no further discussion.

Jeremy's situation suddenly seemed so complicated and sad when compared to Jeannie's own new found joy. Stanley Briggs had become a big part of her life. They enjoyed the same things, shared the same sense of humour, required the same things from life, in short they were in love and neither of them could quite believe it.

Stan broke out in cold sweats when he remembered how close he'd come to tying the knot with Mollie Shakespeare. How could he ever have imagined himself in love with her? What he felt for Jeannie Kirk was love. He loved her more than anyone or anything in his whole life and what's more he didn't mind telling her! Jeannie loved the fact that he told her. Richard her husband had been undeniably charming, educated, a lovely man but he could never have been called spontaneous or romantic, she could never once recall him telling her he loved her. At the time knowing nothing else it hadn't seemed to matter but now she found Stan constantly telling her how much he loved her, how much he wanted to take care of her, intoxicating. Jeannie Kirk had never been so happy. If only it weren't for Jeremy.

CHAPTER SIXTEEN

Her long brightly coloured skirt dipped into the puddles, deep after two days of torrential rain, soaking her hems, dragging them down. The rain now a cold drizzle quickly plastered her waist length black hair to her head and she wrapped her shawl more closely around her shoulders. As her fellow passengers hurriedly made their way through the station yard she pulled the scrap of paper from the pocket of her skirt, hastily thrust it in front of the woman coming towards her, snatching at her arm as she did so. The woman, taken by surprise, stepped back quickly pulling her arm free. Maude Prescott was not a person to be man-handled. Leader of the W.I. Churchwarden, local Magistrate, Chairman of the School Board of Governors, she was returning from a three day visit to her aged aunt, never a happy experience, she was looking forward to being home with her husband.

'What on earth!' she cried. 'Kindly remove your hand immediately young woman.' She looked at her with distaste. Travelling in the same compartment she'd been doing that for the whole of her journey home, had been at pains not to get drawn into any conversation with her, had kept her distance, pretended that reading her "Woman's Weekly" from cover to cover was necessary to her very existence. Maude made to stalk off.

'No, no pleeze, you will 'elp me yes? I need to find this place' and she once again pushed the scrap of paper under

Maude's nose. Maude relenting, straightened out the crumpled piece of paper, peered through her spectacles now beginning to steam up in the drizzle. She looked the woman up and down. She supposed she had no choice.

'Well that's the house over there' she said pointing ahead.

'That OK thank you, that ver good' replied the stranger. Without more ado, tightening her cloth bag around her chest, she strode off in the direction Maude had pointed out. By the time she'd travelled just the short distance water was trickling down her forehead and her clothes stuck to every part of her cold, cold body. She went around the side of the house and tapped on the back door. Lizzie, busy peeling potatoes at the sink, looked up and peered through the window out into the yard to see who the visitor might be.

'Oh lor love us Mrs. Barley, it looks like the gipsies are in town. There's one knocking on t'back door.' Peggy Barley barely looked up from her pastry.

'Well knock on winder and tell 'em to clear off' she said. Lizzie did as she was told, rapped on the window with a dripping hand.

'Ere you clear off' she shouted. The woman turned to the window.

'No, no' she shouted back 'I need come in.' Lizzie shaken by her angry face turned to Peggy.

'Aye did ya 'ear that Mrs. Barley?'

'I certainly did' replied Peggy, already on her way to the door. 'Cheeky piece! I'll send 'er off wi' a flea in 'er ear an' no mistake!' She yanked open the door. ''Tis no good ya knocking 'ere love, we don't want no pegs or paper flowers or our fortunes telling thank ya very much.' The stranger suddenly looked afraid, began to cry.

'I 'ave to see Meeze Kathy' she said through her tears. 'She live here yes?' Peggy was taken aback.

'Miss Kathy, ya say ya know 'er?'

'Oh yes' smiled the stranger through her tears 'I know her ver well.'

'Well I suppose in that case you'd best come in' and she opened the door only slightly against the now heavy rain. 'You just sit yoursen there an' I'll get a towel to dry you off.' Actually she wasn't keen about this. Certainly the woman had the appearance of a gipsy, jet black hair, swarthy complexion. She was sure as her name was Peggy Barley she wasn't English.

Once Peggy had satisfied herself that water was no longer dripping from the stranger she led her to the more comfortable chair next to the fire. Lizzie turning from the sink couldn't help a look of disapproval, she knew full well it was asking for trouble inviting a gipsy across your threshold, it could only bring you years of bad luck. Her Mam always bought a peg off 'em for fear of them casting a spell over the 'ouse but she would never ever have let 'em inside. Peggy saw the look.

'You get back to them spuds my lass. I'll deal with this.' The cook settled herself in her own chair opposite the woman, re-arranged her skirts, straightened her apron. 'So you know Miss Kathy?' she asked carefully.

'Yes, yes I do' nodded the woman enthusiastically, 'I work for Meeze Kathy in India.'

Ah, it all began to fit into place, make sense, she certainly weren't no gipsy then.

'Well you 'ave come a long way then 'aven't ya love an' I'm sure Miss Kathy will be right glad to see ya.' Privately she wasn't too sure. Were people usually pleased when servants suddenly turned up out of the blue on their doorstep? And let's be honest Miss Kathy had been a right hoity toity madam when she'd arrived, so presumably she had been when she'd been out in India. At least she thought she wouldn't have to deal with this for long, Miss Kathy would soon be home. Their visitor was mid-way through a slice of cake and a cup of tea as Peggy heard the front door open and then Kathy's footsteps as she made her way down the hall.

In the doorway Kathy stood stock still, took in the sight of the visitor, then she smiled, a great big beaming smile, rushed across the room and took the stranger in her arms crying tears of joy.

'Ying' she cried, 'Oh my darling Ying, how lovely to see you.' As the two women eventually pulled apart Kathy put her arm around the other's waist. 'Peggy this is my wonderful friend Ying and Ying meet my wonderful friend Peggy.' Peggy held out her hand.

'Very pleased to meet ya love' she smiled 'an' I'm sorry if I mistook ya for someone else.' Kathy looked quizzically at her. 'Nay, don't matter.' She daren't admit to Kathy that she'd mistaken her friend for a gipsy although in truth she'd had every right to do so – the clothes alone, bright, heavily patterned, so clearly out of fashion would've led anyone to the very same conclusion.

In fact although not realizing there was a phrase to describe it Peggy was suffering from a severe case of "déjà vu". Total stranger turning up on the doorstep, turning out to be someone of importance, being integrated into the family, and more importantly to Peggy usurping her position in their affections. First it had been Dannah arriving and getting close to Miriam then along had come Kathy, and now here was this one apparently close to Miss Kathy! Would it never end?

Dannah arrived home closely followed by Patrick and both were duly introduced to Ying. Harry arriving somewhat later was shocked but delighted to be re-united with Ying who had played such an important part in his life in India. There was much to catch up on and it soon became clear that Ying needed a home. And so the household increased yet again, leaving only two rooms free to offer to paying guests.

CHAPTER SEVENTEEN

When Maude Prescott, newly appointed Billeting Officer, called a meeting in the village hall everyone knew what it must be about, evacuees. The inhabitants of Oakfield although keen to do their 'bit' were not at all sure that taking in evacuees would have been their first choice but dutifully sent along a representative from each household. Maude told them in no uncertain terms that it was their "duty", the very least they could do towards the war effort.

'After all' she said, slamming her fist on to the table in front of her, 'some would be giving their very lives!' Maude had a list – a very long list – and first of all she needed to know how many vacant rooms each property had. At the end of a very long evening she told them that they would each receive letters informing them of how many evacuees they would be expected to take into their homes. As they filed noisily out of the hall there was much mumbling and grumbling for this was a very unpredictable exercise and completely out of their control. They had all heard tales of ragamuffin city kids being dragged kicking and screaming into the countryside determined to do their worst, cause as much havoc as they could. No one could truthfully put their hands on their hearts and say they were pleased about it in spite of the payments they would receive from the Government.

Maude Prescott had as usual taken matters into her own hands, decided to do things her way. The directive from the Government was that on arrival the children should be taken to some central point and once there a "pick-your-own evacuee" should be held. Maude wasn't stupid, knew what would undoubtedly happen. Families would haggle over the most presentable children and the sickly grubbier ones would be left until last. She wasn't having any of that nonsense! And so Maude Prescott compiled her own list with no more information available to her than each child's name and age and personally decided who should go where.

Kathy opened the very official looking letter and scanned its contents until she came to the critical bit. Peggy stood by wanting to know the worst.

'Well, it seems we are to play host to a little girl of six, Pearl Pettinger, and a boy of eleven, Colin Clipson' she said finally.

'Oh my gawd' cried Peggy. 'At least they could've given us two o' the same kind, this means two rooms, cos they'll each 'ave to 'ave their own.'

'Indeed yes' agreed Kathy. 'I'm afraid it's looking as if we'll have to close down as a Guest House at least for the duration.' If she'd expected Peggy to argue or be upset she was mistaken. Peggy took it in her stride, was far more concerned with what problems the evacuees would bring.

John Tremmings opened their letter with trepidation. Living above a shop was likely to bring its own difficulties with evacuees, these city kids being notoriously light fingered. And they did only have room for one and that was at a pinch, it would mean Tommy sharing which he knew he wouldn't be too keen about, and who could blame him?

He read that Samuel Beckett aged nine would be their guest. John looked again, incredulous.

Oh no, surely not, not a lad called Sammy. Surely someone should've known, realized what that might do to them having lost their own lad called Sammy. He felt bad enough, what would poor Mavis feel about it? Perhaps he ought to have a word first, see if he could get it swapped around before he gave the news to Mavis? He tucked the letter in his back pocket and that very afternoon took himself off to see Maude Prescott. He told her in no uncertain terms that it just wouldn't do. Explained what it was likely to do to Mavis. She'd come so far recently what with Tommy, Joannie and Gladys to occupy her, he didn't want her setting back he said.

Whilst privately feeling guilty about the unfortunate oversight Maude knew that any change would disrupt all her plans, she'd have to start all over again. She told John Tremmings there could be no change, they would be required to billet Samuel Beckett and that was all there was to it. John Tremmings, whilst liking Maude Prescott and having great respect for all she did in the community, had always considered her to be rather aloof and inflexible. Today she had proved him correct. When Mavis expressed surprise that they hadn't received their letter about the evacuees, everyone else having seemed to have got theirs, John reluctantly pulled the envelope from his pocket, handed it to her without a word. Mavis read its contents, half way down the page she stifled a gasp, put a hand to her mouth.

'Oh a boy of nine that'll be nice, better start getting the room ready then.' She handed the letter back to John. No mention was made that day or ever of the sad coincidence.

Jonas and Maisie found themselves in the unfortunate position of having four empty bedrooms. Due to their age however Maude had deemed it inappropriate for them to manage too many children. A young mother with twin boys and a girl of nine were to stay with them. The young mother would be expected to help with the extra work that would be caused. Jonas and Maisie accepted that they had no choice but Bernie railed against it fearing what such an influx could do to a house as beautiful as theirs.

Luci and Philip were spared at least for the time being due to Luci's imminent confinement.

Luci Richards went into labour three weeks after war had been declared and nearly two weeks over her due date. Her waters broke in the early hours and Philip pedalled for all he was worth to the nearest phone box to summon the midwife. Muriel Parker took one look at Luci and decided that more than her undoubted expertise would be required. It would be a breech delivery and best handled in the hospital.

Jonas crept quietly into the darkened room, bent down beside Maisie. He looked tenderly into the filmy eyes struggling to focus. He put his hand on the snowy white coverlet wrapped so snugly around her and as he did so a little fist appeared and curled two tiny fingers tightly around one of his own. Those tiny fingers clung not only to Jonas Hardcastle's hand but also to his heart, turning it inside out forever. A tear ran unashamedly down his cheek.

'Emily, hello Emily Elizabeth' he whispered.

Luci remained in the hospital with Emily for the compulsory two weeks, resting quietly and getting to know her daughter. Philip went to the bank each day and visited Luci and Emily every evening. In between he with the help of his neighbour Margo, Maisie and Jonas prepared the tiny cottage for their arrival. Although he could quite easily have done so Jonas never once offered to help the young couple acquire a bigger property, he knew without a shadow of a doubt that Philip would have been affronted. The cot was placed in the front bedroom overlooking the beck. Emily would sleep alongside her doting parents.

Maisie felt she had never cried so much in her life. To have been given the gift of her sight back enabling her to see this beautiful grandchild was more than she could comprehend at times, more than she could ever have dreamt of. After Emily's birth the very first person she wrote to was Professor Zeigler. She told him of her joy, how it would always be impossible to put into words what he had done for her. Simone Zeigler opened the letter. Hadn't she always known what a genius her husband had been. There would be no reply. Franz had been killed in a skiing accident only months after Maisie had returned home.

Julia Richards arrived to see her niece clutching a teddy bear bigger than the child herself.

'Oh Phil,' she cried, bursting through the door one evening as he quickly gobbled down his meal, in a hurry to be off to the hospital. 'You're so clever aren't you, both of you. How soon can I see her? I bet she's beautiful isn't she?' Philip rose from the table laughing, surprised but delighted to see his sister.

'You bet your life she is. Looks just like her daddy.'

'I do hope not' giggled Julia. 'I'm sure a moustache won't look good on a baby. And where has that come from?' she asked scrutinizing his top lip.

'Thought it made me look a bit more distinguished' he

laughed, pretending to twirl the ends of something which was actually not much more than a downy covering.

'Well if I were you I should get rid of it' she said in her usual forthright fashion. 'Looks a bit daft to me!' Julia had managed to wangle the afternoon off and so had the rest of the weekend to spend with her brother. Luci was thrilled to see her sister-in-law, working at a school quite some distance away they saw her very infrequently. Luci couldn't wait to get Philip out of the way, have Julia to herself.

'Philip darling why don't you nip along to the nursery? They've taken Emily there for her bath. You really must see her, she absolutely loves it, kicking her little legs, she just looks so sweet!' Philip needed no second bidding, was out of the ward before she'd even finished her sentence. 'Quick, quick sit down' she said patting the chair beside her bed. 'Tell all' she grinned at Julia.

'Well...' smiled Julia, pulling a chain from beneath her jumper and from which hung a beautiful sapphire and diamond ring.

'Oh no!' squealed Luci, 'Oh Julia!' and she clasped her hands together in excitement.

'Ssh' laughed Julia putting a finger to her lips, 'no one else knows.'

'But when? When did all this happen?' persisted Luci, 'Was it a surprise?'

'Well you know, not really, I'd hoped, but he'd never actually asked me and then last time he was over he just got down on one knee and put this on my finger.'

'Oh Julia, come here, let me give you another hug, I'm so, so pleased for you!'

'Yes well not a word to Philip, not yet. This is your

exciting time, mine can come later.' At that moment Philip backed into the room. In his arms he cradled a sleeping little bundle, her thumb tucked into her rosebud mouth.

In her excitement Julia forgot the ring now hanging around her neck, peeped inside the pink and white blanket.

'Oh but she's beautiful, the little poppet. May I hold her, please can I hold her?'

'Well sit down first' said Philip with mock severity. 'You know what a clumsy thing you are, I'm not having you drop my little princess.' As Julia sat down Luci coughed.

'Julia, Julia.' She made to pull at an imaginary chain around her own neck.

'What? Oh yes, yes' said Julia hastily tucking the chain back underneath her sweater. The doting aunt nursed the little bundle through the whole of visiting time. The little body so light really and yet so solid, quietly breathing and snuffling as they talked, was already one of them. It was as if she'd been there forever and they were so, so glad, the terrors of war a million years away.

CHAPTER EIGHTEEN

Nursing Miriam Foster on her return home from hospital after her stroke had been more taxing than Muriel Parker had at first envisaged. It had become clear from the very first day that away from the security of the hospital environment and all the aids close at hand Miriam would struggle, as indeed Dr. Kirk had predicted privately to her. But Miriam had been a proud woman and determined to hide her frailty as best she could for everyone else's sake. Muriel alone was witness to the true complexities of her condition and although sad beyond belief had not been surprised when Miriam finally succumbed, her heart simply not able to cope with the strain.

The sadness of Miriam's death had an unexpected impact on Muriel. Miriam dying at such a relatively young age had made her determined to grasp her own life with both hands. She decided to take her career more seriously. With her mother Beattie no longer there to nurse and with Miriam gone she knew she should do something useful with her time and set up an interview at the hospital. The hospital matron was delighted to see her again and was only too happy to persuade her back into a profession so desperately in need of compassionate, experienced people. However, keen as she was to return to work Muriel was always conscious of her duty to her husband Joe and knew that working full-time on the wards would not allow her any compromise.

After talking it through the matron asked if she had ever considered specializing in midwifery. There was always a desperate shortage of midwives she said. When she married Joe, Muriel had assumed that motherhood would take her away from the work place. When it sadly hadn't she'd found it uncomfortable to be around other mothers and their babies and therefore had never considered midwifery as an option. Now however she could see that it might have its advantages at least in terms of her working commitments. The hours would not be so rigid, would be much more flexible and so she had finally agreed to undertake the necessary training.

That was how Muriel Parker came to be involved in Luci Richards' pregnancy, how it had been she who had spotted early tell-tale signs of a problem with the birth and insisted on Luci's immediate admission to hospital. Only she and Jeremy Kirk knew that that night she had probably saved the lives of Luci and her baby.

Muriel had decided that Luci would be her last call of the morning. The new young mum was having trouble breast-feeding and was becoming impatient and anxious which quite naturally affected the baby, making her fractious and uncooperative. Muriel had made light of Luci's concerns explaining that it was all quite normal and 'would sort itself out'. Muriel propped her bike against the wall, took her bag from the basket on the back and headed up the path to the white washed cottage. She tapped gently on the door and stepped into the tiny living room. All was quiet. The pram was in the corner under the window.

'Hello' she called 'Anyone in?'

'Oh yes, hello, I'm just in here' called Luci bobbing her head around the kitchen door. 'Won't be a tick.'

'It's OK it's fine' answered Muriel tip-toeing over to the pram. She pulled down the sheet. There was the beautiful child, rosy cheeked and sleeping peacefully, her finger under her chin as if she was pondering a problem. Muriel reached out and stroked the baby's head, hair silky like gossamer thread, curly at the back where it sweated slightly on to the sheet. 'Ah' she said. Luci was beside her drying her hands on a towel.

'I know, it's a miracle isn't it.' Muriel laughed.

'It all takes time love, it all takes time. But anyway she seems absolutely fine now, well done.' After enquiring after Luci's own health Muriel said she had better make tracks. As Luci saw her to the door..

'I was wondering if it would be alright now for me to take her out for a walk?' Muriel screwed up her eyes in concentration.

'Now what is she? Three weeks by now isn't she, well I don't see why not. As long as you're both wrapped up against the cold it would probably do you both the world of good.'

'Oh thank you' gushed Luci as if she'd been given a prize. 'I can't wait to show her off.'

'And why not?' laughed Muriel, 'Why not?' Luci stood in the doorway as usual to wave Muriel off.

'Bye' she called. But this morning unusually Muriel didn't turn to wave.

'Hello love' smiled Jeannie as Muriel came into the waiting room. 'How are........ 'Oh no! I must stop staying that' she laughed. 'Jeremy's always telling me off.'

'Oh it's the same for me I do it all the time' agreed Muriel with a smile.

'Well sit yourself down anyway, Jeremy won't be long, you're next and his last for the morning.'

'Good morning Nurse Parker' Jeremy greeted her. 'Sit yourself down and tell me what I can do for you.' Muriel came straight out with it.

'I think I could do with a tonic Doctor, I find myself really tired all the time, falling asleep by eight o'clock as often as not. And my appetite has just gone out of the window, normally I can eat anything but at the moment just the thought of food makes me feel quite sick. And I get hot sweats in the night. I know what you'll be thinking, that at my age it's the 'change' but it isn't, that's long gone with me I can assure you.' Jeremy sat back in his chair, folded his arms across his chest.

'Hmm, any headaches, pains anywhere?'

'No, no not headaches exactly although it does seem a bit muzzy at times.'

'Well I think it would be best if I examine you' he said, 'just have a feel around your tummy. If you'd just get yourself ready on the couch and I'll be right with you.' Jeremy gently prodded Muriel's tummy.

'Ah' she laughed. 'I know what you're thinking, I have put on a bit of weight since I've been working again. You know how it is, every visit I make I'm pressed to have a cup of tea an' a piece o' cake and they're really offended if I refuse. And then, well then when the baby's born there's a huge box o' chocolates stuffed in my hand. Honestly I could stock a shop I really could!'

'I'm sure, but I think you'll have to stop eating them all my dear' he laughed looking shrewdly at her over his half-moon spectacles. 'Anyway if you'd like to get dressed and come back through.'

Muriel regained her seat. Jeremy clasped his hands together.

'Well I can't find anything untoward' he said which in a way wasn't a lie. 'But I think we should start doing a few tests just to make sure. I'd like to take a urine sample and so if you'd do that and come back in a week's time we can talk again, see how you're feeling by then.'

Muriel was taken aback.

'So you're not giving me a tonic then Doctor?'

'No, not at the moment my dear. As I said we'll have the urine test and then we'll talk again.' Muriel rose to her feet.

'Oh, oh, alright then, I'll do that then Doctor' she said hesitantly and made for the door.

In spite of her own medical knowledge Muriel was concerned. Because it was herself, was she missing something? The week seemed a very long time. She made her appointment for a Wednesday afternoon, supposedly her half day.

'Come in, come in my dear' Jeremy greeted her brightly. It couldn't be bad news then surely? He wouldn't be bright and chirpy if he was going to tell her something awful. She hadn't sat down.

'I think you should sit down my dear' he said. Her heart began hammering against her rib cage.

'In my estimation Nurse Parker' – he looked down at a chart on his desk, ran his finger down it – 'You are ten weeks pregnant.'

'What!' Muriel reeled, she went clammy, she thought she was going to faint. Jeremy was beside her in seconds, his arm around her, laughing.

'I gather this is somewhat of a shock then?' he grinned.

'Oh yes, oh yes but the most wonderful shock imaginable.'

She began to cry. But then.. 'Are you sure Doctor? Are you really sure? There's no mistake?' she begged.

'No my dear no mistake, I was as certain as I could be when I examined you but for your sake I had to be absolutely sure.'

'Oh Doctor' she gasped and crumbled very un-professionally into his arms.

Muriel pushed her bike all the way home, she daren't ride it, she felt quite giddy. So much went through her mind. When to tell Joe, how to tell Joe, and then how sad that her mother wasn't there to share it, she'd so much wanted a grandchild. As Muriel nudged the gate open with her front wheel a white feather landed on her handlebar, stuck there. Now where had that come from? But she knew, it was her mother telling her she was there, telling her she knew. Muriel looked up to the skies smiling, blew a kiss.

Joe arriving home to the welcoming aroma of one of Muriel's famous stews gave her a perfunctory kiss on the forehead as he went through into the scullery to have a bit of a wash before his meal. Whilst not being a dirty job the smell of coal and steam seemed to permeate everywhere. Muriel always maintained she liked it but he wasn't too sure.

Muriel waited until after the meal when they were washing the dishes together. Her hands still deep into the sudsy water she turned to Joe.

'Joe' she said 'I've something to tell you.' Joe was busy now drying his hands and hanging up his tea-towel.

'And what's that me darling?' he asked not at all concerned with the answer, already on his way out of the door to see to Betty and Grable his two racing pigeons and his passion in life after Muriel.

'I'm pregnant, we're having a baby' she said to the empty

doorway, he'd gone. Within seconds he was back.

'What?' he asked incredulously. 'What did you just say?'

'I said I'm pregnant Joe, nearly three months, we're having a baby.' Joe was across the kitchen, lifted her from the floor, her hands dripping soapy water everywhere. He spun her round and round until they were both dizzy. When he finally set her down he put his hands either side of her face, looked deep into her tear-filled eyes.

'Oh my love' he said, 'My precious love' and he burst into heartbreaking sobs.

'Oh Joe' she cried laughing, 'don't take on so we're supposed to be happy.'

'Happy, happy' he shouted 'Happy don't describe how I feel. There ain't a word for it!' Muriel and Joe spent the rest of that Wednesday evening laughing and crying together, never ever had they been so happy and yet theirs always had been a happy marriage, one they both said was 'made in heaven'.

Cuddled together in front of the cosy fire they made plans now not for two people but for a precious third. Muriel had to ask.

'There's just one thing love' she said seriously. Joe pulled away from her so he could look at her.

'Aye?'

'It's just that..' Her voice suddenly faded.

'Go on love you've got me worried now.'

'It's just that... if it's a little girl could we call her Beatrice after my Mum?' Joe roared with laughter.

'Love you can call the little'un whatever you want, da ya really think I care! But ya know what?' he said quietly, 'That'd be right nice, your mam was a diamond and I'm sure any little lass o' yours is sure to be too. Come here ya daft 'apporth' and he hugged her tightly, but not too tightly to hurt the baby.

They decided to keep their news to themselves for a while, but now Muriel looked even more tenderly at the tiny babies in her care, imagining that soon she would have her very own.

CHAPTER NINETEEN

The British Government could have learnt a lot from Maude Prescott, Billeting Officer for Oakfield. Maude had instructed the host families of the evacuees to present themselves promptly at Oakfield Station to meet the 3.30 p.m. train. Thirty two children and four young mothers, two of whom were pregnant, were expected. As the train pulled in Maude positioned herself, clipboard in hand, on the edge of the platform so as to be right next to it. As the door of the first carriage flew open and two boisterous boys made to hurl themselves on to the platform Maude stepped forward.

'No, No, No' she shouted. 'You will remain on the train until I say otherwise' and she unceremoniously and very firmly bundled the boys back from whence they had come. 'Now' boomed Maude. 'As each child appears I will read the labels on their lapels and call out the name written there. When you hear the name of your child please step forward.' There was much mirth over Maude's Sergeant Majorish attitude but the residents of Oakfield were well used to it.

First to step down from the train was a pretty curly haired little girl. Maude bent towards her, read the brown parcel label tied to her lapel.

'Pearl Pettinger' she boomed again. 'Who is here for Pearl Pettinger?'

'Oh that's me' cried Kathy taken unawares, she'd been busy chatting to Maisie. She rushed forward quickly anxious not to be subjected to Maude's icy glare.

'Hello dear' she said to the girl. 'I'm Mrs. Watson-Smythe, you're to stay with me.'

'Am not!' replied the girl sulkily 'Me Mam said I only 'ad to stay wi' somebody posh.'

'Oh,' said Kathy taken aback. 'Well I'm sure we'll do our best for you. Let us try will you?' and she held out her hand.

'I ain't going nowhere without me bruvver!' said the girl, planting her feet firmly apart and folding her arms defiantly across her chest, a small battered suitcase by her side. Maude Prescott bustled over.

'What is it?' she demanded impatiently, they were going to be here all day at this rate.

'Well I think Pearl here thinks she should be billeted with her brother.'

'Brother! Brother! She doesn't have a brother' said Maude, quickly consulting her list.

'Aye she does' shouted a voice from one of the carriage windows. 'I'm 'er bruvver and I'm tellin' ya now I ain't going nowhere she's going!' Pearl began to cry.

'There, there dear' said Kathy, kneeling in front of her. 'I'm sure he doesn't mean it.'

'Does, 'e's 'orrible' sobbed Pearl.

'Well in that case perhaps you'd be better apart for a while. Come with me and we'll see what we can do.'

Pearl interrupted her, sobbing.

'But me Mam sez' she whined. From behind, a chorus of 'But me Mam sez' broke out from a group of boys hanging out of the train windows.

'Oh for goodness sake just take her will you' stormed Maude and she once more took up her position next to the door of the train.

It was some time before Kathy's other charge Colin Clipson stepped down from the train to the accompaniment of much jeering and banging on windows from his friends still in the carriage behind. As Kathy stepped forward he looked her up and down and cheekily wolf-whistled, turning round to his pals for the expected guffaws and cheering for his 'lip'. Kathy's heart sank, but not as far as Peggy's who had been standing in the queue with Kathy waiting for their two "cherubic" children to appear. By this time Maude had had enough. Her plan to allocate each child had gone well up to this point but was now in serious danger of being derailed if they all started to make their own choices, make their own demands. No she'd had enough!! Fortunately she'd had the foresight to bring with her her old whistle from her hockey refereeing days. She gave a loud blast on it and everyone was instantly silenced, order restored to the proceedings.

'Stop that right this minute young man' she shouted at Colin Clipson. 'You are to be billeted with Mrs. Watson-Smythe and that's an end to it.' She returned to her clipboard. 'Next' she bellowed.

John Tremmings was beginning to feel some relief as the train now empty had not yielded Samuel Beckett, clearly he hadn't come after all. Maude Prescott however was adamant that thirty two children were to have boarded the train and unless they'd hurled one off on the journey (and let's face it that would hardly come as a surprise) there was still one more to come. She insisted on the train being searched. She set off from one end, John Tremmings from the other and Joe Parker and the Station Master in separate ways from the middle.

Having been unsuccessful in their search Maude, John and the Station Master were already back on the platform.

'He's 'ere' shouted Joe, 'found 'im hiding under one of the seats.'

'Stupid boy!' shouted Maude harshly, thoroughly fed up by now. John Tremmings took one look at the boy, his anxious face, the boy he had so not wanted to arrive, and his heart turned over. He went to him, put his arm comfortingly around his shoulders.

'Aw, come on lad you'll be right fine wi' us, there's nowt to worry abaht, we'll look after ya.' The boy looked up at John. He was freckled, snub-nosed, wore horn rimmed spectacles and was chubby to say the least. 'Aye come on lad, we're right pleased to see ya. I thought for one minute ya 'adn't come and that would've bin a shame an' no mistake.' Maude had calmed down now.

'Thank you Mr. Tremmings' she said politely. John tipped his cap to her, picked up the boy's carrier bag and led him home.

Tommy Fletcher walked home from school that afternoon as if he was going to the dentist. The tennis ball he would normally have kicked all the way home lay forgotten in his pocket. The 'evacuee kid' would be there when he got home and he wasn't looking forward to it. Uncle John and Auntie Mavis expected him to be nice to him and he wasn't expecting that to be possible. Evacuees had already gained a reputation for being 'right uns', in other words trouble! No doubt the kid would already have wrecked his room and half his things! As he passed the shop window about to turn down the alleyway he glanced in, saw Cissie Downs busy with a customer, she looked up and waved.

Cissie hadn't had to give up work on marrying Constable Downs, the war had seen to that. With many of the men 'called up' and away, the women were now urgently needed to fill the gaps in the workforce. With no children of her own as yet Cissie was more than happy to continue working for the Tremmings. With her husband Jimmy away 'God knew where!' she needed to keep herself busy and chatting with the customers all day kept her mind off things. Working as an usherette in the evenings helped too because the nights were the worst for worrying but then there was talk of the cinemas and theatres being closed down for the duration. It was no longer deemed wise to have a lot of people all in one spot. However she would keep going until that was decided.

It was much the same for newly-married Joannie Thorn. Jack had been called up almost immediately and she was left living with his mam Gladys. Not having much money and no savings to speak of they'd had to do the same as most 'newly-weds', move in with their in-laws. Not that she was complaining, Gladys was a love, but just sometimes she longed for a bit of space. Joannie's brother Tommy had decided that he would rather stay with Mavis and John Tremmings when Joannie married and moved out. She'd been surprised, a bit hurt really after all she'd done for him over the years but Jack had persuaded her it was only natural, living over the shop, and in the High Street at that, was bound to be a more interesting proposition for a lad his age. In any case he said 'he could allus change 'is mind, there'd be nowt to stop 'im.' And it did have its advantages, she was able to go to work without worrying about him all the time and that was important now. Joannie no longer existed on a series of cleaning jobs as she'd had to do previously having been left on her own to bring up her little brother following the death of their parents during a nationwide flu epidemic. Quite by accident, Joannie and Tommy's sad plight had come to the attention of the childless Tremmings, who had taken the pair under their wing and now treated them as their own. Joannie now worked at Hardcastles in the 'dipping shop'. Lots of jobs had become vacant as the men had been 'called up' and Joannie had grasped the opportunity with both hands, even feeling a little guilty that she enjoyed it.

Mavis and John Tremmings heard the downstairs back door go, opened and then slammed shut. They heard Tommy's feet coming up the stairs, not running as usual but with a stomp as he laboriously placed each foot on every tread. Samuel Beckett sat at the table, back ramrod straight, hands on his chafed knees as he waited for the milk and biscuits promised by Mavis Tremmings. His mother, anxious to make a good impression, had dressed Samuel for the journey in an old tweed suit she'd picked up on the market for 'next ta nowt'. Samuel being undeniably 'sturdy' the jacket, albeit a man's, had fitted quite well but the trousers had needed alteration. Veronica Beckett had sat up all night chopping the legs off the trousers and turning them into shorts. Not being a seamstress of any note her efforts had not been altogether successful. Whilst indeed the trousers had become shorts the hem around the bottom was so thick that the tweed had ended up gripping Samuel's chunky legs so tightly that they chafed with every movement. With the unseasonably warm weather and the clamminess of the crowded train Samuel was in pain, his poor legs red raw.

Tommy Fletcher appeared in the doorway, hands thrust deep into the pockets of his shorts. Mavis and John glanced anxiously across at each other.

'Ow do' Tommy said gruffly nodding in Samuel's direction. But what was this? This kid looked like a right little toff. Hair slicked back, glasses, tweed suit! Only the incongruity of the parcel label still hanging from his lapel spoiling the picture. Samuel turned, his eyes still glistening behind his spectacles, towards Tommy.

'I'm most awfully well' he said in a plummy voice but one cracking with emotion. Mavis turned away quickly, busied herself arranging the tea tray as Tommy looked across at her. He turned to his Uncle John. On his face too a bemused expression but with it a kind smile telling him without words to be careful, to understand. At that moment something clicked in Tommy, he strangely, intuitively, did understand. Instead of laughing at the boy, 'taking the mick' as he would normally have done, he went over, sat at the table next to him.

'Ow wos yer journey mate? Bet it were 'orrible weren't it?' Samuel Beckett was determined not to let down his guard.

'No, not at all actually, it was frightfully nice' he replied. Fearing that eventually Tommy would give vent to what she knew would be his true feelings Mavis bustled over with the tray and began laying the table for what she'd now decided should become afternoon tea for four. The three of them tried not to stare as Samuel nibbled delicately at the sandwiches she'd prepared, even though he must have been ravenous he still placed the crusts untouched at the edge of his plate. They watched transfixed as he held his cup and saucer high and drank from the cup with his little finger protruding from the handle. Tommy was mesmerized, couldn't take his eyes off him, whilst Mavis and John attempted to make polite conversation.

Was he from a big family they asked? Did he have brothers and sisters? Any pets? What were his favourite things to do? Each question greeted as far as possible with a monosyllabic answer. Once the little tea party was over Mavis decided it was Tommy's turn.

'Tommy' said Mavis, 'We've put Samuel's bag in your room but perhaps you could show him where he can keep his bits and pieces. And Samuel, if you've brought photographs, you know of your family love, then you just put them up where you like, it'll be nice for you, help you feel more at home.'

As Samuel pushed back his chair, rose from the table ready to follow Tommy, Mavis noticed the red raw chafings above the boy's knees.

'Oh love' she cried 'Look at your poor legs. When you've done putting your things away I'll put some cream on them for you 'cos they must be mighty sore.'

'Thank you Mrs. Tremmings, that would be most awfully kind' he said and dutifully followed Tommy.

Mavis looked over at John, raised an eyebrow. He rubbed his fingers across his forehead grinning.

Samuel Beckett along with all the other evacuees was required to attend school the very next day and Mavis knew without a doubt that his demeanour and attire would draw teasing and laughter from the other children. His demeanour she could do nothing about but his attire she could and in any case that chafing could only get worse and would eventually break the skin and become really painful. She knew she had to do something and quickly. Mavis stayed up most of that night inserting elastic into the waistband of a pair of Tommy's old shorts. So different in stature. Tommy now so tall and slim, Samuel so short and well......chubby, the shorts needed considerable alteration and a not inconsiderable length of elastic to accommodate Samuel's girth. Mavis

Tremmings was no faint heart and by morning a presentable and hopefully big enough pair of shorts was waiting for Samuel when he woke up. Not that Samuel had slept much that first night. Homesick, alone and afraid he'd cried silent tears into his pillow. Tommy's sudden burgeoning maturity had made him pretend not to have heard the snuffling coming from the bed opposite his own.

At first when Mavis presented him with the new shorts Samuel had been surprised, obviously hadn't realized there might be a problem but in the end he had smiled behind his spectacles and courteously thanked her. The walk to school with his new friend in tow was painful for Tommy with much taunting. Shouts of 'Hey Laurel an' where's 'ardy' being among the politest.

Quite naturally the evacuees found it difficult integrating with the local children and almost immediately factions were set up. The majority of the evacuees were from the same school in the city and were streetwise to say the least. The local children were unsophisticated and innocent by comparison, they played fair and expected others to do the same. The inhabitants of Oakfield in fact found the evacuees more troublesome than Hitler himself.

The most successful homing of a child had to be little Pearl Pettinger. She liked Kathy, but adored Peggy Barley, when out of school was never far from her side. And Peggy loved it. Even though so much younger than Lizzie, Pearl was a willing student of all of Peggy's many skills. Pearl needed no second bidding to reach for the sewing box or the knitting needles.

Just as Pearl was content and happy Colin Clipson was not, turning out to be a rogue in every sense of the word.

Even Dannah with his calm reassuring ways had little or no success with him. Colin got into scrape after scrape, had been sent home from school on many occasions. Kathy was at her wits end with him, had even contemplated sending him back to his family but was unwilling to accept defeat.

Lizzie had been relieved to no longer be the sole focus of Peggy's attention when little Pearl appeared and besides she had new interests of her own now. Kathy had been intrigued when one Sunday afternoon Peggy had dragged her into the drawing room, insisting that 'she had to come and see this.' They had taken up positions in the bay window and they did not have long to wait. The local Salvation Army band was gathering together outside the Swan Hotel opposite. Several of the lady members were organizing their collection tins. Suddenly Peggy nudged Kathy.

'Aye 'ere she comes, look' she said leaning forward to peer more closely out of the window.

'Here comes who?' enquired Kathy still puzzled.

'Look, look 'ere.' Peggy grabbed her arm pulling her closer. 'It's our Lizzie in 'er bonnet!'

'Lizzie?' asked Kathy incredulously. 'Lizzie's joined the Salvation Army? I had no idea!'

'Aye well none of us 'ad. She jus' went off an' done it. It's the bonnet if ya ask me, the bonnet wot's done it! Even her mother sez so. Apparently she's always bin tekken with that big bow, ya know the one that's abaht 'ere' and she demonstrated where the bow might be on an imaginary bonnet.

'But surely not' cried Kathy. 'You don't join an organization such as the Salvation Army just for the bonnet!'

'Well you might not love, but this is our Lizzie we're talking abaht don't forget!' and she chortled to herself. They continued to watch until the band led by the flag bearer began to march off, the lady collectors, one of whom was Lizzie, bringing up the rear.

'Well, well I never' said Kathy. 'I never would've believed it but perhaps she's found God.'

'Puh' laughed Peggy dismissively. 'Only thing Lizzie's found is the bonnet! She'll soon get fed up you see' and she went back to her kitchen and chores chortling all the way.

CHAPTER TWENTY

Other than the arrival of the evacuees and conscription beginning for the younger men, not much changed in Oakfield in terms of the supposed war. Although the declaration of war by France and Britain honoured a promise to assist Poland in its time of need there was no attempt made to mount serious military action. France merely took up a defensive position while Britain remained wary of bombing Germany for fear of retaliatory air raids. Before long the newspaper headlines began to refer to it as the 'Phoney War' whilst the people christened it the 'Bore War' and debated whether it might be all over by Christmas. The inactivity inevitably began to cause dissention, the restrictions put in place being deemed unnecessary. The residents of Oakfield found the 'blackout' particularly irksome and many argued that it wasn't necessary for small communities such as theirs. It was pointed out to them that, as with many small communities, important military sites likely to be targeted were close by. Also that if rural communities were lit they would show up all too clearly around large pools of darkness indicating more densely populated blacked-out towns and cities.

Christmas was almost upon them and many of the evacuee children had decided they'd like to go home to spend it with their families. Not many voices were raised in objection. Pearl Pettinger most certainly didn't want to leave her cosy billet. Unfortunately her 'bruvver' did. Her brother had turned out to be none other than the now notorious Frank Brook, an even bigger rogue than Colin Clipson (if that were possible) and consequently his best friend. Maude Prescott had been unaware that the two children Pearl and Frank were brother and sister, the two having different surnames. Their mother was the common link, having the two children by different men but marrying neither. Maude's outraged disapproval when she discovered the truth and passed on the information to Kathy caused repercussions she could never have dreamt of. Kathy spent many sleepless nights.

In her anguish over her sister's illness and subsequent death, the struggle to deal with the mystery surrounding Miriam's finances and the even bigger problem of how to solve it, Kathy had been forced to put her personal problems to one side. Maude Prescott's horror at the scandalous revelations over Pearl and Frank's illegitimacy had brought it all back into focus, in actual fact she was no better than the errant Mrs. Pettinger or Brook, whichever name she went by. Having been able to put it all to one side for so many years she'd almost managed to persuade herself it had never happened.

But it had. At only eighteen Kathy had been left to face alone the consequences of a relationship that had always been unwise. As it had finally dawned on her that she was indeed pregnant she had been too frightened to waste time casting blame, anxious only to solve her dilemma. Over the years however she had begun to lay the blame more and more at Jeremy's door. Being so much older than her, holding the position he had held, shouldn't he have been wiser, more responsible? Jeremy now maintained that had he known of her pregnancy he would've moved heaven and earth to find her, marry her, and she had no reason to disbelieve him.

At first she had been thrilled to be reunited with Jeremy, swept along on a tide of emotion, but was the emotion one of love or simply nostalgia? Kathy had arrived in Oakfield full of her own self-importance, used to giving orders and having them obeyed, used to the finer things in life, perfectly matching Jeremy's own persona. But her time in Oakfield had taught her with unrelenting insistence that life could be a trial, fraught with difficulties that you had to tackle head on. To use one of Peggy Barley's pet phrases she'd "bin brought down a peg o' two".

Unfortunately there had been no such change in Jeremy. He had made it quite clear for instance that there could be no question of her working once she became the "Doctor's wife", it simply wouldn't be acceptable he'd said. Initially working for financial gain she now found she "wanted" to work, enjoyed the hustle and bustle, the friendships she made, life had a purpose. Jeremy's plans for her worried her. He was pressing her to agree on a wedding date, but always nagging away at her was the question of whether to explain everything to Harry first as Jeremy wanted. Kathy was doubtful, was it the right time? Surely the discovery of his illegitimacy and her years of deception could only cause untold harm to their already fragile relationships. Harry blithely unaware, was happy, doing well, had excelled at the local school as expected, a private education in India having given him many advantages. He was now studying for exams which would allow him entry into a School of Veterinary Medicine, his target the University of Glasgow. Should he prove successful the five year course would prove extremely expensive and Kathy knew that she would struggle financially. Jeremy was insistent that he would contribute but Kathy, beginning to acknowledge her doubts over their relationship, if only to herself, was unhappy about what it might mean. Was Jeremy's offer conditional upon her agreement to marry? If it was she suddenly didn't feel comfortable with that.

Henry's insistence on her return to England and subsequent divorce once he had learned the truth would have been the end of it if Jeremy hadn't appeared on the scene. Without him she could have made sufficient excuses, there would have been nobody to guess at the truth or even want to. Things she suddenly realized would have been so much simpler.

Little Pearl Pettinger didn't want to go home for Christmas but her 'bruvver' Frank most definitely did insisting 'there weren't no way he wos comin' back neiver!' Maude Prescott was adamant that if one went they both went and so Christmas Eve found the brother and sister jostling with many of the other evacuees on the station platform waiting for the train to take them home for the holiday. Knowing his friend was going Colin Clipson had also wanted to return to the city but word had come back that his parents didn't want him home. For the first time in a long time there was a smidgeon of sympathy in the Ladan Road household for the boy. No matter who or what had been tried Colin had been a pain in the neck and now was pretty much being left to his own devices which they all knew was quite wrong. They were supposed to be good steadying influences on the child – in their defence they had tried but failed quite spectacularly. The only thing Colin was interested in, indeed was passionate about, was the railway, spending many hours tramping alone along the tracks.

With his friend Frank gone and unlikely he knew to be coming back, Colin was at a loss what to do with himself. He had no interest whatsoever in the Christmas festivities and refused point blank to join in anything which might be termed 'fun'. There was no such thing as 'fun' in Colin's life.

Samuel Beckett was another story, blossoming under John, Mavis and indeed Tommy's care. When helping him to unpack the carrier with his few belongings Tommy had discovered four well-thumbed books amongst his things. Samuel was a bookworm and as a result highly intelligent, another reason why he didn't quite 'fit in'. Not sporting in any way he had nonetheless been dragged along by Tommy to many a game of 'footie'. The first time the two of them had turned up there had been howls of laughter at Samuel's attire, he always insisted on wearing his cap and tie whatever the weather and whatever the activity. The laughter had been followed by much jeering as the village team had decided that Samuel should be 'in goal' for them.

'What the 'el!' shouted Freddie Catsnip, captain of the opposing team.

'Wi''im in goal we'll get nowt past, 'es that bloomin' fat! Might as well 'ave a double decker bus in there!' Tommy was undeterred, Samuel was his pal and that was an end of it. Over the months Mavis had attempted to slim Samuel down a bit and was slowly but surely beginning to see some results, he now needed a smaller size in most things. Samuel had remained 'Samuel' not Sammy and that had helped John and Mavis with what could have been a difficult situation. When one day someone had referred to him as Sammy, Samuel had been quick to correct them and they had both heaved a sigh of relief.

Samuel like Pearl had no desire to return home for Christmas, or ever, if he had his way. He loved it in Oakfield, loved the countryside, had no yearning for the dirt and grime of the city, nor for his many siblings most of whom could neither read nor write. His mother always referred to him as the 'runt of the litter' and even though not entirely sure what that meant he knew instinctively that it wasn't complimentary.

Veronica Beckett had had good reason for sending Samuel away 'all smartened up', thinking someone would be more likely to take a shine to him, especially as he was 'quite bright an' all, poor little sod.' No, Veronica Beckett was quite happy that her son wouldn't be home for Christmas, would be quite happy if he never came home again in truth. "e was 'ard work wi' 'is fancy ideas!' She didn't know 'what 'e was talkin' about 'alf the time.'

Lizzie Carson contrary to all Peggy's predictions was still content with the 'Sally Army' as they were nick-named. She stood proudly – bonnet firmly in place – alongside the tree in the village square as the band led the villagers in their Christmas Eve carols. Although not prepared to admit it her boyfriend George Doyle was sneakily proud of her but not prepared to give in to her pleas for him to join them. George had bigger fish to fry, was waiting for his call up papers, they should arrive any day now.

Christmas 1939 passed peacefully for the inhabitants of Oakfield. Little Emily Richards was the apple of everyone's eye and thoroughly enjoyed being so. Luci waited with fear in her heart for Philip to be called up counting every day as a blessing. Just another month she would say, keep him with us for another month.

Muriel and Joe Parker felt it safe to broadcast their good news, Muriel now in her fourth month and beginning 'to show'. They'd thought they'd been happy hugging their secret to themselves, but the joy with which everyone greeted their news was humbling. Joe wanted to wrap Muriel in cotton wool, keep this precious child safe, but Muriel with her experience knew that wasn't what was required and would have none of it. Although no longer cycling in the final months she nonetheless continued her rounds until the last six weeks marvelling anew at the miracle of birth and what she at long last was to experience.

The majority of Oakfield's evacuees, against the general trend, did choose to return after the Christmas holiday. Maude Prescott was on the train bringing them back having felt it her duty to travel down to organize them at the other end. The train being the Friday evening special was packed. Maude had just blown her now infamous whistle, issued the instruction for the children to begin gathering up their belongings, when there was a tremendous bump and then the sound of crunching steel and breaking glass. The carriages reared up, high into the air and then fell with an almighty crash before rolling over and over down the embankment. The noise was unbelievable but heard by nobody on the train. Maude's instruction had meant that most of the children were on their feet as the train collided with a goods train carrying heavy steel girders travelling in the opposite direction. The silence was eerie, only steam could be heard hissing from the engine as it stood firm and tall against the crumpled wreckage of its carriages. Unbelievably although approaching its final run in to the station the train was sufficiently far away for the sounds of the crash to go unheard. A lone fisherman returning home with his catch was the first to stumble across the horrific scene. He pedalled for all he was worth towards the village and help. But his efforts were in vain. The angle at which the first carriage had reared up had meant that it fell completely on top of the second carriage before they both rolled over and over, joined together in a tangled broken mess.

There were no survivors, even the engine driver and his mate being killed as they raced to try and help. What was left of the goods train lay on its side on the other side of the track, its load of steel girders pinning its driver and mate to the ground. The newspapers carried the tragic story for days relating how twenty two evacuee children had been killed returning to their place of safety. The irony lost on no one.

Alongside the twenty two children another thirty locals lost their lives that day. One of those was Maude Prescott. Her husband Wandsworth stood with his head bowed, quickly brushing aside a tear as Maude's poor broken body was carried from the tangled wreckage. As her handbag slipped from the stretcher it was too much and he fell to his knees a broken man. Even if everyone else had viewed her as a figure of fun he had loved her, loved her dearly, Maude's bossiness had been mere bravado masking the low self-esteem of an only child's upbringing filled with loneliness and rigidity.

The aftermath of the crash seemed to go on and on, each day bringing another heart-rending story. A young couple killed had been on their way to break the news of their engagement to the girl's grandmother, another pair anxious to be married before they might be parted by war. Two teachers had been on the train, coming to Oakfield to boost staff numbers at the local school. With the influx of evacuees the class sizes had become unworkable and so reinforcements had been sent for. The Deputy Headmistress, three months away from retirement, had also been on the train, gone to meet her new colleagues, make sure they got to Oakfield safely.

The parents of the dead youngsters arrived in dribs and drabs, some of them unable to immediately get the time off work to come and see to their poor little bodies. Many didn't want to take them home to the squalor of the city, wanted them to lie peacefully, away from the potential bombing. In the end it was decided that most of the young evacuees would be buried in a special plot in the churchyard and that a special monument would be erected listing all their names. It was a tense time because for some unknown reason the children's relatives seemed to blame Oakfield's residents for what had happened. Clearly they weren't to blame but equally clearly something or someone was. Police and special railway investigators were drafted in from surrounding areas to try and assess what had happened to cause such a catastrophic event.

After much painstaking work the conclusion drawn was that it could only have been a signal or points failure, a malfunction of the system. Gilbert Broddings had been devastated. As the signalman for the Oakfield line for the last twenty years he knew his job inside out, could've done it with his eyes shut and his hands tied behind his back. He had been alone in the signal-box he testified, there had been no one else anywhere near. In that he was mistaken, he hadn't seen Colin Clipson lurking in the bushes below his signal box, hadn't seen Colin tamper with the points.

In actual fact Colin hadn't intended any real harm just a piece of childish tomfoolery, give the train a bit of a jolt. He truly hadn't been able to imagine what a tiny jolt would do to a train travelling at speed. Colin was gone long before the consequences of his actions were played out. As word spread around the village of what had happened he returned to the scene of his crime unable to comprehend the enormity of what he'd done. That night for the first time ever Colin Clipson, alone in his room, cried. When Colin once more pleaded to be allowed to return home, no one other than Colin knew why and no one argued.

The village remained the focus of press attention for many, many months but mourned their loss forever. The 'Oakfield Incident' as it came to be known was put down as a tragic freak accident, cause unknown, but with Gilbert Broddings completely exonerated.

Just as things began to return to some semblance of normality in the village there were huge changes looming for the country. Rationing was introduced at the beginning of the New Year bringing its own very unique problems particularly for the retail establishments. In April the Prime Minster Neville Chamberlain stepped down and was replaced by Winston Churchill. Churchill brought a new and much needed wave of confidence to the country.

CHAPTER TWENTY ONE

When Nancy and Edgar finally announced their marriage plans, the announcement having been delayed due to the horrific events surrounding the train crash, there was much surprise, no one had seen this coming. Kathy was first to hear the news from Peggy Barley.

'But Peggy when did all this happen? I had absolutely no idea. I mean it's lovely, but what huge changes for them both.'

'Aye I know' sighed Peggy, the sadness of what would be her loss was sinking in more each day. 'I was right surprised I can tell ya but I don't know, perhaps it'll work out, I do 'ope so I really do. Poor Nancy hasn't 'ad much of a life really, waiting on people all 'er life. But I'll miss 'er I don't mind admitting, she's bin like a sister to me she really 'as.' She quickly wiped away a tell-tale tear. 'And then o' course there's little Pearl, I miss 'er, I thought she might come back but she 'asn't.'

'Hmm I know' replied Kathy. 'From an inauspicious start she turned into a little treasure didn't she? I suppose we must be grateful though for if she had come back after Christmas she would probably have been on the train and that doesn't bear thinking about does it' she shuddered, 'at least she's safe.'

'Aye I know you're right an' I thank the Lord every day for that, but she were such a bonny little thing I'd got right fond of her in the end.'

Nancy and Edgar were married quietly in the Methodist Chapel the Saturday after Easter. Only a small number attended, all friends as neither of them had any relatives, certainly none close at hand. Mr. and Mrs. Desmond moved to their little one bedroomed cottage close to the Haven. The cottage had a south facing garden and the soil was fertile, Edgar could ask for nothing more.

The Desmonds' marriage and subsequent departure left two vacancies in the Henderson household and provided Kathy with a possible solution to her dilemma over Ying. Upon her arrival Ying had seemed to slip into her old role as companion to Kathy, the role Kathy had once so much valued. Ying clearly assumed that Kathy was still a woman of privilege and some means as she had been in India. Even the fact that Kathy worked in the shop every day had not seemed to change her view thinking that it must merely be a pleasant way of passing the time. Kathy had known that eventually she would have to enlighten Ying as to the true situation but her indebtedness to her friend made her fearful of telling her the truth. The household would struggle to support another guest. Harry was studying, earning nothing and about to cost a small fortune when he left for University. Patrick was a low wage earner still and unable to contribute much in the way of his keep.

With his inheritance Dannah had paid off Miriam's debts, a not inconsiderable sum, insistent that it was his final act of love to her. He also paid into the weekly household expenses and so the two of them, Kathy contributing her wage from the shop, kept the household afloat – just.

Salvation came by way of Nancy and Edgar's departure. It had actually been Peggy's suggestion that perhaps Ying could fill at least one of the vacancies next door. Over an early breakfast one morning she put forward her idea.

'I was wondering ya know' said Peggy, settling the sacred tea-pot in its rightful place, 'if Ying might be getting a bit bored. Ya know there's not much needs doing 'ere that me and Lizzie don't tackle an' it's plain to see she's a worker, not one to be sitting around like.'

'No, no, that's not Ying at all' agreed Kathy 'but in all conscience I don't see what we can find for her to do.'

'Well 'ow's abaht next door? They don't need much 'elp now admittedly, 'em not doing much entertaining with 'em getting on a bit, but ya know there's always the cleaning an' laundering an' such, so they're gonna need somebody. I know George is still there to do the 'eavy stuff like, but even then 'ow much longer before 'e gets 'is call up papers?'

Kathy couldn't believe that this hadn't occurred to her, the Hendersons definitely would need some help and when she thought about it Ying would be perfect. The only thing was how would Ying react? She hardly dared to ask. After assuring Peggy she would think it over she decided first to talk it over with Dannah.

'Hmm, well how do you think she'll take it?' he asked screwing up his face. 'I mean as you say she's obviously got used to being more in the way of a companion cum lady's maid to you, might she think it a bit of a come down?'

'Yes, yes I know and I'll hate having to do it, but what else can we do. Our joint incomes just can't sustain our expenditure for much longer.'

'I know and I sympathize with you, it's not going to be a very comfortable conversation that's for sure.'

Comfortable or not Kathy knew it had to be done

but first she needed to find out whether Ying might even be considered by Mr. and Mrs. Henderson. Although neighbours they could not be classed as friends and she was unsure how best to broach the subject.

The Hendersons now getting on in years spent more and more of their time at their house in the nearby town and so it was some while before Kathy was able to approach them. Her opportunity came one Sunday morning as they were leaving church. As their chauffeur helped them into the car and out of a heavy shower of rain Mrs. Henderson spotted Kathy, saw that she was in danger of getting extremely wet and beckoned their neighbour over insisting that she should ride with them. Kathy spent the short journey making polite conversation whilst sizing up when she could make her suggestion. Without looking extremely rude there had been no opportunity, the journey being so short. Kathy bid them good day thanking them for their kindness. It was in the middle of the night that it came to her. She would take a small gift, nothing too extravagant, to thank them for saving her from a thorough soaking.

Kathy closed the shop for lunch the next day and headed for the Tremmings' emporium.

'Ah 'ello love and what can we do for you?' asked Gladys Thorn cheerfully.

'Good afternoon to you Mrs. Thorn. I'm after a small thank you gift and as always a box of chocolates springs to mind, especially when there are few flowers to be had.'

'Aye I know, I love it when we've got some flowers to sell. But nay you're right, there's always chocolates ain't there, or pr'aps a tin o' biscuits?'- Gladys gave Kathy a huge wink – 'what with the rationing an' all.'

'Yes, do you know that's a good idea, but as you say with the rationing will it be alright? Do you have a nice tin of biscuits?'

Gladys Thorn ducked under the counter and surreptitiously produced a small selection for Kathy to choose from.

Kathy didn't go straight home that evening, instead went to knock on the Hendersons' front door. George answered, very smart now in a new suit, bought for him by the Hendersons to indicate if only temporarily his more senior position in the household in the absence of Mr. Desmond. After longing for the post for years George now found himself ambivalent about the whole thing, looking each day for his call-up papers to arrive, wanting to be off with his mates to fight for his country having no idea of what it would really mean. His pal Billy Simmons had already gone, he shouldn't have to wait much longer surely?

'Why 'ello there Miss Katherine an' what can we do for you?' he asked politely, the animosity of their first encounters long forgiven and forgotten.

'I was wondering if I might have a quick word with Mrs. Henderson if she's in George. I've brought this little thank you gift' and she held the wrapped tin aloft.

'Oh aye, she's in Miss an' I'm sure she'll see ya, don't get a lot of company these days. If ya just want ta step inside I'll go an' tell 'er you're 'ere, won't be a tick.' Kathy stepped inside, the first time in fact that she had ever been in what would be termed the family quarters. She heard George knocking very loudly on a door further down the hallway, muffled voices. Within minutes George was back.

'Yep, come this way Miss, Missus sez she'll be pleased ta see ya.'

Unable to get up from her chair easily, Evelyn Henderson nodded her head in the direction of a comfortable armchair next to her own and motioned Kathy to sit down. Before Kathy had chance to speak...

'Will you have a cup of tea with me my dear?' Without even waiting for a reply she picked up a little bell from a table next to her chair and shook it hard. George appeared almost instantly, clearly he'd been waiting outside the door anticipating such an event.

'Do you think you could rustle up a tray of tea and biscuits for us George?' she asked smiling.

'Course I can Mrs. Henderson Ma'am, course I can, just give us ten minutes eh?' he said backing towards the door. As the door closed behind him...

'Oh he's a good lad bless him he does his best' Evelyn smiled 'but I do so hate asking him to do women's work.' Kathy couldn't believe her luck but knew to bide her time.

'I've brought you these Mrs. Henderson' she said holding out the biscuits, 'to thank you for saving me from a certain drenching the other day.'

'Ah yes indeed, the weather was certainly inclement but there was no need of a present my dear I was merely being neighbourly.'

'Oh yes, I know' agreed Kathy 'but nonetheless I was extremely grateful, you saved a pair of shoes I am particularly fond of.'

'Ah yes' sighed Evelyn wistfully. 'I remember being extremely fond of shoes in my younger days, but they don't look nice on arthritic legs and swollen ankles I'm afraid.'

It wasn't long before George returned with a surprisingly well turned out tea tray. Silver tea-pot, china cups, silver sugar tongs, tray cloth, jug of hot water, biscuits. Kathy was impressed but refrained from showing surprise and certainly Evelyn Henderson showed none, clearly expected nothing less.

Having achieved her objective in getting to speak with Mrs. Henderson Kathy found herself uncertain how to proceed in her proposal regarding Ying's possible employment. In the end she decided she would just have to be bold and introduced the surprise marriage of Nancy and Edgar into the conversation.

'Oh my goodness yes, it was certainly a surprise. Of course my husband Cornelius and I had been aware that retirement would soon be approaching for both of them but had allowed ourselves the luxury of ignoring it for a while, knowing how difficult they would be to replace. In truth when they first made the announcement we almost decided to sell this house and use our town house as our sole residence. We're getting on in years and in a way it seemed the best solution, knowing how difficult it will be in the current climate to find staff. Unfortunately though my poor husband's head doesn't always necessarily rule his heart, poor dear' she laughed. 'This house'- she looked around the room, spread her arms wide – 'has been his home since childhood and he's reluctant to let go of his memories. We have Mrs. Hilary helping us out at the moment on a part-time basis but we know if we are to stay we will have to look for a more permanent solution.'

'Oh' said Kathy adopting an air of surprise. 'So you're looking for domestic help? I confess it had never occurred to me but of course you will be, however Nancy and Mr. Desmond will be hard acts to follow.'

'Indeed yes' nodded Evelyn. 'And of course we must have someone reliable particularly when we are away so much ourselves.' Kathy sipped her tea.

'Hmm I wish I could help, wish I could think of someone.'

'Oh I'm sure we'll resolve the matter in due course' sighed Evelyn. 'There's no need for you to concern yourself my dear.' Kathy realized the moment had passed again.

'Well if I do hear of anyone I'll let you know' she said lamely, cross with herself for letting the opportunity slip.

'Help yourself to a biscuit' insisted Evelyn bringing that particular conversation to an end.

The Hendersons returned to their home in the town the next day, not returning to Ladan Road for several weeks. When finally they did return Kathy knew she must waste no time making her move. She called round the very next day. Kathy explained that her friend Ying who had been her companion cum housekeeper in India was becoming restless and was considering moving on to gain employment in the city. She had been reminded she said of their previous conversation when Mrs. Henderson had mentioned that they would need to find a replacement for Nancy.

'I wondered if you might find Ying suitable?' Kathy asked. Much to her delight Evelyn was enthusiastic having not made any progress in that direction. Her only concern was what a loss Ying would be to Kathy. Kathy was quick to reassure her that all she wanted was what was best for Ying but she would be more than happy if her friend were to at least remain close by.

When the suggestion was first put to Ying she was puzzled and embarrassed. Embarrassed because she realized it could be seen that she'd been taking advantage of Kathy's friendship. Kathy was at pains to tell her that wasn't the case at all. She knew the only way to convince her friend was to be totally honest.

'The thing is Ying my privileged position in India was entirely due to my husband. I did come home to England expecting to be reasonably well off, my family having owned a very successful business here, but unfortunately over the years the business had floundered and I returned to find my poor sister in financial as well as physical difficulties. I have done my best alongside Mr. Delaney to resolve matters as best I can but we still find ourselves way, way short of the standard of living we were used to.' Ying was alarmed.

'But miz Kathy why you not say? I would've gone find new job.'

'Yes and that's exactly why I didn't tell you. I was so thrilled to see you as was Harry, so happy to have you back in our lives. I want you to stay more than anything in the world, I owe you so much' she choked.

'And so theeze Missus 'enderson, she would wish that I work for her next door?'

'Well all I'm saying is it's a possibility. I certainly don't want you doing anything you're not happy with.'

Ying was interviewed by both Evelyn and Cornelius Henderson and was offered a trial period. Ying could see that she might enjoy the move. She was allocated a suite of rooms very similar to those of Peggy. Having her own sitting room with its dining table and chairs and more especially her very own radio was certainly an attraction.

Ying loved the music of the big bands and danced her way through her days given the opportunity. She was offered full board and lodgings and quite a handsome wage, she could imagine she might well enjoy her new situation. Pretty much her own boss she took great pride in the house, polishing and cleaning with great enthusiasm and filling it with flowers at every opportunity.

Although freed of financial responsibility for her friend Kathy was aware that it would be no long term solution, they were still nowhere near paying their way.

CHAPTER TWENTY TWO

Muriel Parker's pregnancy much to her surprise was text book. A first baby and at her age, with her medical knowledge she'd anticipated some problems along the way. There had been none. Beatrice May Parker was born kicking and screaming but otherwise perfect on a beautiful May morning. Joe Parker was beside himself, went home from the hospital and the first to be told were Betty and Grable.

Kathy and Jeremy were no longer able to fool themselves that their relationship was as it had been. The heady days of their reunion seemed light years away now. Jeremy although unsure what was happening between them desperately wanted to cling on to the relationship if only because of Harry. He longed to be a father to him, wanted Harry to know that he was his father. Kathy remained unconvinced, no longer secure in their relationship. Harry was studying hard and each day brought Kathy further worries over their financial plight realizing full well that she would find it nigh on impossible to finance his studies out of her own pocket, that Jeremy's offer of assistance would probably prove essential. Was this to be another case of her 'using' a man? Would she need to go through with another marriage, one she was now so unsure of, for the sake of her son? Surely though she argued with herself, the situation was hardly the same? Jeremy did have responsibilities, ones which he had avoided albeit unwittingly all these years. She desperately needed to speak with Dannah, no longer able to deny even to herself that she had feelings for him. Yet was it right? Her sister's intended husband for goodness sake! And she'd end up having to tell him the whole sordid tale, expose herself as cold and calculating, willing to use a man for her own ends. Pregnant outside marriage and then concealing the truth using other people to hide her shame, the truth could hardly endear her to him. And Jeremy, what of him? He could only sink low in Dannah's estimation and that surely would be impossible to hide. Did Dannah in any case have feelings for her? Sometimes she suspected he did, but was it just his innate politeness?

It had been a long time since Kathy had received any correspondence other than the mundane, something she'd initially been grateful for it meaning an end to the missives from the bank and some of Miriam's irate creditors.

When Peggy bustled into the kitchen one morning waving a cream vellum, heavily embossed envelope in the air declaring 'There's somethin' foreign for ya 'ere, looks like from India,' Kathy was surprised and intrigued having heard nothing from Henry since their divorce had been finalized. She took the envelope from Peggy.

'Goodness me whatever can it be?' She examined the envelope, slit it open. The letter was several pages long and typewritten. The heading Saul & Saul Solicitors, Bombay. It began.....

'Dear Mrs. Watson-Smythe' followed by some other pleasantries, but Kathy's eye was taken further down the page. Bold underlined words. 'LAST WILL & TESTAMENT of HENRY WATSON-SMYTHE'. Whatever did it mean? Henry was alive.

Except that he wasn't. The letter went on to inform her that Henry Watson-Smythe had sadly succumbed to a virus which had attacked the muscles of his heart. Henry had died a month ago leaving no will other than the one made following their marriage. Henry had either omitted or decided not to change his will after their divorce. She Katherine was the sole beneficiary. She read that Henry had a not insignificant pension, considerable savings and a large insurance on his life. Clearly Kathy would once again become a woman of means thanks to Henry a man she had so heartlessly misled.

There was no happiness in her heart at the news. How could there be? Mercifully Peggy had left her alone with her letter, was not there to witness Kathy's shock and sadness. She carefully folded the envelope, put it in her bag and gathered the rest of her things ready for work. The handwritten envelope sealed and addressed by Henry to her and included in the paperwork from Saul & Saul she left un-opened to read another time. Trade at the shop that day was brisk, people at long last looking forward to the summer.

Jonas Hardcastle was content. There seemed to be no deterioration in Maisie's sight and he was finally beginning to allow himself the luxury of believing the improvement would last. Maisie had had no such concerns, just delighting in what she'd been given right now and enjoying every single minute. She had insisted he return to work.

'Thought you'd want to see this boss' announced Stanley Briggs entering Jonas' office and slapping a large official looking envelope on his desk. Stan had spotted it amongst the pile of post Edna Harper was busy sorting through. Being his secretary it was Edna's job to sift the mail, determine which letters were mundane everyday business and which

Jonas needed to see. Stanley had picked up the envelope, glanced down and met Edna's eyes, a silent knowing look between them.

'I'll tek this love' he'd said and Edna had simply nodded.

'Why what is it lad?' asked Jonas, lifting the envelope from his blotter. But he knew without even opening it and his heart sank. He opened it gingerly knowing it would simply confirm what he'd been expecting. Hardcastles' Cycles would be no more – at least for the duration. His pride and joy, the epitome of everything he'd worked all his life for was to be requisitioned by the Government, given over to producing military equipment.

'Oh God' he said. Stan took the chair opposite, reached for the letter, raised his eyebrows in query to Jonas wordlessly seeking his permission to read it.

'Aye course lad' said Jonas wearily. He rested his elbows on his desk, clasped his hands together in a fist. Stan having perused the letter put it back down on the desk.

'Well it's just as we thought ain't it? It were always gonna be a matter o' time.' The letter went on to inform them that a specially trained team would be drafted in to instruct the workforce, at least those who wished to remain, the implication being that it was expected that if at all possible the workforce SHOULD remain to do their duty. Jonas was devastated, went home early that day to report back to Maisie.

'Oh love' she said going immediately to wrap her arms around him. 'But you know it might not be for long. You know they're still calling it the 'phoney war'.'

'Aye I know that but with everything ya read in the papers I think the Prime Minister's right, it will all kick off before long.'

'But you did expect it love, you thought they'd take the factory.'

'I did aye but ya know when it actually 'appens, well it knocks ya for six. An' it's not just the changes it'll bring. No what's worse is knowing that my factory will be instrumental in making weapons to kill people, kill other human beings. It's not right Maisie, it's just not right. I've seen it all before, first hand and nothing, nothing is worth that. There's got to be other ways than killing.' Maisie needing to share his heartbreak, rested her head on his chest, with her arms squeezed him as hard as she could.

'I know darling I know,' she whispered.

Jonas was adamant that his workforce should hear the news from him and as soon as possible. At 8.30 the next morning they were gathered together in the newly created canteen. Gasps of surprise and shock greeted his announcement, at least from the younger members, the older ones had been expecting it but were still undeniably saddened. Jonas assured them that he would keep them up to date as more information filtered through from the Government.

In fact more information was slow to reach them and it became quite a problem knowing how best to manage the business. How long did they have before production would end? Could more orders be taken? Would they even have time to fulfil the orders they already had? An already difficult situation was made even worse by what seemed to be a very disorganized Government.

Eventually however the news came, arrangements were made and once initiated progressed at speed. Existing orders were honoured and the stock pile of cycles newly off the production line was taken away and stored in one of the smaller warehouses on the site. Kathy had been informed that once the stock in the shop was sold the shop too would be closed down until the end of the war. Jonas had felt terrible having to tell her, knowing only too well through her friendship with Maisie that the financial situation at Ladan Road was in the main precarious. Jonas had entered the shop with a grim face and heavy heart feeling it his responsibility to personally break the bad news and was therefore pleasantly surprised when she accepted the inevitable with good grace and even a smile.

'Ah well' was all she'd said, patting his arm to reassure him that it was alright, he wasn't to worry. Kathy had always been apt to apply little sayings to things that happened to her and now another one came to mind. She felt like the person who fell in the river and came up with a pocket full of fish. She lost her job and income at exactly the same time as she inherited a huge amount of money! Life was strange indeed.

As yet Kathy had told no one about Henry, not even Harry and certainly not Jeremy. She'd decided she needed time to mull it over, get things straight in her own mind before involving the opinions of anyone else.

To honour her memory Wandsworth Prescott had decided to take on his late wife Maude's role as Billeting Officer for Oakfield. Over the months there had been much to-ing and fro-ing of the evacuees as the state of the war remained uncertain. Jonas and Maisie still had their guests, the Tremmings still had Samuel and others were still scattered throughout the village. It was Wandsworth Prescott who knocked on the front door of Number Two Ladan Road asking to see Kathy. At home now that the shop had been closed Kathy invited him into the drawing room. She expressed her deepest sympathies to him over the loss of his wife and her admiration for him at having taken over her role.

'It can't be easy' she said sadly.

'No, no but it somehow helps to know that I'm continuing her work. I think she would be pleased.'

'Oh but I'm sure she would, how could she not be?' agreed Kathy.

Wandsworth came to the purpose of his visit. He reached down by the side of his chair for his battered briefcase, unfastened the clasp and began to rifle through a sheaf of papers. Kathy looked on puzzled having no idea what business he could possibly have with her.

'Ah yes here it is' he said at last straightening up. 'I gather that you previously had billeted with you a little girl..... Pearl Pettinger?'

'Oh yes we did' confirmed Kathy. 'An adorable child. But she never returned to us after Christmas. You have some news of her?'

'Well yes I have. I'm informed that Pearl's family would like her evacuated once more and I was wondering if before I asked anyone else you might be interested?'

'Oh, yes, yes!' said Kathy. 'We'd love to have her back.' At that very moment the door opened heralding Peggy with the tea tray. Kathy leapt to her feet, went to her.

'Peggy you'll never guess! Little Pearl is coming back to us.'

'Wha'? Oh my lor' that is good news' cried Peggy, hurriedly putting the tea tray down before she dropped it. 'But there's nowt wrong is there? Her family are alright?'

'Yes, as far as I'm aware they are' joined in Wandsworth. 'Reading the information I have here it would seem like a simple case of overcrowding. I gather another family of relatives have had to join them. That seems very much to be the norm in the cities now, and can only get worse I imagine.'

Little Pearl Pettinger returned to Oakfield two weeks later declaring she 'weren't goin' back 'ome nevver!' Kathy and Peggy were waiting as the train pulled in. Pearl was the first off racing to 'Auntie Peggy' and flinging her arms around her.

'Ooh Auntie Peggy I do loves ya' she cried.

'An' me you my pet' Peggy laughed through her tears, ruffling the child's curls.

CHAPTER TWENTY THREE

Within weeks of the factory being requisitioned machinery began to arrive. Huge trucks rumbled down the hill and into the village, closely followed by teams of engineers specially drafted in to set up the machinery and get it quickly operational.

In the end it all happened with breath-taking speed. Once the factory was deemed ready, more specialist teams were brought in to instruct the initially slimmed down workforce in the production of weapons capable of killing and maiming. Jonas was heartbroken as he viewed from the window of his office all that was taking place on his factory floor. He no longer had jurisdiction but was allowed to stay, as was Stanley Briggs, to oversee the site maintenance of what was after all his property.

'By lad this is a sad day an' no mistake' he said shaking his head sadly. There was no argument from Stanley Briggs.

Of the management team of Hardcastle Cycles only Dannah Delaney was to remain on the staff. The new Factory Manager was to be one Ralph Falconer appointed by the Government. It was Dannah who met Ralph Falconer at the station, Dannah who took him to his digs on the Falworth Road slightly out of the village, it not being deemed appropriate for him to fraternize too closely with the locals, his workforce.

Ralph had been anxious to get on with the job, anxious to see around the site and arrived with files full of information and plans, plans which even Jonas hadn't known existed. Ralph Falconer was pleasant but brusque which in a way suited Dannah as he himself wasn't one to shilly-shally. The other man was diligent in his observations and meticulous in everything that was required of himself and others. He spent long days at the factory and long lonely evenings in his digs writing reports.

Eventually though the two men similar in age and temperament and working closely together became friends and often over a pint in the pub would exchange stories of their past. This left Dannah feeling envious of all that the other man had achieved, embarrassed that by comparison he had accomplished so little alongside this highly intelligent, clearly well regarded man. However much to his surprise Ralph Falconer seemed interested in Dannah's everyday life bemoaning the fact that he had never had what could be termed a happy settled home life himself. In sympathy Dannah was lulled into revealing more than he otherwise would have. He told him with great sadness how his intended bride had died on the very day of their wedding. How Miriam's long lost sister had arrived home from abroad and was now on the verge of remarrying after divorcing her husband. How her son Harry was to study to be a vet. Ralph seemed totally absorbed in everything he had to tell him. Dannah supposed him to be just being polite but was nonetheless puzzled when an invitation to a meal at Ladan Road was instantly and firmly turned down.

Kathy mused how she always seemed to have problems of one sort or another these days, how different from her pampered existence in India. On her arrival back in England she had immediately been faced with worries over poor Miriam's health followed by the heartache of her subsequent death and then worries over finances which in all honesty had surprised her the most. In her entire life Kathy had never had to worry about money. With her mother and father she'd led a very comfortable existence and poor Henry had provided the same for her, his position offering her every comfort and amenity, an elevated status in the upper circles of society in Bombay. No, this had been the first time in her life that she'd had to think about money, learn to live life frugally. Now, after receiving the letter from Saul & Saul, she suddenly found herself with money to her name again. The problem this time was how to explain her new found wealth? Did she even need to?

Initially she had decided to simply bank the money, use it entirely to fund Harry's studies, turn down Jeremy's proposal that he would pay or at least share in the costs which would be incurred. She couldn't help feeling that Jeremy's offer was all part and parcel of the continuing assumption that they would eventually marry and the truth regarding Harry be revealed. How could Harry not be angry when he learned the truth, for he too had been made to live a lie? She couldn't understand why Jeremy didn't seem to grasp this, that no good could come of the truth coming out. To coin one of her father's famous phrases she would be deemed a 'trollop' and Jeremy a 'cad' at best. He was so wrapped up in the revelation that his dream had come true, that he was a father. But Kathy knew that this was no fairy tale, that truth invariably carried as much heartache as joy. Kathy grew more and more convinced that the secret should be kept, that Jeremy should remain a close and loving friend, perhaps even eventually step-father to Harry, but no more. Until now Kathy had told no one, not even Harry – especially not Harry – that Henry, the man he believed to be his father, was dead.

The letter from Henry enclosed in the documents from the solicitors, when she finally plucked up courage to read it, made her cry. He wanted he said to have things straightened between them on his death. She would only receive this letter on his death and who knew when that might be, hopefully not for many years. The letter was a precaution, nothing more. So typical of Henry she smiled sadly that there should be no loose ends.

He told her of his fondness for her. She noted he never mentioned love. But then had she had the right to expect that? He explained his surprise when she'd announced her pregnancy. He had assumed he would never father a child, been told as much by the doctors. He acknowledged that he had been less than honest with her, should have acquainted her with that fact when he had proposed marriage. He said how much he had come to love Harry but had always harboured suspicions that he may not be his child. Henry confirmed that as Kathy had suspected it had indeed been Dr. Robeson who had persuaded Henry once and for all that Harry had not been born prematurely as she had insisted. That Harry could not be his child. Dr. Robeson's files he said had finally provided the truth. He had decided not to press her for the true identity of Harry's father feeling it could only add to his heartache. He said that at last he was able to find it in his heart to forgive her treachery, indeed had come to be grateful that he had at least for a time had the joy of believing himself to be a parent. He wanted there to be no lingering animosity between them. He had made a generous settlement on her and in the event of his death everything would be left to her in gratitude for the happy times they had spent together. He wished her well in the future, accepted that they had both contributed towards a very sad situation, forgave her for her part and asked for forgiveness for his. He ended by confirming his love and affection for Harry, as he said 'a fine boy indeed, a young man to be proud of', expressed his heartfelt wish that one day Harry might understand his reasons and forgive his sometimes harsh treatment of him.

She wanted to respond, tell him how sorry she was, assure him that she forgave him, but of course she couldn't she'd received this letter because Henry was dead, beyond any words of forgiveness from her. Kathy folded the letter carefully, pressing it back into its original creases just as Henry would've done – always so meticulous. She put the letter back in its envelope. She found herself dropping a tender kiss on it before tucking it in the bottom of her jewellery box, well out of sight. Somehow she couldn't destroy it, certainly not yet anyway.

CHAPTER TWENTY FOUR

'Ooh Miss, we really shouldn't be 'ere on t'front door step, me Auntie Peggy'll be right mad, she allus shoos kids off if they dares ta come ta front.'

'It's absolutely fine Pearl' Julia Richards assured her as she rang the doorbell. 'I'm with you.'

Little Pearl Pettinger wasn't at all sure, looked around her apprehensively as they waited for the bell to be answered. As the door opened Pearl quickly looked to the ground, anxious not to witness the annoyance she was sure she would see on Auntie Peggy's face. She looked up again as she realized that it wasn't Auntie Peggy but Miss Kathy who had come to answer the door. Kathy's welcoming smile slipped as she saw Pearl standing next to Julia Richards. Pearl was unfortunately still inclined to get herself into scrapes and by the look of it here was another one!

'Hello Miss Richards' she said. 'How nice to see you, but is something wrong? Now what has our little scallywag been up to?' Julia Richards was quick to reassure her.

'Oh nothing, nothing at all, leastways nothing that I know about anyway' she grinned. 'No there's just something I'd like to discuss with you if you have a moment or two. I had intended sending a note home with Pearl but thought that as I would be passing it would perhaps be easier if I explained everything personally.'

'Why yes of course, do please come in won't you?' Kathy said intrigued. She ushered the young teacher into the drawing room and a very relieved Pearl down the hall to the kitchen and Peggy. 'Ask your Auntie Peggy if we could have a tray of tea will you sweetheart?' she called after the child as she sped away.

Julia Richards had returned to Oakfield in the aftermath of the train tragedy, a replacement for one of the teachers who had been travelling on the fateful train to take up her new post. When Luci had written to her telling her of the vacancy she had jumped at the chance, keen to spend more time with her brother and his new little family. Unfortunately Julia had not foreseen the problems which would come following such a harrowing event. There were reminders everyday of someone whose life had been taken, someone who had been there, should be there, but wasn't. The little school indeed the whole community had tried their best to move on, put extra effort into everything they did hoping to alleviate the bad memories and create some new happier ones. It was one such occasion that was the reason for Julia's visit that afternoon.

Julia sat down in the armchair opposite to Kathy, crossed her ankles, brushed down her skirt.

'The thing is Mrs. Watson-Smythe' she began, 'As I'm sure you know Oakfield will shortly be holding its annual Summer Carnival.'

'Oh yes, yes of course' interrupted Kathy 'we're all so looking forward to it, particularly with all the sadness of late.'

'Hmm. Yes it has certainly been a very challenging time' agreed Julia, remembering the many occasions when she had found one of her young pupils sobbing quietly in a corner requiring an explanation as to why their 'little mate weren't comin' back.' 'The thing is Mrs. Watson-Smythe every year apparently the school is called upon to provide a Carnival Queen and her attendants. The names of all the girls in the two top classes are put into a hat, the first name out is the Queen and the following six her attendants. The name first out of the hat this time' – she grinned broadly – 'was none other than little Pearl.'

'Oh! Well oh my goodness! How lovely!' cried Kathy, clasping her hands together. 'Does she know? Does Pearl know? She will be so excited.'

'Well no, she doesn't know, not as yet. We thought we would be best to check first how you felt about it before raising the child's hopes.' Kathy looked across at her puzzled. 'The thing is not all the evacuees are altogether popular with some of the host families, in some cases the relationship is really difficult, particularly where there is another child in the family. Clearly I can see from the expression on your face' Julia smiled, 'that's not the situation here.'

'Oh, no, no definitely not' cried Kathy, 'I couldn't be more pleased, the child will absolutely love it. She will be so thrilled.'

'Well that's wonderful then. There will of course be some expense involved unfortunately. The Queen and attendants are expected to provide their own costumes and obviously being war-time it is more difficult to purchase material and such.'

'Oh don't worry about that' Kathy flapped her concerns to one side. 'We'll find something don't you worry. Oh how exciting! When do you propose to tell her?'

'Well why don't you tell her? Tell her now.'

'Oh really? Are you sure you wouldn't rather do it in school?'

'No, not at all. Why shouldn't you have the pleasure?' Kathy needed no second bidding, went to the door calling down the hall for Peggy and Pearl to join them, telling Peggy to bring a cup for herself.

'Just coming Miss Kathy, tray's almost ready' answered Peggy. Peggy bustled into the room closely followed by a very wary looking Pearl, put the tea tray on the low table.

'Sit down Peggy we have something to tell you.' Inwardly Peggy groaned. She'd honestly thought she'd been making some headway with the little 'un, looked like she'd been wrong and she was in trouble again! Peggy wearily settled herself on the edge of a chair. Pearl stood beside her, leaning into her, arms wrapped tightly around the cook's neck, their heads together as if together they would face the world. But Kathy looked at Pearl and smiled.

'We have some lovely news for you darling. Miss Richards here has come to tell me that you have been chosen to be the Queen at this year's Carnival. Now what do you think to that!' The girl looked back at her startled, unable to say anything.

'Oh love!' cried Peggy pulling the child round to face her. 'Carnival Queen! Well you are the lucky one aren't ya' and she hugged her. Pearl released her arms from Peggy's neck, plonked herself on to her lap.

'Will it mean I gets a new frock?' she asked looking up at her.

'Oh aye love!' laughed Peggy 'a new frock and a CROWN! Ooh I can't wait to get started!' and she cuddled the child even tighter. Julia Richards finished her tea and departed, reflecting on how nice it was to bring happy news to a family for a change.

As the weeks leading up to the Carnival sped by Kathy was hard pressed to decide who was the most excited, Peggy or Pearl! Once recovering from the shock of not after all being in bother Pearl had become quite giddy at the notion of being Queen and had to be taken down a peg or two on more than one occasion. She had adopted a very superior attitude which had not exactly endeared her to the other participants, namely her six attendants. After a fight in the playground one day when one of the attendants as usual came off worse Pearl had had to be threatened with having her 'Crown' handed to someone else. Peggy had been mortified and had a serious heart to heart with the child. It worked, and from then on all Pearl's energies had been put into learning to 'walk proper' and 'smile nicely' as instructed by the cook. As anticipated material was becoming scarce and so old sheets stored away for future spring cleaning cloths were brought out and the best bits cut away from the rest. As Peggy said 'it was allus the trimming that made the difference any road.'

Ying although resident next door was a constant visitor to the house and spent many hours with Peggy mercifully helping to fill the huge gap left by her friend Nancy's departure. Ying was much changed from the Ying who had first arrived in Oakfield. Her hair was no longer waist length but cropped into a very fashionable and becoming bob. Her clothes she either made herself or were hand me downs from Kathy. She was no longer the rather stout verging on chubby build she had once been, now she was svelte-like and as a result appeared much taller. An accomplished seamstress like Peggy, Ying was keen to assist in the making of Pearl's

Carnival Queen robes. Ying loved shopping at the open air market much preferring it to the regimentation of the indoor retail establishments and spent most of her Saturday mornings leisurely browsing the various stalls set up in the centre of Oakfield looking for field fresh produce and bargains. It was Ying who brought home from the market various braids and ribbons for Peggy to choose from with which to trim Pearl's dress.

The whole household became involved in Pearl's 'big day'. Even Dannah joined in saying that he would make the crown! This he did, crafting it out of chicken wire and then carefully covering it with cotton wool padding and silver paper. Initially Pearl was at her usual graceless best. When hearing how Dannah proposed to create this most precious of items she point blank refused to accept it saying she 'weren't goin' round wi' no bleedin' chicken wire on 'er 'ead for nobody.' When presented with the finished article however she had a swift change of heart. The make-shift crown was beautiful. With glass drop beads – taken from an old necklace of Miriam's – hanging from its wired curves and an old costume jewellery ruby coloured brooch of Peggy's adorning the front it was a work of art. Once finished it had pride of place on Pearl's little dressing table so that it was the first thing she saw every morning when she woke. She no longer drew the curtains in her bedroom, wanting to glory in the early morning sun falling on her crown lighting it up as if it were indeed made with precious jewels.

After a long hot spell the weather the week before the Carnival left everyone despairing. Heavy rain followed by ferocious winds and thunderstorms was rapidly reducing the showground to a quagmire. The organizing committee led by Violet Prendergast wondered whether they should cancel, never before in the history of the Carnival had it been threatened by such atrocious conditions.

It was important that this particular event designed to 'turn the face' of the village after the abject despair following the train crash should take place. It was to herald a new dawn. Violet took soundings from her committee as to what to do. Wandsworth Prescott, Oakfield's newly elected Mayor, was adamant that it should go ahead.

'If the news is correct we will have far worse than this to deal with' he insisted. 'Time to show our metal.'

Julia Richards had been encouraged to join the organizing committee by her Headmistress. Young, artistic, enthusiastic she was just what they needed according to Adele Blanchard. Julia herself wasn't altogether sure but was all too aware that she needed something to take her mind off her own woes. Julia threw her weight behind Wandsworth, supported him in insisting that the Carnival should go ahead as planned. There were many dissenting voices but in the end they won the day, the Carnival was to go ahead. The local farmers offered to provide bales of straw which every night would be spread across the site to soak up the water. Early each morning the straw was to be lifted leaving the air to get to the ground allowing it to dry out during the day before being replaced with new straw each evening. Mercifully there was no shortage of volunteers as it was a huge undertaking. Both Patrick and Harry were keen helpers, there on the dot of five in the morning and returning at eight o'clock in the evening.

One very unhappy person was little Pearl Pettinger, Carnival Queen elect. She no longer woke to the sun glinting on the jewels of her crown, casting colourful patterns on her wall. She'd heard everyone saying that the Carnival might have to be cancelled.

'If I doesn't do it this time I'll not get another chance. I'll be too old an' me looks will've gone' she'd protested much to everyone's amusement as she'd tossed back her tight curls. Patrick had burst out laughing, ruffled her hair.

'My you're a right little madam aren't ya? I think this 'Queen' things gone right ta yer 'ead' he grinned, bowing as he did so.

'Aye well you're only jealous! An' ya needn't think I'd be 'aving ya as me King neiver! Kenneth wud be me King so there!' Whoops of laughter greeted this announcement, clearly Pearl had taken a shine to the biggest bully in her class.

Once it had been confirmed that Pearl was to be Carnival Queen Kathy had pondered over whether the child might like her mother to witness the event. She decided to discuss the matter with Peggy, see what she thought.

'Oh well, ya know I'm not too sure. If it was anyone else I'd say yes, but she don't seem right fond of 'em, her family, does she? But then again if it was me, if I was 'er mam I'd want to be there, pr'aps be best jus' to ask Pearl.'

'NO, NO, NO!' was Pearl's shrill reply. 'I don't want none of 'em. Me mam, nor none of 'em! Our Frank 'ud only want ta come an' 'ave a laugh at me and I ain't 'aving 'im not no way.'

'Well I think that's quite clear then don't you?' Kathy grimaced at Peggy.

'Certainly looks like it.' agreed Peggy. 'An' we don't want to spoil her day do we. Best leave it. Leave well alone.'

The idiosyncrasies of the English weather prevailed and somehow seemed to be rewarding them for their fortitude. After a brief shower in the early hours Oakfield awoke to bright sunshine. Once again Pearl's crown glistened. Having cried herself to sleep for several nights this came as a relief to everyone. Peggy had begged her not to cry telling her she'd look a very 'unregal' Queen indeed if she ended up with puffy eyes through crying. Each and every one of them had been called into service reading to Pearl each night to try and get her off to sleep. Her favourite had been Harry who she insisted had the 'bestest' voice. Pearl's costume hung on her wardrobe door, where she could see it, see the colour from the crystals of her crown playing on it as the sun rose.

Peggy and Ying had spent many contented hours creating Pearl's gown. That it was made from old sheets could never have been guessed at covered as it was by ribbon and jewelled trimming. Pearl had watched in awe as the two women had created from nothing the most beautiful dress she could ever have imagined. When the train, made from some long discarded drawing room curtains, was attached at the shoulders by some scarlet bows Pearl was speechless. The evening before the Carnival when the weather was still in doubt Pearl was allowed to try on the finished garment. The kitchen was full, the entire household present as she emerged from Peggy's bedroom. The gown so heavily adorned weighed her down but she nonetheless held herself straight, her head held high, so proud, so very proud. Behind her Peggy stifled a little sob, reached for her handkerchief as everyone began to applaud, the boys wolf whistling and whooping with congratulation. It was left to Dannah to provide the finishing touch, placing the crown reverently on to her curls.

'Cor Uncle Dannah yu'd nivver fink it wos ju' ole chicken wire, wud ya?' she said and everyone burst out laughing.

Lizzie too was 'dressed and blessed' (as Peggy would insist on calling it) for the great day. Lizzie had eventually decided she'd like to become one of the famous 'Sally Army' band but with no discernible musical talent had been assigned the cymbals. This had caused Peggy much mirth especially when she came across Lizzie practising with her saucepan lids. Even her own mother Ruby declared that was what she'd allus bin best at, creating a racket! Lizzie however was by now immune to the constant barbs about her new found interest, revelling in being suddenly visible in the community and the bonnet still being an added incentive! She proudly took her place among the shining instruments of the band as it gathered in the station yard, waiting as the lorries only recently employed transporting bales of straw duly arrived bedecked now with balloons, banners and bunting, 'floats' for the various organizations taking part in the procession.

Pearl and her attendants were the last to mount their float. Pearl sat atop "Dredgings Fertilizers" lorry resplendent on the chair from Adele Blanchard's office, which was now covered with crepe paper as near to the colour of gold as possible. It was hoped there would be no more rain. As Julia pointed out colour so easily 'ran' from crepe paper! Happily there was no more rain that afternoon and the Carnival was a huge success, at last giving the villagers something to cheer. It was tradition that the bouquet so carefully and proudly carried by the Carnival Queen was hers to keep. Julia however had other ideas and gently suggested to Pearl that she might instead like to lay it on the memorial to the train crash victims in the adjacent churchyard. The little girl was instantly agreeable realizing that it would be yet another little ceremony where she would be centre stage. And so it was that the man who had lost the love of his life and the child who if fate hadn't decreed otherwise would almost certainly have lost hers, walked hand in hand to lay the bouquet and pay their respects to all those who had lost their lives that fateful day. Respectful applause rang in their ears as they turned and walked away.

George had walked alongside the band all the way to the showground suddenly feeling an overwhelming need to be close to Lizzie. They had been boyfriend and girlfriend for some considerable time now and inevitably the threat of war and parting had lately brought them even closer together. That very morning George's 'call up' papers had dropped on the mat. At first eager to join up, anxious to be with 'is mates', when one of them had arrived back home only six weeks later minus most of his toes George had begun to think differently about the whole thing. Perhaps it wasn't quite the lark they'd all assumed it to be? And even if they called it the 'phoney war' was it? It seemed to be going on and on 'phoney' or not.

George had decided not to tell Lizzie that day that his 'papers' had arrived. He knew how much she was looking forward to it, didn't want to spoil it for her.

Kathy followed behind the procession walking with Dannah, keeping a watchful eye on Pearl. Peggy had gone on ahead with Ying to be there when Pearl dismounted from the float, not wanting any mishaps. As Kathy and Dannah paid their dues at the gate they came upon Jeremy and Jeannie, Jeannie with her arm tucked through that of Stanley Briggs. Apparently they were a couple now, their relationship flourishing as quickly as Kathy and Jeremy's appeared to be faltering. It was only a matter of time it seemed before they would marry and Jeannie vacate the surgery. Dannah although still confused as to Kathy's relationship with Jeremy decided to make himself scarce leaving them to spend time together. Jeremy was grateful, Kathy less so. No matter how much she tried to deny it to herself she no longer felt the love she had initially felt for Jeremy, no longer yearned for his company, found him interesting and exciting. Was it he who had changed? She had to admit surely not? She now supposed it to have been mere infatuation, unfinished business even from so many years ago. As soon as the thought surfaced that it might have been convenience on her part – a need swept away when once again thanks to Henry, the man she had so heartlessly duped, she became a woman of independent means – she had to swiftly dismiss it.

Kathy was not only troubled by her feelings for Jeremy, but also her feelings for Dannah. She found herself looking forward to seeing him, revelling in his company, laughing with him. Dannah could see humour and ridiculousness in everything where Jeremy could only see rigidity, mirthless rigidity. Nonetheless Kathy took his arm, chatted amiably as they perused the many side-shows and attractions laid on by the Carnival committee.

As later that day Peggy burst into the kitchen, Pearl's gown draped over her arm, she saw Kathy looking anxiously at something in her lap.

'What is it love, what's wrong?'

'Oh nothing, it's just this bracelet. Jeremy would insist that I had a turn on the hoop-la stall and as I took aim my bracelet caught on my sleeve and fell off on to the grass. I think I've damaged the clasp, it won't seem to close properly anymore.'

"ere let's have a look' said Peggy, pulling her glasses from her pocket. 'Oh aye, you've must've given that a real good yank love. That needs seeing to properly. Take it up to ol' Mr. Garsides, he'll put it right for ya, an' he won't be expensive neither. Wants doing properly or you'll be sure to lose it again.'

'Yes I'm sure you're right and I am especially fond of it. I'll nip upstairs and put it in my jewellery box until I can take it to Mr.?'

'Garsides love' replied Peggy 'in the market place.'

CHAPTER TWENTY FIVE

George waited until the day following the Carnival to give the news to Lizzie. He had just ten days he said before he had to leave for the training camp. He would be away for six weeks after which he would have a week's leave before being sent away to God knows where. It being a Sunday they were out for their afternoon stroll, walking hand in hand.

'Oh no George, oh no!' she cried, putting her hands to her face.

'Yep' he replied with a bravado he no longer felt. 'We knew it were gonna 'appen dint we.'

'I know, I know but when it 'appens it's different ain't it.' She hastily pulled a handkerchief from her pocket. George put his arm around her shoulders, pulled her close. They walked along heads together towards the Haven, sat down when they found a bench empty. George knew that it was up to him to be brave.

'Any road, probably won't be for long, ya know what they're all saying.'

'Aye an' they've bin saying that for a long time now 'aven't they' she said annoyed. But the annoyance was soon forgotten, replaced by the sadness over what was to be. It was a very red-eyed Lizzie who arrived home that afternoon for her tea. Ruby coming through from the kitchen with a plate of thinly sliced bread took one look at her, knew immediately what must have happened, nodded meaningfully at Cissie.

Cissie uncurled her legs from beneath her, got up from the lumpy sofa, went to her sister.

'Is it George darlin'? Is 'e off?' Lizzie couldn't even answer, shrugging Cissie off went to her father, the man who had become just a shadow in their lives, no longer able to grasp quickly what was being said and even slower to respond. Lizzie sat herself on his lap, she could feel his painfully thin legs through her skirt. He pulled her to him, tucked her head under his chin.

'There, there lass,' he said simply, the most meaningful words he'd spoken for years. Lizzie stayed in her father's arms sobbing quietly, wetting his grubby shirt. Ruby turned on her heels, went back to the kitchen, took the kettle off the range. Cissie joined her.

'Oh Mam' she said sadly, resting her arm across her mother's shoulders. 'First my Jimmy and now George.'

Knowing only too well that eventually George would be called up Edgar Desmond had volunteered to return to his duties in the Henderson household in his absence, realizing that Ying couldn't be expected to remain alone in the house when the Hendersons also were away.

Nancy having come to enjoy the close companionship which marriage had quite unexpectedly brought her was adamant that if Edgar was to move back then she would too. Their little cottage was to be rented to one of the new managers at the munitions factory who happily was also apparently a keen gardener.

It was a very emotional day when George and several of his pals climbed aboard the dusty army truck taking them goodness knew where. Having no proper family George had ended up with a large make-shift one and there were no dry eyes as the truck pulled away. Lizzie waved until the truck was out of sight, wishing him God speed, realizing once and for all how much she had come to love him.

CHAPTER TWENTY SIX

When Luci's letter had arrived telling Julia that there were two teaching posts vacant at Oakfield School she had known that she must apply immediately. She needed to be away, away from all the memories. Julia's romance with Claude Dubois had continued apace once she had moved to the city, she had imagined herself in love and on the verge of marriage. Until that was she discovered quite accidentally from one of his work colleagues that Claude was in fact married with two young children. Julia had been devastated, couldn't bear to think about him let alone see him. He had said he wanted to explain. Just how did you explain away an engagement ring!

The School at Oakfield was so desperate to replace the two teachers killed in the fateful crash that having applied and been successful she was allowed to commence work with immediate effect. And so Julia had moved once more into the small back room in Philip and Luci's tiny cottage. Philip completely unaware of Julia's romantic entanglement was simply pleased to see her, it was Luci who had wanted to ask questions. Julia just wanted to get on with the job, throw herself into work and so she had not been averse to joining the Carnival Committee when Adele Blanchard, her Headteacher, proposed it. She'd been surprised how much she'd enjoyed it and afterwards realized how much she would miss the meetings. Julia had got on particularly well with Wandsworth Prescott. Many years different in age they nonetheless found they had much in common. Intellectually they were amazingly well matched. Wandsworth, an amateur artist himself, admired and encouraged Julia's artistic talent constantly telling her, just as Claude had, that it was wasted. They discussed literature, music, politics, found they shared the same tastes and principles.

It had been a long time since Wandsworth Prescott had first fallen in love. Married to Maude for nearly twenty five years – they had been due to celebrate their silver anniversary the very next year – Wandsworth was taken by surprise by how much he looked forward to meetings when Julia Richards was to be there. He found himself scouring the room for her, anxious for her to arrive, and when she did, settling happily as everything suddenly mattered so much more. Once the Carnival was over and the necessary meetings no more he found himself lost, a miserable old soul indeed. It took him some while to recognize what was missing. In any case how could that be? The mere idea was totally absurd! He busied himself so as not to allow these ridiculous thoughts to enter his head. He threw himself wholeheartedly into the role he'd taken on as the evacuee Billeting Officer. With heavy bombing now in the major cities – the 'phoney' war seemingly at an end – more and more families were seeking safety for their children. Oakfield was once more in great demand.

Julia Richards as primary school teacher was as much involved with her young pupils' home lives as she was with their education, recognizing only too well how their personal circumstances impacted on their ability to learn. In the end it was Julia whom Wandsworth consulted over the possibility of a new little family being accommodated in the school. Much to his amazement and delight she had seemed pleased to see him. He was almost certain she wasn't just being helpful. When she herself suggested they might get their heads together over supper one evening his old heart did more than skip, it did a backward somersault. Wandsworth suggested they should meet at his house.

Whilst being wary not to look as if he'd gone to too much trouble he nonetheless took great care with the small supper he'd prepared. Having noted previously she was a vegetarian it had somewhat challenged his culinary skills. But that was the thing with Julia, everything required that extra effort and he knew it was good for him.

Unknown to Wandsworth Julia had butterflies in her stomach just contemplating the evening ahead. She had brushed aside Luci's questions regarding Claude Dubois which only served to make Luci even more curious, normally Julia told her everything. When Julia had first arrived back in Oakfield Luci, much pre-occupied with her own problems, namely a very demanding baby daughter and a husband awaiting call up papers any day, had accepted Julia's casual dismissal of any reference to her affair with the Frenchman. In any case it had been difficult to pursue any sustained line of questioning with Philip being totally unaware of what had been going on. Julia had known Philip would disapprove and Luci had had to agree. Although highly intelligent Philip had a perverse dislike of all foreigners and nothing would persuade him otherwise, and so Luci had been left in the dark as to what was happening between her sister-in-law and Claude Dubois. She had noted however the lack of correspondence. Conscious that Philip would be certain to disapprove of any such liaison Luci had made it her business to pick up the post every morning anxious that Philip might ask questions if he saw letters to Julia with a French postmark. She needn't have worried, there never were any.

When Julia rang the bell Wandsworth jumped, the cat curled up on his lap woke with a start and shot off into a far corner of the room. Wandsworth stood up, brushed himself down to remove any cat hairs, straightened his tie and walked briskly through into the hall.

'Ah, hello my dear, how good to see you, come in do. Let me take your coat.' Julia shrugged off her new camel coat, handed it to Wandsworth.

'This way my dear, I thought we might have a little aperitif before supper if that would be agreeable.' Julia picked up her briefcase from the floor and followed him into what was obviously his study. The room lined from floor to ceiling with overflowing bookshelves was a typical man's bolt-hole. 'Here have a seat whilst I get you a drink. Now what shall it be?' he smiled. Julia laughed.

'You'll have to forgive me I'm afraid but I'm not a drinker. An orange juice would be just fine for me.'

'Oh! Well yes' said Wandsworth caught unawares. 'In that case you'll have to excuse me whilst I just venture into the kitchen. I won't be a moment.' Julia used his absence to have a good look around the room. Although now a man on his own he clearly took great pride in his home. The furniture shone, the windows sparkled. Paintings adorned the walls, framed photographs covered every available surface. The cat came in, closely followed by Wandsworth carrying a jug of orange juice and two crystal tumblers on a tray.

'Oh please don't let me stop you having a proper drink' cried Julia as he began to fill both glasses.

'Not at all, probably a whole lot better for me anyway' he grinned. He sat down taking the chair opposite to hers. Suddenly it became difficult, both tongue-tied not knowing how to break the ice with the initial pleasantries dispensed with. In the end Wandsworth laughed. 'Oh dear you must think me an old fool' he said, 'But it's a very long time now since I entertained anyone other than to discuss business.'

'I know' said Julia simply, understanding immediately. 'But anyway we do have some business to discuss don't we, the Starling family and what is to become of them.'

'Ah yes indeed, but I had hoped that this evening would be more of a social evening' he said feeling the need to say it but at the same time extremely embarrassed.

Something soft and wonderful washed over Julia. She wanted, needed, to make things right for this man, wanted to see him smile, hear him laugh, watch him be happy.

'And so it will be' she smiled. 'So it will be, I've looked forward to it so much' she found herself admitting. Wandsworth gazed across at her, his heart no longer thumping but slowly, very slowly, melting.

'Have you my dear? Have you really? Because so have I.'

Over their supper taken in the rather splendid dining room the two discussed the Starlings. A large family it would not be a simple matter to accommodate them either in someone's home or in the tiny School.

Afterwards in the drawing room side by side on the sofa they talked about themselves, their lives up until that moment. Wandsworth had heard her sadness, her disappointments, had wanted to make everything right for her. Thinking to comfort her he had taken her hand and she'd let him, wanted him to.

Wandsworth insisted on walking Julia home. When they parted on the corner of the Beck – just out of sight of Philip's cottage – Wandsworth quite uncharacteristically found the courage to take her in his arms and kiss her. Julia's heart turned over. Had she really imagined what she had felt for Claude to be love? Oh no! This, this was love! Wandsworth walked home with a new spring in his step, his heart no longer heavy but full of dreams.

What an old fool I am said Wandsworth to himself as he looked hard at his reflection in the mirror the next morning. At least I suppose I have my own teeth and although it's grey I still have a few strands of hair left, but look at the rest of me, I'm almost old enough to be her father for goodness sake! Wandsworth had fallen asleep a happy man but he'd woken with a start to reality. Had he been drunk? No even that wasn't a possibility the most they'd consumed was orange juice and coffee and neither of those were known for causing hallucinations! Whatever had he been thinking of! Poor Julia, poor girl. Although alone he found himself colouring with embarrassment.

As he sipped his first coffee of the day Sheba the cat appeared on the window-sill outside, anxious to be in after a night on the tiles. She peered in at him and then proceeded to prowl backwards and forwards along the window-sill tail in the air, she wasn't at all used to being ignored. Eventually he took pity on her, went to pull up the sash window to let her in. As he did so he saw Julia about to lean her cycle against the porch. She saw him, grinned, waved and he automatically did the same. The cat jumped down into the room and then followed him to the door. He wished he didn't have to do this, didn't have to open the door, face her.

He knew it was up to him to take the awkwardness out of the situation, clearly she'd come to put things straight, get them out of the way quickly. The poor, poor girl. Nonetheless he managed to open the door with a smile on his face. The sun shining behind her blonde head was like a halo he noted, and his heart melted all over again. She bounced past him into the hall, immediately held out her arms to him.

'I've come before you get any ideas in your head that last night was a mistake' she smiled, 'Because it wasn't, at least not on my part' she added hastily. Wandsworth went to her, let himself briefly be enfolded in her arms and then suddenly lifted her from her feet and carried her giggling into the kitchen.

'You know I can't believe it' he said. 'I can't believe this has happened. I feel as if I've known you always, as if you've always been there alongside me and yet it's only now that I can see you.'

'I know' she cried happily. 'I feel exactly the same!'

Eventually Luci noticed. They were out pushing the pram through the park one day.

'You seem to be seeing an awful lot of Mr.Prescott these days' she said, 'I thought all this business with the Carnival had finished?'

'It has' answered Julia.

'Then why?' Julia looked her straight in the eye.

'Erm' she said.

'What on earth do you mean 'Erm?' persisted Luci.

'I MEAN Erm...' repeated Julia looking hard at her.

'What! I don't understa.........' and then the penny dropped. 'You don't mean..... You can't mean you're SEEING him' she exclaimed. Julia was instantly cross.

'And why not?' she cried.

'Well…… I don't know' Luci stammered. 'I suppose for one thing he's old enough to be your father. Whatever are you thinking of Julia? Philip will be so cross.'

'Well Philip can be what he likes' Julia shouted. 'I really don't care what he thinks!' Emily, woken from her nap, began to cry.

'There, there darling' cooed Luci, 'It's just Aunt Julia being cross.'

'I am NOT,' cried Julia stomping off in the opposite direction.

Philip was more than cross when Julia herself told him about Wandsworth. He was furious.

'But how can you? He's old. If you were to marry there'll be no children, you'll end up a young widow!'

'Oh for goodness sake Philip!' cried Luci suddenly entering the fray, surprising even herself. 'That's ridiculous and you know it. People can die at any age, and lots of older people have babies.' Luci wondered where this had come from, up to this point she too had been against the relationship. But did they really have the right to dictate what Julia did? If it worked that would be wonderful and if not then she knew that Julia would blame no one but herself. Suddenly Luci was on Julia's side and when she saw the grateful loving expression on her sister-in-law's face she knew without a shadow of a doubt that she'd been right to support her. But even Luci's intervention made no difference to Philip's view, he was adamant it wouldn't work, was ridiculous.

Luci discussed it with her mother.

'Julia's seeing Wandsworth Prescott Mummy, she says she loves him.' Maisie bouncing Emily on her knee stopped mid bounce, settled the child on her lap.

'Is she? Well how lovely. I must confess she's seemed rather down since she came back, but I put it down to all the stress at the school. I'm so pleased if she's happy again.'

'But you're not shocked then?' asked Luci. 'There's a huge age gap.'

'Well yes undoubtedly but sometimes that's right for people. For some people it works out beautifully and Julia is in spite of being very bubbly very mature in her interests. No I can see that working out well, very well indeed, and Wandsworth is such a dear man. He plays bowls with Daddy you know. I wonder if Daddy knows?'

Philip's 'call up' papers arrived some weeks later, the disagreement with Julia ongoing, they were barely able to speak to one another. Luci was distraught, terrified that her husband was going to war and heartbroken that he would leave on bad terms with his sister. In the end she suggested he should meet with Wandsworth, see the pair of them together. She had, and had recognized true love. At first Philip refused but when reminded of the reality that he might never come home, finally gave in.

Wandsworth had been desperate. Knowing that Philip had every reason to be protective of his sister, telling Julia that perhaps Philip was right and it was wrong for her to become involved with him. Julia was incandescent. She wasn't 'involved' with him she said. She was 'in love' with him', head over heels.

It was Philip who pushed Emily's pram up the short gravelled driveway to Wandsworth's house. Luci held on to the pram handle, Julia's arm through hers. Wandsworth opened the door. Emily now in Philip's arms, turned, and with a toothless smile immediately reached out to him.

Wandsworth, uncertain, looked to Philip. Philip suddenly capitulated, smiled.

'Well if she thinks you're OK you must be' and he handed over his beaming daughter. Wandsworth felt it his duty to reassure him that he would do everything in his power to make his sister happy. He fully understood Philip's reasons for being uncertain, of course he did, in the same position he would've felt the same. By the end of the afternoon they had arranged to all meet again. Luci was to cook a meal.

In the evening following their visit to Wandsworth Luci excused herself saying she was tired out and needed her bed. Julia sat with her brother, reconciled at last, told him how much he meant to her, how she would look after Luci and Emily until he returned. She had no intention of marrying she said until that happened, she needed him to give her away she grinned.

Philip left only a month later. Jonas and Maisie were there to support their daughter and wish him well. 'Come back safe lad' said Jonas gripping his shoulder. 'Come back safe.'

In the end Luci had had to turn away, simply couldn't watch as he climbed into the back of the truck.

CHAPTER TWENTY SEVEN

Things at the factory were going well having already progressed to a twenty four hour shift. Oakfield though seemed a very different place. There were few young men around most having been shipped off to learn how to fight for their country. Already two had been killed and several returned injured. Oakfield was now populated by women, children, and old men.

Cissie and Lizzie had much to everyone's surprise given up their respective jobs and gone to work at the armaments factory. In truth they couldn't afford to turn down the money. Cissie having spent only two months being Mrs. Downs and sharing her husband's rented rooms had returned home to live with her parents whilst Jimmy was away. It made no sense she said to be 'forking out on rent when she could live with her Mam and Dad.' Ruby was pleased to have her company once more, poor Charlie not able to be much of a companion these days. Lizzie although still living at home was actually seldom there. Enjoying her job at the factory she delighted in the company of so many other young women of her own age. And of course she had the 'Army'. In spite of much ribbing from her new workmates she was still just as committed. Peggy although missing her young charge had another one to take her place albeit much younger. Little Pearl was her constant shadow and actually surprisingly helpful.

Mavis Tremmings had seemed not to mind that she would once again be needed in the shop, more than happy to fit it in around caring for the two boys in her life, Tommy and Samuel.

As things had begun to settle down at the factory, with everyone getting into the swing of things, Dannah and Ralph Falconer's relationship had become much more relaxed and Friday evenings would usually find them sharing a pint or two at the 'Feathers'. It was one such evening when walking home in the blackout about to go their separate ways they heard a whimpering, wailing sound, the sound of an animal clearly in distress. Dannah reached in his pocket for the ever present torch and shielding the light with his hand cast the beam around trying to locate the animal. It was a cat clearly having been hit by a vehicle of some sort, presumably unseen in the blackout. It lay at an odd angle and was obviously barely conscious. The two men knelt down.

'Well she's still alive at any rate' Dannah said. 'You stay here and I'll run and fetch young Harry, he'll know what to do' and he was off running for all he was worth. When Dannah and Harry arrived back at the scene Ralph was gone and the cat dead. Harry had examined the animal carefully.

'Aw, her poor back's broken Dannah, there would've been nothing we could've done.' The next morning at the factory Dannah went looking for Ralph.

'Where did you get to?' he asked tersely. 'I thought you'd wait until we got there.'

'Oh I can't bear the sight of blood. It turns my stomach' Ralph replied. 'How is it by the way?' So the poor creature had still been alive when he'd left it. Dannah walked away hands in pockets, disappointed in the man and puzzled. There had been no blood.

Kathy had been concerned as to how her friend Ying would react to the return of the Desmonds, Edgar being very proprietorial and Nancy famously 'bossy'. She had foreseen problems. Ying had become used to being in charge of the house, thoroughly enjoying herself and wouldn't like to be usurped. Besides she'd seemed to be doing an excellent job. However Kathy had found that all seemed to be well. Returning home after calling on Ying she found Peggy avidly perusing her newspaper.

'Hey, 'ave ya seen this?' she demanded. 'Reckon the so and sos 'ave gone an' bombed the Palace, and the family there an' all! Sez 'ere the Queen reckons she's glad, feels like the rest of us now. I 'ave to say it was never gonna be any good 'er just parading around in 'er furs an' jewels. Don't look right 'em walking among the bomb sites and then getting in their posh car.' Kathy leaned on the back of the chair, peered over Peggy's shoulder to read the story for herself. 'Didn't 'ear anything abaht it on the radio last night though did ya?'

'No, no I didn't' replied Kathy. 'But I think they're supposed to be keeping things very quiet so that the Germans don't think they're winning.'

'Well fat lot o' good that is then if they 'ave it plastered all over the papers!' Peggy exploded. 'Who on earth's running this country!'

Christmas passed without the anticipated announcement of Kathy and Jeremy's engagement. Even Harry had been expecting it, not entirely supporting it but reconciled to what had seemed inevitable.

By February Jeremy had had enough, decided he must have an answer one way or the other. He chose his moment when they walked back from a Sunday visit to the

Hardcastles. Kathy had her arm through his but it may as well have been wrapped around the nearest lamp post for all the feeling of closeness it conveyed.

'This can't go on can it my dear?' Jeremy said simply, not even looking at her. Kathy stopped in her tracks momentarily and then continued on with a determined step.

'No, you're right it can't.'

'So I'm right in thinking that you no longer care for me?' he asked. They carried on walking.

'Of course I care for you, how could I not after all you were to me, after all you've been to me. And you're the father of my son!'

'But that's not enough, not enough for you to want to marry me?'

'Oh Jeremy I thought it was, I truly did. But you know as things have settled down I have a different perspective, my life has changed so much. I honestly feel that I will never marry again. And I have no wish to be so cruel as to use a man again. I have never forgiven myself for what I did to poor Henry. How could I do the same to someone as dear to me as you?'

Jeremy stopped, turned to her. 'But in what way would you me using me?' he asked. 'I don't understand.'

'Well suddenly allowing you to be father to my son at a critical stage in his life. When his education needs funding and so much more. I couldn't expect you to do that if I can't give you what you want from me. I just couldn't do it Jeremy. To my shame I used a man once before and I'm not about to do it again.'

'But it's hardly the same. How would it be 'using' me?' he persisted. 'It surely is my duty to support my son irrespective of how you may feel about me. I accept, I have to, that your feelings for me have changed and that perhaps in the end we may not marry, but I beg you to consider what my role could be in my son's life. I want to be part of his life Kathy. I need to be.'

'Oh Jeremy I understand I really do and I wish so much that things could be different, but at the moment they just can't be. I have no wish to marry again.'

'So there is no one else?' he asked with a perceptiveness he wasn't even aware of.

'Why no! Of course not. I've told you I have no wish to re-marry.'

'Well I shall just have to cling to the hope that one day you might change your mind.'

After such a difficult conversation Jeremy surprised Kathy by accepting her invitation to stay for tea. He was in fact finding things quite lonely at home, Jeannie so occupied these days with Stanley Briggs. Not that he had any objection he fully recognized that Stan was good for her. Jeremy wanted to spend time with Harry, with his son. They got on well enough but their relationship remained distant. Over the tea table Kathy noted with concern how Jeremy constantly glanced over to Harry, showing obvious approval of everything the boy said. She hoped no one else had noticed, especially Harry. When finally Jeremy took his leave of her on the doorstep he quite uncharacteristically these days took her in his arms, held her close.

'I'm going to be away for a few days my dear' he said, 'possibly a week but I'll see you as soon as I'm back.'

'Oh really? You never mentioned you were going away.'

'It's something that's just come up. More Government

mumbo jumbo for us poor GPs to contend with I expect' he grimaced.

'Oh right, well we'll see you when you're back then. Take care my dear, take care' she said watching as he went down the steps.

Kathy felt trapped realizing that now if the truth came out about Henry's death and her subsequent inheritance, it would look as if she'd only been prepared to marry Jeremy in order to secure Harry's education and once that was no longer necessary she'd rejected him. Oh what a mess!

CHAPTER TWENTY EIGHT

Wandsworth propped the letter from his brother behind the clock. The letter told him that his older brother Reginald and his wife Davinia would be paying their annual visit. He'd expected it but dreaded it in equal measure. His brother he was sure would be fine about Julia, Davinia he knew would be an entirely different proposition. Before he'd even had chance to tell Julia of their intended visit he wrote back saying how much he was looking forward to seeing them, saying he had someone he'd like them to meet. Reginald relayed this information to his wife.

'It'll be another cat! He'll have got himself another cat!' she said dismissively.

Wandsworth spent the two weeks leading up to the visit reassuring Julia that there wouldn't be a problem, they would love her as he did. This was unfair because he knew with cast iron certainty that although Reggie would accept it Davinia would most certainly not. Similar in age to Maude the two had got on famously. Davinia would be disapproving of any new relationship, appalled at one with someone so young.

Wandsworth heard the car pull up, gravel spitting from its tyres as his brother put his foot down hard on the brakes. Before he could even get to the door he could hear the stentorian tones of Reginald issuing instructions to Davinia. Fixing a beaming smile on his face he opened the door.

'Ah Reggie!' he cried reaching to grasp the other man's hand. 'Good to see you, good to see you.'

'And you too old boy, and you too' boomed his brother, slapping him hard on the back. 'Come on Davinia old girl, what're you doing? There's no need to be fussing with the cases I'll sort 'em later.' Wandsworth's heart sank to hear the plural. Cases? He'd thought it was merely an overnight stay! Davinia bustled up to her brother-in-law, presented one powdered cheek and then the other for the perfunctory kisses.

'How are you Wandsworth my dear?' she asked pityingly, clearly still expecting him to be in deep mourning for Maude.

'Oh you know, getting along. Now come inside both of you, the kettle's on and I've made sandwiches.'

'Well thank gawd for that! Me stomach thinks me throats bin cut!' said Reggie pushing past Wandsworth and into the drawing room where he promptly flung himself on to the sofa. Davinia after a gentle perambulation of the room checking what was new, missing or neglected, settled herself in the window seat waiting for her brother-in-law to appear with the tea trolley.

Reggie was already asleep, exhausted after the journey and cat-napping. Reggie was famous for his cat-naps, able to fall asleep instantly and then wake immediately refreshed and raring to go even after the shortest of rests. Davinia went to shake him as Wandsworth arrived with the trolley.

'What? What's going on?' mumbled Reggie crossly.

'Tea up darling, tea's ready' she said returning to her seat in the window. With a dainty plate of sandwiches in her lap and the china saucer in one hand she deftly lifted the cup to her lips. She thought she caught something out of the corner of her eye, leant her head back to see more easily. Through the window she saw a young girl cycling up the drive. She watched as the girl carefully propped her cycle against the porch.

'You have a visitor Wandsworth my dear' she said.

'Oh that will be Julia, I'll just go and let her in' and he hurried from the room. He could see from her face she was anxious. He took her hand. 'Don't worry' he reassured her.'Here, come with me.' He went into the room ahead of her pulling her after him. Both heads turned towards them.

'I said there was someone I wanted you to meet and this is she' he announced proudly, 'Julia, my friend Julia.' Davinia's cup returned to its saucer with a clatter, there could be no mistaking the implication. And he was holding her hand for goodness sake! Reggie rose to his feet, a broad grin on his face.

'Pleased to meet ya my dear, pleased to meet ya.' Julia returned a nervous smile looking beyond him to Davinia who had not risen to her feet. 'Davinia come here old girl and meet Wandsworth's friend' Reggie insisted. Had he really not realized what was meant by 'friend'? But then at times he could be so unworldly thought Davinia, reluctantly going to take the girl's hand, smiling a tight smile.

'Delighted to meet you I'm sure.'

'Here sit over here and I'll get you some tea and something to eat' fussed Wandsworth, trying to ease Julia's discomfort.

'Thank you but I'm fine, I'll eat later at home' insisted Julia.

'Julia's just come from school haven't you?' smiled Wandsworth.

'Oh yes and which class are you in?' asked Davinia tartly. Reggie as usual was oblivious to the barb but his brother was not.

'Julia is a primary teacher at the School aren't you my dear?' He grinned trying to deflect his sister-in-law's sarcasm.

'Oh yes and how long have you been at the School? Not long I would imagine' Davinia continued her questioning.

'Oh long enough' responded Julia at last finding her tongue. 'I taught for a while in the city and then came here to cover for one of the teachers killed in the train crash.'

'Julia's a very experienced teacher and also an accomplished artist' interjected Wandsworth, 'shortly to have her own exhibition.' He looked hard into Julia's eyes as she turned to him in amazement. 'Go with me on this' he said silently. Julia simply wanted to escape, she'd known it would be like this, known they would be disapproving.

'Well good for you my dear' said Reggie suddenly resurfacing. 'Love to see your stuff sometime my dear. If Wandsworth reckons you're good then you must be.'

'Oh no not really, I think Wandsworth gives me more credit than is due' she grimaced.

'I'm sure' said Davinia quietly and tartly.

Wandsworth heard and was furious. When Julia eventually offered her apologies citing lots of homework to mark he did not try to dissuade her, wanted her away from an embarrassing encounter. After seeing her out he stormed back into the drawing room.

'That was extremely rude and unforgivable even for you Davinia' he exploded. 'How dare you be so rude to a guest in my house.'

'Hey, hey just a minute' boomed Reggie, 'Ya mustn't go on at the old girl like that, what's she done?' Wandsworth realized that Reggie actually didn't know what his wife had done, yet again was oblivious to her cutting remarks and cruel asides.

'She has been extremely rude to Julia and I simply won't have it' he insisted. Reggie looked from one to the other still puzzled.

'Oh Reginald for goodness sake join the human race! Your brother is carrying on with a young girl barely old enough to be his daughter and poor Maude barely cold in her grave.'

'What? What? That's not true is it Wandsworth?'

'Certainly we have a great fondness for each other yes, but what it has to do with either of you I have absolutely no idea! If you'll excuse me I'm due at a meeting, help yourselves to anything you may need. I will see you in the morning.' And with that he slammed out of the house.

It was much later that evening when he went in search of Julia. He knew where to find her, at home with Emily. She babysat each Thursday whilst Luci attended one of her W.R.V.S. meetings. He tapped gently on the door. Julia heard him immediately for she'd been expecting him, knew he would come. After checking on her sleeping niece she crept quietly down the darkened staircase feeling her way, not wanting to stumble and wake Emily. She inched the door open, had no need to invite him in.

'Oh Julia, my darling girl, I am so ashamed of Davinia. I will never forgive her.'

'Oh you will' smiled Julia 'because she's right isn't she? And maybe it is all just too soon in any case apart from the age thing.'

'Oh Julia' he sighed and pulled her on to the sofa beside him and began to tell her everything.

Reginald and Davinia had eventually taken themselves off to bed realizing Wandsworth had truly meant what he'd said 'he wouldn't see them until the morning'.

'You know you had no right to say that to him Davinia, no right at all. He has a perfect right to do as he pleases, whatever makes him happy.' Davinia, busy at the dressing table with her Ponds face cream, turned to him.

'But it's the principle of the thing!' Reginald got off the bed, went and stood in front of her, eyes blazing.

'Any principles one decides to adopt are personal and not for one to demand of someone else. Principles won't give you a warm glow Davinia but gratitude for love and understanding just might!' With that he climbed into bed and pulled the sheet tightly round him indicating he wanted no more discussion.

Reggie was sound asleep and snoring when Davinia still awake heard Wandsworth returning, the front door closing quietly behind him. She waited and listened, he hadn't come up to bed. With the greatest of care so as not to wake her somnambulant other half she pulled on her dressing gown, put her feet into her slippers and silently made her way downstairs. Half way down the stairs through the bannisters she was able to make out Wandsworth slumped over on the sofa head in hands. She crept down the remaining stairs.

'I'm so sorry Wandsworth' she whispered from the doorway. 'So very sorry my dear, I had no right.' He looked up, smiled his gentle smile.

'Are you my dear? That's kind.' In her floral dressing gown she sat down beside him, took his hand between her own.

'It just all seemed so sudden you know, Maude being gone such a short time.' He turned to her, pain and anguish plainly etched on his face.

'She was going to die Davinia. She had been diagnosed with terminal cancer, had been given only a year at best....'

'What! But no surely not, what are you saying?' cried Davinia, stunned beyond belief. 'Surely we would have known, should have known, why didn't you tell us?'

'She wanted no one to know' he said shaking his head sadly. 'She said everyone would begin to treat her differently and she wanted to live her life for as long as possible as a normal person. And she did you know she'd already had six good months. She was beginning to tire a little but there was no wonder really she was so determined to fit everything in. She'd always been a busy person but still managed to increase the tempo. Of course everyone thought she'd lost the plot a bit, got even more bossy and demanding.' He laughed. 'But she hadn't you know, she was just trying to fit everything in before it was too late.' Tears glistened along his eyelashes.

'Oh my dear, dear boy, whatever can I say' begged Davinia, tears beginning to fall steadily, tears hastily wiped away very inelegantly in the absence of a lace trimmed handkerchief with the cuff of her dressing gown. He allowed her to hug him in his grief, the first time that had happened since he'd lost Maude. In the end he pulled away.

'So you see in a way it was a relief, she was so afraid of what was to come and that fear was taken away, she never had to face all the things she had been so frightened of.'

'But why did you never say?' she protested. 'Surely, surely there was something we could've done?'

'There truly was nothing.' He tried to smile. 'We just locked ourselves away in our little cocoon and enjoyed the time we had left. And we did enjoy it believe it or not, it's amazing what having a time limit on something can do.'

'And so no one else knew?'

'Only the doctor and of course the consultant at the

hospital. At that point there had been no need for anyone else to know.'

Davinia subdued now sat staring into the fire, looked along the mantelpiece at the many reminders of Maude. The china cats one each end of the mantelpiece. The Coronation mug stamped either side with pictures of the King and Queen. The shell photograph frame strangely out of place amongst the finer things, enclosing a sepia photograph of her long dead parents. A crystal rose bowl given to her and Wandsworth on their wedding day. And centre stage next to the ornate clock a little wooden box carved apparently by one of the evacuee children inscribed simply with the words 'fanks'.

'Oh dear' she said straining to hold back the tears again, holding her cuff once more to her eyes.

'It's alright my dear. Of course I understand your emotions, but knowing what she knew Maude had assured me that when the time came she wanted me to move on, enjoy my life even though it would be without her. She had an enormous heart as you well know. Admittedly we neither of us could've imagined I would find happiness with one so young and at first I couldn't believe it, couldn't accept it for Julia's sake. But you see I do love her, I really do and I know, I'm sure, I can make her happy.'

'Well of course we all should take any happiness life can offer us' sighed Davinia. 'Life is very, very short but you just don't realize it until you get to our age.' She tried to laugh.

When she eventually returned to bed she found Reggie still snoring, oblivious to all that had taken place.

The next afternoon found Davinia lined up with the mothers on the pavement opposite the school. Most of the mums eagerly taking the opportunity for a gossip leant against the wall which bounded the bakery. Davinia did no such thing, standing ram-rod straight and dressed very smartly she kept herself at a discreet distance. It had been a long walk down to the school and she had had to ask for directions several times. Julia finally appeared pushing her cycle through the gates, a child hanging on to her handlebars one each side. In animated conversation with her young pupils she was more than surprised to see Davinia waiting for her. She went across the road to her smiling uncertainly and then turned to her companions wishing them good night and assuring them she would expect to see them bright and early on Monday.

The two women watched as they skipped off, happy it was Friday and therefore no school for two whole days. When Davinia quietly slipped her arm through Julia's she really had no idea what to do – shrug it off or leave it there? Davinia didn't give her time to decide. She gently urged them both forward.

'I wondered what you might think to a little tea party?' she said. 'For Wandsworth and Reggie I mean. They've gone off for a round of golf so there'll be plenty of time.' She rolled her eyes as if in despair. 'Neither of them are any good at it you know!' She'd broken the ice.

'No I didn't know' laughed Julia.

'Well will you come then? Come and help me, let me show you how very sorry I am.' Julia stopped pushing the bike, turned to her.

'Of course' she said simply. 'I'd love to.'

After stopping off for provisions which were loaded into the basket on Julia's cycle, and the long walk home, they didn't have as long as they had expected before the two men appeared. Already alerted to Julia's presence by her cycle in its now customary place propped against his porch, Wandsworth was at first apprehensive wondering what on earth could've brought her there. Davinia quickly went to him, put her hand on his arm.

'It's alright my dear all is well. I have apologized profusely' and she turned to Julia standing across the room as if for confirmation. Julia's beaming smile told him all he needed to know.

CHAPTER TWENTY NINE

After two weeks and having heard nothing from Jeremy Kathy decided she must take the bull by the horns and seek him out at his surgery. The waiting room was full as she entered and Jeannie was busy registering patients. Kathy had not at all been looking forward to encountering Jeannie. Great friends whilst her relationship with Jeremy had been at its best, that is at the beginning, Kathy had noticed a distinct cooling between herself and Jeremy's sister-in-law. Jeremy had dismissed her reservations saying that Jeannie simply wasn't like that, was just so totally absorbed with Stan Briggs and their impending marriage.

'She really has thoughts for nothing and no-one else' he'd laughed good naturedly. Kathy wasn't so sure and felt she definitely detected a very false tight-lipped smile when Jeannie finally looked up from what she was doing and acknowledged her. Kathy waited patiently in the queue for her turn.

'I was wondering if I might have a quick word with Jeremy?' she asked. 'But' – she turned and looked round the crowded room – 'I can see he must be tremendously busy.' Jeannie frowned.

'Jeremy's not here' she said rather stiffly. 'I assumed you knew that.'

'Well yes he told me he would be away for a week. I was just wondering if he was unwell.'

'No he's not unwell' answered Jeannie sharply. 'As to when he'll be back I really can't say, but I'm sure he'll contact you as soon as he is.' With that she looked to the next patient as if indicating their conversation was at an end. Kathy had no hesitation in taking the intended hint and exited the room as quickly as she could. Oh no doubt I deserved it she chastised herself. Jeannie would be only too aware of the situation between herself and Jeremy and obviously she would be none too pleased. On returning home she relayed the news of Jeremy's prolonged absence to Peggy.

'Oh aye love I must've forgot to tell ya. I 'eard t'other day that that there Doctor Whitstable was standing in for a while. Sorry love, I thought you'd know.'

It was in fact another two weeks before Jeremy finally called to the house, immediately asking if he could have a private word in the drawing room. Kathy didn't even ask for a tray of coffee to be brought through, sensing that this conversation was one which shouldn't be interrupted.

'Of course, come this way' she said leading him into the room. 'Have a seat.' There had been no kiss of greeting between them, neither of them seeming to want it. Jeremy hesitated, toyed with his cuff link, a clear indication that he was feeling uneasy. Kathy noticed immediately.

'You might as well come out with it Jeremy, whatever it is you've come to say. Just say it.'

Jeremy suddenly jumped to his feet, went across the room to the bay window, twitched the curtain slightly looking out. He let go of the curtain, turned to her.

'I've enlisted, Kathy. I went down to London initially just to have a chat but they immediately asked if I would consider going down to Chenebrook, the military hospital, for some specialized training and now I'm to go to the front. I leave for France next week.'

'What?' Kathy was stunned. 'But why have you done that? Surely you needn't have? You're needed here and besides aren't you too old?' He couldn't help a wry smile at her outspokenness. Jeremy came back into the room.

'Medics are never too old' he grimaced 'particularly with things as they are. Reading between the lines I don't think things are going too well. There are many, many casualties and doctors and nurses would seem to be in short supply. In any case I feel it is my duty and I have no family to consider' he said somewhat pointedly. 'Far better that I go instead of a family man when it could result in a tragedy.'

'But what a thing to say!' cried Kathy. 'It would be just as much a tragedy if something were to happen to you.'

'Would it?'

'Why of course' protested Kathy. 'How can you even think such a thing?' Jeremy had regained his seat now and Kathy went to him, knelt in front of him and took his sad face in her hands, looked into his eyes.

'This isn't because of me is it Jeremy? It just mustn't be' she pleaded.

'Of course not!' he lied even now still concerned for her feelings. 'I just feel it's my duty, something I must do.' Kathy sat back on her heels.

'Oh Jeremy my dear' she sighed 'how has it come to this?'

'There are many, many questions we don't have answers for' he smiled tenderly 'and this I'm afraid is one of them. Anyway I just wanted to tell you, I wanted you to hear it from me. But I really must go now, as you might imagine there is a lot that needs attending to.' He rose to his feet and as he did so he pulled Kathy to hers.

'But I will see you again won't I? Before you go I mean.'

'Of course, I wouldn't leave without saying goodbye.' Kathy followed him to the door.

'Should I tell everyone then or do you want to?'

'No you tell them my dear, it's not exactly an easy thing for me to explain. Jeannie was extremely cross, it's taken a lot to persuade her that I'm doing the right thing and even now I can tell she's just humouring me, not wanting us to part on bad terms.'

'Well no, I'm sure she must be heartbroken, you've always been so close.' Privately Kathy knew that Jeannie would probably be blaming her, thinking that if she and Jeremy had still been close he wouldn't have even considered doing what he was about to do. With the promise of a proper farewell she closed the door behind him and went in search of Peggy. She found her with Pearl, heads together over a piece of crochet. She took a seat at the table. The door to the yard was open, a light breeze blowing through from the warm afternoon. In the end she decided to keep her news not wanting detailed discussion in front of the child.

Harry was out, Patrick also, busy at the farm. It was Dannah arriving home unexpectedly early from the factory with whom Kathy eventually shared her news.

'I don't suppose you'd care for a walk would you?' she asked.

'Aye, do you know I would. Just let me give meself a quick wash and I'll be at the front in ten minutes.'

He was waiting at the foot of the front steps. With one hand in his pocket he crooked his arm, silently inviting her to link arms. She felt embarrassed and guilty at the thrill it sent through her body as he did so.

'The Haven?'

'Why not' she smiled. Too engrossed were they to notice the figure lurking just out of sight behind one of the sheds in the station goods yard opposite.

They found 'their bench' occupied by two fishermen taking a breather on their way home, their tackle propped against the back of the bench, the baskets at their feet evidence of a successful day's fishing. Kathy and Dannah continued on along the bank, the water sloshing on to the polished stones just beyond the long grass.

'Jeremy has joined up Dannah' said Kathy suddenly. 'Did you know?' Dannah stopped walking.

'Ah! No, I didn't but I pretty much guessed that he would eventually.' He was careful with his next words.

'And how are you about that?' he enquired gently.

'Oh you know, apprehensive for him of course.'

'I meant about yourself. How do you feel about it for yourself?' he persisted. Kathy shrugged her shoulders noncommittally, there was no use pretending any more.

'I'm not sure it really has anything to do with me' she replied. 'Sadly things are not as they used to be between us. You surely must have noticed?'

'Well... it's not been for me to notice one way or the other, but if that's the case I'm really sad to hear it. I'd thought the pair of you were a match made in heaven. I think we all did.'

'Hmm, it was probably a bit too good to be true. Fairy tale endings are usually just that aren't they?'

'So what now?' he pressed gently.

'Nothing' she replied flatly. 'Business as usual, he'll go off to do his duty and I'll continue as before on my own.'

'You're not on your own love, you're really not, we're all here for you and Harry. Does Harry know by the way? I guess he must've assumed like the rest of us that you would marry.'

'I suppose he did, but to be honest I don't think he particularly cares one way or the other. As hard as he's tried Jeremy has never really succeeded in getting close to him the way you have. In any case Harry's head is so full of other things' she laughed.

'Ah well things will sort in the end' said Dannah sadly. 'War certainly is a terrible time for everyone, throws everything out of kilter.' A thought suddenly came into Kathy's head. She pulled abruptly away from him.

'You won't go will you Dannah, you won't go too?' she asked urgently.

'No love, I'm too old for 'em, they don't want me for fighting. I'm more use at the factory, especially as things are going.'

The week leading up to Jeremy's departure sped by and once more the Ladan Road household found themselves gathered together, this time at the station to wave him off. Kathy received a rather brusque 'good morning' from Jeannie as she arrived to say her farewells. Of all of them Harry, although present, seemed the least concerned, a fact that did not go unnoticed by either Jeremy or Kathy. Once the train had pulled out Jeannie walked sadly back to the surgery alone. She constantly reflected on the turn of fortune for herself and Jeremy. It had been Jeremy for whom married bliss had seemed to beckon but now he was away to war whilst she waited patiently to wed her beloved Stan. Life was so very strange with all its twists and turns.

Jeremy had not been sent immediately to France as expected, instead he spent another three weeks at Chenebrook. It was from there that he sent Kathy's birthday card, a little early but he'd wanted to send it from England, be more confident that she would get it. Knowing full well what it was when it dropped on the mat Kathy placed it behind the clock waiting for the day, the 14th October. Noticing the card one day Harry had been reminded of his mother's birthday and was anxious to buy her something nice. He knew full well he was being rather neglectful these days. But then he was so busy! Although still not earning and with little money at his disposal he was keen to get something she would really appreciate, especially as the departure of the doctor had left her a little 'down'. He decided to broach the subject with Peggy asking for suggestions. She had no hesitation.

'Well I think I know what she would really like love an' I'm sure it wouldn't cost too much either.'

'Oh yes, what is it?' asked Harry, eager to solve his dilemma.

'Well a few weeks ago at the Carnival your mam had an accident with her bracelet, broke the clasp I believe and being specially fond of it she'd intended getting it fixed. I asked her about it only the other day as it 'appens and she said she 'adn't got round to it, it was still in 'er jewellery box. Pr'aps you could get it mended for 'er as a surprise, I'm sure she'd be pleased as punch with that love' she nodded.

'Peggy that's an excellent idea' he said. 'So if I sneak it out of her jewellery box you don't think she'll notice?'

'No, I'm sure she won't pet and if you tek it up to Mr. Garsides in the Market Place I'm sure he'll do it cheap for ya. Tell 'im Peggy Barley sent ya.'

Harry took his opportunity one afternoon a few days later when he knew Peggy and Kathy were at a school event with Pearl. Rarely visiting his mother's room he nonetheless spotted the jewellery box straight away placed as it was on a small chest of drawers next to her bed. He sat down on the floral quilt, picked up the box and placed it on his lap. In the box he found several pairs of ear-rings, a pearl choker, a silver filigree necklace and yes there at the bottom laid on a vellum envelope was the bracelet. Harry picked up the bracelet, popped it into his trouser pocket. About to replace the contents of the box curiosity got the better of him and he lifted out the envelope. It obviously contained a letter. Whilst bearing no post mark it clearly bore his father's unmistakeable hand, a flowing itallic script. One word beautifully written across the front, 'Katherine'.

He couldn't resist, he pulled the single sheet from the envelope, unfolded its creases and in that single act changed his life forever.

Harry read the letter, discovered the unbelievable truth that Henry Watson-Smythe was not his father, and what was more must in fact be dead. From what he read his mother had tricked his supposed father for years and years. Now he had the real reason why his mother had returned to England and why he had had to follow. His 'father' had discovered the truth of her treachery and wanted rid of her. He read the letter to the end in disbelief realizing that in spite of everything Henry Watson-Smythe had eventually found it in his heart to forgive his mother for all that she had done. In shock Harry folded the letter, having read it once more just to be sure, and placed it back in its envelope. Tucking it back in the box he carefully covered it with all its contents including the bracelet which he returned from his pocket, no longer feeling any desire to do anything nice for his mother.

When the three returned from their outing he was missing. Harry pondered long and hard over the contents of the letter exposing as it did his mother's deceit. Certainly it probably answered why Henry had seemed not to like him, particularly latterly. No one could truly comprehend being disliked by their own flesh and blood and so in a way the truth brought him some comfort. He was left with feelings of fury and total disgust with his mother but ones which he needed to hide until he'd decided what to do. Overriding all these thoughts was his desire to know the identity of his real father. He was desperate to know.

To find some answers Harry needed to delve into Kathy's past. He began with Peggy quizzing her over the family history but she was unable even unwittingly to provide any clues. He learned that she had had no knowledge of his mother's very existence until she had arrived back in England. If Peggy didn't know then Lizzie certainly wouldn't and Dannah wasn't part of his mother's history, so who was there to ask? He thought about Ying. Perhaps she would know something having been with his mother in her early years in India. But as a servant she obviously wouldn't have been party to secrets of her private life. Desperate, he nonetheless decided that Ying would be worth a try.

On the morning of Kathy's birthday Peggy raised a quizzical eyebrow as Harry handed his mother a box of chocolates and not the repaired bracelet as she had suggested. With no answer to the questions permanently in his head Harry became angry and estranged from his mother although she had absolutely no idea why, putting it down to growing pains or the thought of impending important exams. He shared his discovery with no one, not even Patrick who in any case had recently made his own discovery – girls! – and was enjoying a special relationship with one of the twin daughters of Farmer Dearing. Gail had suddenly become a very important part of Patrick's life.

Harry used the pretext of borrowing some fishing tackle to call at the Henderson household and speak with Ying. Dannah and Ralph Falconer had discovered a shared interest in fishing, had taken to going off to the grounds quite regularly, work permitting, and after Patrick had joined them and seemed to enjoy it Harry also was being pressed to join them.

Since the incident with the cat Dannah had found his regard for Ralph Falconer tested. Ralph however was still keen to share Dannah's company although still reluctant to join in any activities at Ladan Road. He just wasn't a family person was his perennial excuse. When Dannah had turned up one day for a fishing trip with Patrick in tow Ralph had expressed surprise and pleasure but was privately a little concerned. When a subsequent trip was planned and he learned Harry was to be included he claimed pressure of work was going to make future trips more difficult and the trio went without him.

Harry had at least managed to secure the loan of some fishing tackle when he had called to see Ying but his questions over his mother albeit subtle remained unanswered. Clearly Ying had been what he'd always imagined, a close and trusted servant but no more.

Actually Ying had trained herself many years ago to 'forget' that Henry Watson-Smythe was not Harry's father, she'd found it easier that way. Of course once re-united with

Kathy, seeing her closeness to the Doctor, hearing that they had once been close friends had raised her suspicions. But whatever her suspicions she kept them to herself and always would. Kathy was aware of the conclusions her old friend might come to but nothing was ever mentioned between them, she knew without a shadow of a doubt that it wasn't necessary, her secret was safe with Ying. Harry was careful to keep the knowledge of his 'father's' death to himself and it became clear to him that Ying was not aware of it, why should she be?

With another Christmas almost upon them Luci received the wonderful news that Philip should be home for a brief spell of leave. Julia and Wandsworth hastily arranged their wedding more in hope than expectation that he would actually be there. But he was there. Philip gave his sister away on a cold snowy day just before Christmas, his tiny daughter clutching a posy of Freesia and Lily of the Valley taking her first uncertain steps behind them. When Wandsworth turned and saw his young bride he quite clearly heard Maude. 'I love you my darling, be happy.' His eyes were moist as he took Julia's hand, looked round her to Philip.

'Thank you' he mouthed. Philip nodded, smiling, scooped up his little daughter and took his place alongside Luci in the front pew. As they left the church there was no confetti, just rice thrown a little too enthusiastically by many of Julia's young pupils. Reggie went to his brother, slapped him on the back, gave Julia a huge bear hug. Davinia took Wandsworth's hand as she kissed his cheek, eyes bright with tears.

'Be happy my love' she said simply. Wandsworth wiped away a tell-tale tear, looked up to the sky, smiled.

'Thank you Maude my darling' he said, 'Thank you.'

CHAPTER THIRTY

Six months later Oakfield found itself much changed. The war was no longer dismissed as the 'phoney war', hostilities had intensified, major cities were bombed relentlessly and each day brought lists of more casualties, several from Oakfield. Being such a small community each one was taken as a personal assault. George had not returned, had immediately been sent to the front. The letters to Lizzie were sporadic, there being none for several weeks and then three or four would arrive together. They said very little of what was happening to him, mostly were reminiscences, reflecting back on what at the time had seemed insignificant events but which now seemed momentous and unbelievably happy.

Edgar Desmond's appearance at the Carson household one winter's evening took everyone by surprise. He needed to speak to Lizzie he said. As Lizzie was out at one of her Salvation Army meetings Ruby said she shouldn't be too long if he'd like to wait and offered him a cup of tea and a currant bun.

It wasn't long before they heard Lizzie coming down the alley at the side of the house, the echo of her steel tipped boots bouncing off the walls.

'Mr. Desmond's 'ere to see ya love' Ruby greeted her as she fell through the door. Ruby had noticed that these Army meetings always seemed to exhaust her, she was always high as a kite when she got back, goodness only knew what they got up to! Lizzie instantly rallied at the mention of Edgar Desmond's name.

'Eh! What for?' she asked much surprised, looking anxiously towards her mother as she carefully removed her bonnet. Edgar Desmond seated at the table inclined his head indicating she too should take a seat. Ruby was becoming increasingly alarmed. Edgar Desmond she knew was named as George's next of kin, this could surely only mean one thing! Please God no! She took the chair next to Lizzie so as to be ready. Edgar Desmond, pulling an official looking envelope from his breast pocket, cleared his throat.

'I've had news of George Lizzie and I thought you should be the first to hear it.'

'Oh no, Oh lor!' cried Lizzie. 'Oh Mam!'

Ruby reached for her daughter, put her arm around her. Charlie looked on unconcerned, continued rolling his cigarette paper between his fingers, his machine having finally given up the ghost. Edgar Desmond knew only too well what reaction his little speech would produce, but he loved a bit of drama. He didn't get to be centre stage very often these days. In the end he said

'Ah, no you mustn't concern yourself my dear. George as far as I know is safe and well. What I have here is notification that George is to receive a commendation for bravery.'

'Oh my God!' shrieked Lizzie 'I thought you'd come to tell me 'e was dead!'

'No my dear' smiled Edgar at last. 'Not dead but exceedingly brave, apparently he saved the lives of an entire French family and two of his comrades. George is indeed a hero, we should all be immensely proud of him.'

'Oh Mam' cried Lizzie, beginning to sob, the relief suddenly overwhelming her.

Word soon spread through the village of George's bravery and award, the citizens proud beyond measure of George Doyle, thankful that for once they were celebrating on someone's behalf instead of mourning them. Lizzie by connection found herself the centre of a great deal of attention and thoroughly enjoyed every minute counting the days until George might be allowed some leave.

CHAPTER THIRTY ONE

Wandsworth Prescott as the Evacuee Billeting Officer for Oakfield was the first to hear of Gloria Pettinger's intention to pay a visit to her daughter Pearl. From the very outset Maude had been most particular about who should visit the evacuees and when, had insisted that all requests for visits should be made to her. Maude had compiled a register of all the children concerned and had meticulously noted all visits made to each one, who had visited and when. Wandsworth went to the top drawer of the desk, took out the register so painstakingly filled in by Maude. He opened it, straightened out the pages so they laid flat, saw the simple but clear hand of his wife and wanted to weep, so much attention to detail, so typically Maude. Running his finger down the page, arranged in alphabetical order, he saw immediately that the line alongside Pearl Pettinger's name was completely blank. Pearl had had no visitors in all the time she'd been in Oakfield.

'Poor little soul' he muttered to himself. 'Surely someone must've wondered about her, wanted to see her. What a cruel world we do live in.'

'What is it darling? What's wrong?' Julia coming into the room had seen the register laid out before him, noted the concerned look on his face.

'What? Oh nothing really you know! I've had a request from a parent for a visit and I see that the poor child hasn't seen a single member of her family in all the time she's been here. That's just so sad, how can they do that?' he asked.

'Oh my goodness, that's really awful, the poor little mite. Am I allowed to know who it is?'

'Well of course, I know you're the soul of discretion my love. It's little Pearl Pettinger, you know the Carnival Queen.'

'Oh yes I know alright!' laughed Julia, 'That child's never been the same since, imagines she's some film star, certainly has adopted some airs and graces!'

'Hmm, well her mother has decided she wants to see her and it says here "as soon as possible." Wonder why it's suddenly so urgent.'

'So what are you going to do?' asked Julia. 'I imagine it could be very unsettling for Pearl not having seen her for such a long time. Do you have to see if it's what she wants too or is it a fait accompli?'

'Pretty much I guess. After all she is the child's mother, I suppose we could hardly refuse but I'll have a word first with Mrs. Watson-Smythe. I'm sure she will be able to prepare her, but it seems as if time is of the essence. It says here' – he waved the letter in the air – 'that she needs the visit to take place within the next few days.'

'Huh!' scowled Julia. 'Why the hurry all of a sudden?'

'Why indeed' mused Wandsworth thoughtfully, closing the register and returning it to its rightful place.

With his car in mothballs for the duration Wandsworth pulled his cycle from the shed at the side of the house, clipped his cycle clips around his notoriously skinny legs and set off the very next afternoon for Number Two Ladan Road. He had decided to time his visit when the little girl would be at school not wanting her to be party to any decisions made on her behalf until it had all been thoroughly talked over amongst the adults. Having propped his cycle along the front wall of the house and in the process of removing his cycle clips he was taken by surprise by Peggy Barley arriving home from her afternoon's marketing, her bulging basket over her arm.

'Why Mr. Prescott and what might you be doing propping your bike along our wall like that? That ain't allowed ya know' she said sternly.

'What? Oh I am so very sorry!' he flustered, 'Perhaps if I take it round the back into the yard?' Peggy smiled.

'No, no love I'm only kidding, put it where ya like, but are ya wanting to see us?'

'Yes I am actually if that would be possible? I need a word about little Pearl Pettinger.' Peggy's heart sank, she'd been dreading this and yet knowing it might come.

'Oh aye, well 'spect it'll be Miss Kathy you'll be needing, you come on in and I'll see if she's at home.'

Wandsworth followed Peggy into the hall and waited as she tapped on the drawing room door.

'Come in' called Kathy.

'Sorry to disturb you love but Mr. Prescott's here, wants a word with ya abaht little Pearl.'

'Oh! Right.' Kathy was on her feet as Wandsworth entered the room. 'There's nothing wrong I hope?' she asked concerned.

'No, no indeed' he smiled 'it's just that........'

'Oh please, please do sit down. And you too Peggy dear for if it's something concerning Pearl then I know it will concern you too.'

'Aye well yes, it would' agreed Peggy, happy that her relationship with Pearl was properly acknowledged. The child had become the nearest she would ever have to her own daughter and she loved her dearly.

Wandsworth settled himself in his chair, took the envelope from his inside pocket.

'I've had correspondence from Pearl's mother, Mrs. Gloria Pettinger' he said. 'She wishes to visit young Pearl with the utmost urgency.'

'Really, but why?' asked Kathy. 'She's shown absolutely no interest in the poor child in all the time she's been here.'

'Calls 'erself a mother!' scoffed Peggy quietly.

'Well of course I have absolutely no idea' answered Wandsworth. 'I did check my register of visits and so I am aware as you say that Mrs. Pettinger has not paid any visits to Pearl, but I'm not able to cast any light on why she should suddenly want to do so.'

'Pr'aps decided she might be useful now she's a bit older' joined in Peggy bitterly.

'Hmm, well we should certainly hope that's not the case' frowned Wandsworth. 'The thing is there really is no way I can prevent her seeing her own daughter if that is what she wants.'

'No of course not, of course you can't' Kathy reassured him.

'Suppose Pearl doesn't want to see 'er Mam?' interjected Peggy. Slightly surprised Wandsworth turned in his seat to face the cook.

'Do you have reason to suppose that might be the case Mrs. Barley?'

'Aye I wouldn't be a bit surprised an' who could blame her? Poor little mite.'

'Oh I see' said Wandsworth, slightly ruffled now. Kathy knew she needed to intervene.

'Well whatever the rights or wrongs clearly these problems are not yours Mr. Prescott.' She smiled kindly at him. 'You're here merely to organize a time agreeable to everyone when Mrs. Pettinger for whatever reason may be re-united with her daughter.'

It was agreed that Kathy and Peggy together would tell Pearl of her mother's impending visit. They broke the news to her just before she went up to bed that evening. They both agreed afterwards that it had been the most spectacularly bad timing. Pearl opened her mouth wide, aghast at what she was hearing.

'She's comin' to tek me away i'nt she! Well I'm bloomin' well not going no way, so there!' she screeched sticking out her tongue. Peggy went to put her arms around her to comfort her but she shrugged her off. 'Gerroff!' she cried 'You promised I'd niver 'ave to go back.'

'Now I'm sure I never did that' Peggy said anxiously. 'I couldn't love for yer not ours.'

'Whatever Pearl I will not have you being rude to Auntie Peggy, say you're sorry at once.'

'Will not!' screamed Pearl.

'Well in that case I suggest you go straight to your room, and there'll be no story tonight young lady.'

'But....' began Pearl.

'No buts, off you go NOW!' Pearl turned on her heel, stomped to the door, slammed it behind her. They heard every single thud of her footsteps on the stairs, followed by the slam of her bedroom door which shook the chandelier in the hall beneath.

'Ah well I guess she ain't too pleased at the thought of seeing her Mam again' said Peggy in a massive understatement.

'No it would seem not' grimaced Kathy. 'But I'm afraid we're going to have to deal with it one way or another.'

The meeting between mother and daughter was arranged for the Saturday of the following week-end. Pearl was in the front bedroom helping Peggy change the beds when the doorbell rang. She went over to the window, popped her head under the sash. Resting her arms on the sill she leant over on tip-toe, looked down.

'Don't reckon it's me Mam Auntie Peggy' she called over her shoulder. "ho ever it is is too posh for me Mam, she's got this daft little 'at perched on 'er 'ead, looks like she's off to a wedding or summat!'

Peggy joined her at the window just in time to see the woman who surely must be Pearl's mother being ushered inside by Kathy.

'Do come in Mrs. Pettinger, how nice to see you. Did you have a good journey? I know the trains can be very unpredictable these days?'

'Well weren't too bad I suppose' Gloria Pettinger conceded. 'Leastways I got 'ere which is more than can be said for some' she said with an oblique but nonetheless pointed reference to the train crash. Honestly thought Kathy indignantly it was as though Oakfield had been in some way responsible, it really was so unfair. She decided with a struggle to ignore the woman's crass comment.

'Please do take a seat Mrs. Pettinger, Pearl will be down in a minute. I'm sure she will have heard your arrival.'

'Ah come 'ere pet let's just straighten yer 'air up shall we? Make ya look all bonny like' said Peggy reaching for a hair brush on the dressing table.

'But you sez I allus look bonny' countered Pearl. Peggy laughed.

'And so you do! Let's jus' say bonnier than usual shall we' and she hugged the child to her and then tapped her behind giving her a gentle push. 'Go on then love, let's go see yer Mam.'

Gloria Pettinger, sitting very elegantly, ankles neatly crossed, handbag perched in her lap and wearing a very smart up to the minute costume along with "er fancy 'at' was to Pearl unrecognizable. There had been a total transformation. When she had last seen her her mother had been a curly haired brunette, not overweight but definitely not thin and her clothes although the best she could afford could in no way have been described as stylish. This woman purporting to be her mother was a sleek haired blonde, thin to the point of being gaunt, and dressed with class. The only thing remotely recognizable to Pearl was her voice. The shrill cockney twang remained.

'Oh my gawd an' look at you!' she shrilled, not even rising from her seat. Pearl, speechless, stared straight back at her, didn't run to put her arms around her, stayed stubbornly rooted to the spot. Gloria Pettinger had come to tell them that she was taking her daughter back. She had managed to claim one of the infamous GIs who wanted to marry her and take her back home to America. As his term of duty in Britain was about to come to an end Gloria was anxious that nothing should stand in her way, nothing would stop her going with him. Pearl's elder brother Frank had told his mother in no uncertain terms, and much to her relief, that he was going nowhere and so that only left Pearl. Don had said it would be fine he'd look after both the 'little ladies' but Gloria was doubtful. Did she really want a kid cramping her style, spoiling all her dreams of a new life? As soon as she'd set eyes on Pearl she knew she didn't, knew Pearl would spoil everything! She smiled half-heartedly at her daughter.

'I 'ope you're being a good girl and be'aving yourself for Mrs...... .' She floundered around for Kathy's name. Good heavens thought Kathy we've fed, watered and looked after her little girl for months and months and she doesn't even know my name.

'Watson-Smythe.' supplied Peggy witheringly.

'Perhaps we could have some tea Peggy if you wouldn't mind. I imagine Mrs. Pettinger must be thirsty after her journey' suggested Kathy. Peggy was only too happy to escape, fearful she might say something she would regret if she stayed in close proximity for much longer. Pearl followed Peggy only too happy also to escape.

'Actually I'm pleased they've both gone' began Gloria 'because I've come to ask ya somefink.'

'Oh so it's not just to see Pearl, see how your daughter's getting on?' She almost added 'how she's GROWN!' but thought better of it.

'Aw, Naw,' answered Gloria dismissively as if she'd never heard anything so ridiculous in her life. 'Naw it ain't like that, I can see she's well looked after.' Not a word of thanks Kathy noted.

'It's just that I'm gonna be 'aving a change of circumstance so to speak.' She began to look uncomfortable. 'Thing is ya see I'm getting married again. Well not again really cos I've never bin married, but ya know! Anyways he's a yank, a GI and he's due back 'ome any time soon and wants me to go wiv 'im. Our Frank don't want to go any road but Don, that's 'is name, sez it'll be alright for our Pearl to come wiv us.' How very good of him thought Kathy! 'Thing is I ain't too sure Pearl 'ud like it so I was wondering like if you could 'ave 'er.' Kathy blinked back her astonishment.

'Have her? Quite how do you mean have her? Until you're settled do you mean?'

'No, no I mean 'ave 'er like for always.'

'You mean adopt her?' asked Kathy incredulous.

'Well yeah if that's the word for it.' Kathy watched as Gloria got to her feet, began pacing the room, she was certainly agitated. Gloria catching sight of herself in the mirror above the sideboard even in her agitation was still able to admire her reflection, gave her hat a little adjustment. Kathy was lost for words. Surely no mother worthy of the name would give up her child so readily.

'So what do ya say?' demanded Gloria Pettinger almost angrily.

'What I say' replied Kathy, herself on the verge of anger but knowing she must stay calm. 'Is that I can only imagine you haven't thought this through properly, you surely cannot want to leave your daughter behind. And if your future husband is happy for Pearl to be included then surely where's the problem? Pearl might find it difficult at first, but eventually she would settle with you to help her, and what promise of a wonderful future.'

'So ya won't 'ave 'er then, is that what yer sayin'?'

'Mrs. Pettinger' began Kathy 'we love Pearl dearly but we can't just adopt her. I myself am divorced, I can't offer her the proper family life that she deserves.'

Kathy had never seen anything happen so quickly. Gloria spun round, snatched up her bag, headed for the door and was gone, closing the front door very firmly behind her. Peggy, hearing the door, rushed down the hall, Pearl on her heels.

'What on earth?' Kathy shrugged her shoulders.

'I'll go after her' she said. She found Gloria Pettinger leaning on the wall of the station waiting room puffing hard on a cigarette.

'What've you come for?' sneered Gloria. 'You ain't gonna 'elp are ya so clear off!' Kathy was indeed tempted to do just that but held her ground and her own temper for the sake of the child.

'But Mrs. Pettinger you surely must understand it just isn't that simple? A person can't just take another one's child, the law doesn't allow it for a start.' Gloria thought she detected a slight weakening, a chink of light. She tossed her cigarette on to the platform, ground it out with her heel.

'Adoption ain't against the law' she insisted.

'No certainly it isn't' Kathy conceded. 'But it's certainly a very lengthy and complicated process. Surely wouldn't you at least be better to give it a try, take Pearl with you to America. I'm sure she'd love it, you'd all have a wonderful life together, land of opportunity and all that.' Gloria couldn't be bothered to argue any more, realized that she would be better to let Kathy think that she had been persuaded.

'Oh expect you're right, I'll talk it over again wiv Don and then we'll come an' get 'er. But it won't be for a while' she added hastily.

'No, no, well that'll be fine, give us all chance to come to terms with it. But are you going to come back with me now so that you can explain all this to Pearl?' Never ever had Gloria Pettinger been so pleased to see a train and nor would she again.

'Naw, naw, train's 'ere look an' I don't wanna miss it. I'll come again another time when we're a bit more sorted. Don't wanna upset 'er again.' Kathy was shocked.

'But surely ..... she's barely seen you.' Gloria pushed past her towards the train against the tide of disembarking passengers. By the time Kathy caught up with her she was in a carriage, the door shut, leaning out of the window.

'Jus' tell 'er I'll be back' she said. 'Jus' tell 'er I'll be back.' Kathy knew any further discussion was pointless, walked away from the carriage, and back down the platform.

Kathy entered the drawing room, found Peggy and Pearl enjoying the tea and buns they had prepared for their visitor. Pearl quickly put down her beaker of juice.

'Where is she then? Where's me Mam?' Kathy sat down beside the child.

'Oh dear, do you know it was such a shame, your mother suddenly realized there was somewhere she needed to be and she had to catch the very next train. But she promised to be back very soon, that'll be nice won't it!'

'Oh aye,' said Pearl dismissively, clearly not caring one way or the other. Peggy looked across to Kathy, raised her eyebrows. 'Later' mouthed Kathy, 'later.'

Both Kathy and Peggy were aware that although Pearl hadn't especially been looking forward to seeing her mother it nonetheless had been an 'event', an event she had now been deprived of. Peggy desperately wanted to make things right for her.

'Tell you what love when we've had this and tidied up why don't you and me go along to Mr. Doughty's. I 'ear tell he's got some baby rabbits, I'm sure you'd like to see 'em.'

'Oh yes Auntie Peggy, oh yes!' she cried excitedly and then suddenly looked downcast at the floor. Pearl was shrewd enough to recognize the right moment. 'But I've always wanted one o' me own.' She allowed her bottom lip to tremble. Peggy looked over to Kathy, raised an eyebrow. Kathy gave an imperceptible nod of her head.

'Well .... we might be able to see about that' smiled Peggy, 'If there's one you really tek a shine to.' Pearl stopped her quivering lip, looked up from the floor, her eyes shining. She rushed to Peggy, flung her arms around her neck, hugging her.

'Oo Auntie Peggy I loves ya. If ya weren't me own Auntie I'd 'ave to steal ya!'

Pearl paid several visits to Mr. Doughty's house to view the rabbits before he deemed it to be OK for them to be parted from their mother. Mr. Doughty loved the countryside, loved everything it had to offer and considered shooting and fishing as merely a fact of life, just part of the food chain and so although allowing the rabbits to roam his home like kittens he wouldn't think twice about one ending up in his cooking pot. Pearl had kept the name of her new pet a secret, one not to be revealed until it was safely ensconced in its hutch in the backyard, the hutch so carefully made by Dannah.

It was a Sunday afternoon when the rabbit finally arrived at Ladan Road. Transported in a cardboard box Pearl was told that she might have a little cuddle before it was put in its hutch providing she sat nice and still on a chair brought into the yard for the occasion. All the family were there including Lizzie having taken on the role of 'big sister' as Patrick lifted the frightened animal from the straw and placed it carefully on Pearl's lap.

'So go on then pet tell us what she's to be called' urged Peggy.

'Margaret! She's called Margaret' answered Pearl lovingly stroking the rabbit's back. The adults looked at one another bemused and amused having expected the animal to be named Mrs. Bunnykins, Hoppy, or something equally unoriginal. Peggy was the first to speak.

'Oh, Margaret? Well that's certainly an unusual name for a rabbit love, why's that then?'

'It's for Princess Margaret, cos I allus feel right sorry for 'er, cos she ain't niver gonna be Queen is she? And it int right fair! An' she's jus' as pretty as t'other one.'

'Well I'm sure the Princess would be thrilled to know that you've named your rabbit after her Pearl' Kathy managed through trembling lips. It was Harry who started it, trying desperately to choke back his laughter. It began as a ripple but it quickly spread and then they were all laughing unable to stop. Pearl confused as to what could be so funny momentarily loosened her hold on Margaret and sensing its opportunity the rabbit leapt from her lap and was through the gap under the gate before anyone had chance to stop it. Lizzie was first to the gate, yanked it open.

'Anybody lost a rabbit?' asked a familiar voice. George stood there, huge grin on his face, clutching the trembling animal.

'Oh my God George! Oh George!' cried Lizzie. Poor Margaret was squashed between the delighted pair so pleased to be re-united at long last.

There was a huge celebration that night to welcome George home and to celebrate his bravery. No one asked when he was due to return to the front, no one wanted to know.

CHAPTER THIRTY TWO

The joy surrounding George's return and the arrival of Margaret had temporarily put Kathy's many problems to one side but they soon came back to haunt her. Harry was still being uncooperative, even surly at times and it seemed to be his mother alone who bore the brunt of his unpleasantness. With his exams taken, these could no longer be used as a reasonable excuse. Kathy knew she must speak with him but by now was even afraid to do so. The problem of Pearl and her mother was still far from settled. It had been several weeks since Gloria's visit and her promise to 'be back' had not materialized. Kathy eventually decided she must discuss it with Wandsworth Prescott. She found him in his garden pruning his roses.

'Ah, Mrs. Watson-Smythe, what a pleasant surprise.' His home being on the edge of the village and not what would be deemed in 'strolling' distance Wandsworth knew that something of importance must've brought her here.

'I wondered if you might spare me ten minutes?' asked Kathy. 'I would be very grateful. I'm rather worried.'

'Oh dear, well we can't have that. Just come with me whilst I rid myself of these tools and wash my hands and then we'll see what I can do to help' he said kindly.

Once settled in Wandsworth's study Kathy explained her unease surrounding Pearl and her mother's visit.

'And so you have heard nothing from her since she suggested you might 'take on' the child as it were?' asked Wandsworth, mystified.

'No absolutely not. I felt sure when she left that I'd persuaded her that it simply wasn't an option, that she should take Pearl with her to America.'

'Hmm, it's certainly very awkward' said Wandsworth rubbing his chin. 'In all honesty I don't really know what I can do. Perhaps we should write to her, try to clarify the situation. I will have an address for Mrs. Pettinger somewhere amongst my papers but I assume so will you?'

'Well I thought I had, but I tried that, tried writing to her I mean, to ask what was going on but the letter came back "not known at this address". It's all very strange I must say.'

'Oh dear. Well clearly we'll have to try and track her down another way. I seem to recall, correct me if I'm wrong, but wasn't there another child, a boy?'

'There was yes, Frank. He wasn't billeted with me, was only in Oakfield for a short while, wanted to return home and to be honest I imagine he could be anywhere, he was certainly an unpredictable character to put it mildly.'

'Then I think my dear this might call for some intervention from the police, surely they will be able to trace the lady. They will be able to at least call at the house and speak with the neighbours.'

'I suppose you're right' sighed Kathy, reluctant to bring in the police but recognizing there probably was no option. 'The only other thing I could think of would be to try Colin Clipson. He lodged with me for a while, was an absolute tearaway but Frank's best friend. I suppose there's a chance he might know where the family, or at least Frank, has gone.'

'Now that sounds a very good idea. Just one moment and I'll check and see if I have his address. Yes indeed here it is' said Wandsworth, settling himself on the sofa next to Kathy having quickly located the necessary file in his desk drawer. "Clipson, Colin, 18 Chaplin Court, Blinsgate."

'I think what we should do, or rather I if you prefer, is have a word with Sergeant Credland and see what he suggests.'

'Well I should be really grateful if you would do that' said Kathy. 'It would take a weight off my mind if you're really sure.'

'Of course I am Mrs. Watson-Smythe, no trouble at all, and I suppose it could be deemed my responsibility in any case.' Kathy left him, feeling that at least someone else was sharing THIS problem.

Sergeant Credland, accustomed to problems of a more parochial nature, was intrigued when Wandsworth called at the station the next morning to discuss the problem of Pearl.

'Ah! Expect it'll just be a case of 'em doing a moonlight flit. Expect they owe the rent or summat, ya know what these city folk are like! But you leave it with me Mr. Prescott. I'll get on to it, get our city lads to see what they can find out. I'll get back to you the minute I hear anything.'

'Good man, good man' said Wandsworth, rising from his chair and taking the man's hand. 'I'll look forward to hearing from you.'

Harry remained tortured by the revelation that Henry Watson-Smythe was not after all his father, puzzled by the fact that the man was apparently dead, had been obviously for several months and yet his mother had chosen to tell no one. He desperately needed his mother to tell him who his real father was. Although not his biological father Henry had managed to instil into Harry many of his own characteristics, tenacity, patience and yes ruthlessness. Harry used them now to good effect knowing that if he was to ever learn the truth of his parentage he had to at least keep lines of communication open with his mother, difficult though that was. He wanted to shout at her, rave at her but knew he must stay calm if he was to ever unearth the truth. He eventually decided upon a plan that would surely ensure she had to at least be honest with him about one thing. He found her at her desk in the drawing room one afternoon.

'I was wondering Mother if I might have a word, there's something I would like to ask.' As Harry had seemed disinclined to exchange a civil word with her for some time now Kathy was relieved and delighted. Had it really been exam pressure after all as she'd hoped?

'Why of course darling' she smiled turning towards him, away from the desk. 'Go ahead.'

'I've been thinking for a while now that I would actually quite like to return to India, you know just for a short while, just for a holiday. I do have many friends out there and sometimes if I'm honest I feel that I may have been a little unfair to my father, no doubt I misunderstood, perhaps he was being strict thinking to do me good in the long term.' Needless to say Kathy was stunned, he could hardly visit Henry and if she told him now that he was dead, had been for quite a long time, how would she explain her secrecy? She put her hand to her forehead, rubbed her temples desperate to think of a convincing reason why this couldn't happen. She glanced at the clock, saw behind it on the mantelpiece yet another envelope containing a bill. The answer came to her, sealing her fate – perpetuating the lies even further.

'Well that really is a lovely idea and I'm sure your father would appreciate a visit from you but I'm afraid my love that it is quite out of the question.' Inside Harry was furious, still, STILL she was lying. With enormous difficulty he remained calm, drew on all his reserves.

'But why? It would seem to be such a good time, before I go away to college. If I went now I would easily be back for the beginning of the term.'

'The thing is Harry' said Kathy shaking her head sadly. 'We simply don't have the money, you know I would love nothing more than for you to go but we just can't afford it.' Harry was not prepared to let her off the hook so easily.

'Well perhaps if I wrote to my father, let him know what I'm thinking, perhaps he might consider paying for my ticket.'

'No, no!' Kathy almost shouted. 'Absolutely not, I won't hear of it, your father and I parted on less than amicable terms and that just wouldn't seem appropriate.' Harry wanted to turn the knife.

'But Mother' he said in a reasonable, placatory tone, 'the animosity between you and my father has absolutely nothing to do with me and as I said perhaps it was me who misconstrued his intentions. I feel sure he would like to see me. I am his son after all' he couldn't help adding. Kathy knew she had to put a stop to this once and for all. She rose to her feet.

'I said NO Harry and let that be an end to it! You have far better things to be doing, studying for instance, rather than flitting around the world!' Harry too got to his feet, stared hard at her.

'So that's your final word is it?' he asked calmly.

'Indeed it most certainly is!' she shouted. 'Now get out of my sight!'

'Don't worry, I'm going!' he shouted back and stormed out slamming the door behind him.

Little Pearl, busy at the kitchen table doing a jigsaw puzzle, clamped her hands to her ears and whimpered. She'd become unused now to the shouting and slamming that had previously been so much a part of her life. Peggy went to her, put her arms around her.

'There, there pet, nothing to worry your pretty 'ead about.'

When Sergeant Credland eventually rang Wandsworth to say that he might have something interesting to tell him he could hardly get to the station quickly enough. 'The City Lads' as Sergeant Credland would insist on calling them had apparently drawn a blank when they had called at the home of Gloria Pettinger. According to her neighbours she'd been there one day and 'gorn the next', off they suspected with "er fancy Yank." Of Frank there was no sign, hadn't been apparently for months. Colin Clipson's address given to them by the Sergeant had however yielded some disturbing news. Having called at the flat to ascertain if Colin might have any idea of the whereabouts of any of the Pettingers his sister had told them that he was out with his pals, would be back later and she would tell him they'd called.

When told that the police wanted to speak to him Colin had assumed that the game was up, that the truth of the Oakfield crash had come to light. That night in the darkness he laid on the track and allowed the eight forty five to Jenisbrough to bring to an end his torment. It wasn't until daylight the next morning that the blood splattered wheels of the train gave a clue as to what had taken place, and the track maintenance team made their gruesome discovery.

Wandsworth had naturally been horrified to hear what had taken place but neither man had any idea of its true significance. Sergeant Credland went on to tell him that enquiries had been made at the American Air Base where Don Dueringer had been stationed and it had been confirmed that one Donald Dueringer and his wife Gloria had departed for America over six weeks ago. The case of little Pearl Pettinger would now be on file as child abandonment and pursued as such.

CHAPTER THIRTY THREE

Harry's surliness towards his mother increased daily and Kathy was at her wits' end not knowing how to resolve the situation. With Jeremy away the only person she felt she had left to confide in was Dannah but he was so busy these days. The factory was working twenty four hour shifts following the disaster of Dunkirk. Although thankfully so many men had been rescued it had left a huge shortage of weapons, the men having no choice other than to leave them behind. The country was now vulnerable with so little artillery at its disposal and all armament production sites were working hard to replace what had been lost.

In the end it was Dannah himself who initiated the conversation. He was worried about her he said, one could hardly miss the tension there was now between her and Harry. He'd chosen the sunshine of the backyard to have their heart to heart, another cloudless blue sky in a glorious summer darkened only by war.

'You're quite right' began Kathy. 'Harry and I have certainly 'had words' so to speak. The thing is he's suddenly decided he'd like to return to India for a holiday, you know look up a few friends but most bewilderingly to see his father. I've told him that we simply can't afford it and he's not at all pleased.' Dannah took his time considering what she'd said.

'Well it certainly seems a bit strange when you think back to him running away for fear he was going to be sent back...... but I suppose he's older now.'

'Apparently he now thinks he might've misjudged Henry, that perhaps he behaved as he did for his own good after all.'

'And do you think that could be right?'

'Who am I to judge?' shrugged Kathy 'but in any case he can't go.'

'Perhaps we could try to find the money' Dannah said doubtfully 'if he's so desperate. It would be difficult I know but we could at least try if you think we should.'

'Well I don't! And we can't.' Kathy almost shouted. 'Harry can't go back to India to see his father.' Dannah was shocked by her tone, she was more than just angry.

'But wh........?'

'Because his father is DEAD! Henry is dead, has been for months!'

'What?........ DEAD? I don't understand' said Dannah totally at a loss. 'But when did that happen? You've never said. Why have you kept it to yourself? How long have you known?'

'Oh for months' Kathy replied almost nonchalantly before bursting into floods of tears. Dannah was on his knees in front of her. Margaret peered curiously at them through the wire mesh door of her hutch.

'There, there love, don't go upsetting yourself' he said gently, trying to comfort her. He handed her his handkerchief, waited as she brushed the tears impatiently away. 'But let's go indoors shall we? There's surely lots to get off your chest so let's go where it's more comfortable. Come on darlin'' and he helped her up from the hard wooden kitchen chair and led her inside. Ying, busy with her knitting on the other side of the wall, heard it all, was relieved.

With the house mercifully to themselves Dannah chose the drawing room for them to continue the conversation.

Hesitantly at first, knowing she had to be very careful what she said, how much she could actually tell him without incriminating herself, Kathy relayed the contents of the letter she had received from Henry's solicitors in India.

'Apparently' she said 'poor Henry died quite suddenly from a virus which had attacked the muscles of his heart. The solicitors advised me that either by accident or design Henry had not changed his will after our divorce and for that reason I am the sole beneficiary. The thing is I know it was by design. Henry had written a letter to be given to me in the event of his death telling me exactly that. Apparently it was to be my reward for the few happy years I had given him!' she added wryly.

'Was there nothing for his son then? No mention of Harry?' asked Dannah. Kathy hadn't been prepared for this.

'No, no' she blustered, 'no mention of Harry. I suppose he just assumed I would deal with that.'

'And you're saying that you haven't told Harry? Why? I don't understand. He'll have to know sometime won't he?'

'Yes, yes of course but it's just all so difficult you know with things.........' Dannah waited, making her continue.

'Well with Jeremy really. It's all rather awkward. You've obviously noticed, I think EVERYONE has noticed that things between us are not as they were. With our plans to marry Jeremy would naturally have taken over our finances relieving me of the burden and I can't deny I was grateful knowing that. But over the last few months I'm not so sure that that is what I want to do, marry Jeremy I mean. Now I'm worried that when everyone hears of Henry's death and the money he has left me it's going to look as if my change of heart over Jeremy is simply because I no longer need his money.' Privately Dannah couldn't help but agree, but knew that the truth had to come out, would come out sooner or later. 'So you understand my dilemma' persisted Kathy, 'why I haven't told Harry?'

'It's certainly a bit tricky, I can't deny that' agreed Dannah 'but the lad has to know his father's dead love, you can't hide it from him forever and the longer it goes on the worse it'll be.'

'Oh I've been over and over it. I hardly get a wink of sleep worrying about it and the only solution I come up with is to simply get on with it, marry Jeremy and then I can't be accused can I?'

'Oh love no, you mustn't do that. It wouldn't make for a happy marriage for you or Jeremy would it? A marriage just for convenience sake can't work can it? Can't be happy.'

'No, no it can't' said Kathy almost to herself. 'I thought it could once but I know it can't.'

'Well there you are then that's not the answer, you can't condemn yourself or Jeremy to that just because of what other people might think.'

'So what is the answer then?' she asked sadly.

'Right at this minute love I don't know. I wish I did, but at least you've shared it with me and I hope that helps a bit.'

'Oh yes' Kathy smiled at last, 'it helps a bit.'

Jeannie Kirk although still aggrieved over Kathy's treatment of her brother-in-law nonetheless quickly came to realize that she was depriving herself of something she'd come to very much enjoy, being in Harry's company. Jeannie knew that in her coolness towards Kathy she was actually cutting her nose off to spite her face.

Being receptionist cum secretary to the Doctor rather pleasantly gave her a position of some standing in the community and Jeannie was usually considered a 'shoe in' for any committee or organization looking for members. Currently she was embroiled in arrangements for the forthcoming Oakfield Show, primarily organizing the various competitions which played a huge part in the Show's overall success. It was whilst perusing the list of last year's events that her eye was drawn to the dog section, "Best turned out dog, Dog looking most like its owner, Most obedient dog", there were so many categories! That was it, Jeannie knew exactly what she must do! She would ask Harry to judge some of the classes. It was well known that he was soon to be away studying to be a vet and the local vet old Clarence Treadwell was notoriously curmudgeonly and therefore would prove an unpopular choice even were he to agree.

Jeannie decided she would have to be brave and face Kathy's response to her own coolness. Calling at the house one afternoon she was surprised when Kathy, greeting her quite warmly, invited her in to share a cup of tea. After exchanging news of which there was little about Jeremy, Jeannie came to the purpose of her visit. Kathy's attitude immediately changed. She wasn't at all sure she said, Harry was very busy with his studies, in fact busy all round, she really didn't feel he could spare the time.

'Well could we perhaps just ask him?' persisted Jeannie.

'Well unfortunately he's not in at the moment and........' The front door slammed and Harry's voice could be heard laughing over something with Patrick. Kathy knew she was left with no choice. She went to the drawing room door, opened it.

'Harry dear I wonder if you might spare me a moment?'
Harry entered the room clearly reluctantly, made no move
to sit down.

'What?' he asked sourly in spite of seeing that his mother
had a visitor. Kathy knew this exchange was going to be
unpleasant – they always were these days – but this really
was beyond the pale, being rude in front of a visitor and
especially Jeannie of all people.

'Mrs. Kirk has called to ask if you might consider helping
with the judging at this year's Show Harry. I have already
said that of course you are much too busy with your studies
but she is quite desperate and so insisted that I should at
least ask you.' Jeannie was stung by Kathy's addition of the
word 'desperate', she had never said she was desperate but
it quite cleverly gave Harry the idea that he was not her first
choice, a last resort.

'But I.........' began Jeannie keen to correct the impression
Kathy had given. However she had no need. Harry had
quickly sized up the situation, realized that his mother didn't
want him to do this, probably wouldn't even have mentioned
it to him if she'd had the choice.

'Why Mrs. Kirk' he said, the broadest of grins across his
face, 'I'd absolutely love to do it! I can't thank you enough
for thinking of me' he gushed.

'Oh, oh well that's lovely then' replied Jeannie taken
aback. She had known just as well as Harry that it was the
last thing Kathy wanted her son to do. 'Perhaps we could
arrange a time when we might meet and discuss one or two
things?'

'Of course. Any time that suits you. Just let me know.
I'll look forward to it.' With that he gave a cheery wave

and left the room. The two women were left with a rather uncomfortable few minutes before Jeannie gathered up her gloves, thanked Kathy for the tea and took her leave. She waited until she was half way down the street before she allowed the smug expression to claim her face.

Harry rather cruelly but in his book deservedly was delighted with the opportunity Jeannie Kirk had presented him with to antagonize his mother. He really couldn't wait for her to contact him, it could be ages, the Show wasn't for weeks yet, he needed to put his plan into action now. Jeannie was surprised but delighted to find him on her doorstep not two days later.

'Why come in, how lovely to see you' she smiled opening the door wide. 'Let's go into the sitting room shall we?' and she led the way down the hall.

'Now, what can I do for you? But first do sit down, and can I get you a drink?'

'Something cool would be nice if you have it.'

'Home made lemonade?'

'Excellent.'

With Jeannie busy in the kitchen Harry had a good look round. There was evidence of Jeremy everywhere even one of his jackets still draped around the back of a chair. Jeannie appeared with the drinks and settled herself in a chair opposite Harry. She saw his eyes ranging over the many photographs scattered around the room.

'Oh I know what you're thinking' she laughed, 'I've got too many photographs!'

'Not at all' said Harry getting to his feet. 'They're so interesting aren't they photographs, especially old ones, they tell us so much don't they.' Indeed they do thought Jeannie, indeed they do. Harry picked up a small silver frame, in it a picture of two young boys smiling, one sitting in a wheelbarrow the other ready to push.

'Jeremy and his brother' supplied Jeannie. Harry went to another photograph. This time, a man, probably mid-twenties, looking smilingly into the camera. 'My husband Richard' she said, 'Jeremy's brother.'

'Good looking chap' smiled Harry, 'almost feel I know him from somewhere.' I bet you do thought Jeannie, try looking in the mirror. Although it was generally considered that Harry had his mother's looks, certainly he had taken almost nothing from Jeremy in that direction, Jeannie had always been able to see her husband Richard in the boy. Not just looks either but the way he tilted his head, the way he stood, but mostly in his grin and the way he laughed.

'Anyway' she asked, beginning to feel uncomfortable, 'what can I do for you?'

'Well it's more what you want me to do for you with the Show' he grinned. 'I know it's early days but I like to be prepared, I don't want to let you down.'

'Oh there's no danger of that my love' she smiled. They went on to discuss the various classes which had been used in the past and their apparent success or otherwise. Harry said he would go away and think about what would be best. They probably needed to introduce something new to freshen things up a bit. They agreed to meet regularly to update each other on any ideas they might have.

Jeannie was delighted to have achieved her objective as was Harry, his increasingly frequent visits to Jeannie annoying his mother more each day.

CHAPTER THIRTY FOUR

Jonas Hardcastle was at a complete loss without his factory to run, there had never been a time when he had nothing to do and it didn't suit him, Maisie even less! He'd tried a few hobbies but he 'couldn't see the point in 'em unless there was summat at t'end o'it.' In desperation he'd tried the Home Guard but if he was being honest had found it a poor substitute for the real thing, unless positioned near to the coast where they were utilized manning the anti-aircraft guns they seemed to do little of real value. Stanley Briggs and John Tremmings had enthusiastically joined him but they too were left feeling totally ineffective. In the end the trio decided to try their hands at being Air Raid Prevention Wardens. Although there had been no bombs dropped on Oakfield itself, when a raid took place on the city just over the river they were called upon to ensure that all residents were safely in Anderson shelters at the bottom of their gardens or in Morrison shelters inside their houses, and out of the way of stray incendiaries. The Black Out introduced even before the official announcement of war was also their responsibility and strictly enforced as was the carrying and wearing of gas masks.

Harry and Patrick still too young to be conscripted were disappointed not to be able to do 'their bit' whilst their respective families were relieved beyond measure that they were unable to. At their age the only thing that they could usefully do they were told was Fire-Watch. Naturally it would be Hardcastles, now the armaments factory, that would be the focus if God forbid Oakfield were to be targeted, closely followed by the school. New to the job the boys were initially given sites considered to be of lesser importance, the two churches and the biscuit factory being among this number.

Ying of all of them was probably the least affected by war. Happy running her own little household, at least she WAS running it until the Desmonds reappeared – and even this she found she could just about cope with – Ying's main preoccupations were her many handicrafts, at which she was excellent, and also shopping. Ying loved shopping, looked forward each week to her Saturday trip to the market. It was during one such Saturday expedition that Ying experienced her first stirrings of unease. Busy at the fish stall her attention was caught by a commotion taking place in the far corner. Someone was clearly upset and shouting the odds. It was a man who it would seem had been bitten by someone's dog and was none too happy about it. The dog's owner was obviously apologizing profusely but the man was having none of it, was threatening to call the police. Several of the stall holders began remonstrating with him trying to get him to calm down but he continued shouting and waving his arms in the air. It was only when the market superintendent arrived notebook in hand ready to take down particulars that the man seemed to have a sudden change of heart and stalked off. It had been the stance initially which had drawn Ying's attention and then the walk, the quite unique gait. Once the fuss had died down she put it to the back of her mind and moved on to her favourite stall – haberdashery. It was the very next weekend on her usual visit to the market when seeing that same man again in the distance she was reminded. She was puzzled, curiosity got the better of her, she decided to get a bit closer, follow him.

Harry occupied his time whilst waiting for his examination results accompanying Patrick to the farm, fire watching and annoying his mother. The latter he did by spending as much time as possible with Jeannie Kirk supposedly organizing events for the Show. On the day his examination results arrived it was Jeannie he went to. She opened the door to him, could see he was clearly distressed.

'Oh my dear boy' she said 'Whatever is it? Come in, come in.' Harry slumped down into what had now become 'his chair', put his head in his hands. Jeannie sat down in the chair beside him.

'Whatever is it love?' she asked gently, 'Can't you tell me what's wrong.' Eventually he was able to, told her he'd failed his exams, wouldn't be going away, wouldn't be able to become a vet. Now what was he going to do with his life?

'But surely that doesn't have to be the end of it darling, surely you can re-sit them can't you?'

'If things weren't as they are maybe I could've but ....' He broke off despairingly.

'I'm not sure what you mean Harry. If things weren't how exactly?' Harry suddenly jumped to his feet furious.

'With my mother. She's lying to me all the time, never stops lying!' Jeannie was taken aback.

'I'm sorry love but you're going to have to tell me what you mean. What is she lying about?'

'Oh about everything! I asked her if I could go back to India, you know for a holiday and to see my father but she said I couldn't because she couldn't afford it, that's all she said! She didn't tell me even then about my father. But you see I KNOW! I know about my father and yet she's still not telling me, still not telling me the truth.'

Unfortunately in her joy that the truth was finally out Jeannie didn't stop to wonder exactly how he knew. Her heart stopped. At long last he knew that Jeremy was his real father!

'Oh love what can I say except I'm relieved. Relieved that you know and I know Jeremy will be too.' Harry turned to her.

'You knew? And Doctor Kirk, he'll be pleased?'

'Why yes love of course. He's wanted all along, ever since he found out himself, for you to know. He's so proud that you're his son.'

'WHAT? Dr. Kirk's my father!' Jeannie was flustered now.

'Well yes love, that's what you're telling me isn't it, that you know?' Uncertainty was beginning to creep into her mind. What HAD she done?

Harry was ashen, went to the door, formed a fist as if he was going to smash it.

'No, that wasn't what I was telling you! I've discovered that the man I had always understood to be my father actually wasn't and what's more he's dead, has been for some time, and yet my mother' – he said the name with a curl of his lip – 'has seen fit to tell me none of this. But no, Mrs. Kirk I had no idea at all that it is Dr. Kirk who is my real father' – again the curl of the lip. 'It would appear that everyone keeps secrets from me, things that I of all people should know. You've all known and yet none of you have seen fit to tell me the truth!' Jeannie got shakily to her feet, the enormity of what she'd done overwhelming her. She knew she had no alternative now other than to tell him the whole truth.

'No, no love, it's not like that, really it isn't. Jeremy had absolutely no idea of your existence until your mother returned to England and even then she didn't tell him, he guessed. Ever since he found out he has pleaded with her, begged her to tell you the whole story but she has refused. Keeping it a secret believe me is the last thing Jeremy wants. More than anything in the world he longs to recognize you as his son. His much loved son' she added. 'Oh my dear boy.' She went to him holding out her arms but he turned and ran from the room, ran from the house.

Jeannie was distraught, unable to concentrate, during surgery even managing to incur the wrath of the mildest of men Dr. Whitstable, waiting for the visit from Kathy which she knew must surely come. By the time Stan arrived for his tea there had been no sign of Kathy. By tea-time the next day there still had been no sign.

Kathy didn't arrive because she had no idea what had taken place.

Harry had known instinctively that he shouldn't immediately confront his mother, that he needed time to digest everything that he'd learned. At least he now had the one piece missing from the jig-saw, but what was the picture he was left with?

Jeremy had had no leave since leaving for France, his skills along with all medics urgently needed. Things were clearly not going well for the country. Operation Dynamo – the Dunkirk evacuation – had in Churchill's own words been a 'massive military disaster', the rescue of so many of the troops – approaching 400,000 – 'a miracle of deliverance.'

When Jeremy arrived home completely out of the blue several weeks after Jeannie's disastrous disclosure there had still been no word from Kathy. All Jeannie had received was a polite but curt note from Harry saying that he would not after all be able to help with the Show as planned. When Jeannie arrived home one evening to find what could only be Jeremy's kit bag in the hall she didn't know whether to laugh or cry. She pushed open the living room door.

'Oh Jeremy, how good to see………' She got no further, burst into tears. Jeremy although expecting an emotional reunion was somewhat nonplussed however when her sobbing went on and on, she literally couldn't stop. Surely this was more than the normal show of relief one would expect? Exhausted Jeremy slept for the rest of that day and all of the next.

Jeannie had seen nothing of Harry since receiving his curt note and had only exchanged the briefest of pleasantries with Kathy when they had met unintentionally either in the street or at the church. The expected confrontation had never arrived and she was left mystified as to why.

In fact Kathy still had no knowledge of what had taken place between Harry and his aunt, was embroiled in arguments and accusations with her son as to why he had not delivered the expected exam results and also critically, what to do next. Even Harry didn't know what to do. He felt like telling his mother it was all her fault, how could he have been expected to concentrate, give them his full attention when he'd had so much whirling around in his head? But for that he'd have to tell her that he knew everything and somehow he still wasn't prepared for that. Kathy was still maintaining that the expense of another year's study was unmanageable when he knew that the opposite must be true.

Jeannie was uncertain what to do, didn't know whether to tell Jeremy what had taken place, that she had accidentally but quite innocently revealed to Harry that he was his real father. If Kathy didn't know, and it certainly seemed that she mustn't, then Harry for some reason must be keeping it to himself and if that was the case then perhaps she owed it to him to remain silent. She decided perhaps cowardly to do just that.

Jeremy arrived at the house in Ladan Road to find Kathy out but Peggy and Dannah delighted to see him and anxious for all his news.

Kathy had been looking forward to when she might see Jeremy again. In his long absence had missed him, had decided that marrying him might after all work, be the best thing for them all. Kathy opened the drawing room door, found herself overjoyed that he was here at last. But this wasn't the Jeremy she remembered. He was greyer, older, looked absolutely exhausted, his skin was sallow and seemed to be hanging from his face. She couldn't help it.

'Oh my love' she cried, going to him, putting her arms round him. 'Whatever has happened to you?'

'War has happened to me Kathy' he said quietly. In that moment Kathy knew she had come to the right decision. She no longer had doubts over what her answer would be if he once again asked her to marry him. They sat close together on the sofa interrupted only by Peggy discreetly arriving with afternoon tea on a tray. Kathy encouraged Jeremy to tell her all that had happened to him since they had last been together. He tried but most of it was just too terrible to contemplate recounting, was the stuff of his nightmares and need not be hers. In the end he turned to her, took her hand between both his.

'Kathy........' he began. She could barely wait now for him to ask her, the response ready and waiting on her lips. Yes Jeremy she would say, I will marry you.

'Kathy, I have some news, something to tell you, something which I hope you will be pleased to hear.'

'Oh yes?' Oh please God he doesn't have to go back, her mind was racing ahead.

'I hope you'll be pleased, happy for me. I am to marry. When I return to the front I will go as a married man'

She was stunned. Even she didn't know what was going to come out of her mouth.

'Wha.....? Well how lovely, how wonderful for you' she stammered. 'And who..... Who is the lucky lady?'

Jeremy smiled fondly just at the need for her name to be mentioned.

'Geraldine' he said. 'Geraldine McKay, she's a nursing sister, we work together in the field hospital. She's a wonderful person Kathy' he said quickly as if reassuring her.

'I'm sure she must be' replied Kathy, quickly gathering herself together. 'If you've chosen her my dear then she absolutely must be.'

Even Jeremy didn't know why Kathy had been the first to hear about his forthcoming marriage. Why he hadn't first broken the news to Jeannie his beloved sister-in-law? If he had, and if she'd told him what Harry now knew, things probably would have turned out very differently.

Jeannie on hearing the news was lost for words, her brain scrambling around as Jeremy relayed his plans, trying to imagine what the repercussions might be. She told him how delighted she was, how all she'd ever wanted was for him to be happy, as happy as she and his brother Richard had been. She said she'd be delighted to attend the ceremony in London, wouldn't miss it for the world. Inside she was in turmoil, should she tell him Harry knew everything or was it too late? Would Harry say something? Clearly he hadn't told his mother what he knew.

CHAPTER THIRTY FIVE

After Jeremy had left, to Kathy's sound assurances that she was delighted for him, couldn't wait to meet Geraldine, Kathy went up to her room to compose herself. She really didn't know how she felt. Only a few months ago determined that she wouldn't marry Jeremy she now perversely found herself with feelings of rejection and hurt. The thing was could she really blame him for looking elsewhere? She'd told him quite plainly how she felt, that she had no desire to marry. It would seem also as if he'd finally given up on his wish to have Harry's true parentage revealed. Harry had not even been mentioned. Obviously he was now prepared to walk away not just from her but also from his son.

If Kathy assumed that Jeremy had found it easy to accept that he wasn't after all to figure in either her life or Harry's she couldn't have been more wrong. Working until mentally and physically exhausted, with all around him heartache and despair, Jeremy had in the end come to accept that his own problems were as nothing by comparison. He wasn't about to lose a leg, an arm, his mind, he was in one piece and should be glad of it, his despair was emotional and he should be man enough to move on. He WOULD move on, let Kathy and Harry get on with their lives, he'd managed without them for all this time, he could manage again.

It was at this point with this new determination uppermost in his mind that Sister Geraldine McKay arrived at the camp.

Geraldine was everything you wouldn't imagine a nurse at the front to be. She was beautiful. Long dark hair, when it wasn't in a chignon at the nape of her beautiful neck, beautiful eyes, beautiful skin, tall, exceptionally tall, beautifully tall. Every description of Geraldine would necessarily begin with that one adjective. She suddenly and unexpectedly brought light into the darkness of Jeremy's days. Never even imagining that she could be anything other than a working colleague he watched from the sidelines fascinated as every hot blooded man in camp tried their damnedest to ingratiate themselves into her affections. Geraldine was anything but naive, knew exactly the effect she had on the opposite sex, had known it for most of her life, had enjoyed it for most of her life but now she needed more. When widowed in the very early days of the war and left with a young son she had had to change, had to take over the reins, become a proper parent to Euan no longer having her husband Alastair to take care of everything. In her younger days Geraldine had seen nursing as being 'glamorous'. The smart uniform, the dashing red cloak, the drama that surrounded it, she'd decided that she wanted to be part of it and had worked hard to make it happen. She had quickly had her misconceptions surrounding the job swept away but a deeply compassionate nature hitherto hidden had been unearthed inside her. It had only been with her own family that Geraldine had been unable to show affection and commitment and when Alastair McKay arrived on the scene, sweeping her off her feet and quite obviously wanting to take absolute control of her life, she saw him as heaven sent. Even when Euan was born it was Alastair who took control, Alastair who paraded him around proudly to their family and friends, Alastair who without asking her hired a nanny.

Alastair's sudden and tragic death had not as her family anticipated reduced her to a crumbling wreck. Amazingly overnight she found a steeliness she'd never known she possessed, became as a tigress protecting her young as far as her son was concerned. She now revelled in caring for him, immediately sacking the nanny. She suddenly controlled everything in his life and knew that this was what had been missing. With the best of intentions Alastair had removed from her life all responsibilities, and therefore he thought all problems and worries in order to give her what he wanted for her, a very pampered life.

Although loving her little son more than life itself, when the news began to filter from the front of huge loss of life and thousands upon thousands of casualties Geraldine was conscious that she had skills that were needed desperately, skills that should be put to good use. She knew without having to ask that her parents, although often bewildered and deeply hurt at her treatment of them, and also Alastair's parents – who no doubt felt the same – would have no hesitation in taking on her little son so that she might do her duty for her country.

It was in the middle of the night, humid, noisy with aircraft screaming overhead, that Geraldine had gone albeit reluctantly in search of Jeremy Kirk. One of his patients was quite clearly painfully but courageously coming to the end of his short life. Harry Braithwaite was twenty years of age, had not seen much of life, had never married, never had a child, possibly never even been in love, and here he was dying. Dying due to the whims of strangers, people who were anxious to stand by their principles but not quite as anxious to face the horrors of the consequences.

When Geraldine lifted the flap on the tent that was Jeremy's sleeping quarters she found him awake. He had been unable to sleep, unable to find any peace, the tortured cries of patients sleeping through their nightmares or crying out for fear of what was to come haunting him.

'Doctor' she whispered. 'I think it's probably 'time' for young Harry Braithwaite, his breathing has suddenly got so much worse. It's very shallow and he's starting to gasp......'

'Of course, of course, thank you Sister I'll be right there.' She waited outside as he put on his boots, straightened his hair and covered his uniform with a more casual sweater – this young lad's last view of the world wasn't going to be of a sterile medical coat. Together in the darkness they slithered and slid in the mud that was a constant of the site. Jeremy went to the boy, he was no more than a boy.

'Now then young Harry' he said gently taking his hand, 'I've come to see if there's anything I can do to make you a little more comfortable.' Jeremy indicated to Geraldine that Harry might find it easier to breathe with his head a little higher on the pillow. He went to lift him gently as Geraldine bent down to carefully rearrange the pillow, as she did so she smiled tenderly at Harry and he looked back into her eyes.

'Tell me mam I lo.........' he rasped, and was gone. Jeremy closed the boy's eyes, thankful that the last they had seen was a look of absolute tenderness from Geraldine. Together they laid his tussled head on the pillow, made him comfortable as if he still knew what that meant. They sat either side of the bed each holding one of his hands, so recently warm but rapidly, so quickly, turning cold. Their thoughts were identical, of his mother somewhere blissfully unaware that she no longer had a son, that his last words on earth had been to tell her that he loved her. Jeremy promised himself he would find out who she was, would personally write to her, make sure she knew how much her son had loved her.

'I know a Harry' he said quietly. Geraldine looked across the bed, wiped away a tear threatening to fall on to the sheet now tightly tucked under Harry Braithwaite's chin.

The sadness they all too often shared over the loss of one of their patients was heightened somehow by the loss of Harry Braithwaite, what they had so intimately shared that night. They began to seek each other out, Jeremy suddenly no longer fearing her beauty, her popularity, realizing that beyond all that she was just a normal person and one that he was increasingly coming to care for.

To Geraldine McKay Jeremy was a breath of fresh air. She was tired of being flirted with, she found it shallow, patronizing in a way, always had done. Jeremy Kirk treated her with dignity and respect, didn't seem at all interested in how she looked, more interested in how she felt, what she thought, what she had to say. They fell in love. In spite of the horrors facing them every day neither of them had been happier. Jeremy felt embarrassed now at what he'd considered to be his 'love' for Kathy, realizing all too clearly that his imagined 'love' had been merely nostalgia. No, Katherine had done him a huge favour turning down his proposal of marriage, what a disaster that would've been! Even thoughts of his son Harry were not as painful as they had once been. He had a son and he should be grateful for that alone. He would always know who he was, might even know where he was, and that had to be enough. Kathy had been right when she'd insisted Harry was best left in ignorance.

Jeremy and Geraldine's feelings for each other although kept secret – relationships between personnel being strictly forbidden – simply grew stronger. They intended to marry as soon as possible. SOMEHOW they promised themselves they would wangle – by fair means or foul – home leave at the same time. In the end they managed it and after a blissful few days together in a very blitzed London they each went their separate ways heading for their respective homes to give the news of their impending marriage to their nearest and dearest.

CHAPTER THIRTY SIX

When Kathy finally went downstairs to break the news of Jeremy's impending marriage she was surprised when no one seemed to be as shocked as she had been. Privately though everyone present had their own very different views.

Peggy was sorry, very sorry, had been looking forward to the new household which would have been created. Also she felt it would have been the happiest outcome for everybody. Why Miss Katherine would dilly dally over someone like Dr. Kirk and now miss out 'cos he'd found someone else was beyond her, there would've been plenty who would have snatched his hand off. No it was criminal and no mistake.

Dannah was more circumspect about the whole thing. After his conversation with Kathy, when she'd expressed her reservations about marriage, no more had been mentioned of it between them. At the time he'd been pleased that she'd had the courage of her convictions, not just given in and gone ahead for all the wrong reasons. No, he'd admired her determination not to have her life ruled by the opinions of other people, he was quite proud of her really. And it wouldn't have worked out for Jeremy either, not if she hadn't loved him, and now happily he'd found someone else – and good luck to him. The thing still bothering him was that Kathy had as yet told no one of Henry's death and her subsequent inheritance. That certainly did trouble him, no good came of lying you just caused yourself more bother in the long run. And in any case why was she keeping it from young Harry? In fact why hadn't she told him in the very beginning? The lad would've been upset obviously but he would've got over it. Everyone learned to cope with the things life threw at them eventually. They had no choice.

Ying, spending the afternoon with Peggy making new bedroom curtains for the spare room, heard Kathy's news with sadness. Although never having had her suspicions confirmed over Harry's real father she was convinced enough to feel sorry that there wouldn't after all be a happy ending. Aware of Henry's death after accidentally overhearing the conversation between Kathy and Dannah, Ying remained puzzled as to why Kathy hadn't told everyone else. Not being party to the rest of the conversation once Dannah had suggested they went inside she supposed there must be a good reason why Kathy had kept it to herself but she couldn't for the life of her think what. Anyway at least it had laid her own fears to rest so that was a good thing.

With Harry missing Patrick was the only other person present when Kathy had relayed Jeremy's news. Patrick understandably was not much concerned. Deeply in love for the very first time he found only conversations either with or concerning his beloved of the slightest interest. Gail Dearing had become the focus of his life and poor Harry once so close had had to take a back seat. The only time the two really had a proper conversation these days was when they went Fire Watching together which despite the frightening need for it they both enjoyed. Indeed that was where he was heading now, to the biscuit factory to meet up with Harry.

It was far too early yet of course, the light only just beginning to fade, but they always tried to get there without those pesky kids following them. The kids had taken to hanging around the High Street until they spotted them and then following them to whichever site they had been assigned.

It was simple hero worship on the part of Tommy Fletcher and Samuel Beckett. They had often come across the two older boys having a kick around on the OVO and as young boys were apt to do became admiring of everything they did. Of course they knew Harry and Patrick didn't want them around but they didn't care, they just followed at a safe distance whenever they could, wouldn't be shaken off.

Dannah had taken himself off to the graveyard to sit awhile with Miriam, tell her what was happening, silently ask her what she thought of all the goings on. He found himself alone as usual amongst the gravestones. Most people chose the afternoons to visit their loved ones, pay their respects, but Dannah found the time with the sun just beginning to drop, the light just beginning to fade, the most peaceful, the best time for him to enjoy the communication he was able to have with his 'darlin'.

He sat on the rickety wooden bench between Arnold Chappell "Beloved husband of Rosemary and much loved father of Gertrude, Janet, Peter, Gladys, Rene, Ronald, Jacob and Kenneth" and his poor dear Miriam.

"Here lies Miriam Foster much loved wife of William. Beloved sister of Katherine, taken from us this day..........." He tried every time to read it to the end but he never could. Where was he? It was as though he'd never existed, never been part of her life. He wished with all his heart that even if she'd had to die why couldn't it have happened even one day later, that's all it would've taken and then it would've said "Here lies Miriam Delaney Beloved wife of...........!" He choked back the tears that still threatened after all this time, all this time now that he had been without her. He twirled the gold ring, the ring that he wore as a wedding ring, round his finger. It had been unusual to decide to have a wedding ring for himself, not many men did, it was usually just the women who announced to the world their status. He was glad he had the ring, a constant reminder and therefore comfort knowing that although what they had shared had been so short it had been real, had indeed been wonderful.

The Fire Watching that night at the biscuit factory was mercifully uneventful. The only bomb dropped the one by Patrick. After finally sending the two younger boys off home with fleas in their ears Harry and Patrick settled themselves down for the night, sleeping bags and thermos at the ready. It was a cloudy sky, they doubted there would be any bombing tonight.

'Sure 'tis good news about Dr. Kirk' said Patrick casually over his shoulder as he rooted in the bottom of his sack for the pack of playing cards.

'Good news? What good news?' asked Harry.

'Ya know about him getting married.'

'Dr. Kirk's getting married?' So his mother had finally agreed!

'Yeah, some nurse he's met out at the front I think.'

Harry's world abruptly fell apart yet again. Just as he was getting used to the idea that his real father might become part of his life it seemed it was all to be smashed to smithereens. It was a long uncomfortable night for Harry.

The following morning Pearl hung out of the bedroom window anxious to see what all the noise was about.

'Hey Auntie Peggy 'ave ya seen what's goin' on arht 'ere?'

'What was 'goin' on arht there' was to change the look of Oakfield not just for the duration of the war but for many years afterwards, in some cases forever. The Government had decreed that all metal must be used for the war effort and subsequently all metal railings, gates etc. had to be removed. That morning Pearl witnessed the removal of the ornate iron railings which surrounded the station yard. It was suddenly bare, had lost its elegance, its own sense of importance. Only one stretch of railing was left behind the buffers in the event of a train not stopping, which although rare certainly had been known. Peggy joined Pearl at the window.

'Oh tis only Arthur Storey' she said.

'Arf a Story? Auntie Peggy, why arf a story, why can't wiz 'ave a full 'un?' Peggy Barley looked hard at Pearl at first not fully understanding, and then the penny dropped. She ruffled the child's curls, laughed.

'Not HALF A STORY love. It's Arthur Storey, Arthur Storey and his lads 'ho are tekkin up yon railings.'

Arthur Storey and his 'lads' spent many weeks scouring the village removing metal railings wherever they found them. The railings which for as long as anyone could remember had adorned the front of Number Two Ladan Road were removed leaving just holes where they had once been. Holes which would remain empty all through the war and beyond gathering dust and grime in the summer and rain followed by ice during some of the worst winters in living memory.

Even Jonas Hardcastle's precious store of cycles was removed from the small warehouse on the site and taken away on the back of a truck – not for much longer Hardcastle Super de Luxe – reduced to scrap metal. Jonas' heart was heavy as holding Emily in his arms he watched the truck drive off, little Emily clapping her hands excitedly as if something nice was happening. Luci had known how difficult this would be for her father, the very last vestiges of his business being removed for once and for all. She had known the only person in the world who would be able to help him was his precious granddaughter. And so she had found an excuse. Could he possibly look after Emily for the afternoon? She had some shopping she needed to do. Emily turned in his arms.

'Gwan Pa, Gwan Pa' she said 'Gone!'

'Yes my poppet' he said sadly. 'All gone.'

Old railway sleepers were eventually found to replace the railings around the station, marking, although rather haphazardly, the boundaries beyond which you entered only on station business. Joe Parker was not at all happy at what had happened to his place of work and told his little daughter this as he pushed her along in her pram.

"Tain't right all this ya know Beatrice, all this messin' ahaht. This war's spoiling everything an' I want it over before you gets ta realize what's goin' on.' Beatrice nodded her head solemnly at her daddy as if she knew it was important that she agree with him and then giggled. He leant across into the pram, chucked her under her chin. 'Ah little 'un' he said 'God love ya, where did ya come from eh?' Beatrice threw herself backwards in the pram squirming with pleasure.

Muriel Parker was with Dr. Whitstable, having confirmed what she'd suspected but dared not believe. Beatrice was to have a little brother or sister.

'Well Nurse Parker' he grinned as he took his seat after his brief examination. 'I'm delighted to tell you what you quite obviously already know. In approximately six months' time you will have another bundle of joy to brighten your days and disturb all your nights' he laughed.

'Oh Doctor' she began and burst into tears. Tears of absolute joy, he'd been witness to many of those, they were what made the job worthwhile.

'Well' he grinned, 'am I right in thinking that it's good news?'

'Oh yes' she smiled through her tears. 'But so unexpected, we hardly dared hope you know……. we waited so long for Beatrice, had given up hope really and now to be blessed with another child. Well……' She was overcome with another bout of weeping.

'Indeed' smiled David Whitstable leaning forward, putting his hand over hers. 'And how often does this happen, no buses and then they come along in threes? I assume your husband is equally delighted?'

'Oh no, oh no' Muriel cried. Momentarily disconcerted the doctor removed his hand.

'Not pleased? I don't understand, I thought Joe would be over the moon.'

'Oh he will be when I tell him' laughed Muriel wiping away her tears. 'It's just I daren't tell him until I was sure, I didn't want him disappointed.'

'Ah' he sighed sitting back in his chair, clasping his hands together across his chest.

Muriel broke the news to Joe once they had settled Beatrice for the night thinking that the child might be confused by Joe's shouts of delight which would surely come. She wasn't disappointed. The shouts of joy came immediately and so did Joe across the room, lifting her high into the air spinning them both round and round.

CHAPTER THIRTY SEVEN

Harry was tortured over what was happening in his life. His mother was not to marry Jeremy Kirk after all. His real father was actually going to marry someone else. Were they all crazy? And why, oh why, was it always him in the middle? The only father he'd ever known was dead and had turned out not to be his father in any case! To top it all the one thing that could've removed him from all this mayhem had also been denied him, his poor exam results meaning there was no way he could go up to Glasgow and study to be a vet, the one thing he wanted more than anything in the world, more than FATHERS, more than people not being DEAD, more than anything!

Jeremy had purposely kept his distance from Harry whilst he'd been home on leave. He'd been shocked and surprised to hear of Harry's exam results but had felt powerless to help. He had assured Kathy that he would happily contribute to a further year's study if that was what Harry wanted but she would hear none of it, seemed to feel that it was all his own doing and he should pay the price. The way she was behaving reminded Jeremy of her own father's attitude towards her and her ambitions so many years ago. Privately Jeremy thought she was cutting her nose off to spite her face. No matter what had happened it would still be better all round if the boy was allowed to try again. After all that was all he wanted to do, surely he wouldn't fail again.

Kathy knew only too well what she was doing. Harry had behaved appallingly to her over the past few months, had been insulting, hurtful, insolent and this was her retribution. Oh she knew she was being childish, immature, would spoil things not only for Harry but equally for herself, but somehow at the moment she just couldn't help it. Kathy found herself deeply unhappy. Having in the end changed her mind, determined to try and make a go of things with Jeremy, accept his proposal of marriage, she had been forced to accept that actually she wasn't 'his world' as she'd rather arrogantly assumed. He'd found someone else and was planning a new life which did not include her. Jeremy had told her that after the war – when it finished – he and Geraldine intended to return to Oakfield and that he would hope to resume his practice. She rather hoped he wouldn't. She didn't know how she would cope with that, especially when he'd told her that Geraldine's young son Euan would be joining them. Why was it that she now wanted more than anything else in the world for Harry to know his real father when she'd previously been so against it? Why now when it was probably the worst thing that could possibly happen? She wondered if Geraldine knew about Harry. Had Jeremy told her?

Jeremy and Jeannie set off for London. It had been arranged that Geraldine, her parents and young son Euan would meet them there and in a quiet civil ceremony Jeremy and Geraldine would become man and wife. Afterwards Jeremy and his new wife were to return to Oakfield for two weeks before they both went back to the front.

To her surprise Jeannie found she liked Geraldine very much. At first, as with most people that Geraldine came into contact with, she had assumed that a beauty as she undoubtedly was could only be self aware, conscious of what she carried with her, probably be very shallow. Geraldine was none of these things, not shy exactly but extremely self-effacing. Jeremy had offered, very unwisely in Jeannie's view as he was exhausted himself, to take over his old practice for the two weeks to give young Doctor Whitstable a much needed break.

Harry and Patrick had found themselves promoted. Hardcastles old cycle works, now the armaments factory, was to be their next assignment.

Ralph Falconer had been surprised but delighted to receive a congratulatory message from high command. Probably the only thing that the powers that be had been good at so far, not exactly having much success on the military front, was in replacing all the weapons and artillery left behind during the Dunkirk evacuation. Oakfield's factory under Ralph's leadership had been instrumental in that and along with their appreciation came the instruction that the factory should no longer operate twenty four hour seven day shifts. The site was to revert to a twelve hour six day shift. Although good news for the workforce this left the factory more vulnerable at night and on Sundays with no one other than the normal security staff around. It had been decided therefore that the factory warranted two Fire Watching teams instead of the usual one. On their first night amid great excitement the two boys had taken up their allotted place on the ledge behind the huge clock which overlooked the archway entrance. The building was not high, just a single storey, with three sides surrounding the yard.

It was almost half way into their shift and Patrick had already fallen asleep when Harry was alerted by a noise down below. A man appeared in a doorway, lit a cigarette, began drawing hard blowing smoke rings. In between puffs he put his hand down by his side, held the lighted cigarette in the palm of his hand, his fingers curled round it as if to hide it from view. To hide it from view in the Black Out? Instinctively Harry knew differently, he'd only ever seen a cigarette held like that by one person. He watched carefully, curiously as the man paced up and down until the cigarette was gone, ground it under his shoe and went back into the building.

The very next morning over breakfast Dannah asked how the two boys had got on, aware that they needed the opportunity to boast of their new responsibilities. Patrick much to Harry's amusement assured his uncle that it had been 'a doddle'. He'd been asleep for most of it but Harry decided not to mention that!

'It was really quiet' Harry had replied to Dannah 'but the factory wasn't completely deserted. Someone was in the offices I think, came out for a cigarette.'

'Oh aye that would've been Ralph' laughed Dannah. 'Can't leave the place any more than he can leave his cigarettes. That man'll smoke himself to death that he will. He said he'd be there last night tying up the figures it being the month end an' all.'

CHAPTER THIRTY EIGHT

In a small community such as Oakfield in spite of the address written on the envelope Ted Jefferies the postman knew that Mrs. Luci Richards would not be found at the white-washed cottage by the beck. Luci had eventually given in to her parents' pleas to move in with them for the duration, or at least until Philip returned home. At first Luci wouldn't hear of it insisting she must be there as Philip walked up the path kit bag over his shoulder.

Bernie bent down to pick up the post from the mat in the hall, let out a small gasp as she saw amongst the envelopes a brown official looking one addressed to Mrs. P. Richards. Certainly it wasn't the dreaded telegram, but still.... She went in search of Jonas, she knew he was in his study. She tapped gently on the door, didn't wait for a response, popped her head round.

'Jonas' she said quietly. He looked up from his papers. Unused to anything other than her withering references to him as 'Sir' Jonas was instantly alert, instantly concerned.

'What is it love?' he asked. Edging her way into the room, for reply she held out the brown envelope, went to hand it to him.

'For Miss Luci' she said. Jonas took the envelope, his hand shaking, looked to the scene outside the window. Emily was playing 'throw' with Lennie, giggling whilst her mother looked fondly on.

'Oh God no!'

'I'll leave you with it' said Bernie, shaking her head sadly, and went to the door. As she did so..

'Is Maisie around love?' asked Jonas.

'Upstairs I think, sorting some clothes for the homeless charity. Do you want me to get her?'

'No, no, it's fine. I'll go and find her myself.'

Jonas found Maisie in their bedroom, clothes spilling from every drawer. Jumpers, shirts, trousers, skirts covered the bed. Jonas sat down on a pile of clothes.

'Oh Jonas for goodness sake, look what you're doing! I've just sorted that lo.......' She turned, saw his face, instantly ceased her recriminations.

'Oh love, what is it?' she cried. Her eyes darted from his face to his hands, saw the envelope, her own hands flew to cover her face. 'Oh God! Oh no!' Jonas got up from the bed, went to put his arms around her.

'It's alright darlin', try not to upset yourself, it's probably nothing.' He patted her shoulder trying to reassure her. Maisie pulled away, took his place on the pile of clothes.

'What is it?' she begged.

'Well other than it's for our Luci and it looks official I don't know and I can't open it can I? It's addressed to her.' Maisie sat up, straightened her shoulders back.

'We'd better get it over with hadn't we? I think she's in the garden with Emily.'

'Yes' answered Jonas 'she is and they're having such fun' he added sadly. The pair went out on to the wide landing, looked through the arched window down into the garden below. Indeed they were having fun, and they were going to have to spoil it. They went into Jonas' study, he opened the french windows.

'Luci love, you got a minute?' he called. Luci looked up from their game, came to the door holding Emily by the hand. Wordlessly Maisie bent down, took the child in her arms and turned back to the garden. Luci looked to her father.

'What? What?' she asked anxiously. Jonas put his arm around her, led her into the room.

'Sit down love.' Jonas led her to his chair, the comfiest in the room. 'It's this' he said handing her the envelope. 'It's probably nothing.......' his voice faded away. Luci didn't speak, took the envelope from him with trembling hands. She tore at the envelope so fiercely she ripped the sheet of paper inside. A single sheet. A formal almost curt letter informing her that her husband – Sergeant Philip Richards – had been captured in action and was now a prisoner of war. As far as they were aware it said he was in good health and uninjured and by rules of The Geneva Convention should remain so. The letter went on to inform her that she would receive no further news from them. However the Red Cross would provide her with details of how she might be able to correspond with her husband. Sergeant Richards should be allowed to correspond with her but this was by no means certain.

'Oh Daddy!' She handed the letter to her father who quickly skimmed its contents, bent down by her chair, took her in his arms and rocked her stroking her hair as she cried and cried.

Bernie hovering anxiously in the corridor, heard Luci's crying, went quickly outside to relieve Maisie of her granddaughter allowing both parents to be with Luci, comfort her in her distress. Much later when she had quietened Luci was prepared to listen to the wisdom of her parents. At least he was safe they said. In all probability away from the fighting. Prisoners were bargaining tools, had to be kept alive and well.

'Dear God let it be true.'

News soon reached them that the very same fate had befallen young Jack Thorn. It was more than likely they all said that if they had been captured at the same time they would be in the same camp. The news of Jack had been met with the same initial dismay and then slow relief that he wasn't dead by his mother Gladys and his new wife Joannie, they realized that things could have been worse, much worse.

When months later identical grainy, creased photographs arrived for both families sure enough there they were. In the middle of the group Philip and Jack stood side by side in the sunshine smiling. Luci and Joannie both wept over it but were relieved. 'They looked OK' they said.

Jonas and Gladys didn't enlighten them that in all probability guns had been trained on them in case they didn't feel like smiling. Luci pinned the photograph on a cupboard door alongside Emily's tiny bed. 'Daddy' she'd say to Emily each morning pointing him out, she did the same each evening as together they said their prayers for Daddy's safe return, Emily's chubby little hands pressed together, her eyes squeezed tightly shut.

Philip's internment meant many things to Luci. Although in all probability and God willing he should be safe it also meant he wouldn't be coming home until the war was over and that meant no more babies. Luci desperately wanted another child, a brother or sister for Emily. She had had a wonderful childhood, been spoilt by two doting parents, but there had been many times when she'd longed for a sibling and strangely she found not least of all now. She wanted someone to share her worries with who wouldn't be made even more unhappy through her own fears. She tried her best to keep her worst fears and nightmares from her parents knowing how much they cared for her and little Emily. Julia had become the nearest she'd ever have to a sibling and yet how could she unburden herself to her? As Philip's sister she had her own burden of worries over him.

Muriel Parker had become a close friend after seeing Luci through her pregnancy and having babies so close in age it was natural that they would have a lot in common. The announcement of Muriel's latest pregnancy had momentarily rocked Luci bringing to the surface her own longing, but she had pinned a bright smile on her face, hugged her friend and told her how delighted she was.

Julia was distraught, didn't know what to do, where to turn. It had to be Luci.

Julia had been amazed, overjoyed when she realized with total shock that she might be pregnant. She couldn't be she told herself, 'pull yourself together, it's wishful thinking.' And it was that too, wishful thinking, because if asked what her greatest wish in all the world would be it would be to give Wandsworth, this dear, dear man who had come into her life so late into his own, a child. She had kept her idiotic suspicions to herself. It was just too incredible she'd told herself, she would wait a while longer before telling Wandsworth, it was just too good to be true, things like that didn't happen. She immersed herself in her school work. Towards the end of a very intense afternoon of English grammar Julia began to experience severe stomach cramps. Taking herself off to the staff cloakroom she saw the blood, she guessed the unmistakeable signs of a miscarriage. Going back to her classroom as if in a nightmare she urged her pupils to hurry clearing away their paraphernalia and dismissed them very uncharacteristically early without any explanation to her head teacher or any other member of staff. Julia hurried to the cycle shed, she dared not ride the bike, knew she'd have to walk – quickly – to Luci's.

Once news of Philip's imprisonment had been confirmed Luci had decided to return to her own home, Philip would imagine her there and so that's where she needed to be she had insisted. Julia found Luci and Muriel in the middle of afternoon tea, the two babies playing happily on the rug between them. She didn't even knock just fell through the door weeping. Luci was instantly on her feet.

'Julia, Julia, whatever is it? What on earth's the matter?' She guided her sobbing sister-in-law to a chair.

'I can't, I can't!' cried Julia. 'I'll make a mess, I'm bleeding!'

'Bleeding! What do you mean bleeding?' gasped Luci. Muriel in her professional role was much more perceptive, guessed almost immediately, but quite naturally was unable to pose the question, for what if she was wrong! Practicalities took over, Muriel picked up the two children and put them in the playpen with their toys where they could come to no harm and then she went to Julia, knelt down beside her. Luci had insisted that whatever she must sit.

'What is it love?' Muriel asked calmly. 'Can't you tell us sweetheart?'

'I think.... I think it's a miscar.........' Julia broke off, crying again, couldn't bring herself to say the words.

'Ah' said Muriel gently 'you suspect you're miscarrying, well we'd best have a look at you darling.' Luci couldn't help herself.

'What? Miscarrying? What do you mean? I didn't know you were pregnant!' Muriel turned, shushed Luci putting a finger to her lips.

'Will you let me have a look at you then? Let me check.' Julia nodded her head mutely, allowed herself to be led upstairs into Luci and Philip's bedroom. Muriel carefully laid some towels she had found in the airing cupboard on to the bed and after a brief examination had to confirm to Julia that yes unfortunately that was what had happened.

'It's obviously very early though my love so you won't need any treatment, it's all come away naturally.' Julia was heartbroken. Muriel said she'd get Luci to come to her, she'd look after the children. Luci had no idea what to do, what could she do other than hold her hand, 'there, there' her like a child. Julia was insistent that no one else should know what had happened. Muriel was adamant that she would walk her home, Julia walking alongside Beatrice's pram pushing her bike, heartbroken. Mercifully, she thanked God, Wandsworth was not at home, out at a meeting. She had a few hours to sort herself out, compose her thoughts, pretend to her husband that all was well, that he hadn't lost the child he would so have loved.

He had never said he wanted a child, never having had one with Maude it had never appeared on the horizon of his thinking and Julia had convinced him that she wasn't the 'maternal type' otherwise he never would've married her, couldn't have robbed her of the opportunity. She'd told him that she wanted him all to herself, didn't want to share him with anyone and she'd thought she'd meant it. Julia had convinced Wandsworth, had convinced herself, but the very first day it occurred to her that there might be a little person, a product of her and Wandsworth growing inside her, her world had turned around. To have lost this precious little soul was more than she could bear but she knew she had to, had to hide it from the man who was the love of her life.

'Hello darling' she greeted him cheerfully as he came through the door much later that evening. 'Had a good day?'

'Yes, yes' he replied smiling 'And you?'

'Oh yes fine' she said and turned back to the stove.

Julia had done as Muriel had said she must and in great secrecy went to visit Dr. Whitstable. He examined her, expressed his sympathies and assured her there was absolutely no reason why she couldn't conceive again. She was young and first pregnancies he told her were notoriously precarious.

When only three months later Julia had missed two of her monthlies and more significantly was feeling distinctly unwell in the mornings she dared to hope once again. She immediately stopped cycling to school convincing Wandsworth that suddenly she preferred to walk. Luci out of kindness had not enquired as to her health or thoughts on her miscarriage knowing how it could only distress her. Julia once again hugged her secret to herself until into what she judged to be her fourth month she knew she must seek medical advice. Julia to quote her brother was 'as thin as a rail' and so up to press had held her shape and gave no clue as to the miracle that was occurring inside her. Out of sight she stroked her tummy loving this child already. When she first felt the fluttering her heart almost stopped. Was she imagining it? When later the same day it happened again she knew she hadn't been mistaken and made an appointment with the Doctor. A week later her pregnancy was confirmed.

That same evening she went in search of Wandsworth. She found him busy in his greenhouse at the bottom of the garden.

'Have you got a minute darling?' she asked. He grinned, put down his tools, took off his thick gloves.

'What a question!' he laughed. 'I always have time for you, you know that!'

They sat down together on the wooden bench in front of the greenhouse. The sun after a glorious day was setting behind the house. They looked down the garden to the rose beds in front of the dining room which were Wandsworth's pride and joy.

'Darling, I have some good news, at least I hope you'll find it good news.' Wandsworth imagined the news to be something to do with school, perhaps a promotion? She really was a very good teacher, he couldn't be more proud of her. He leant to one side, dead-headed a Petunia.

'I'm sure if it's good news for you then it can only be good news for me' he said turning to her, all the time smiling.

'I'm pregnant' said Julia, 'we're having a baby darling.' Wandsworth dropped the poor dead Petunia to the ground.

'What did you just say?' He looked into her eyes incredulous, disbelieving.

'I'm pregnant' Julia whispered. Wandsworth didn't know what to say, what to do. Kiss her? Squeeze her? But he didn't want to hurt the baby. In the end he pulled her to him, kissed her forehead, stroked her cheeks, laughed, smiled, finally cried, he just had no words. Eventually…

'When?' he asked almost reverently.

'Oh I think in time for Christmas' she laughed. 'I think you and I will have a very special present.'

'I already have that my darling, the day I met you' he smiled.

CHAPTER THIRTY NINE

The news of Julia's pregnancy and the marriage of Jeremy Kirk whilst wonderful for the parties involved had raised anxieties amongst those of a superstitious nature. A marriage, a birth? There was bound to be a third and the only one missing was a death.

Jeremy and Geraldine were spending their honeymoon with Jeannie, Jeremy at the same time standing in for Dr. Whitstable. The work was not arduous, how could it be described as such when compared to his work at the front. It was almost as though people realized that in the main most of their complaints, their ailments, were nothing in the face of war, their fellow men dying in battle in strange lands or being bombed and all too often now killed in their own homes. No, what had previously seemed so urgent, so important, ceased to be so.

Jeremy Kirk had had a quiet surgery that evening, was contemplating a convivial few hours playing a hand or two of cards with Geraldine, Jeannie and Stan.

It was those living closest to the river who saw it first. Saw the sky above the city on the opposite bank lit up a brilliant red, saw the flashes. Heard the sirens, felt the very ground shake beneath them. Oakfield itself being such a small place had no air raid siren and so the inhabitants were taken completely by surprise, had no chance to get to their shelters before the roaring overhead began.

Before heading for the factory Dannah checked that all the Ladan Road household were safely in the cupboard under the stairs. It had long ago been agreed that this would be safer than any shelter, the massive staircase above would surely survive even if the rest of the house should crumble around it. Peggy pushed little Pearl ahead of her the child clutching her teddy, rarely used but today her best friend. Margaret too was found a place in the corner where she crouched in her cage looking every bit as startled as the adults squashed in around her. Lizzie and her mother Ruby were there along with Charlie, Ruby having rushed home to collect him, finding him confused and distressed, not at all sure what was going on. Concern for Charlie's welfare meant he was made comfortable on the only chair, a rug around his knees. Kathy was the last in bringing sandwiches, cake, a thermos. For once they had remembered the playing cards but in doing so had forgotten the books and magazines. Kathy imagined it could be a long night for the six of them and Margaret. Miriam's old commode was placed just outside the door in the hall in case of emergencies.

Mavis and John Tremmings were in the downstairs back room counting the day's takings, the radio on, when Cissie burst in from the shop.

'Hey did ya 'ear yon sirens?' she gasped. John jumped to his feet.

'Sirens, what sirens lass?' He asked the question but already knew, his heart sinking, the answer.

'Sirens' said Cissie urgently ' over the river,'an' that means........'

'Get the boys down Mavis an' then you all get into shelter owt back. I'll just get me 'elmet.' As John struggled with the strap under his chin he heard Mavis' anguished cry.

'They're not 'ere John' she called, 'neither of 'em's 'ere.' John looked anxiously across at Cissie.

'Tis alright Mr. Tremmings, I'll 'elp find 'em an' get 'em in t'shelter, you get off an' do yer wardening.' The girl saw his hesitation. 'Go on' she urged pushing him towards the back door. 'You've yer duty to do!' She made to close the door behind him but had second thoughts, pulled it sharply back. 'An' you tek care o' yoursen!' she shouted.

Cissie headed up the narrow staircase to Mavis. 'They're not 'ere' she cried. 'I've looked everywhere, where in God's name are they?' Cissie took control.

'Well in that case they're in t'yard or up street. You look in t'yard Mrs. Tremmings and I'll run quickly up street see if I can see 'em. They can't be far and this'll scare living daylights out of 'em any road.' Cissie returned not five minutes later and on her own. 'I've looked everywhere' she gasped, bending double getting her breath, 'down alleys an' everywhere but what's for sure is they'll have found somewhere safe. They can't 'ave missed this racket.' Mavis looked at her unconvinced.

'Honestly they will've' the girl insisted. 'They ain't daft. We'd best get ourselves in t'shelter any road like Mr. Tremmings said' and she took charge of the older woman shepherding her towards the door. 'Oops Mrs. Tremmings' she laughed, 'we nearly left box wi' takings, 'ere stick it up yer jumper.' Mavis took the metal box from Cissie.

'Ya know you're a good lass Cissie, we didn't 'alf miss ya. Thank goodness you've come back to us.' In spite of what was going on around them Cissie stopped in her tracks, glowed, she wasn't much used to compliments these days with 'er Jimmy being away.

'Aw go on wi' ya' she flushed.

'No, no I'm serious' said Mavis, 'deadly serious.'

Cissie had returned to work at the Tremmings' shop almost as soon as the factory had achieved its targets, the reduced shift patterns allowing it to function with fewer workers. Cissie hadn't enjoyed her time at the factory as much as she'd anticipated. The work was repetitive and tedious, she often thought a well trained monkey could do it just as well. She hadn't particularly enjoyed the company of all the other girls either finding their eternal gossiping not to her liking. Overriding all that though was the fact that she'd had to give up her job at the cinema, something she really loved. Of course there was talk of places such as cinemas and theatres being closed down for the duration, but it hadn't happened yet and she was rather hoping that Edie Timpson who had taken her place would get herself pregnant before long and have to leave and then she Cissie could return to her rightful place. Ruby her mother was also happier having her home for more regular hours. Lizzie was still at the factory but in the absence of George now spent a lot of her time with little Pearl who absolutely idolized her.

'It must be that pesky bonnet wot affects 'em' Peggy Barley was apt to say 'for wot else can it be?' Actually Lizzie's thoughts were increasingly turning to joining up. She rather fancied being a WAAF. She certainly didn't fancy the Army's get up. The Wrens looked alright but she was prone to getting sea-sick on the park lake so perhaps that weren't such a good idea.

As soon as the distant sirens had begun to wail Jeremy and Stan packed Jeannie and Geraldine into the Anderson shelter in the small courtyard behind the surgery. Jeannie ever resourceful was prepared for all eventualities, a bag packed with food, drinks, knitting, books, cards and a lamp. Once they had the two women settled Stan donned his ARP helmet and headed off to HQ to receive his orders, always supposing there were some. In all honesty they weren't very well drilled, very organized, they hadn't had to be. This would be their first attempt at the real thing. He spotted John Tremmings in the distance, hurried to catch up with him. Before too long they were joined by Jonas Hardcastle.

Dannah Delaney set off for the factory cursing under his breath that this had to happen so early into Harry and Patrick's prestigious new posting.

CHAPTER FORTY

Harry had been first to climb the narrow metal-runged ladder leading up to the ledge on the first floor. The ladder – put there to enable the clock which faced on to the street below to be changed twice yearly and maintained as befitting such an eminent establishment as Hardcastles – had been spared, the scavengers of the metal collecting team deeming it to be insignificant in the scheme of things. Arthur Storey commenting that 'It wun't sa much as mek a tent peg!'

The rungs were wet and greasy and as he reached the ledge Harry bent over using the decorative concrete cornice surrounding the clock to rub his hands dry. As he did so he glanced down and saw two figures scurrying through the archway below, it was those pesky kids! Obviously they'd followed him and Patrick again even though they'd thought they'd warned them off. As Patrick's head appeared above the ladder he was about to sound off about Tommy and Samuel but then thought better of it knowing full well Patrick would go berserk and probably go hurtling down after them. He supposed it didn't really matter, they'd go home as soon as darkness fell. Harry signalled to Fred Archer and Bernard Crowther, the other two fire watchers on duty, that they were in position and Fred on the other side of the building responded with a thumbs up indicating that they could all settle down for a peaceful night. Harry was keen to see if the 'secret smoker' put in another appearance, he'd found that very disturbing especially after what Dannah had said. But he was being ridiculous, fanciful, how could it be?

Without warning all hell broke loose, planes squealed overhead seemingly coming from nowhere their target clearly across the river. Harry and Patrick were on their feet shocked and instantly frightened, their previous bravado forgotten. The distant sky became a blaze of reds, blues, purples, the noise unbelievable. They stood mesmerized just watching and then suddenly from behind them came a mighty roar and they were hurled to the ground as the section of roof beneath them collapsed. Fires broke out all around them, inconsequential at first but rapidly spreading, the smell of fuel permeating the air. Mercifully the boys by now were aware of neither, already unconscious. A plane, a German fighter, had ploughed into the building reducing it to rubble instantly, the walls falling as playing cards fall when balanced one on the other.

About to close the door of the shelter, the skies roaring above him, Jeremy looked up, saw the Stuka making a nose dive and could tell exactly where it must land.

'I'm going' he shouted into the shelter.

'I'm coming too' cried Geraldine scrambling out. Jeannie made to follow.

'You stay right here' shouted Jeremy above the noise, 'there'll be nothing you can do at the moment, you stay safe' and with that, much to Jeannie's annoyance, he slammed the door shut.

Jeremy and Geraldine arrived at the factory, or what was left of it, to find the tail end of the plane sticking up like a dolphin's tail, its nose buried somewhere deep into the ground. Around them everywhere were flames licking closer and closer to the fuselage of the plane.

Dannah having run all the way from Ladan Road arrived breathless.

'The boys!' he screamed as he saw Jeremy. 'They're on duty here tonight!'

'What?' shouted Jeremy. 'Oh my God no! Where?'

Harry was the first to come round but hadn't a clue where he was. Knew it was hot, the noise unbelievable, the smell! Well what was that smell? He knew he was out in the open and his boggled brain was telling him from somewhere that Patrick should be with him. He realized he was pinned down by something, he tried to wriggle his feet, pull them from under whatever it was that held him down, he couldn't. He tried his left arm, but there wasn't one, at least he couldn't feel one. He tried his right arm, at least he could feel that – just! But it felt wet and sticky. He struggled to open his eyes and then even more to keep them open, in the end it was too much effort. He felt around next to him, there were rocks, rubble and then something soft, felt like material, felt like wool. He poked around, he was sure he felt skin next to it. Suddenly he remembered what Patrick was wearing when he came out, the sweater his Mammie had knitted and sent for his birthday last week.

'Patrick, Patrick' he croaked, the heat and dust beginning to sear at his throat. 'Are you OK Patrick?' There was no response. He tried to turn on his side but was unable to. He edged his right arm a bit higher feeling for more flesh, a face. In a brief moment of comparative quiet he was sure he heard a faint groan.

'Patrick, Patrick, is that you? Are you OK?' he croaked again.

'Does it bloody look like it?' managed Patrick before his voice faded and he lapsed again into unconsciousness. Alone once more Harry suddenly became aware of a persistent ticking.

'Oh my God' he cried 'it must be a bomb.' With his one good hand he tried to shake Patrick knowing that somehow they must get away from there, as he did so a piece of reinforced concrete previously so elegantly surrounding the clock face lost its balance and fell to the ground with a glancing blow to Harry's head. He too was granted the blessed relief of unconsciousness.

The majority of the rescuers headed automatically for the far side of the building where the plane had nose-dived. Fred and Bernard, although bloodied and crushed, were at least conscious.

'The boys' Bernard managed faintly, 'they're ovver there, on yon side, on t'ledge behind t'clock.'

Dannah, scrabbling at the rubble surrounding the man, heard, looked at Jeremy. They both screwed their eyes up against the smoke, peered over the great hulking body of the plane. As one they turned and ran scrambling over the fuselage, the wheels, now a mass of burning, searing rubber. They saw the clock, its face on an angle, almost bent in half but on end and mercifully giving some protection to the two boys as it ticked relentlessly on. In front of them on his knees in the rubble, flames licking round his boots, was Ralph Falconer scraping rubble and dust from Harry's face. Jeremy clawed his way up next to him as Dannah and Geraldine went to the other boy.

'Uncle Dannah? Is that you?' gasped Patrick desperately as he felt someone take his hand. Geraldine tenderly took

Patrick's head in her lap all the while scraping away bits of burning rubber which clung to the boy's clothing.

Jeremy, kneeling next to Ralph in front of Harry, saw the boy struggle to open his eyes.

'Father' he whispered, but he wasn't looking at Jeremy, he was looking at Ralph.

Although the 'Duguids of Dundee' clock had done its job, bending as it had and acting as a protective helmet around the boys, the glass face was altogether another story. A blast had sent fragments of the glass into Harry's face and crucially into Patrick's neck. Dannah made to brush away a shard of glass lodged to one side just under Patrick's chin. His hand was swiftly knocked away by Geraldine.

'No' she said quietly but insistently, 'better left.'

Only women with children to care for and those too old stayed in their shelters that night, all the rest becoming heroines and heroes as they struggled to save their neighbours. King's Terrace, a row of fourteen houses which ran parallel to the factory, had also been doused with fuel as the plane made its fatal dive, the vapour trail it left in its wake almost immediately erupting into flames. The auxiliary fire brigade eventually arrived to find a human chain passing buckets of water from the nearby dyke in an attempt to overcome the blaze. Patrick was man-handled on to a door which had been blown off and now served as a make-shift stretcher. Geraldine had assessed his injuries to be major and spinal insisting he should be moved as little as possible.

Harry deemed to be the least injured of the two was temporarily left with Ralph Falconer as Jeremy joined in the careful lifting of Patrick. In the glow of a dangerously close fire Harry looked again at Ralph, screwed up his eyes in pain, his blistered lids making it almost impossible.

By the time Harry joined Patrick in the road, the kerb edge acting as a pillow, he was dipping in and out of consciousness. Eventually he came round to find Patrick unconscious on the door next to him, a crowd of people gathered round them.

'The bomb' he gasped, 'there was a bomb, I heard it ticking.'

''Twas the clock' said Bernard 'an' bloody thing's still goin.'

Geraldine and Dannah knelt either side of Patrick, Jonas Hardcastle paced up and down cursing the time it was taking for the ambulances to arrive, John Tremmings doing his best to calm him down. In the middle of the commotion someone ran from the crowd grabbing frantically at John's arm. He turned his blackened face.

'Cissie? Cissie love, what's up?'

'It's the boys Mr. Tremmings, Tommy and Samuel, they 'aven't come back.'

'What! Oh my God no! Where the 'ell are they?'

Harry more alert now heard Cissie's screaming, unable to move either of his arms kicked out at John Tremmings' leg. John looked down at him, was about to turn away as Harry kicked out once more. Jonas grabbed John's arm.

'Hang on a sec I reckon he's trying to tell us somethin'.' Jonas bent down to the boy.

'What is it son?' he asked urgently.

'In the factory, the boys in the factory' croaked Harry before he lost consciousness once more.

Ralph Falconer was first into the inferno that had once been the factory, scrambling desperately over the rubble. He knew where they might be, he'd seen them several times before heading for the store rooms at the back. Oh he'd known they shouldn't be there but he'd turned a blind eye believing them to be doing no harm, just boys being boys, he'd left them to their adventures. But now he was fierce in his determination to find them, rescue them. He hadn't been wrong, they were where he'd expected them to be, crouching in fright behind the newly installed steel door of the smaller of the two storerooms, the door having protected them so far from the searing heat, the flames licking all around them. Finding strength he'd never known he possessed Ralph hoisted a boy on each shoulder and made a dash for it, his boots already beginning to smoulder. As he emerged in the gaping hole that had once been the ornate archway of 'Hardcastle Cycles' a cry went up and rippled all around. John Tremmings was first to him followed closely by poor slight little Cissie. They each wrenched a weeping boy from Ralph's shoulders, but Cissie unable to bear the weight of Samuel eventually fell to her knees in the road cradling the boy in her arms as if he were her own, her tears falling on to his soot blackened face.

'He's dead!' she wailed. Geraldine raced towards her, fell on her knees grappling for the boy's wrist.

'He's alright love, he's not dead he's just fainted. His body is telling him it needs a rest' she reassured her. 'He'll be fine don't worry.'

'Oh you little sod!' cried Cissie over Samuel's sleeping face, 'You little sod!'

Tommy was equally blessed suffering a few bruises and blistering on his hands but nothing worse thanks to the quick thinking bravery of Ralph Falconer.

Ralph sat on the kerb, his head in his hands, as they waited for the ambulances to arrive. Jim Sanderson was driving that night. Having very quickly given up on the Home Guard his driving skills were put to good use and he felt as if finally he was 'doing his bit'. The boys were lifted into separate ambulances. Dannah and Jeremy went with Patrick and Harry, John Tremmings accompanied Tommy and Samuel. Cissie was dispatched to break the news to Mavis that the boys had been found safe. Stan Briggs said he would go to Kathy. Jonas Hardcastle went over to Ralph, sat next to him on the kerb edge, put his arm across the other man's shoulder.

'My God lad, that was heroic, you deserve a medal you really do.' Without warning cold, brusque Ralph Falconer burst into tears. Geraldine saw, went to sit at the other side of him on the kerb. She reached for his hand gently rubbing it with her thumb trying to avoid the raw patches which would eventually cause him even more pain. The three of them sat in silence as the cacophony around them continued. Eventually Ralph shuddered, straightened his back and impatiently wiped away the last of his tears, there would be no more he told himself, no more.

CHAPTER FORTY ONE

Wandsworth Prescott, having attended a late afternoon Council Meeting, had no inkling of what was taking place as he boarded the last bus to Oakfield. He was on his own and immersed in reading papers from the meeting, all the other passengers having disembarked at outlying villages, when the shout went up from the driver Gilbert Baggings.

'God, God, Oh bloody 'ell!' screamed Gilbert as arriving at the brow of the hill he saw the furnace that was now the sky above Lanchester and in the foreground and even more frightening was the bonfire that was Oakfield. He slammed hard on the brakes and the bus slewed to one side. Wandsworth looking up had no need of explanation. He struggled from his seat to stand next to the driver frantically holding on to the pole as the bus lurched to a halt.

'Oh no!' he cried 'Oh no!' Gilbert hurriedly let go of the brake, slammed the gear into place and set off, the bus bumping and banging erratically, unused to being driven at such speed. Wandsworth had to sit down, unable to keep his feet as the bus careered its crazy way down the hill. At the market place it was all too obvious the bus had reached the end of its journey. There was no way ahead, debris was scattered everywhere and other vehicles lay abandoned. The two men leapt from the bus, Gilbert towards the fires, Wandsworth to Luci's beck side cottage where he expected to find Julia. From a distance he suspected that the cottages being at the opposite end of the factory to King's Terrace were as yet unaffected but he could see clouds of smoke billowing up menacingly behind them. As he ran along the beck he saw Luci's neighbours running from their homes clutching whatever valuables they could. Luci's immediate neighbour Margo had Tiddles her cat cradled, terrified, in her arms. Spotting Wandsworth she called out to him.

'Gone to her Mam and Dad's and your Julia's gone with 'em!' Wandsworth thanking her let out a sigh of relief, said a silent prayer. 'Ere tek Winnies bike!' called Margo, 'she won't mind, she's already gorn to 'er Dad's.' Wandsworth needed no second bidding, hauled himself on to Winnie Colman's "sit up an' beg" which was leant against the fence and pushed off as hard as he could. He knew full well he wouldn't manage the hill up to the Hardcastles' place, he'd have to get off at the bottom, he just wasn't up to that anymore and so he pedalled hard whilst he was able. He had to get to Julia!

When Julia had arrived at Luci's house that afternoon she'd found her sister-in-law in a strange, restless mood. When asked why Luci admitted she had absolutely no idea, she just felt full of restless energy. When she suggested a walk to her parents' home Julia now in her final month of pregnancy was none too keen but realized she'd have to go for Emily's sake if not Luci's.

'Well OK then' she grinned, 'as long as we take it slowly.'

'As if we have a choice' laughed Luci looking Julia up and down. 'You look like a ship in full sail all of a sudden, you've certainly piled it on lately haven't you?'

'Don't I know it?' answered Julia ruefully 'Can you check if I have matching shoes, I can't see my feet anymore!'

When the blasts had started, even though they were at some distance and over the water, Jonas had insisted there was to be no nonsense, everyone had to go immediately to the shelter at the bottom of the garden. With the evacuees temporarily absent that meant five of them plus Lennie the dog.

Once satisfied that his loved ones were all where they should be Jonas donned his ARP helmet, mounted his bicycle and pedalled as hard as he could, free-wheeling most of the way down to the ARP headquarters.

It was uncomfortable in the shelter squashed in as they were. Maisie and Bernie had their knitting and of course Emily demanded her mother's full attention. Julia stretched out as best she could and opened her book. Something was niggling at her, a nagging pain came now and again. But it disappeared so she guessed it was the cramped conditions. Having been in the shelter for two hours Julia was no longer convinced. She beckoned Luci over from the corner where she was happily stacking coloured wooden bricks with her increasingly fractious daughter.

'What?' cried Luci 'not the toilet, please don't tell me that bladder of yours is playing up again. If it is you're going to have to make a run for the house, we've forgotten the commode of all things!!'

'I wish it was!' gasped Julia as a pain overwhelmed her. 'I think I'm in labour.'

'What?' shrieked Luci 'You can't be! How can you be? You're not due yet. No Julia not now!' she screeched. Maisie looked up from her wool winding. Bernie with the wool wrapped around both hands as if tied up in some old western film looked on in dismay.

'What on earth's the matter?' asked Maisie. 'What are you screaming about? You'll frighten Emily if you're not careful.'

'It's Julia!' shrieked Luci, if anything even louder. 'She thinks she's gone into labour!' Maisie dropped the half wound ball of wool and Bernie tried to free herself from the wool hooked so expertly round her hands by Maisie. The two women, bent double due to the limited height of the shelter, shuffled over to Julia.

'Are you sure darlin'?' asked Bernie apprehensively.

'Well if it's not!' squawked Julia on a spasm. 'I don't know what it.........!' Maisie took control.

'Right well we need help or to get you to the hospital.........' As she spoke the ground beneath them shook and a mighty blast followed. Emily, curious, crawled across the muddy floor to see what all the fuss was about.

'Brick for mantie Julha' she smiled and launched the said item on to Julia's tummy.

'Emily!' scolded Luci horrified.

'Thank you darling' smiled Julia grimly 'my favourite colour.'

'I think we do need help and quickly' said Maisie noting Julia's pallor and rapid breathing.

'I'll go for Muriel!' cried Luci, 'she'll be at home I'm sure she will, she'll come.'

'But that will take ages' interrupted Bernie. 'She lives way out of the village, how will you get there?'

'I'll take the car' replied Luci. 'I'll get the keys and go.'

'Oh I'm not sure about that' whispered Maisie. 'We're all supposed to stay in the shelter, and would you be able to see where you're going in any case you're not allowed lights you know.'

'I do know that Mummy!' replied Luci witheringly, 'but what else can we do? I'll manage somehow.' With that she was through the door slamming it behind her. Lennie went to the door after her, scratched at it with his paw.

'Well first I think we need to sort out Emily' said Maisie. 'Poor little mite must wonder what's going on. Let's put some of these chairs on their sides, make a kind of playpen and at least then she'll be contained.' With Emily hopefully settled they turned their attention once more to Julia. She was doing a magnificent job trying to hold herself together, but each pain seemed to get frighteningly closer together.

'Do you think we need to get hot water and towels?' Maisie asked Bernie. 'That's what they always seem to do in the films.'

'Aye very likely' agreed Bernie 'but question is what do they do with 'em?'

'Yes quite, I take your point. Have you never had anything to do with delivering a baby Bernie?' Maisie asked anxiously.

'I'm sorry to say now that I 'aven't, have you?' Maisie shook her head, went back to hold Julia's hand.

Luci drove slowly but determinedly through the blackout to the Parkers' house out on the top road. Actually it wasn't dark, the sky illuminated by the blasts and fires that seemed to be breaking out everywhere down below in the village. Joe answered Luci's hammering on the door, crawling from the Morrison shelter which dominated their kitchen.

'For God's sake luv,' cried Joe. 'Get yoursen inside' he said pulling on her arm.

Muriel lay on her side behind the wire mesh walls of the shelter, her little daughter fast asleep in the crook of her arm contentedly sucking her thumb, oblivious to what was going on around her. Muriel saw Luci, sat up on one elbow.

'Whatever's wrong?' she asked. Luci knelt down on the other side of the mesh.

'It's Julia' she whispered, anxious not to wake the sleeping child. 'She's gone into labour in our shelter, do you think you could come?'

'She's what?' gasped Muriel. 'She's.........' She got no further as yet again the ground shook beneath them. Muriel extricated herself, first from the sleeping child and then the Morrison shelter. She brushed herself down.

'I'll have to go Joe' she said, looking to her husband, knowing he would have concerns for her in her condition.

'Course ya will darling' answered Joe. 'I'll look after Beatrice, don't you worry.'Ow did ya get 'ere luv?' he asked turning to Luci.

'In Daddy's car' replied Luci. 'I know I'm not supposed to but this is an emergency and otherwise we would've had to get an ambulance and I imagine they're pretty well occupied tonight.'

The two women had an even more arduous journey back than Luci's solitary one had been. Vehicles and water pipes were everywhere now seeming to block every entrance and exit. Eventually Luci pulled on to the driveway and both women raced round the side of the house down to the shelter hidden behind the rose arbour at the bottom of the garden. Luci was first through the door. Little Emily, safe in her makeshift playpen but becoming more than a little bored, clapped her hands together at the sight of her mother. She held up her arms to her wanting to be lifted out.

'Mammie' she cried.

Muriel went to the truckle bed where Julia lay, sweating profusely but ashen, her lips bleeding where she'd bitten down to quieten her pains. Muriel only just made it, she knelt down beside an anxious Bernie just as Julia screamed out and the baby's head popped into the world, a look of utter surprise on its pinched little face.

'Oh' squeaked Bernie equally surprised, making to get up, give Muriel some room.

'No, no' said Muriel squeezing her arm gently. 'Your privilege, you've done all the hard work.' She looked down the bed to Julia furiously biting her lips and squeezing Maisie's hand, desperately trying to hold back the screams she wanted to let go.

'One more big push' coaxed Muriel, 'one more and you'll be there.' Julia grimaced, pushed with all her might and Christopher Wandsworth Prescott slithered into Bernie's waiting hands.

'Oh my God! Oh my God!' cried Bernie. 'I've delivered a baby!'

'You have too' smiled Muriel. 'Well done, you've been wonderful.' Bernie carefully laid the boy on a towel as Muriel cut the cord that bound mother and son. Muriel cleaned him off, tucked a clean pillowcase around the child and handed him to Bernie.

'You do it' she smiled, 'you give him to his mummy.' With tears spilling down her cheeks Bernie moved to the head of the bed, handed the still wide-eyed child to his mother.

'Oh my angel' whispered Julia, 'my angel' and then let out an ear splitting scream. Muriel at the other end of her patient put her hand on Julia's still extended tummy.

'There's another one love' she said. 'There's another one in there.'

'What! But there can't be.........' A loud wail came from Julia as she was gripped by another wave of pain. Maisie hastily took the boy from his mother's arms, handed him to a shell shocked Luci, Emily clinging on to her skirts entranced at all that was taking place.

'What Mammie? Is mantie Julha being silly again?'

'Yes, yes she is darling, now you just get on with mangling Nana's wool again' said Luci leading Emily back into the playpen.

'Only mantie Julha' Emily sang to herself. 'Naughty mantie Julha!'

Even Lennie had ambled over, curious as to what was going on. Luci looked down at him.

'Oh for God's sake!' she cried 'we've even got the bloody dog now, it's worse than Jesus and the manger.'

'Luci!' cried Maisie, instantly indignant, 'Please mind your language! I know things are rather awkward' she said in a massive understatement, 'but there's no need for that!'

'Oh naughty Mummy!' Emily muttered from her corner.

It was Muriel who finally delivered Julia's daughter Lydia Rose Prescott.

CHAPTER FORTY TWO

Wandsworth was able to cycle the last bit of the way, the lane leading to the Hardcastles' house being relatively flat. He found the house in darkness as he had expected but unexpectedly Jonas' car slewed across the front of the house. Whatever was Jonas thinking of? It wasn't like him to flout any rules. In spite of the urgency of the situation Wandsworth tutted to himself. He had to feel his way around the side of the house, the overhanging trees managing to block out even the blazing skies beyond. He assumed, hoped, they would all be in the shelter, but actually he had no idea where it might be, it was quite a large garden! After much stumbling he thought he could just make out the shape of a shelter in the distance and edged his way towards it. He eased the door open not at all prepared for the sight that met his eyes. At the far end of the shelter he could just make out what he took to be a bed. To one side a row of wooden chairs draped with towels seemed to be providing some sort of screen. Amidst the commotion no one had noticed him. Lennie was the first to spot him, relinquished his place at the foot of the bed, padded over. Luci pleased that the animal had at last had the good sense to move, turned to watch him and in doing so saw Wandsworth.

'Wandsworth, oh Wandsworth! Julia went into labour' she cried.

'What?' Unable to stand upright due to the height of the roof, in shock Wandsworth jerked up his head banging it hard on the corrugated panels. 'What did you say?' he asked frantically.

'I said.......' Luci began. But she said no more. Muriel came over, took Wandsworth's arm not able to let him suffer one more moment of anxiety.

'It's alright love' she said gently. 'Everything's fine, come and look.'

An exhausted Julia was fast asleep, a beautiful downy headed baby cradled in her arms. Wandsworth fell to his knees beside the truckle bed, unable to believe what he saw.

'Oh my darling' he gasped. At his voice, tender and low though it was, Julia's eyes popped open. She held out her hand to him. He kissed her cheek, his tears wetting her face, put a finger to the cheek of his first born child, stroked it with such tenderness. The child tucked under his mother's chin, her arm reassuringly around him, looked through his filmy eyes to his father with suspicion. Wandsworth laughed, there was no mistaking that look – his brother Reginald all over again!

'Meet Christopher darling' whispered Julia.

'My much longed for, wonderful, unbelievable son' cried Wandsworth. Julia looked beyond him, nodded her head at Muriel.

'And your much longed for, wonderful, unbelievable daughter' laughed Julia as Muriel Parker laid the now mercifully quiet little girl next to her brother.

If Wandsworth hadn't already been on the floor he certainly would have ended up there. He gazed at Julia, from her to his two children. The words whirled round and round in his head 'my children, not my child, my children!' In the end 'But I don't understand' he said, 'we weren't told we were expecting twins.'

'No, for the simple fact that no one knew' smiled Muriel. 'It does sometimes happen that the babies lay one behind the other. It's certainly unusual but not unheard of, they're a pair of rascals and no mistake' she laughed. Wandsworth said no more, just knelt there his knees hurting on the cold hard floor, his arm around Julia, gazing with adoration at his wonderful little family, he felt he might burst.

Eventually Muriel had to reluctantly insist that some semblance of order should be brought to the proceedings. Julia and the babies were absolutely fine as far as she could tell but she'd be happier she said if they all went to the hospital as soon as possible just to be sure, the babies understandably being slightly under weight. As it happened Julia and her babies didn't make it to the hospital until the following afternoon. With the catastrophe which had unfolded at the factory and King's Terrace on their hands a newly delivered mother with seemingly healthy twins was not top priority for the emergency services. Due to the bravery of many people that fateful night, although fourteen families lost their homes only three sadly lost their lives.

Harry and Patrick were the most seriously injured. Harry had broken both an arm and a leg and cracked several ribs and his collar bone as he plummeted from the ledge. He had lacerations all over his face and upper body from the splintered clock face. In agony he spent days drifting in and out of consciousness, the high doses of morphine making him cry out with wild imaginings. Thankfully however when he was conscious he seemed to have forgotten along with many other things his antagonism towards his mother. On the rare occasions when Kathy found him awake he seemed pleased to see her. Harry 'would mend' she was told.

Patrick's prognosis however was totally different. He lay in a coma, one he'd lapsed into almost as soon as he'd arrived at the hospital. His poor body battered and mangled, almost every bone broken or twisted. Seriously damaged, his spleen had been urgently removed. He had lost three toes.

Geraldine had been right when she had insisted the shard of glass embedded in his neck shouldn't be removed, if it had been he would've bled to death there and then amongst the rubble. At the hospital it was removed with the utmost care and his life for the moment had been saved.

Sarah had been sent for. The journey from Ireland which once would have taken three days, during war time took two long weeks. She travelled alone knowing Christie and Nial would have hindered her journey even further, the two children were happy in any case to remain with her parents. Nearly three weeks after the accident Patrick was still unconscious, not expected to survive. Dannah was with Patrick at the hospital when Sarah finally arrived. Kathy had tried to persuade her to rest for a while but Sarah would have none of it insisting that she went to Patrick immediately.

'I'm not tired' she'd said almost crossly. 'You're only tired if you are ill, old or dead and I'm none of those.' Dannah rose from his chair next to the bedside and went to Sarah, holding out his arms. Feeling his strength, his arms around her, she crumbled, sobbing as if her heart would break. Eventually she went to her son, his bandages still bloodied, the wounds even now not properly healed. She brushed back a strand of hair from his forehead, planted a tender kiss.

322

'Oh darlin' she cried in despair. 'Oh darlin'.'

Kathy left them, made her way as usual now to the general ward where Harry, deemed to be improving, had been moved. His broken bones had been set, fragments of glass removed from his face and body and the lacerations were slowly beginning to heal. Daily he pleaded to be able to see Patrick, he did so today as soon as he saw his mother.

'Sarah's with him' she told him, 'best leave it for the time being.'

On Sarah's very first night the priest was called, Patrick not expected to survive until morning. Harry was woken, begged and pleaded to be allowed to say good-bye to his friend. He was wheeled into the darkened room, sat by Patrick's side, took his hand now free of tubes, them no longer deemed to be of any help, removed out of kindness to give him some dignity in death making him look as Sarah said 'like me own darlin'.'

The sudden removal of all medical support seemed to galvanize Patrick's system, it was if in some way he'd been rejecting all help, 'he'd fight this himself'. His eye-lids fluttered, he began to mumble, the mumbling slowly turning to something discernible. He spoke to his dead father Fin but it was a wholly one-sided conversation.

'Aye I know Pa. No I won't be leavin' 'em. I'll look after 'em all I promise, din't I say so!' As the others looked on in shock, speechless, Harry squeezed his friend's hand.

'What you on about you daft so and so?' he gulped. Patrick's eyes so long closed now flickered open, a make-shift grin appeared on his poor disfigured face.

'An 'who 're you calling daft! That's rich that is!' Exhausted he fell back against his pillows. Sarah rushed to his side convinced as was everyone else that this was the last rally before death. Her tears fell on his face, his eyes flicked open again momentarily.

'Tis alright Mammie' he smiled. 'I love you.'

Sarah turned to the nurse standing close by, her question unspoken. The nurse recognized her fears, went to the now sleeping boy, checked his vital signs, knew instantly that some miracle had occurred

'Do you know what?' she smiled, turning to Sarah, squeezing her arm. 'I think this lad of yours is going to prove us all wrong.'

Harry was slowly improving physically but his mind lacked clarity, his thought processes were confused although he didn't realize it. In the early days he'd asked continually for his father insisting he'd seen him, wanted to see him again. He'd been so adamant Kathy had mentioned it to Jeremy who had dismissed it as just his mind playing tricks after the trauma he had suffered. Jeannie being party to this exchange in the hospital corridor had been secretly alarmed. Harry must have meant Jeremy when he'd said he'd seen his father, but only she knew that he'd learnt the identity of his real father. Kathy must still be unaware as if she knew surely she would have told Jeremy. Obviously no one believed Harry, thought he was just talking rubbish, his mind playing tricks so perhaps it was OK but she felt so very guilty, it was such a secret to keep. Jeannie had pondered on whether to share it with Stan, really she should be able to, she was marrying him for goodness sake. But was it fair to burden him? And would it make him think less of her?

CHAPTER FORTY THREE

Along with the eventual good news of Patrick came some good news for Jonas Hardcastle, indeed for all the residents of Oakfield. The factory being only a single storey building had not been as decimated as it would've been if there had been multiple floors. Large parts of the roof had caved in, the front and one of the long courtyard walls had also gone, but the rest was mainly fire damage and much more easily put right. It was decided that the walls could be rebuilt and a temporary roof could be arranged. It would undoubtedly be cold, definitely draughty, but as long as it could be made waterproof that was all that was required, the factory could be operational once more. The workforce would put up with virtually anything anxious to work as they were. They needed to work, needed to earn money to provide for their families. No, a new roof for Hardcastles' was a main priority. Gangs including old men and young girls worked twenty four hour shifts to clear the site under the supervision of Ralph Falconer, Dannah, Jonas and Stan.

The body of the German pilot was removed from the Stuka under cover of darkness, laid reverently on the ground and before being covered with tarpaulin Ralph emptied the man's pockets of anything which might identify him or be valuable. These he put in a brown envelope which he sealed and handed to the Reverend Price. The man in death no longer an enemy was buried out of respect for the war dead and wounded of the village to the back of the churchyard, his grave marked out of compassion should one day his family seek him out. Everyone knew that even though he had been attempting to inflict damage on them he had been a mere puppet of the cynical elite, those sitting in their palatial offices whilst sending others to their brutal deaths fighting for their high blown principles.

With the rubble cleared, the remains of the plane taken away for scrap, work began in earnest to rebuild the walls, construct the temporary roof and get at least some of the damaged machinery functioning again. Luckily the plane had more or less dive-bombed into the central courtyard, its wing and tail end had settled over the administration block. The residents of King's Terrace had been found new homes, some with relatives and others in the rooms vacated by the evacuees. Once again the people of Oakfield joined together in their troubles, their sadness, and survived.

The many alterations made to Number Two Ladan Road for Miriam proved to be a blessing in disguise once Patrick and Harry were allowed home to recuperate. The two boys shared the drawing room, a bed for each being set up in there, along with a radio, a whole library of books and anything else which might entertain them. Pearl was especially pleased to have them home and did her very best to keep them happy and entertained forever popping in and out of their room. Pearl continually attempting to emulate Lizzie had got it into her head that she would like to be part of the school choir. There were to be auditions she told Peggy the following Monday.

'Ah well that'll be nice for ya pet' smiled the cook. 'An' what is it yus gotta sing?'

'Oh we've gotta pick a song out o' t'ymn book oursens' the child replied airily.

'An' 'ave ya decided which one it's gonna be then?' Peggy enquired.

'Yeh I'm gonna sing the one about the kid what flies away.'

'The one about the kid what flies away? Which one's that love? Don't think I've heard that one' she said growing anxious.

'Oh Auntie Peg! Course you 'ave! Anyways I'm gonna sing it for Patrick and Harry to cheer 'em up, so ya can come an' listen if ya like.'

'Wild horses wouldn't keep me away' muttered Peggy under her breath.

Later that evening Pearl stood in the centre of the drawing room ready to perform. Patrick and Harry sat on the end of their beds, Peggy, Kathy, Dannah and Lizzie perched together on the sofa.

'Which hymn is it she's going to sing?' whispered Kathy to Peggy.

'She reckons the one about the 'kid 'ho flies away.' Peggy raised her eyebrows.

'The kid who flies away?' asked Kathy, 'I didn't know there was one' she said slightly incredulous. Lizzie overhearing this conversation joined in.

'There ain't!' she said simply.

'Well we shall soon see' said Kathy primly, settling herself more comfortably.

'Aye an' that's what I'm worried abaht' sighed Peggy.

Pearl cleared her throat, placed her feet firmly together.

" 'e 'ho wud valent be 'genst all disaster,

Lerr 'im in constant tea foller t'master,
They's no............"
Pearl warbled on.
"We knows we at t'end shall life inerit,
Then Francis flee awa' I'll fear not wot men say.............."
The two boys turned quickly away so as to hide their laughter, Lizzie's lips quivered, Dannah had a sudden bout of coughing. Peggy's heart turned over.

'Oh bravo, bravo' cried Kathy, clapping for all she was worth.

'Will you tell her or shall I?' she said out of the corner of her mouth to Peggy.

'Tis alright, I'll do it' answered Peggy resignedly.

CHAPTER FORTY FOUR

Word of Ralph Falconer's heroics on the night of the bombing raid and the subsequent plane crash had quickly spread and he was feted everywhere he went. The Tremmings particularly were anxious to express their gratitude for the rescue of their 'two boys'. Tommy and Samuel miraculously had suffered no more than singed hair and burns to their hands and feet along with extreme fright! John and Mavis along with the boys had gone in search of Ralph to personally thank him and invite him for a special meal. They eventually tracked him down to what had previously been a storeroom off the factory's canteen kitchen, now his makeshift office. Ralph accepted the invitation with as much enthusiasm as he could muster not being a social animal but appreciating that they needed to see that he acknowledged their gratitude. As it turned out Ralph spent a surprisingly pleasant Sunday with the family enjoying a hearty roast of beef and playing Ludo and Tiddlywinks with the boys.

Ralph's almost enthusiastic acceptance of the Tremmings' invitation was in sharp contrast to the one he gave when a similar invitation was issued by the residents of Ladan Road, who also felt they would like to express their heartfelt thanks.

Both Kathy and Dannah had been surprised that in all the weeks that Harry and Patrick lay in hospital recovering Ralph Falconer had made no request to visit them. When

Dannah had finally hinted at the possibility Ralph had replied that he couldn't stomach hospitals. He had enquired as to their progress but no more. When Dannah reported back that Ralph had turned down their invitation to a meal, Kathy was incandescent and even Dannah had felt slightly hurt and confused himself if he was being honest.

'But why?' stormed Kathy, 'I know for a fact that he's been to the Tremmings, Lizzie told me, so what's wrong with us? What have we done to the man for heaven's sake? In all the time he's been here I've never even set eyes on him, so what can I possibly have done?'

'Now calm down darlin', it's got nothing to do with you, nothing personal, how could it be!'

'But he's fine with you, you work alongside him. He's fine with the boys, it's got to be me!! I'm going to see him, sort this out once and for all.'

Privately Dannah had to agree it was all a bit odd but daren't admit it to Kathy. Ralph had insisted he didn't like hospitals, accounting for his reluctance to visit the boys in hospital, which he supposed you could accept. But why couldn't the man accept a simple invitation to a meal? Certainly there was 'nowt so queer as folk' as Peggy was so fond of saying.

Kathy was determined to seek Ralph out, make him change his mind, or at the very least explain himself, it became her mission.

The question of Pearl remained unresolved. Don and Gloria Dueringer had been traced to an army base in the United States but despite several letters from Kathy asking for clarification on what Gloria's long-term plans were for her daughter no response was forthcoming.

'Looks like we've got 'er like it or no' opined Peggy, hoping with all her heart that this was true for she loved the child so much it hurt. Kathy decided that the best thing she could do would be to have another word with Wandsworth Prescott. She doubted very much that there would be anything he could do but she couldn't think of anyone else to ask.

Davinia Prescott opened the door to Kathy's knock, a baby girl draped across her shoulder, asleep now, exhausted having brought up her last feed all over Davinia's cashmere twin set. There was the sound of another child crying in the background.

'Oh I'm so sorry' said Kathy, hastily making to turn away. 'You're obviously very busy, I'll call another time.'

'It will be Wandsworth you're wanting I assume?' asked Davinia.

'Mr. Prescott, yes. But I can see this is a bad time for him and my business isn't urgent, it will keep for another day.' Davinia grasped her arm to stop her leaving.

'Wandsworth no longer has "bad times" dear' she smiled. 'Every day is wonderful' and she jerked her head towards the sleeping infant.

'Oh yes, yes, I imagine they must be' Kathy acknowledged with a grin.

'Anyway come through' continued Davinia 'I'm sure he'll be pleased to see you.'

Wandsworth was desperately bouncing Christopher on his knee in an attempt to stem the child's squawking. Christopher however would have none of it, arching his back and flinging his arms all over the place. When he saw Kathy, Wandsworth rose to his feet.

'My dear Mrs. Watson-Smythe' he greeted her. 'How wonderful to see you.'

'Er, I rather think not' laughed Kathy. 'You look to me to be extremely busy!'

'No, no not at all' he insisted as a chubby fist hit him in the eye.

'Reginald' they heard Davinia boom. 'Reginald! Come and take your turn with your nephew, do something useful for a change.' Reginald dutifully arrived and removed Christopher from the arms of his father, the child instantly falling silent.

'Don't know what they do to you my little lad' he tutted. 'You and me we're just fine aren't we? We don't need all that crying do we.' Nothing more was heard from Christopher for the rest of Kathy's visit.

Once order had been restored Wandsworth offered his profuse apologies and then went on to ask Kathy what he could do for her. Kathy outlined the position as succinctly as she was able, reminding him of what had happened such a long time ago now and how subsequently even though Pearl's mother and step-father had been traced and she had written to them, there had been no response. Wandsworth rubbed his chin thoughtfully.

'It's certainly a mess isn't it?' he said. 'Quite outrageous when you think about it, but I fear that situations such as this will become all too common once the war is over. It's very, very sad and of course very perplexing for you. I wish I knew what to suggest.'

'The thing is I don't know where it leaves me legally' said Kathy. 'I certainly never had any intention of adopting a child. As you know I am divorced with no prospect of remarrying and to fund a child such as Pearl would be a very heavy commitment and one which I don't necessarily feel I could sustain.'

'Quite, quite, my dear. I fully understand all that you are saying' sighed Wandsworth sympathetically. 'But unfortunately at the moment I don't have any answers to your dilemma, all I can say is that I will certainly look into it for you and see what I can find out. I suppose it could be that the authorities will just put her up for adoption through the normal channels if they hear nothing further from her mother.'

'Oh but I don't think we'd really want that. We've all grown really fond of her, and I'm sure, well almost sure' – she laughed – 'that she likes us too, likes being with us.'

'I'm sure that must be the case' grinned Wandsworth, 'but her long-term future will have to be looked at eventually. She can't remain an evacuee forever, the war can't go on forever. But anyway leave it with me for the moment and try not to worry, I imagine you have plenty of other things to worry about at the moment. How are your son and his friend? Coming along nicely I hope.'

Kathy took her leave of Wandsworth feeling that at least some information regarding Pearl's future might eventually be forthcoming.

CHAPTER FORTY FIVE

Ralph Falconer swiped away another drop of rain from his papers on top of the filing cabinet. Although the temporary tarpaulin roof served its purpose most of the time, today wasn't one of them. Rain was falling heavily and the skies above Oakfield were thunderous, much like Kathy's mood. The inclement weather did nothing to side track Kathy's mission. She was going to find out once and for all exactly why Mr. Ralph Falconer persisted in his insulting refusals to have any social interaction with the residents of Ladan Road, in particular with her. If she'd taken the time to consider it properly she would have realized that it wasn't actually just her he'd seemingly chosen to ignore, but her anger at the situation had made her not quite as perceptive as she otherwise might have been.

With his 'office' nothing more than a small storeroom off what had once been the canteen kitchen and with a door ill-fitting due to the damage inflicted on the factory and therefore unable to be closed, Ralph was instantly aware of raised voices. Katherine Watson-Smythe, at her pompous best and adopting an air of unquestionable superiority, went to work on poor Edith Hobbs his secretary. She clearly was demanding to see him, 'insistent upon it' she said. Edith was equally insistent that she wouldn't, but politely said that she wasn't at all sure Mr. Falconer would be able to see her right now.

'He most certainly can and will' Kathy shrilled, pushing past Edith and towards the door she seemed to be shielding. Ralph straightened up from the filing cabinet, remained facing the wall, his back to the door. And then as the door was flung open it came.

'Mr. Falconer I have come for an explanation.......'

'Sit down please Katherine' said Ralph interrupting her, still not turning round.

'Edith' he called out, 'a good time for your break.' He waited until he heard the door closing behind his very reluctant secretary.

'........as to why you persist in trying to ignore us' continued Kathy, 'refusing all our invitations. Apart from being very irritating I also find it extremely rude. I would like to know why!' she exploded, her voice beginning to tremble with annoyance.

'Sit down Katherine' Ralph said once again but more firmly this time. Still highly agitated Kathy began to look around for somewhere to sit, found a rickety chair. And then it hit her! Not Mrs. Watson-Smythe! He'd called her "Katherine"! And the voice!

Ralph Falconer slowly turned round to face her. His hair long now and almost curly, not closely cropped as before, greying as was his full face beard. He sat down opposite her, perfectly still, looked her in the eye. Kathy's hands flew involuntarily to her face. She screwed up her eyes. My God, it couldn't be!

'Oh my God it can't be' she whispered. 'Henry?'

'Yes my dear' he said with a wry smile, 'One and the same.'

'But, but.....' Kathy stammered. 'But you're DEAD!' she screeched.

'Yes I am aren't I!' He couldn't help grinning. 'And for the moment' – he put his fingers to his lips nodding as he did so towards the door – 'I must remain so, I beg you not to ask any more questions, not now, and not here.'

'But wha....? You can't expect that surely?' she gasped. 'I don't know what's happened, what's going on? I feel as if I'm dreaming and I'll wake up, I just don't understand.....' her voice faded away.

Across the wooden packing case which served as a desk he reached for her hand, rubbed his thumb slowly over her knuckle the way he always used to do.

'I see you still wear your wedding ring' he said almost tenderly.

'Why yes, yes of course' she stuttered. 'Why wouldn't I?' Henry's mood suddenly changed.

'I need you to trust me Katherine' he said stiffly. 'Allow me to explain to you in my own way, in my own time. Anything else could make things extremely awkward for me.'

'Awkward? How awkward?' persisted Kathy. 'You haven't done anything awful have you? You're not in any kind of trouble are you?' she asked, her voice beginning to rise again. He had to laugh.

'Trouble? Does that sound like me Katherine? Didn't you always say what a plodding old bore I was!'

'Did I?' she sighed.

'You did!' He nodded his head, smiling.

'Then I'm sorry' she whispered, 'Very, very sorry.'

'No need to be' he shrugged, 'You were probably right, I am what I think is euphemistically known as a "boring old sod"!' He laughed. 'But please, if you'll just give me time to think things through. This wasn't supposed to happen, my cover shouldn't have been blown, I will tell you everything I promise.'

'But when? You can't expect to leave me like this. Cover? What do you mean your cover shouldn't have been blown? It's quite the most extraordinary thing I've ever heard.'

'I know, I'm sure it must be' he said softly, sympathetically, taking her hand once more. 'But it certainly must be away from here and away from anyone else. You must tell no one else what you have discovered. My future depends on it Katherine, it could be extremely dangerous for me.'

'Dangerous! Dangerous!' Her voice went up a notch once more. 'In what way dangerous? I just don't understand.'

'Of course you don't, how could you? But you will eventually I give you my word.'

'Well when? When am I going to hear the preposterous story, learn what has been going on?' He leaned closer.

'Is there anywhere we could meet? Out of sight of prying eyes and sensitive ears.'

Kathy could think of only one place, the Haven. Over the years through all her troubles it had almost become her very own confessional, there could be nowhere else.

'Well I often take a walk to a place called the Haven. I go there when I want some peace and quiet, time to think. There's a bench there......'

'I know' he interrupted her. 'I've seen you often.'

'You have! But how? When?' He grinned.

'Shall we leave that too for another day?' How could he tell her of the hurt in his heart every single time he'd seen her?

'Yes alright' Kathy agreed reluctantly, 'but I can't wait forever for an explanation, it will drive me mad, it already is!' Ralph looked up to the make-shift roof, the rain still hammering on to the canvas.

'Obviously not today' he said. 'What about tomorrow, during the day? About two o'clock? Everyone else should be busy at that time.'

Although unwilling to end the interview without any explanations forthcoming Kathy knew of old that Henry would not be persuaded otherwise once he'd made up his mind. Caution was Henry's middle name, he would need time to consider everything very carefully.

'Well alright then, tomorrow at two at the Haven' she agreed reluctantly. Kathy got to her feet finding herself somewhat giddy. From the doorway she called a curt 'Goodbye, thank you for your time' over her shoulder, one designed to indicate to the returning Edith Hobbs that the meeting had been a business meeting and no more. Henry could but admire her quick thinking, so typical of Katherine, so clever.

'Goodbye Mrs. Watson-Smythe' he called in reply, 'I'm so sorry not to have been able to help you.'

'Good day to you' said Kathy frostily as she passed through the kitchen, reaching for her umbrella which Edith had thoughtfully placed in one of the sinks.

Kathy walked home in a daze, the more distance she put between herself and Henry the more ridiculous it all sounded, there must be some mistake, it was all just too incredible. But it WAS Henry! Very changed admittedly, but there was one unalterable feature, you couldn't change a person's eyes. They were very definitely Henry's eyes.

As she hurried home in the still pouring rain her thoughts swung crazily one way and then the other. She looked up from under her brolly as she passed the drawing room window of Ladan Road, saw the two boys in the bay playing cards. They both waved to her, both! Even Harry! She waved back as if everything were normal, as if her world hadn't just been turned upside down!

Impatient for the meeting with Henry to come Kathy busied herself for the rest of the day and then feigning a headache took herself off early to bed. After a restless night imagining every possible scenario as to why Henry might have to "die" and then reappear as someone else, she woke with a start, saw through the gap she always left in her curtains the grey skies of yesterday. She slipped out of bed, went to the window pulling back the heavy drapes. Across at the station Joe Parker was already busy sweeping the puddles from the yard, fighting a losing battle. Once the cracks and crevices had been swept and as much of the rain as possible removed from them he would painstakingly fill each one with ash taken from the waiting room boiler in an effort to even out the yard and prevent anyone tripping. Unfortunately it would be a thankless task, a deluge such as this rendering his hard work useless, merely turning what concrete remained into an alarming kaleidoscope of pinks and purples.

Kathy rested her arms along the length of the sill and pressing her forehead on to the window pane looked up at the leaden skies. If the weather continued like this there would be precious chance of her meeting with Henry. There was no let-up in the rain, if anything it got worse and by lunch-time she knew there would be no meeting that day.

Peggy noticed her fractious mood as she always seemed to these days and suggested that if she had nothing else to do perhaps she could sort through the old tea chest which housed old curtains, bedding and unwanted clothes.

'Some pr'aps need chucking out' she said 'but some might do for Mrs. 'ardcastle, she's 'aving another one of 'er sales for the 'omeless so I 'ear.'

The next morning brought more rain but there were at least some hopeful breaks in the cloud. At five minutes to two Kathy decided that there was a possibility Henry might risk the weather. No doubt he wanted this over and done with just as much as she did. She donned her hooded raincoat, put on her boots and called out to whoever might be listening that she was 'just out for a breather.'

CHAPTER FORTY SIX

Ralph had been grateful for the bad weather, offering as it did a temporary reprieve, knowing Kathy couldn't expect him to turn up on such a day. Whilst half suspecting one day it might happen he'd done everything in his power to ensure that neither Kathy nor Harry ever came across him. True on the night of the factory fire when he had gone to Harry's assistance the boy had looked at him as if he'd recognized him, even called him 'father', but being in the state he was he must have simply assumed it was his mind playing tricks and forgotten about it. Ralph pondered long and hard over what to do, but he knew he had no choice other than to meet Kathy. He had contemplated bringing forward his departure from Oakfield to avoid the confrontation but realized that even if he was able to do so Kathy would somehow seek out explanations and if he wasn't around to give them she would stir up a real hornets' nest in her quest for the truth. There was no way that she could be told the truth, if she were many months of planning, in fact his whole future, would be put in jeopardy. He realized he had already frightened her and was convinced that the only way to keep her quiet, stop her asking questions, demanding answers, was to frighten her some more and possibly.............?

Kathy was eagerly anticipating her meeting with Henry, expecting explanations but Henry knew she wouldn't be getting any. She assumed that he would try to be there at the same time the following day but when she arrived at the Haven there was no sign of him. She sat down on the bench tucking her raincoat beneath her, the bench was understandably sodden, the old rotting wood having soaked up any rain.

Suddenly a watery sun dared to break through and a pale shadow was thrown across the gravel path in front of her. She turned round, looked up.

'Good afternoon Katherine,' smiled Henry. The old Henry would have raised his hat but there was no hat, "Ralph Falconer" didn't favour hats. Kathy realized that he must have been following her, been close behind.

'I didn't see you,' she said 'and yet you must have followed me?'

'Yes,' he replied. 'I often have.'

'You often have?' she asked incredulously. 'But why?'

'Because I wanted to see you' he answered quietly.

Kathy patted the bench next to her, it scarcely moved as it took his weight, his frame so spare now compared to how he had once been, Henry having grown corpulent after many years of lavish entertaining in Bombay.

'It's very different here isn't it Katherine?' he mused. 'Very different to what we were used to. Have you managed to settle? Has Harry?'

'Oh well...... you know. It was all very difficult' she sighed. 'I arrived back in England to find Miriam seriously ill. She has since died' she added choking back the tears. He reached out for her hand.

'I am so sorry.' She vaguely noted he wasn't surprised.

'At least we did finally get to spend some time together. She wasn't in the best of health, but at least we were together again and able to make up for some of the time we'd lost. She was about to marry you know, she died on the morning of her wedding.'

'I know.' He shook his head sadly. 'Such a tragedy.'

'You knew? But how?'

'Dannah Delaney' he said. 'Dannah told me.'

'Ah, so Dannah has spoken to you about us has he?' She sounded not altogether pleased.

'Only with encouragement from me' insisted Henry. 'I couldn't resist finding out what you and Harry were up to, I wanted to know that you were both well and happy.'

'You cared how we were?'

'Of course, how could I not? You both meant the world to me, you still do.'

Kathy was shocked at what she was hearing. Henry had temporarily succeeded in making her forget the purpose of their meeting.

'Well maybe then you won't be surprised to hear that it's all been quite hellish' she said. 'I also arrived here to find that no one knew I existed, no one knew that Miriam even had a sister, my father had very successfully expunged me from the family. And then on top of that I discovered that Miriam had serious financial difficulties which she'd chosen to ignore.'

'Oh my poor Katherine I am so sorry, that must have been absolutely terrible for you. But now? Everything's alright now?'

'Oh yes, it is now, but it took some time I can tell you, with Miriam unable to vouch for me they all took a lot of convincing.'

'Your father was indeed very cruel wasn't he?' mused Henry. 'Being sent to the other side of the world for some minor misdemeanour, at least I understood it was minor, seemed harsh in the extreme.' Kathy immediately caught his drift.

'Oh it was' she said quickly, 'minor I mean. I truly had no idea when I left England that I was pregnant. I was removed simply as I told you at the time because I had gone behind his back over my chosen career. God only knows where he would've sent me if he'd known I was pregnant! It doesn't bear thinking about!' she shuddered.

'Oh well, that's all in the past,' said Henry patting her hand. 'All in the past and best left there. But what about now? What are you up to now? I heard that you'd intended to marry?'

'Hmm, that's right' she sighed 'but we both decided it wouldn't be right for us. He's gone on to marry someone else anyway, so I can hardly have been the love of his life can I?' she laughed wanly.

'Oh my dear Katherine, you mustn't say that, I always found you infinitely loveable.'

Her sad sorry tale told him without any shadow of a doubt how much she had changed, how she'd had to change.

Although strangely enjoying what she was hearing, enjoying his flattery, Kathy was conscious that as yet they were no nearer an explanation as to why Henry had suddenly and mysteriously come back to life.

'And Harry?' he said quickly 'tell me about Harry.'

'Oh well I don't know how much you know, how much Dannah has told you. He wanted to become a vet you know, but well.... he failed his exams and somehow he seems to inexplicably blame me. He can barely bring himself to speak to me at times. I've tried putting it down to teenage temperament but really I'm not sure, it's as if he's got a permanent chip on his shoulder. If I'm honest I really don't know what to do about Harry. I did have to tell him that I couldn't afford to fund another year of study along with the actual degree and of course he didn't take kindly to that but....'

'But surely?' Henry interrupted feeling slightly uncomfortable. 'The money you 'inherited' from me would've paid for all that?'

'Well yes of course but how could Harry know about that when he doesn't know you're dead?' Henry turned to her in astonishment.

'Harry doesn't know I'm dead? You didn't tell him, but why?' Kathy had no desire to get into explanations over Jeremy and his proposal of marriage forever linked in her mind to him then feeling obliged to pay for Harry's education.

'Because..... because I couldn't bear to tell him, I thought he'd been hurt enough.'

'You're telling me that you imagined Harry would care whether I was alive or dead?' Henry asked, stunned. Kathy gazing into the far distance had no hesitation.

'Oh yes, I realized in the end that he would care very much. Oh there were issues when you first sent him back to England. He had thought you'd ill-treated him, treated him badly but I think he slowly came to accept that it was simply the way you'd been brought up, the disciplinarian in you.' Whatever else he might be Henry was an honest man, honest especially with himself.

'I think we both know don't we Katherine that that wasn't the way it was? Once I knew categorically that Harry wasn't my son I couldn't cope, I did find myself treating the boy differently and yes for my sins with a certain degree of if not cruelty then callousness, the guilt for which I shall carry deservedly for the rest of my life.'

'Oh' sighed Kathy. 'I had treated you so badly, it was just a pity that you had to use Harry to hurt me.'

'It didn't take long believe me to realize what a huge mistake I'd made in sending first you away and then Harry. I soon realized how much I loved you both in spite of everything.' Kathy turned to look at him unable to believe what she was hearing.

'You loved me?' she whispered 'in spite of what I'd done, you loved me?'

'Oh yes my darling – and I still do.'

Henry suddenly reached for her, took a very puzzled Kathy in his arms. She knew she should pull away but somehow didn't.

'I don't understand? I thought you hated me, you wanted rid of me and even I could understand why. What's changed?'

'Nothing has changed for me that's the point. As soon as I saw you, even in the distance, I knew how much I still loved you. Surely my "in the event of my demise" letter told you that I'd forgiven you?'

'Well yes....' she stammered 'but I must admit I found it rather strange. You'd been so cruel and you had gone through with the divorce after all.'

'I know, I know' he said sadly shaking his head, 'and how I regretted that. Regretted it every single day.'

'Really?' she asked, amazed.

'Never regretted anything more' he whispered.

Kathy had no idea why she was feeling susceptible to Henry's protestations of lasting affection, after all theirs had never been what could be termed a 'love match'. Certainly and to her shame not on her side. Perhaps he was just catching her at a time when her need was so great. She needed some reassurance that she was worthy of someone's affection, the business with Jeremy had left her feeling very vulnerable

Kathy wanted to be loved. She was so lonely, everyone around her seemed to have happy relationships of one sort or another and yet even her own son seemed to dislike her.

'So what now?' asked Kathy through sudden tears, frantically wiping them away as fast as they came. He laid his arm across her shoulders pulling her close to him again and she found she didn't mind. It had been a long, long time since Kathy had felt loved and she enjoyed the feeling.

'Ah well my darling' he said, 'as far as you and I are concerned that is up to you, only you can decide that. My dearest wish would be that we could become what we once were to one another. I know that would take time and much hard work on my part, but my darling Katherine you must believe me, I never ever stopped loving you.'

Still unable to quite take in what he was saying and even less her reaction to it she was nonetheless acutely aware that she still had no answers to what he was doing in Oakfield and under an assumed name.

'But Henry you still haven't explained what you're doing here, and you say you could be in danger? I don't understand, you're going to have to tell me what's going on.'

'I'm afraid the telling of that is not quite so simple' he answered grimly, 'and in order not to also put you in danger by relating the tale I must ask you for a little more time. I will tell you everything my love – all in good time. And when it is safe' he added.

'Safe? So you really are in danger? But how, why? I need to know. How can I rest now you've told me what you have?'

'Not in danger right now but I could be if my new identity is compromised. My whole future could be put in jeopardy, and that of others. Katherine for the moment you must simply trust me. You know I hope that I would do nothing to hurt you and it is safest believe me that you know as little as possible. For me I am just so happy to have found you again just when I need you the most, and to find also that you might still have a little bit of regard for me if not affection' he grinned ruefully. 'I know I have no right whatsoever to expect that.'

'Oh Henry we have both in our own ways treated one another very badly and I think we might be better just to accept that and move on if we can.'

'As long as that means we can see each other again then yes my dear Katherine, I could wish for nothing more.'

They arranged to meet again, wanted to meet again as soon as possible. Henry had to tell her though that as the factory was to be subjected to a governmental inspection over the next few days their meeting would have to be delayed until the following weekend. It would mean all hands to the pumps he said and he wanted it all out of the way so that he could concentrate all his energies on her. He had missed her so much he said, never ever stopped loving her. They had both parted reluctantly.

'You really must go my darling, it's getting dark and they'll be sending out a search party.'

'I know, I know' she sighed. He turned away to hide the curl of his lip.

The next week was the longest Kathy could remember, thoughts of Henry going round and round in her head. She listened more carefully now when Dannah related events from the factory waiting for mention of "Ralph", hoping that the inspection was going well, he'd told her how important it was – 'Dear Henry'. Unfortunately for her Dannah had returned to his old ways of being a man of few words. In the early days he had been so quiet, barely opening his mouth unless asked to. Peggy had frequently traduced him saying that it was like a book never being opened.

'We've all bin made different for a reason an' if we aren't prepared to show oursens then the good Lord 'as wasted 'is time jus' like a writer whose book's never opened.'

Dannah strangely never once mentioned the inspection, clearly thought Kathy that must be top secret too.

CHAPTER FORTY SEVEN

Kathy met Henry the following weekend with a new determination, looking forward to getting some answers. She had returned to earth with a bump the day following their last meeting wondering just how she had allowed herself to be fobbed off over something so important. After all it wasn't as though he was simply telling her he'd lost a set of keys for God's sake – he'd died!!! And then been reincarnated as Ralph Falconer!! She was annoyed and frustrated with herself for not being more insistent. This time she WOULD get the truth but for the moment he had sworn her to absolute secrecy. It was imperative he'd told her that she behaved exactly as she had before, she must not give him away, it could be dangerous for them both. Having frightened her Henry had then quite cleverly sweetened the pill. Refusing to be drawn over his mysterious re-birth he had managed to persuade Kathy that alongside their new found joy in each other the mystery surrounding him was of little consequence, what really mattered was the two of them, everything else could wait. Whilst knowing that this was completely ridiculous Kathy had been prepared to accept almost anything just to have someone seem to care about her, even if it was Henry. He had promised that he would tell her everything, he just needed a little time. It was safer for the moment that she knew nothing he'd said because no one else must find out the truth. Completely mystified Kathy had felt she had no other option than to agree.

Henry had arrived before her this time. He said he'd been 'unable to wait a moment longer'. Immediately taking her hand he suggested they took a walk, strolling along the embankment like any normal couple. Kathy enquired as to how the inspection had gone.

'Insp..?' He hesitated. 'Very well thank you, extremely well, better than we could even have anticipated.' With that out of the way she felt able to pursue her own agenda.

'Henry' she smiled, 'you did promise you were going to tell me what has been going on. This can't be kept a secret from me forever.'

'I know I promised my love but I've turned this over and over in my head Katherine and I'm afraid it must, certainly until the war is over.'

'But Harry, surely Harry?' she persisted. 'He's never supposed you to be 'dead' anyway.' Henry stopped walking.

'This has nothing to do with you, me or Harry' he answered firmly. 'This is to do with the war.'

'But surely you can – must – at least tell me' she cried. 'If I don't know the truth it is all very difficult for me.'

'EVERYTHING has to be kept secret Katherine! No one must know anything other than that I am Ralph Falconer.'

'But........'

'There can be no 'buts' Katherine. And in any case' he added quietly 'I shall soon be gone.'

'Gone? Gone, but gone where?' she shrieked. 'Where is it that you're going? You've only just turned up again, from the DEAD!' she added theatrically 'and now you say you'll soon be going! I thought you were telling me we might have a future together again.'

'I know' he said sadly 'and I sincerely hope that one day we will, but it won't be now and it won't be here.' A couple walking the other way stopped to let them pass on the narrow track. Henry nodded his head in acknowledgement to thank them. Once the other couple were on their way and out of ear-shot..

'But why will you be gone? Where is it that you're going?' she asked again. 'You can't be! Just when we've found each other again.' Even to her the 'again' didn't quite ring true. There had never been a grand passion between them in the past, never that special frisson of excitement between them, at best just a certain contentment and comfort. Now she was close to committing herself to him on what basis? Could she really believe that he had always harboured these feelings for her? The very fact that he'd reneged on his promise to tell her everything, or at least part of it, left her feeling uneasy.

'Sadly Katherine I can' he almost whispered, catching hold of her hand as he did so. 'I have no choice. I have my duty to do. If I were to walk away now it could impact on a great many other people and I could be looked upon as a coward and you know me well enough to understand that I could never allow that to happen.'

'Not even for me? Not even for the future you're telling me we might have?'

'Not even for you' he replied tenderly, 'not even for you. My purpose here was simply to establish a new identity and my superiors have decided that I have had sufficient time to do that.' He grimaced. 'And hopefully other than with you I have succeeded.' His mind recalled the hours he had spent in the pub with Dannah, the hours fishing with him, practising, practising until he was word perfect, his past persona just that, a thing of the past. Kathy lowered her voice.

'But when then? When will you have to go? This war is so wretched our lives are being ruined, they are no longer our own!'

'Our lives during war time belong to the person to the right of us, the left of us, to the front, behind' he said. 'Our lives belong to each other my dear, fighting this danger together until FINALLY – and we MUST – we win.' This was the mantra Henry preached to himself every single day.

Kathy knew she would get no further with her cross-examination of Henry.

He asked could they just spend a little time together being 'normal', that was what he needed more than anything. In her new found fondness for him she could do nothing other than agree and they spent a pleasant hour talking for once of what their future might be instead of their past. They parted having arranged to meet the following Saturday afternoon. It couldn't be the morning he'd told her because that was when he did his shopping. He frequented the market he said to avoid the intimacy of shops, people at the market were less inclined to want to chat, less inclined therefore to learn your business.

'Although' he added ruefully, 'that was where Ying almost caught me out.'

'Ying?' gasped Kathy. 'How did you know she was here? And how do you mean she almost caught you out? I don't understand.' Henry decided that there could be no harm in at least relating this tale.

'Oh I was doing my usual shop one Saturday morning, buying a few bits and pieces when this mangy dog decided to nip my ankle. I was so surprised that I unfortunately committed the ultimate sin and objected loudly and kicked the thing away, needless to say drawing attention to myself. And you know how the English are about their pets!' He laughed. 'You'd think it was the other way round and I'd bitten the dog!! Anyway amongst the crowd which had gathered to express their disapproval of me I noticed this dark haired, foreign looking person who seemed particularly interested in what was going on. In all honesty at first I barely recognized her, she was so... what shall I say.... chic?, fashionable hairstyle, fashionable 'un Ying' like clothes. It was sometime later when I became aware she was following me and I realized incredibly that it was indeed Ying. I just never dreamt after I'd dispatched her from our home that she would find her way to you here in England. But I can't imagine why not' – he shook his head – 'she was devoted to you, adored you.'

'Not altogether' interjected Kathy. 'Ying didn't always admire me as you seem to think.'

'No?'

'No' she reiterated firmly, 'most definitely not. And now?' she went on, 'has she stopped following you, stopped looking?'

'I believe so yes, certainly I haven't been aware of it now for quite some time. She's walked past me a few times since and seemed to show no special interest.'

'Well that must be a relief then' said Kathy 'Under the circumstances.'

Ying had in fact ceased paying any particular attention to 'Henry' after accidently overhearing Kathy reveal to Dannah that Henry had died. She had been relieved beyond measure to learn that Henry was dead, that her fears Henry had followed Katherine to England to cause trouble had been unfounded, that she had been mistaken when she had thought she had recognized him at the market.

Kathy enjoying the closeness that she and Henry suddenly seemed to have between them was finding the 'whys and wherefores' of the situation beginning to matter less. They parted once more looking forward eagerly to their next meeting.

CHAPTER FORTY EIGHT

The following Thursday evening over dinner Dannah had some news. Ralph Falconer had gone and he had been put in charge of the factory.

'What!' Kathy couldn't help herself, was on her feet at once seemingly outraged. Dannah was a little put out, a trifle insulted that she obviously had so little confidence in him, patently regarded him as incapable of managing the factory. He looked down at his plate clearly embarrassed and annoyed.

'I'm quite capable' he said indignantly. Kathy was instantly contrite, realizing that her concern had been misconstrued. It had absolutely nothing to do with Dannah's capabilities but the abrupt departure of Henry without so much as a word. She was anxious to repair the damage between them without revealing the true nature of her worries.

'Oh Dannah no, no I didn't mean I was for one minute doubting your expertise, how could I?' she tried rapidly to back track. 'No I meant what a cheek to suddenly drop it on you like that. The nerve of these people – REALLY !' Dannah, slightly mollified said, it was 'fine', he'd handle it, they all had to accept all sorts these days, these were strange times. Everyone around the dinner table nodded in agreement. Kathy took herself off to her room, she had correspondence to deal with she said. Everything was so confusing she no longer felt she could make sense of anything. The mystery over Henry had still not been explained and now it seemed even less likely to be. And his sudden disappearance! Where had he gone? And most importantly why hadn't he told her? She assumed that he must have been ordered away at short notice unable to get a message to her without arousing suspicion. But what now? Supposedly he would get a message to her somehow.

With Henry's reappearance Kathy had begun to think that perhaps Harry now need never know what had transpired, Henry's supposed 'death', nor of her sudden wealth. She had lately imagined that one day it could simply be revealed that she and Henry had become reconciled and they all might be able to pick up the pieces and move on. However she acknowledged that to be naive in the extreme. Life, as had been shown to her time and time again, was no fairy tale. It would seem too that Harry need never know the truth about Jeremy. Jeremy had returned with Geraldine to the front, may or may not eventually return to Oakfield. Certainly he seemed to have turned his back on any notion of Harry being told the true identity of his father. It seemed fortuitous now to Kathy that she had chosen to keep these secrets to herself.

As far as Harry was concerned his brush with death had made him view things in an entirely different light. Although remaining surly and at times uncooperative he didn't seem to have the same appetite for arguments, for which his poor mother was truly grateful,

Henry's incredible and dramatic reappearance had a profound impact upon Kathy. She had a new found confidence, was happier and more decisive. She'd decided that she would suggest to Harry that when he was sufficiently recovered he should try again to pass the exams he needed to get into Veterinary College. She was acutely aware that she had been unreasonable, vindictive, and what's more – and probably worse – like her own father!

Unfortunately the latest development, Henry's sudden and unexplained disappearance, left her once again feeling vulnerable and ill-used. But she told herself she must get on with things until he returned or at least contacted her.

Henry's tale of when Ying had come close to recognizing him at the market had puzzled Kathy. Once upon a time Kathy had been Ying's closest confidant, Ying would have told her anything, particularly anything which troubled her. Kathy decided she would attempt to get Ying to confide in her, tease out of her what had been going on in her mind – if indeed anything had – over Henry. She suggested a companionable stroll to the market one Saturday morning in the hope that it might remind Ying of her earlier suspicions. After all Henry had said the woman had followed him and she wouldn't have done that without good cause. However once having overheard the conversation about Henry's "death" Ying had erased it from her mind, not given it another thought. Why would she? The only thing which had puzzled her was why Miss Kathy had clearly told no one other than Dannah of Henry's demise, but she was sure there must be a good reason, Miss Kathy always had good reasons.

Kathy soon realized Ying was not overly enthusiastic about their proposed shopping expedition to the market. She was surprised but soon found out why. Ying even with Kathy alongside her was intent on a flirtatious exchange with the fishmonger in the corner of the market. Her eyes sparkled, her chic jet black bob was continually patted and pushed back to reveal her sultry stunning eyes framed by long luscious lashes. In the end Kathy deduced that Ying had nothing to tell her and, feeling like a gooseberry, said she would make her way home.

Kathy's decision regarding Harry and his future had originally been made when she had felt better, more optimistic. Now with so many uncertainties again she could seriously have had second thoughts but knew she mustn't, mustn't punish anyone else because of her own dissatisfaction.

Kathy expected to find Harry alone in the drawing room, Patrick having been pushed out in his wheelchair for a breath of fresh air by Dannah. She tapped on the door, popped her head round.

'Harry?'

Harry looked up from his book, didn't smile, it still didn't come naturally to be nice to her. He couldn't forget what she'd done and she was still perpetuating the lie. He merely raised his eyebrows.

'Yes?'

'I wondered if I might have a word?'

'Of course' he said with exaggerated formality laying his book on the table beside him. Kathy settled herself on the sofa.

'You're looking well darling, much more your old self, and your walking's coming on a treat don't you think?' For God's sake thought Harry to himself she surely hasn't just come for an update on my condition! Mercifully she quickly changed tack.

'I'm wondering if perhaps now you're showing such improvement we should give some thought to the future and what you might like to do.' Harry tossed his head impatiently, looked away from her.

'You know perfectly well what I want to do' he replied coldly. 'But you tell me it's out of the question financially. We can't afford it!' Knowing what he knew he couldn't resist the insinuation. Kathy was totally ignorant of his implied criticism.

'Well I've been working things out, doing a few sums and I think if that is really still what you want to do, then you must. We'll make ourselves afford it.' Harry privately remained cynical but knew if he were to achieve his objective he must hide his true feelings. With difficulty he rearranged his face into what could be termed an appreciative smile.

'Really?' he gushed. 'That would be excellent.'

Kathy, totally unaware of his true feelings, the sarcasm behind his words, was overwhelmed with a great sense of relief, relieved that at long last the troubles between them might be over. At the end of their conversation she went to him, playfully ruffled his hair.

'I give you my word I will make it happen' she smiled. Kathy closed the door quietly behind her but then popped her head round at the last minute and gave a little smile and a wave.

'Oh for God's sake!' Harry muttered under his breath as the door finally closed on his mother. Kathy had suggested that one of his old college tutors might be engaged to assist him in revising for the examinations. As if he needed a tutor!! There was no way he would fail. He needed to be away, he was determined to be away – he wouldn't fail again!

'You'll never guess what' said Harry pushing a piece of game pie into his mouth as he shared his evening meal with

Patrick. Since returning from hospital the two boys had been given the special dispensation of taking their meals in the drawing room, temporarily their private living quarters.

'My mother' he continued with a twisted smile, 'has decided that I am to be allowed to continue with my studies after all.' Patrick raised an eyebrow.

'Yes indeed' Harry said sarcastically. 'Apparently we can now afford it!' Patrick, having thought that Harry's hostilities with his mother had become less acrimonious, was surprised to hear his unpleasant tone.

'But well then surely that's for the good isn't it? What ya wanted?' Suddenly something in Harry burst – he'd had enough! He leaned forward over the table.

'The thing is we've always been able to afford it.......' He paused for effect. 'Ever since my father died!' Patrick was beginning to lose patience with Harry.

'What on earth do ya mean, since yer father died? When did 'e die?' Harry leant back in his chair adopting a nonchalant air.

'Oh ages ago' he said dismissively, waving his hand in the air as if it was of no consequence.

'Ages ago?' asked the other boy, 'but ya never said, why's nobody mentioned it?'

'It has not been 'mentioned' as you put it because my mother for her own mysterious reasons chose not to tell anyone.'

'So why now then?' queried Patrick. 'Why 'as she decided to tell everyone now?'

'Oh she hasn't' Harry curled his lip. 'I only know because I found a letter from my father's solicitor which she'd hidden away. She's known for months that he was dead, pleading poverty when all along she has been left a merry, very merry widow!'

'But that's plain daft, why would she do that?' puzzled Patrick.

'Well who knows what goes on in my mother's poor addled brain?' sneered Harry. 'But it certainly provided her with an excuse to prevent me following my ambitions.'

Patrick although a loyal friend – perhaps because he was a loyal friend – was nothing if not fair.

'Aw come on Harry, that ain't fair, it was you who messed up the exams remember not yer Mammie.' Harry bristled.

'Well with what I'd discovered going round and round in my head what do you expect? It wasn't the easiest thing in the world to be able to concentrate.'

'Aye well I'll accept that. What an awful thing to happen, I'm real sorry that I am, and for yer Mammie not to tell ya.' Patrick shook his head sadly. 'But why on earth didn't you tell 'er ya knew, surely that would've straightened things out a darned sight sooner than this!' Harry knew that he couldn't take that extra step and reveal what else he'd discovered. Not yet!

'Because how could I? She'd realize then that I've known for ages about her lying, and besides I'd end up looking as bad as her, snooping about, reading her private letters.' Patrick turned to the window.

'What a mess' he said, 'what a bloody mess.' Further discussion was interrupted by a tap on the door announcing Peggy's arrival to collect the pots, closely followed by Gail who had come to visit Patrick. Harry was quick to make himself scarce, he couldn't bear to witness the sickly sweet exchanges which would pass between the love-struck pair.

Reaching for his crutches he hobbled to the door saying he would be in the dining room across the hall revising.

CHAPTER FORTY NINE

Patrick had long ago learned that much as he liked him Harry could at times be his own worst enemy. Look at the time when he'd run away for goodness sake, what had that been about? All over nothing in the end, he'd just got the wrong end of the stick. After mulling it over Patrick had decided that in all probability this was just another of those occasions, but he felt the need to confide in someone, after all if it was all true it was one 'helluva' secret. There could only be one person, his Uncle Dannah.

Dannah had got it into his head that although Patrick was healing physically, albeit it slowly, he needed to be out and about more. Dannah had great faith in the healing properties of simple fresh air, and so whenever he could be spared from the factory he would settle the boy in his wheelchair and push him out. The fishing grounds were a particular favourite. Patrick had always been a keen fisherman and it required no particular attributes other than being able to sit a long time in comparative silence. Patrick was good at this, one thing he must at least have inherited from Dannah. His father Fin had as a boy been described as a 'chatter box' and as an adult 'gregarious'.

One particular day with the sun making a rare but welcome appearance Dannah suggested they make the most of the opportunity and go fishing. He carefully arranged Patrick in the chair and set off, pushing hard along the often muddy and deeply rutted tracks to the fishing grounds some distance away. Patrick was transferred with some difficulty to a folding green canvas chair, a rug tucked around his knees. Whilst Dannah erected the obligatory umbrella behind him Patrick examined the contents of the rucksack. Peggy was notoriously generous with her 'packing up' and Patrick was not disappointed, just the sight of her homemade pasties made his mouth water and his tummy go into free-fall.

With everything finally arranged for Patrick's comfort and with the rod safely in his hands Dannah lay on his side in the long grass resting on his elbow. He watched silently as a water vole popped it's head above the bank and then surprised to see them took fright and slithered back down the muddy slope and plopped into the water.

'Uncle Dannah' Patrick dropped into the silence. 'Can I talk to you about something, something's bothering me.' Dannah had been fearing this, waiting for this since Gail Dearing had appeared on the scene. He'd assumed, or rather he had wanted to assume, that Sarah would've had a 'chat' with Patrick about the 'birds and the bees' but he'd never been quite sure. The boy could be a bit immature, a bit naive at times, and so in spite of his growing misgivings over Harry – who always seemed to have something to whinge about – Dannah was actually relieved when Patrick revealed that it was Harry who was troubling him.

'It's Harry, I'm real worried about Harry.'

'Why, what's the matter now?'

'It's 'is Da.'

'His Da?' asked Dannah, suddenly interested.

'He reckons 'e's dead.'

'Oh, an' 'ow's he come by that information?'

'Apparently he found a letter from some solicitors in India telling his Mammie that 'is Da 'ad died.'

'And does anyone else know this? Has he mentioned it to anyone other than you?' It suddenly dawned on Patrick that his Uncle didn't seem surprised at the news, he was being very calm, very matter of fact about it. He screwed up his eyes.

'You knew didn't you? I can tell you did!' Dannah decided there had been enough lying.

'Yes I did' he admitted. 'Harry's mother told me only recently.' Patrick was dumbfounded, he'd almost convinced himself that it was all a 'flight of fancy' on Harry's part.

'But why did she tell you and not Harry?' he wanted to know. Dannah sat up, plucked a blade of grass, automatically split it to make a whistle, a habit from childhood still not lost.

'Well he's a nice enough lad but we all know he can be a bit highly strung don't we and she apparently decided it would upset him too much, disrupt his exams.'

'Well it certainly did that anyway!' scoffed Patrick. 'He couldn't 'ave made a bigger mess of it if he'd tried!'

'No pr'aps not' grimaced Dannah.

'The thing is' continued Patrick, 'she's kept on lying to him, not telling him about 'is Da and telling him she couldn't afford for him to go to do 'is studies. He knows his Da left 'er bags o' money!'

'Well I don't have the answers to most of that' sighed Dannah. 'When she told me I said Harry should know but she disagreed. Anyway what does Harry intend to do about it?'

'That's the thing. Apparently the other day out of the blue his Mammie told him she would find the money so that he could go away after all. She didn't tell him how of course, just that she would. Harry is steaming, furious that she's still lying to him.'

'Hmm' said Dannah, gently blowing through the grass whistle. 'So is he going to tell her now that he knows?'

'Don't think so' he shrugged. 'Harry just sez he wants out of it, wants to be out of 'ere as quick as 'e can.' In truth Dannah couldn't help but share Harry's sentiments.

The one certainty after the accident was that neither Patrick nor Harry would be conscripted when the time came. Patrick it was predicted would have a permanently weakened arm, fortunately it was his left one, and a pronounced and painful limp at the very least. Harry might just pass muster if they were desperate but could never be classed as A1. The shard of glass from the clock face which had embedded itself in Patrick's neck had left a deep scar, mercifully only seen by Patrick himself with great difficulty, but which served as a constant reminder to Dannah as it did today, of how close they had come to losing this precious child of Fin and Sarah. He would remain eternally grateful, they all would, to Geraldine Kirk for her quick thinking and prompt action that night. Without her there would have been no fishing trips.

With more time on his hands than he knew what to do with Patrick found himself constantly musing over Harry's woes. Harry hadn't seemed to particularly like his father, had even run away thinking he was to be sent back to him in India. It must have upset him to find out he'd died, but HE'D lost a Da he had adored and he'd had to get on with it. The difference he supposed was that unlike Harry he had good male role models in his life. Uncle Dannah, Grandda'

O'Keefe his Mammie's Da, and her brothers Sean and Liam, all of them strong but compassionate men. He was sure that was Harry's problem and was why he always ended up feeling sorry for him.

CHAPTER FIFTY

Jeannie Kirk, shortly to marry, had at first insisted that she 'wouldn't dream' of walking down the aisle without her brother-in-law Jeremy present. Jeremy had written her a very strong letter saying she must do it as soon as possible, he wouldn't countenance her waiting, it could be months, years, before he was home again. Jeannie's accidental disclosure to Harry over the true identity of his father was on her mind every single day, never able to forgive herself for what she had done, what she might have caused. She knew that before she was able to enter into this marriage with Stan she must somehow clear her conscience, nothing must blight this second chance she had of happiness.

Peggy answered the door, Pearl as ever at her side.

'Ah hello love, long time no see. Don't see so much o' ya now Dr. Kirk's not 'ere an' the cards finished. Blessed cheek that don't ya think? They reckon it's cos of the war! But what's war got to do wi' a game o' cards! Never 'eard nowt like it! Naw tis jus' cos we beat 'em. Poor losers that Lower Solesby lot!' she huffed.

'Oh yes indeed, I certainly miss our little gatherings' agreed Jeannie gamely. She really didn't want this conversation, she just wanted to get what she'd come for over and done with.

'Erm, I was wondering if Katherine is in, if I might have a quick word with her?'

'No I'm afraid she ain't' replied Peggy. 'She's at the school, got called in to have a word about Madam 'ere ain't she miss?' and she looked at Pearl shaking her head. Pearl put her thumb in her mouth and turned away sulkily. 'I'll tell 'er ya called though shall I?' continued Peggy.

'If you will I would be most grateful, I'll call another time.' Jeannie making to turn away was met by Kathy coming up the steps.

'Hello' Kathy greeted her, not quite frostily but pretty close. 'Can I help?'

'Well I was just wondering if you might spare me a few minutes?'

'Yes of course, why not?' said Kathy sidling past Jeannie and into the hall. Unbuttoning her coat she beckoned Jeannie to follow her into the dining room now used as a small sitting room.

'Take a seat won't you' gestured Kathy indicating the high backed armchair in the window. 'Now can I offer you a drink?'

'Oh no, not for me thank you, it's not long since I had one, unless of course you're desperate for one yourself?' she checked.

'No, no!' Kathy screwed up her face. 'I had one with Pearl's teacher Mrs. Appleyard along with a very large slice of humble pie! Pearl really is a wonder to me, when she's at home and certainly when she's with Peggy she's a nice little thing, at least most of the time, but at school she just seems to cause mayhem, I must admit I find it all rather embarrassing!'

Jeannie was anxious to be as pleasant, as agreeable as possible.

'Well I'm certain that can be none of your doing Katherine, you've taken the child in and done a wonderful job as far as I can see, I'm sure her problems can't be laid at your door.' Kathy returned her smile, happy to receive some support. Mrs. Appleyard had been quite scathing really, rather unfairly Kathy had thought.

'The thing is you don't get support with these children once you've taken them on, they arrive and you're just left with them. But anyway I'm sure you haven't come to talk about Pearl. Is it Jeremy? I do hope he's safe and well, and Geraldine of course.'

'Yes, as far as I'm aware they're both safe thank you. No, it's another matter which has been troubling me for some time, something I need to get off my chest.' Kathy leaned forward intrigued, with Jeremy's marriage to Geraldine she and Jeannie seemed to have little to unite them these days.

'It's Harry' began Jeannie. Kathy's heart sank. That dreaded phrase 'It's Harry' seemed to pop up all the time and was always the precursor to something unpleasant, some bad news. It was second only to 'It's Pearl', and as with the latter always followed by the query as to what he had done.

'What has he done?' she sighed.

'Harry hasn't done anything' said Jeannie, fiddling with the clasp on her handbag. 'It's me!' She hesitated, seemed unable to continue.

'I'm sorry? You've quite lost me.' Jeannie took a deep breath.

'The thing is Katherine Harry believes that your husband is dead and he knows that he wasn't his real father, that Jeremy is his real father.' Kathy turned pale, sat bolt upright in her chair.

'But.... no, I'm sure you must be mistaken. How could he possibly know either of those things?' Jeannie raised her head, looked Kathy straight in the eye.

'I have no idea why he thinks the way he does about your husband, but he knows about Jeremy because I told him.' Kathy was instantly on her feet, instantly furious.

'What! What do you mean you told him? You had no right to tell him, no right at all!'

'I know, I know, but it was accidental, I only confirmed what I believed he already knew.' Jeannie went on to relate the conversation she had had with Harry when he'd told her how his mother was lying to him, how he knew about his father. 'Of course I had no inkling of what he'd actually discovered, that your husband Henry was dead. Having no knowledge of that myself I assumed he meant he'd found out about Jeremy and I quite unwittingly confirmed it. I am so very, very sorry Katherine, if I could only turn back the clock!' Kathy looked down at the heartbroken soul before her. Without warning her anger turned to pity.

' Oh how is any of it your fault?' she almost whispered. 'You've done nothing wrong other than try to cover up other people's mistakes, mainly mine' she added ruefully. 'You should never have been put in that position in the first place.' She went over to Jeannie, bent down before her, took her hands in her own, Jeannie's tears flowing freely now dropping on to them. In the end Jeannie dared to look up.

'You mean you forgive me?' she asked incredulously.

'There is nothing to forgive' smiled Kathy, 'Absolutely nothing.' Kathy waited until Jeannie's tears had begun to subside and then went to fetch a small stool so that she could sit more comfortably beside her. Slowly but surely beginning to feel a little better Jeannie had one more thing to say.

'There's something else.'

'There can't be' laughed Kathy grimly, 'there just can't be.'

'I didn't tell Jeremy that Harry knew that he was his father, and now I wonder, I wonder if he had known if maybe he wouldn't have gone off and married Geraldine. You two might have been together and Harry would've had his family complete. I feel so dreadfully guilty.'

'Oh Jeannie, Jeannie my lovely Jeannie' sighed Kathy. 'What a sweet person you are, but it wouldn't have been like that believe me, well if it had been we wouldn't have been happy. We'd both realized that our love belonged in the past, and we were both able to see that by falling in love with other people. It could never have worked out well.' Jeannie was unsure what she was hearing.

'But I thought Jeremy had married Geraldine on the rebound, that you'd turned him down and he'd settled for her.' Kathy couldn't help laughing.

'Settled for her' she grinned, 'with her stunning looks? I don't think any man would 'settle' for Geraldine do you Jeannie! Oh no you have it quite, quite wrong' Kathy assured her. 'When Jeremy returned I had decided for Harry's sake to accept his proposal, but you see his proposal never came, he'd met Geraldine and was deeply in love and in a way I was grateful.'

'And you? You say both of you. So you have found someone to love too?'

'Oh yes' replied Kathy somewhat sadly. 'I too have found someone to love very deeply.'

'Well what can I say my dear other than I am delighted.' Jeannie decided not to probe any further, she suspected Kathy wouldn't have been forthcoming.

'So' said Kathy, 'are you feeling better now? Because I know I am!'

'Are you? Are you really? In all honesty I can't understand why after what I did.'

'As I said before you should never have been put in that position and I am so sorry as I'm sure Jeremy would be if he knew. The only mystery is how did Harry find out about Henry's death?'

'So it is true then?' asked Jeannie. 'He is dead.'

'Oh yes' said Kathy without hesitation, 'Henry Watson-Smythe is very definitely dead.'

'In that case I am very sorry for your loss' sighed Jeannie.

'Ah yes thank you, but things were over with Henry a very long time ago. But anyway now we've got that all over and done with I want you to stay and have tea with me like the good friends we used to be. Will you? Please.'

'Oh Katherine I would love nothing more.'

Blow the fact that Stan would be waiting, wondering where she'd got to, turning up for his tea and finding her missing, this was far more important! Kathy went off to find Peggy, see if she could rustle up something to eat.

Later, about to leave, Jeannie paused as she put on her gloves.

'I don't suppose.....? No........' She stopped what she was about to say.

'What? Come on' urged Kathy, 'what were you going to say?'

'I don't suppose you'd consider being my Matron of Honour would you?'

'What? What? Oh of course I would, I'd love to' and she held out her arms to Jeannie and hugged her.

374

Jeannie returned home to find the house in darkness, Stan sitting on the now low front wall with its iron railings removed, his legs stretched out in front of him.

'Oh Stan' she cried, 'what on earth are you doing out here, you should've gone home, I'd assumed you would.' He stood up.

'Not till I knew you were safe' he smiled. 'But I'll go now.'

'You will not.' She grasped his arm. 'I want you to come in with me and I'll tell you where I've been.'

'Aye well if you insist' he grinned with a pretended nonchalance.

'Oh I insist alright' she giggled.

Over cups of warming cocoa Jeannie told him everything, explaining what had been troubling her, causing her so much pain over the last few months. At the end of the evening they'd determined to make an appointment with the Reverend Price hoping to set a date not too far distant for their wedding.

CHAPTER FIFTY ONE

Kathy had felt better after spending time with Jeannie, putting right a few misconceptions, but of course she was now faced with the problem of Harry. How exactly had he discovered Henry had died and possibly more importantly why hadn't he told her he knew? And then again did he care? Until recently he'd seemed to have no liking for Henry, had barely mentioned his name. She knew she must address it immediately.

Kathy rapped on the drawing room door, not quietly because she knew she would be unlikely to get a response. In spite of her assurances concerning his long term studies Harry had, to her great distress, for some reason reverted to his old ways, being distinctly frosty with her, merely being civil. As she expected there was no reply. She popped her head around the door. Harry was seated at the table in the window, books and papers scattered everywhere. She stepped into the room. He ignored her. Kathy crossed the floor, took the chair by the side of the table.

'You look busy' she ventured brightly. Harry still didn't look up, flicked the pages of his book.

'I believe that is the general idea' he said sarcastically. Kathy gave up any idea of light heartedness.

'Oh Harry please. Please don't be like this' she begged. 'We have to talk.' Harry at last looked up, his pencil between his teeth.

'Do we? Do we indeed?' he almost snarled. She determined somehow to remain calm.

'Yes, yes we do.' She fiddled nervously with her fingers in her lap. 'I've been speaking with Jeannie Kirk, she came to see me.' He sprawled back in his chair tapping his pencil on his teeth. Kathy felt as if she were being interviewed for a job.

'How commendable!' he smirked, 'How very riveting! And what did you talk about? Knitting? Your newest hats?' Kathy had had enough.

'For God's sake Harry stop it!' she stormed. 'I think you know perfectly well what Jeannie came to tell me.' Harry shot to his feet.

'Yes I think I do too, but perhaps you should tell me. AT LAST!' he added furiously. He went to the marble fireplace, leant against it resting his elbow, in the same way reflected Kathy that Henry used to.

'Well please will you at least sit down' she pleaded.

'Why? What difference does it make whether I'm sitting down or standing up?' he sneered.

'Well I don't know it just seems more civilized' she ploughed on. As the word was out of her mouth she knew it had been a mistake.

'Civilized!' he jeered. 'Oh now we want to be civilized do we? That's rich!' He detached himself from the mantelpiece, went across the room towards her furious and then suddenly, inexplicably, dropped down on to his chair as though defeated. He put his elbows on his knees, his head between his hands. 'I think it's a little late for that don't you?' he sighed wearily.

Kathy's heart turned over, her mind going back to the time when he'd run away for fear of being sent back to India.

For a while after that they had seemed close, but she had to acknowledge that their relationship had always been fraught with difficulties, never an easy one. Harder still to bear was that it was all her fault, based on her lies, her need to cover up the many, many mistakes she had made in her life. Her instinct was to reach out, hold him in her arms as she had done that last time, make everything right, but she knew that this time it wouldn't work, he wouldn't allow it.

'I've come to tell you the truth Harry, right from the very beginning.' He looked sideways at her.

'Really?' he asked quietly, 'because it's about time.'

'Yes, you're right my love' she whispered. 'It is about time.'

And so the long sorry tale of Kathy's life was told. Her difficulties with her father, echoed in their own relationship. Her banishment to the other side of the world. Her pregnancy although unknown at the time, her subsequent deceit convincing Henry that he was Harry's father. Henry's understandable outrage when he'd discovered the truth finally and he'd sent her back home to England, the heartbreak when her hopes of a new life were dashed finding her sister so ill. Harry sat in disbelief as she told him how her father had so comprehensively removed all trace of her from the family. How hard she had had to work first of all to get everyone to believe who she was and then how she had struggled to gain their trust and friendship. The relationship with Jeremy, when they'd both assumed they could just carry on where they'd left off, she told him had been a mistake. What they had at first taken to be love had been mere nostalgia. Jeremy she assured him had no inkling that he had a son until Harry himself arrived in England and he began to put two and two together. Once he had discovered the truth he had wanted nothing more than to claim him, tell the world he had such a son.

'Well then why, why didn't you marry him? We could at least have all been together' he said sadly.

'Oh my love, how simple you make it all sound. At first when Jeremy and I got back together and believed ourselves in love it WAS simple, we had every intention of marrying. But I soon came to realize that what we had wasn't love at all, just a wonderful friendship built out of memories of the past. I had been about to tell Jeremy when I learnt of your father's death and my subsequent inheritance. I was convinced that if everyone knew of it and then I changed my mind about marrying Jeremy it would look as if I'd changed my mind simply because I no longer needed financial support. I had two choices, marry Jeremy after all or keep silent about your father's death. I married for convenience once before and knowing only too well the consequences of that I decided to keep quiet about your father's death, after all it was of no importance to anyone here, allowing me to turn down Jeremy's proposal. The irony is that I had eventually changed my mind, thought it might be the best thing for you in the end, but by this time Jeremy had changed his mind, met Geraldine and fallen madly in love.' She had to laugh.

'Serves me right really! And of course by this time it was rather too late to announce your father's death. I certainly hadn't intended to keep it a secret for ever but things have a tendency to run away with you and then the "right time" seems impossible to find, too late.'

'But surely' queried Harry 'Dr. Kirk being my father he had every reason to support me, whether you married him or not, would be expected to?'

'Had everyone known that, yes of course. But they didn't, still don't, all kept a secret to cover up my mistakes.' Kathy grimaced.

'But surely his too, my father's too?'

'Yes of course but even today, such a long time later, if the truth were to come out he could be ruined. Your father's career could be ruined, and really would it be worth that? I'm sure it wouldn't be.'

'So does he know? Is Dr.Kirk aware now that I know he's my father.'

'No, he doesn't and that's why Jeannie came to see me. She has been distraught, worrying that had he known, had she revealed what you had told her, he wouldn't have married Geraldine, that there would've been the "happy ending". I assured her that would never have been the case.'

'So that's it then is it, the whole story?'

'It is my love yes, and the only thing to be decided now is do you want Jeremy to know that you are aware he is your father?'

'I think I would' said Harry quietly. 'I think I would very much.'

All of this Kathy had told her son with tears falling down her cheeks, making futile attempts to dab them away with the sleeve of her gown. As she finished he went to her, knelt before her and taking her hands in his whispered 'Don't worry Mum.'

There was just one piece of the jigsaw left. How had Harry learned of Henry's 'death'?

'Oh that's simple' he said. 'Nothing intriguing about that. I found the letter in your jewellery box. Peggy had suggested I had the clasp fixed on your bracelet as a birthday present and that's when I found it.' Such a simple explanation, one Kathy could never even have guessed at, her imaginings had been wide of the mark.

Did Kathy still have one more secret to reveal? She decided not. Henry had forbidden her to tell anyone of what she knew, had persuaded her that it could be a matter of life or death.

CHAPTER FIFTY TWO

Kathy had known it would come. At first puzzled and hurt at Henry's sudden and unexplained departure she had slowly come to accept that it would have been something out of his control. He clearly was involved in something very important. She must bide her time, be patient. She found the letter propped behind the clock in the kitchen.

'Came this morning' said Peggy as Kathy reached for the cream envelope. She recognized neither the handwriting nor the postmark. 'Bletchley', she knew no one there. She took the letter along with her coffee cup into the drawing room, now returned to its former state, no longer a dormitory for the boys. Seating herself in the sunshine of the bay window she turned the envelope this way and that, until it was actually opened she could imagine all sorts. In the end she could resist it no longer.

"My dear Katherine," it said. *"I do hope I find you well. I shall be in England for a short visit very soon and would adore it if we might meet – India seems such a long time ago now. I wonder if I contact you with a date if we could perhaps spend a few days together in London. I realize that travelling is such a bore these days, but I would so like to see you. As I shall be travelling around there would be no point in my giving you an address to which you might reply and in any case in these uncertain times who could guarantee that*

*it would reach me anyway. I will just trust that when I
send you the date you will be able to come.*

Lots of love darling, Petronella xxx "

Clever thought Kathy, very clever.

Jeannie and Stan were now well on with preparations
for their wedding. The church was booked, Mrs. Barber was
making Jeannie's dress, the reception arranged at the Swan
Hotel, everyone was looking forward to a happy occasion
amidst all the depressing news of the war which continually
leaked out in the press.

One evening with Peggy out at one of her 'knitting
socks for soldiers' soirees Kathy found herself alone with
Pearl, the child being particularly annoying, sulking when
beaten at any of the many games they had played and being
particularly obstinate over learning her letters. Kathy was
pleased when it came to bed time.

'Go and get ready for bed, clean your teeth and then I
shall be up to read you a story' she said.

'Huh!' scoffed Pearl, dragging her feet and eventually
stomping up the stairs.

As Kathy approached Pearl's room she stopped as she
heard what she took to be Pearl in mid-prayer. She peered
through the crack in the door. Yes indeed Pearl was on her
knees beside the bed in earnest conversation with Jesus.
Kathy leant against the wall to listen.

'An' dear Jesus, it ain't right fair ya knows that bloomin'
Miss Kathy gets ta be a bridesmaid an' I dusn't. She's too
old an' not 'alf as pretty as me. Even me Auntie Peggy sez
so' she added quickly as if that would surely convince him.
'Any road' she went on 'I's telled ya now so tis up ta ya, but

I bet ya can't sort that even if ya can turn whatter inta wine. 'An by the way Jesus can ya jus' stop our Margaret throwing up alt time, it fair turns ya stomach when she dus it an' yus 'aving yer breakfast. Lots o' love Jesus. I 'opes yus 'avin' a right nice time.'

With that Pearl scrambled into bed, patting the eiderdown next to her when she saw Kathy come into the room with the book of fairy tales.

'Which one shall it be tonight?' asked Kathy kindly, her previous irritation forgotten. 'Goldilocks and the Three Bears?'

'Naw, naw, don't like that un' said Pearl. 'She's a right spoilt little cow she is.' Pearl was as surprised as Kathy herself that she wasn't severely reprimanded.

The next morning Kathy set out with a mission. She found Jeannie in the surgery waiting room tidying the magazines after morning surgery.

'Do you think I could have a quick word?' she asked. 'It won't take long, I can see you're busy.'

'I'd love to take a breather' grinned Jeannie. 'It's been unusually busy this morning. Everyone seems to have suddenly realized that they can still be ill even if there's a war on. Come through to the back.'

With a cup of tea in her hand Kathy broached the reason for her visit. She repeated what she'd heard of Pearl's prayer the previous night. Jeannie couldn't stop laughing, had to put down her own cup she was shaking so much.

'Oh dear, she obviously thinks you're over the hill then does she? Goodness me, she's a character isn't she!'

'That is certainly one way to describe her!' agreed Kathy primly, pretending to be aggrieved.

'But anyway the reason I'm here......'

'You can stop right there!' said Jeannie holding up her hand. 'There's nothing I'd like more than for Pearl to be a bridesmaid. I'll get on to it right away. What colour do you think she'd like best?'

'But are you sure? I don't want you to feel I've railroaded you.'

'Oh you haven't and if you had why should it matter? A little girl's happiness is all that matters.'

'Oh Jeannie, you're such a friend!'

'Well I hope I'm a little more than that' she laughed. As she saw Kathy to the door she couldn't help asking, had to know.

'Kathy' she said 'have you told Harry about..... you know?'

'Harry knows everything' smiled Kathy grasping the other woman's arm. 'He knows everything and what's more wants Jeremy to know that he knows.'

'Oh but that's wonderful!' gasped Jeannie. 'Jeremy will be so pleased, when will you tell him?'

'Oh I think we'll leave that for when he's home don't you? I'm sure he's got more than enough to cope with at the moment. And anyway' she grinned 'we've got a bridesmaid to sort haven't we?'

'We have indeed' laughed Jeannie as she closed the door behind her visitor, 'we have indeed.'

It had been agreed that Jeannie would call to personally invite Pearl to be a bridesmaid. The child was summoned to the drawing room expecting to have another of her misdemeanours exposed. Peggy was close behind her also expecting the worst.

'Sit down please Pearl' said Kathy. 'Mrs. Kirk here has something she'd like to ask you.'

'Pearl dear' began Jeannie. 'I was wondering if you might do me the honour of being a bridesmaid for me.'

'Wor? Wor ya say?' asked Pearl astounded. 'Well I'll go ta our 'ouse.' She ran to the door.

'Pearl, Pearl where are you going?' cried Kathy. 'I'm gonna thank 'im', say ta' answered Pearl. 'I'm gonna thank Jesus, an' I can unly dus that wi' me slippers on next ta me bed.'

'Oh yes, right' said Kathy, nodding her head and turning in exasperation to Jeannie who had tears of joy and laughter streaming down her face.

Jeannie and Stan finally tied the knot on a bright and breezy day in November. November 10th had been chosen, Stan's birthday. Needless to say Jeremy wasn't there, wasn't there to give Jeannie away. But Harry was, having volunteered himself for the job and therefore so very special. Jeannie remembered feeling excited on her first wedding day but this was different. Her happiness was beyond anything she'd previously known. With the support she had all around her how could it be anything other? Her wedding to Richard had been simple, in a registry office, just the two of them and witnesses brought in from a nearby office, he had wanted it that way, 'not wanted a fuss' and perhaps Stan too felt that way, but if he did he wasn't saying. Jeannie had to have everything just as she wanted.

For once although excited Pearl behaved herself and walked sedately behind the bride next to Kathy.

Most of the village were there, both the bride and groom being important cogs in the wheel of Oakfield. Jonas, standing as best man for Stan, caused a slight stir when in the silence of the church, awaiting the arrival of the bride, he caught sight of his sister Philly as she made her way down the aisle to take her seat next to Maisie. He nudged Stan in the ribs.

'My God son tek a look at that will ya! 'If ya can't fight wear a big 'at!' he said at the top of his voice.

The newly-weds spent their honeymoon at Inchcombe-on-Sea, enjoying it in spite of the barbed wired coils now stretching along the beach to ward off invaders.

CHAPTER FIFTY THREE

Finally it arrived. Kathy tore open the letter from 'Petronella' inviting her to meet 'her' in London in a week's time.

'*Please bring something spectacular to wear*' wrote 'Petronella'. '*I have something special planned.*' Kathy smiled to herself, there was only one thing that 'something special' could be. She planned her trip carefully, it was strange she mused how before the war not many people would venture as far as London and yet now with all the complications involved in getting there, and the perils involved when they actually did, more and more people seemed to head there. Head into the very heart of danger. 'Petronella' told her 'she' would be staying at the 'Curzon' and would book a room there for Kathy.

Two days before she was due to leave Kathy informed Peggy that she would be away for a few days, going to spend a few days in London with an old girlfriend. Peggy was surprised but decided against advising her not to go, 'she'd only do as she liked any road.'

As everyone had been advised to do before travelling in war-time Kathy left an envelope in her jewellery box containing the name and address of where she would be staying. The journey to London was hellish in the extreme, Kathy and most of the other passengers having to exit the train on no less than three occasions in order to make room for servicemen on the move.

Kathy arrived at the hotel late in the evening after an arduous and complicated journey. She went straight to her room and was about to settle down for a much needed rest when a knock came on her door. She opened it to find a liveried footman, a message for her laid on his small silver tray.

'A gentleman sent this for you Madam' he said handing her the envelope. 'A Mr. Clifford Wallace I believe.' Kathy stifled a giggle. Oh he was being very clever, using aliases familiar to them both.

"Please would you meet me downstairs in the cocktail bar in half an hour" the message read.

She dressed with care, out to impress. Thirty minutes later she entered the extremely busy cocktail bar of the 'Curzon', saw him immediately.

'Katherine my dear' he smiled 'how good to see you.'

She nodded her head graciously.

'And you too' she answered formally just in case anyone should overhear. He suggested dinner and ravenously hungry after her long journey she readily agreed.

Over a candlelit dinner in an alcove tucked away from the main body of the room, Henry told her of his plans. How he had arranged these few days in the hope that she would do him the honour of agreeing to marry him. Here in London, now! He loved her deeply he told her taking her hand, had always done so in spite of everything and wanted nothing more than to spend the rest of his life with her. Responding tenderly she told him that she felt exactly the same, could think of nothing more wonderful. But first she said she must have some answers to her questions. Henry albeit reluctantly agreed, he knew he really had no choice.

Kathy listened to all he had to tell her with amazement and increasing admiration for his courage over what was to come next for him. Confident of what his answer would be she knew it would be quite safe to query the timing of their wedding.

'But surely it would be better to wait until things are more settled darling?' As she'd expected he immediately dismissed the idea of a postponement.

'No, no my dear, I need the thought of you to come home to, to get me through.'

'Oh Henry darling.' She smiled lovingly at him.

Having finished their meal and both slightly tipsy Henry very boldly asked if he might visit her room that night. His room was on the floor above hers, he felt sure he could manage it without being seen.

'Oh darling I think not if you don't mind awfully. I'm so very tired it's been a long day and besides I need my beauty sleep, want to look my best don't I?' she teased him with a smile.

'Of course, of course' he smiled. 'One more night won't make any difference.'

'One night?' queried Kathy, startled. 'You mean the wedding is planned for tomorrow? That's very soon isn't it? How in the world have you managed that?' Henry smiled broadly, tapped the side of his nose.

'Who ya know Katherine. It's who ya know.'

'Oh well yes, how lovely, well done' she said reaching across to cover his hand. 'But surely there must be quite a lot that needs attending to, you know legal, financial things.'

'Yes indeed my sweet, we have an appointment with my solicitor at four o'clock immediately after the ceremony.'

'Oh darling' she gushed, 'you are so, so clever, how lucky am I to be marrying you for a second time. How have I ever managed without you!'

After wishing him goodnight Kathy left Henry in the bar of the hotel downing a double brandy. In the ostentatious highly gilded lift she quickly made her way to her room, glancing at her reflection in the mirror of the lift as it rose effortlessly between floors.

'Can I really be doing this?' she asked the flushed face that stared back at her. Kathy had been taken by surprise, knew she had no time to lose.

CHAPTER FIFTY FOUR

London had been the target that night and the German bombers more than up to their task. The centre of the capital had been decimated, bombed out of all recognition. Kathy had mentioned to no one other than Peggy about her proposed trip and so when she was missing the next morning Dannah had thought nothing of it. Gathered round the table for breakfast, the radio on in the background, he was therefore not unduly concerned at Peggy's gasp of shock when the news of last night's blitz on London had been reported, she could sometimes be a bit hysterical. That was until Peggy's gasp turned to a wail.

'Oh God! Oh no! Not Miss Kathy!'

'What do you mean? Not Miss Kathy?' he asked, suddenly sensing that something was very wrong. 'Where is she?'

'London' cried Peggy. 'She's gone to London for a few days to meet up with a friend.'

'What? But she never said! When did she go?' he demanded.

'Yesterday, she went yesterday, on the early train.'

'Did she tell you where she was staying? Did she leave an address?'

'Well no, she didn't say but I'm sure she will have left it somewhere, you know how we're supposed to.'

Harry, equally shocked to hear his mother was missing, was next to the radio, banging it, urging it to crackle into life. He knelt down in front of it, his ear next to the mesh.

'Shush' he said 'they're giving out details of what was damaged.' A plummy BBC voice told them that the centre of the city had been severely damaged and hundreds of people killed, many of them guests at the hotels in the area.

'Oh my God no!' cried Peggy again. Dannah was round the table to her.

'Are you sure she didn't tell you where she was staying?' He gripped her shoulders.

'Aye I'm sure, to be honest I thought she was being a bit secretive like so I knew it'd be best not to ask.'

'Well then where would she have left the address? Come on think!' With the anxiety of it all Peggy couldn't think of anywhere, her brain being completely scrambled.

'Her jewellery box' suggested Harry suddenly, 'it could be in there.'

'Well quick lad, go an' have a look.' Harry had already gone.

The envelope containing the address of the hotel where Kathy would be staying was in the jewellery box, just as he had suspected it might be, under the bracelet which still needed repair and on top of the infamous letter from Henry's solicitors in Bombay. Harry put the bracelet in his pocket. He would have it repaired for her if.......... It didn't bear thinking about! He raced downstairs.

'Here it is' he shouted waving the paper in the air. 'She's staying at the 'Curzon'.' Dannah quickly snatched the paper from his hand.

'Right I'll go and find her.'

'But how?' wailed Peggy, 'How ya gonna get there? There'll be chaos! You'll never get there, the trains are bad enough at the best of times, they'll be even worse now!' Dannah having had the same thought was suddenly inspired. Snatching his jacket from the back of his chair he headed for the door.

'I'll hitch a lift on one of the trucks, one of 'em's bound to be heading there or least in that direction. I'll get somewhere close anyway.' Harry pulled his own jacket from the hook on the door.

'I'm coming with you.' Dannah halted in his tracks, although in a desperate hurry the agony etched on the boy's face made him stop, this was important too.

'No son, you stay here' he said gently. 'It'll be quicker just one of us. I'll find your mammie and she'll want to come home and find you safe.'

'But....' began Harry.

'No buts son' said Dannah, gripping the boy's shoulder, looking him in the eye. 'You're too important, you've got to stay here.' With that he went, slamming the door behind him. For the first time that anyone could remember Harry, usually so reserved, slumped down at the table, wept openly. Peggy Barley went to him and put her motherly arms around him.

'Hush luv' she soothed, 'yer ma will be OK you see.'

Pearl, not really sure what all the fuss was about, went to stand next to Harry, began patting his head saying 'there, there' whilst raising her eyebrows and looking over to Patrick as if needing some explanation of what was going on. Patrick in his wheelchair was reminded once more of his frailties, not so very long ago he would've been out of the door with his uncle, he felt so damned useless!

Dannah was in luck. He raced into the yard of the factory just as one of the huge army trucks was about to pull away. Standing in front of it he waved his arms, flagging it down, motioning for the driver to stop. He wrenched open the door, climbed up on to the step and swung himself into the cab alongside the driver.

'I need a lift to London' he said breathlessly, 'or at least as close as you can get.'

'Now mate ya know that's "no can do"' said the driver shaking his head and turning off the engine. 'We're not allowed passengers! The powers that be'll 'ave me guts for garters.'

'We'll I'll 'ave more than your guts for garters if you don't!' answered Dannah fiercely, 'So ya can take yer pick!' The driver didn't reply, restarted the engine and slowly pulled out of the yard.

During the course of the journey Dannah explained the emergency, enquiring of the driver if he had any idea where the 'Curzon Hotel' might be. Bob Barrett scratched his head.

'Well I've certainly 'eard of it, know it's in the middle somewhere but can't say I can really 'elp ya. An' besides' he added – not entirely helpfully considering the situation – 'Sounds like there's not much left of it thanks to them buggers!'

Dannah decided he was probably best left to his own thoughts after that and settled himself in the corner of the cab as if trying to sleep. The journey was long, tedious and depressing, passing as they did through towns and villages most of which to some extent or another bore the scars of war.

Daylight was fading when Dannah jumped down from the cab, thanking Bob profusely for his help. Although having to be dropped some distance from the centre of the city it wasn't long before he could see stretched before him the damage inflicted by the German bombers. It went on and on.

He eventually reached the heart of the city, its skyline dominated by St. Paul's Cathedral, which miraculously seemed to have survived the onslaught. His feet blistered, his eyes already sore from the dust and smoke which seemed to be everywhere, he finally emerged into something that looked as if it might once have been a major thoroughfare. It was now just a pile of rubble, people scrambling over it like ants, looking, looking for God knows what. Having stood awhile in disbelief, incredulous at the devastation before him, he eventually realized that there was some sort of organization, were people in charge. He stumbled over the mountains of rubble, went to the nearest 'tin hat'.

'I'm looking for the 'Curzon', the 'Curzon Hotel'?' The 'tin hat', although he didn't want to, knew he had no choice. He straightened up, pointed to the biggest mountain of bricks and stone.

'There mate, that's what's left of the 'Curzon'.' He moved away shaking his head in despair. 'Sorry mate' he said as an afterthought.

Dannah looked around him dazed, sat down amongst the rubble, the fires, the noise. Wondered how he was going to tell everyone. How was he going to tell Harry? And how was HE going to go on.

After a while he got to his feet once more, dusting himself down, although knowing it was pointless. And then.. He must be seeing things! Amidst the fragments of curtains and upholstery blown to shreds and now hanging almost festively from lampposts and shattered doorways he'd seen a hat- a ridiculous hat but one frighteningly which he recognized.

Bits of it were missing but he still knew it to be hers. Did he want it? Was he sure? If he didn't retrieve it would he one day be sorry? His feet took him towards it, stumbling all the way he had to look down so as not to fall.

As he straightened up he couldn't believe what he saw. She stood there amongst the rubble, her coat dusty and soot marked, her hair dishevelled, just staring into space.

'Kathy?' he called unsure. Could it really be? Was it his mind playing tricks? She heard him, even above the racket, she heard him, turned.

'Dannah?' she cried. 'Dannah? Oh my God!' They scrambled desperately towards one another and then were in each other's arms, laughing, crying, Dannah pushing the tears from her face, kissing her cheeks, her eyes and then finally her lips.

'Oh my darlin'' he cried over and over again. 'Oh I love you, I love you.'

When finally one of the wardens came over to tell them they were in the way Dannah, with one arm tightly holding on to Kathy, reached out to retrieve what was left of the hat.

'I think we need this' he grinned, 'to remind us.' Kathy smiled tenderly in agreement whilst in her heart knowing that she would need no reminders of the moment when all her hopes and dreams had finally been realized and Dannah Delaney had taken her in his arms and told her that he loved her.

CHAPTER FIFTY FIVE

Picking their way through the devastation, wanting to get as far away as possible, Kathy and Dannah walked and walked. Walked until their feet were sore, their legs weary, their noses and throats choked with dust and smoke from still burning buildings, there seemed to be nowhere where they might rest.

'We should see about getting home, see if there are any trains running' said Dannah.

'I don't think there will be much chance of that, do you?' grimaced Kathy. 'We could try my hotel, my things are there anyway.' Dannah turned to her puzzled,

'Your things? Your hotel? I thought.... I thought you were staying at 'The Curzon'?'

'Oh, well I was supposed to be. I did for a while. I had a room booked for me there, but I also had one booked at the 'Rodreigal'. That's where I should've been last night if it hadn't been for the raids. We were advised to take shelter in the basement of the hotel, but I've never understood why being in the basement of a tall building could be a good idea with all that to fall on top of you. No I'm afraid I disobeyed the commissionaire's advice and went to the underground station, that's where I've just come from.'

In the middle of all this, all this confusing information, Dannah found himself obsessed by one thing.

'But your hat' he said, twirling it around his finger. 'How did it come to be where I found it?'

'Oh the hat!' she laughed. 'I think I lost that clambering down the fire escape.'

'Clambering down the fire escape? I don't...' he began.

'No, and nor will you' she laughed, taking his hand. 'Until I've explained everything.'

They arrived at the 'Rodreigal' to find it damaged but in the main habitable. The windows on one side of the building had been blown out but fortunately the other side where Kathy's room was situated had survived more or less intact. They picked their way carefully over the broken glass through to the entrance. The commissionaire, busy at his desk, looked up as they came though the revolving door.

'Ah Madam, Madam' he cried recognizing her, 'you are safe and well! You had us quite worried, you were unaccounted for in the basement.'

'Oh yes' smiled Kathy, feeling guilty for having ignored his instructions. 'But I had a most urgent appointment you see and I actually ended up taking shelter in the underground station.'

'Oh dear, Madam' he sighed. 'I imagine that can't have been at all pleasant with all the.... what shall I say? With all the ordinary people.'

'The ordinary people were just fine' said Kathy indignantly. 'In fact it was quite fun. Anyway can I assume that my room is still available? Because if so I would like to clean myself up.'

'Of course Madam' he replied, feeling stung. 'Everything is quite in order, your room is quite in order.'

'Good, good' said Kathy haughtily, sweeping past him towards the lift which surprisingly was still functioning.

'Katherine!' said Dannah reprovingly as the doors slid to behind them. 'That was really wicked of you, the poor man' he laughed.

'Well, he deserved it! Who does he think these ordinary people are? Honestly these days the staff are more snooty than the guests!'

Whilst Kathy tidied herself in the bathroom, Dannah took the comfy armchair in the window which looked out over the still burning devastated city and breathed a sigh of deep sadness.

Kathy knew that the time had come for explanations. Settling herself in the chair opposite to Dannah's she waited for his questions.

'So then tell me, why is it that you came to London?' he asked. 'Surely it must be a strange time to be visiting the city? And your friend, how is she, is she safe?'

'I came to meet Henry' she said simply. 'He thought I'd come to London to marry him!' Dannah should have shouted 'HENRY!' That would have been the natural thing to do but he didn't.

'You came to London to meet Henry?' asked Dannah as if he were merely slightly surprised, as though Henry hadn't hitherto been considered dead. Kathy smiled, laughed at him.

'Oh Dannah, you behave as if everything is fine, so normal, so calm. I do so love you.' She went on to tell him Henry's story, how and why she'd been told he was dead, of his mysterious appearance in Oakfield. That the man he knew to be Ralph Falconer was in fact Henry Watson-

Smythe. Understandably Dannah struggled to take it in. It couldn't be more improbable, but she assured him it was the absolute truth and he believed her.

Kathy went on to tell him that when she'd accidentally discovered the truth about Henry, uncovered his new identity, he had professed undying love for her, said he wanted nothing more than to remarry her, spend the rest of his days with her. She'd gone along with it she'd said, not believing a word of it, knowing Henry was just out for ultimate revenge. She knew Henry well enough to know he never forgave anyone for anything. She suspected that he thought he could frighten her, get his money back and break her heart. She laughed out loud at that.

'As if Henry could have broken my heart!' she scoffed. 'I wanted to make him squirm, let him think that he had fooled me. I'd guessed correctly that he wanted me to come to London to marry him. He had it all arranged, we were supposed to be married yesterday, followed by a visit to his solicitors transferring back everything which had previously been left to me. He thought I loved him of all things, was going to marry him, but I never had the slightest intention. I'd already booked a room here and after we'd dined I excused myself saying I would see him in the morning and left hurriedly by the fire exit. Of course I no sooner arrived here than the sirens went off and we all had to flee.'

'But the 'Curzon' he said. 'If you'd stayed there as you should have...'

'I know' she trilled, 'I'd be dead!'

'But Henry? What about Henry?'

'Oh Henry' she said nonchalantly, hardheartedly. 'Well by the look of it Henry will be dead. AGAIN!' Both knowing that the whole tale was too incredible for words and would take a very, very long time to sink in, they agreed to temporarily put it all to one side and enjoy their very own story.

'How long have you loved me?' she asked.

'It seems like forever' he said. 'How long have you loved me?'

'Oh, I don't know' she answered mischievously. 'Not QUITE forever!'

He picked her up from her chair, laughing threw her on to the bed.

'Are you staying?' she asked meekly.

'I most certainly am not!' he said in mock admonishment. 'Look where that got you the last time young lady! I'll be making an honest woman of you first!'

'You will?' she asked, smiling.

'I most certainly, definitely will' he replied tenderly.

CHAPTER FIFTY SIX

Henry Watson-Smythe had been pleased to be 'dead'. In fact his 'death' couldn't have come at a better time. His life was in ruins, in fact hadn't even been much of a life up to press, certainly his personal life anyway. His career? Well he supposed he'd done fairly well with that. No, Henry was happy to say goodbye to Henry Watson-Smythe, pleased to be able to make a fresh start.

When Henry's immediate superiors, about to withdraw him from his diplomatic post in Bombay due to the imminent war, had chanced upon his impressive credentials they had realized that Henry Watson-Smythe might be just what the proposed Special Operations Executive were looking for. Well educated, highly intelligent and importantly multilingual, he could prove invaluable in carrying out espionage and acts of sabotage against German forces. Senior officers in India had been sent to sound Henry out. They had found him instantly agreeable, in fact keen to pursue their plans for him.

If those plans were to succeed it was imperative that Henry adopted an entirely new persona. Henry Watson-Smythe had to die. A bogus firm of solicitors "Saul & Saul" acting in Bombay had proceeded under governmental instruction to execute the "Last Will & Testament of Henry Watson-Smythe Esquire". Mercifully – and a factor which had encouraged Henry's selection – there was not a lot to be done, few people to convince of Henry's demise. Although now divorced from him Katherine Ava Watson-Smythe had been named as his sole beneficiary and as such had stood to inherit Henry's estate which when all put together was not insubstantial. Henry meanwhile had been categorically assured that he would be more than handsomely compensated for what he was about to do.

Henry Watson-Smythe's sad and sudden 'death' had been orchestrated by the authorities, apparently dying in a military hospital far from his few friends and acquaintances.

For what he was about to do Henry had needed training and also a new identity. He was to become Ralph Falconer, consolidating his new identity by infiltrating an entirely new situation. He was to be placed as an armament factory manager close to a special training establishment where he would be instructed in all he needed to know for his top secret role with the planned S.O.E. He had been offered a choice of locations and had hardly been able to believe it when he saw that his S.O.E. training could take place at Lullesham Hall not far from Oakfield and Katherine his ex-wife. He had decided it must be fate, just reading the name had made his lip curl, he couldn't wait to get there.

Henry had never been able to forget nor forgive what Katherine had done to him. In the early days of their marriage his suspicions over Harry's true parentage had haunted him, giving him no peace. When his long held suspicions were finally confirmed he had been incandescent but also heartbroken. Henry had always 'played a straight bat' and expected others to do the same, he felt that in many ways life had cheated him. His father had taken his own life to escape punishment for massive embezzlement over many years, leaving Henry and his poor mother to bear the shame and consequences of what he had done. At the time he had been grateful that his mother had been spared long lasting ignominy due to her husband's deeds by her own early death but he had missed her, he'd had no one left.

When Henry had met and fallen in love with Petronella Wyatt he had thought perhaps the tide had turned for him, but he had been mistaken, she hadn't loved him enough to move to India with him and leave her family. Henry had never ceased to wonder should he have turned down the diplomatic post for love? Would his life have turned out a good deal better if he had? In many ways it certainly couldn't have turned out much worse. Katherine's appearance on the S.S.Narkunda bound for Bombay had seemed heaven sent at the time, he'd considered her a malleable little girl, would never have considered her capable of such deceit. In actual fact if when he had finally confronted her that fateful day she had denied his accusation he would have gratefully accepted it, because he had wanted with all his heart to believe he was wrong. But she hadn't. Her silence had told him he was right, confirmed all his worst fears and instilled in him an anger, a hatred so strong he knew it would never be assuaged. The letter he had had to write to her pretending he had forgiven her, wanted there to be peace between them, had been the hardest he'd ever written, had turned his stomach, made him physically sick. He had known in his very soul that one day he would have his revenge.

Henry had arrived back in England on a perfect summer's day. He'd walked in the London parks, breathed in the air, wondering why he hadn't returned sooner, this was where he belonged. With two weeks to re-acclimatize himself, do as he pleased, he'd visited his old family home, visited the graves of his parents side by side in the little village churchyard. He'd read the headstones. They could have been two people who had loved and laughed all their lives, there was nothing there to tell the truth. How his father whilst adopting an air of superiority, of self-righteousness, had obviously been a crook and a cheat, how his mother had so clearly been betrayed. Was it right that people departed this life with their sins expunged by the few simple words carved into a headstone?

Two weeks after arriving in England Henry had begun his intensive training. First of all he'd had to learn to be Ralph Falconer, quiet, conscientious bachelor, only son of dead parents. Then he'd had to learn all there was to know about armaments and their production. Ralph Falconer was to become the manager of the Oakfield armaments factory. A newly established factory, it had been hoped that any problems which might have arisen due to Ralph's hitherto lack of knowledge would be hidden alongside everyone else's inexperience. Ralph had spent his days in the study rooms and his nights in his hotel room reading everything he could find to read about weapons and their production. Also being aware he would need to converse with people in a way which would convince them that he had spent most of his time in England he had known he must find some interest which he would be able to share. Although always a keen fisherman he'd known such a solitary pastime would not suffice and so had cultivated an interest in cricket and football, in the end being able to recall the names and achievements of English sporting heroes of the previous decade.

On his arrival in Oakfield Ralph Falconer had been greeted by Dannah Delaney, a quiet unassuming but nonetheless intelligent man, someone Ralph had felt he could get along with. Dannah had been part of the management of what had previously been Hardcastles' cycle factory and his knowledge of the site and its workforce had been considered to be useful, he was to be Ralph's right-hand man. They had worked well together, Dannah having been totally taken in by Ralph, been more than happy to stand in for him when he'd been called in for frequent briefings at Lullesham Hall whilst having no idea of their true purpose.

The two men so similar in temperament after a slow start had become friends, often sharing a pint together at one of the local pubs. His tongue loosened by drink Dannah had eventually begun to tell Ralph snippets of his home life. Ralph had heard of the tragedy of the man's wedding day, of the surprise return from India of his intended wife's sister followed by the surprise arrival of her son. Dannah had spoken with seeming fondness for them both and Ralph's determination for revenge had intensified.

Unknown to her Ralph had followed Katherine, often seeing her take a stroll with Dannah, tucking her arm through his, smiling so sweetly up at him. In an effort to be friendly Dannah had frequently tried to involve Ralph in family gatherings, but on each occasion Ralph had declined, saying he had 'work to do'. He'd claimed he wasn't good at family gatherings, he'd never had to be.

The two men had however enjoyed fishing trips together until after a while Dannah's nephew Patrick had been included instantly sending out warning signals to Ralph. The day Dannah had told him that Miss Kathy's boy Harry was also to come along Ralph had known the fishing trips must come to an end. Harry would most certainly have recognized him, disguised though he was. He'd known he wouldn't bear close scrutiny.

He'd known it would come eventually. He thought he'd got away with it the night the plane had crashed into the factory. He had had to do his best to save Harry. As he'd struggled to help him the boy had looked into his eyes as if he had recognized him, had called him 'father', but seemingly had subsequently either forgotten or imagined it to be delirium as a result of his injuries. His seeming neglect of the boy following the accident, not being able to visit him in hospital in case Harry recognized him, had been his ultimate downfall. Katherine had become so incensed at his apparent lack of concern she had been determined to seek him out. As soon as he'd heard her voice as she marched through to his office he'd known what he must do. He'd had no alternative other than to admit the truth whilst at the same time frightening her into silence. He had admitted the truth, had frightened her and as soon as he had seen her had known how his revenge would come. He would convince her that he still cared for her, had cared for her all along, loved her, after all what woman could resist that he'd thought bitterly.

Katherine had been more compliant than he could have even wished for, falling immediately for his protestations of love. How very, very naive he had mused. Henry had taken great delight in playing with her affections, leading her on, what a little fool! Well she'd made a fool out of him once. Now it was his turn.

He had left Oakfield in a hurry without even leaving her a message hoping it would tantalize her even more. He'd left it several weeks before sending the letter from 'Petra' suggesting they might meet in London at some future date.

The second letter some while later entreating her to meet with her friend would, he'd been sure, have the desired effect.

When Katherine had appeared that night in the doorway of the cocktail bar of the 'Curzon' Hotel Henry had realized it was the culmination of years and years of planning. At last revenge would be his! She had been delighted to see him, anxious to accept all his plans, thrilled that they would remarry, live happily ever after. Even being told he had arranged the wedding for the very next day had seemed to please her, she'd told him she 'couldn't wait'. The planned visit to the solicitor immediately after the wedding hadn't perturbed her either, seemingly assuming it was all quite normal. What a fool! What a little fool!

When Katherine had excused herself saying she needed her beauty sleep, gone up to her room, Henry had sat back in his comfy chair congratulating himself on a plan well executed, tomorrow he would humiliate Katherine as she had humiliated him for so long. He would regain all his assets and then leave her high and dry with nothing to her name. He had downed two more whiskies, died with his glass in his hand too drunk to get himself to safety as the German bombers concluded their deadly business for the night. At least Henry had died unaware that revenge would never have been his, that Katherine had long ago guessed at his plan and had initiated an act of revenge of her very own.

It hadn't taken her long to pack. The maid had been in, unpacking and hanging up her few clothes, carefully laying out her nightdress on the bed. Kathy had quickly gathered them up and bundled them back into her valise. Closing the door quietly behind her she had taken the very helpfully indicated fire exit, carefully but quickly negotiating the steel rungs of the fire escape and emerging into the hustle and bustle of the street below. Hailing a taxi she had quickly headed for the 'Rodreigal' hotel where she had a reservation. Had Henry really believed her to be that stupid!

CHAPTER FIFTY SEVEN

As they had anticipated Kathy and Dannah struggled to get a train home and spent the next two days worrying that they had been unable to contact anyone to let them know they were safe. In spite of that they revelled in being in their own little bubble, walked by the Thames, the river it seemed being the only thing Hitler couldn't destroy. In the evenings it was beautiful, in the mornings it was beautiful with mercifully a temporary respite from the bombing.

On the third day they checked out of their rooms at the 'Rodreigal' and slowly, painstakingly, made their way to what was left of the station. After hours of queuing in the bomb ravaged terminus they eventually managed to find a train with two seats together but ever the gentleman Dannah was constantly on his feet in the corridor relinquishing his seat to women, children, old men. From the corridor he gazed adoringly at Kathy. In the reflection on the window she saw and turned to jelly. Two stops from home the passengers had thinned out considerably and Dannah was at long last able to take his place beside her, holding her hand as if he'd never let go.

Whilst on their own in London they naturally had discussed all that had taken place between them, how their feelings for one another had seemingly sprung from nowhere and each believing that their feelings were not reciprocated. The important thing for both of them had been their love for Miriam, Kathy feeling that it was somehow wrong that she should love the man who would have been her sister's husband. Dannah too being deeply troubled finding himself falling in love with someone who should have been his sister-in-law. Now they were faced with telling everyone else and then worrying how they might react.

'We can't do anything other than be open and honest with them' was Dannah's view. 'It wouldn't be fair to be anything else.'

'But when? When should we tell them?'

'Soon, as soon as possible. I need you to be mine' he smiled, lifting her hand and kissing it tenderly.

'Oh Dannah.'

They found the family around the table enduring another meal when they walked through the scullery door.

'Oh my lor!' shrieked Peggy, immediately on her feet. 'Oh you're still alive!' and she flung herself at Kathy sobbing as if her heart would break. Pearl joined them and began to cry too, thinking that was obviously what she was supposed to do. Grown-ups did an awful lot of crying!

Dannah went to Patrick, knelt down beside his wheelchair.

'Alright son?' he asked gently, tears glistening along his lashes.

'Aye, fine Uncle Dannah' he said, choking back the lump in his throat. Dannah hugged Patrick to him and the dam burst. Tears over the terror of the last few days wondering if his uncle and Miss Kathy were dead or alive mingling with previously unshed tears over the catastrophe at the factory and his resulting injuries.

Only Harry had dry eyes. Dry eyes that is until his mother broke free of Peggy and Pearl and went to him arms outstretched.

'Harry, my darling, darling Harry' she smiled.

'Mum' he croaked and then his shoulders dropped and he joined the rest of them crying until they felt they'd never stop.

The news of Kathy and Dannah's love for each other was announced over cups of cocoa around the drawing room fire later that evening. The drapes were drawn against a cold night, they were all cosy, together again and happy, there could only be good news.

'Well an' abaht time too!' cried Peggy. Harry cheered and Patrick struggled to his feet to shake his uncle's hand.

'What?' asked Dannah, amazed to see him standing.

'I've bin practising,' smiled Patrick.

The one dissenting voice was Pearl's.

'I'm not gonna be a bloomin' bridesmaid agin am I!!'

CHAPTER FIFTY EIGHT

The morning of the wedding found Harry, due to give his mother away, still not arrived. His journey from Glasgow subjected to the vagaries, cancellations and deviations of any form of transport in these difficult times. Edgar Desmond still in temporary residence next door was on standby to do the honours should Harry not make it, as was looking extremely likely.

Dannah, haunted by memories of his last wedding day when he had scoffed at any idea of superstition, had moved out with Patrick – who was once more to stand as his best man – so that there could be no chance of him setting eyes on his bride until they met at the altar. The pair had taken up the very generous invitation from Jeannie and Stan Briggs to stay overnight with them.

And so Number Two Ladan Road once more became an all – female household. Kathy, Peggy and Lizzie – just as it had been at the very beginning – but now joined by Ying and little Pearl.

Kathy's wedding outfit, a pale blue slim fitting calf length dress with matching cloche hat made in the thirties style she so loved, hung next to Pearl's blue chiffon ballerina style dress, her tiny satin slippers lined up oh so carefully beneath.

It was March and a cool breeze skudded the clouds across a blue grey sky. Choosing a date for the wedding had not been easy, so many dates having particular significance, bringing back to mind so many unhappy memories. They had finally chosen Easter, although with Easter being early that year it had never been anticipated that the weather would be kind to them. However in spite of a poor winter the daffodils had done their best to struggle through and a few stood tall among the snowdrops and deep purple crocuses along the church path.

The four women, and the little girl trying so hard to be one of them, sat around the kitchen table enjoying their last 'cuppa' before they would all go their separate ways and prepare for the wedding.

Thank goodness – in Peggy's eyes – this wedding would bring no significant changes to the household she had served so well and for so long. She would remain as cook, Patrick would stay until he was fit and ready to fly the nest, it would be Harry's home whenever he needed it, and Pearl would be....... well whatever Pearl was! The only thing different would be that these two very special people would be as one, and that in her eyes 'could be no bad thing, they both were due a little happiness'.

'Don't look like Harry's gonna make it love does it?' said Peggy.

'No I'm afraid it doesn't' said Kathy sadly, glancing anxiously at the clock. 'And I suppose we'd better get a move on.'

Ying, now become almost a fashion plate in her determination to hook the fishmonger, was to help Kathy and Pearl with their hair and a little make up. Peggy was left to tidy the kitchen before getting herself ready. Busy upstairs none of them heard the door and Peggy's rapturous greeting. When finally bride and bridesmaid were ready they went downstairs to join Edgar Desmond. Except it wasn't Edgar Desmond waiting at the foot of the stairs.

'Harry!' cried Kathy, and despite her finery ran down the stairs and into the arms of her son.

'Now don't cry mother' he laughed, 'you know what you always say.....'

'I don't cry prettily' they said in unison laughing. Harry reached into his pocket, gently took his mother's hand and slipped the bracelet on to her wrist.

The church was quiet awaiting the arrival of Kathy, Harry and Pearl. There was to be no organ. Mr. Bates had been unable to return after breaking his wrist and with Philip a prisoner of war there had been no one else to replace him. With no prior intention to do so however Luci Richards, having taken her seat in the pew alongside her parents, suddenly handed Emily to her mother and mounted the steps to the organ dais. Her fingers roamed tentatively at first over the keys and then as Kathy appeared she threw caution to the wind and began to play 'Jesu, Joy of Man's desiring'. As she began her walk down the aisle Dannah turned to look at Kathy, gave her a huge loving wink and her heart turned somersaults.

Immediately after the service, once photographs had been taken and congratulations given, Mr. and Mrs. Delaney slipped quietly away round the side of the church. Dannah stood by solemnly as Katherine laid her bouquet of Freesia and Lily of the Valley on Miriam's grave. She looked up at Dannah with tears in her eyes.

'She would be happy for us wouldn't she?' she whispered. Dannah gathered her to him, kissed her hair through her ridiculous little hat.

'I'm sure of it me darlin'.'

Unheard, Pearl had quietly tip-toed up alongside them. Kathy felt a small hand slip into hers.

'Can I's put me flowers on too Miss Kathy?' Kathy bent down beside the child, put her arms around her.

'Of course darling, that would be so lovely' she said, smiling through her tears.

'The Chimney Sweep's Daughter', due to be published later this year, tells the background story to some of the characters who finally emerge in 'The Polished Stone' and 'A Little Sunshine A Little Shade'.

Who would have guessed there was a musical hall star amongst them?